The Cowboy Who Looked Again

Second Chance Romance & Small Town Saga

Second Generation in Three Rivers Romance™
Book 2

Liz Isaacson

feel-good fiction

ELANA JOHNSON

ISBN-13: 978-1-63876-338-3

Reader Note

Hello Fabulous Christian Cowboy Readers!

I'm thrilled you're back in Three Rivers with me!

This is a second chance romance between Link and Misty. In it, you'll get sweet and swoony kisses and nothing more. Lots of inside jokes between the two of them, which I think are so amazing and so fun.

Misty comes from a broken family, with a history of neglect. Her brother is in jail. All of my books address real life situations without fear or shame, because I believe we all make mistakes, our Savior suffered for all of us, and we can all repent, be healed, and come back to God.

So are you ready for true-to-life romance, family saga, and the small town goodness you might've come to expect from me?! I hope so! If you're new, you're in for a treat!

xoxo

~Liz

The Small Town of Three Rivers

Welcome to Three Rivers! There have been three complete series here already - Three Rivers Ranch, Seven Sons Ranch (Walker Brothers), and Shiloh Ridge Ranch (Glover Family).

That's 37 books. Loads of characters. I'm going to list them here, but you don't need to know them all comprehensively for this book. I just know some of you like seeing these amazing small towns and who lives here!

Three Rivers Ranch:

Frank and Heidi Ackerman - patriarch and matriarch. Frank died 15 years ago; Heidi is remarried to Malcolm Rust.

Squire and Kelly Ackerman

Son: Finn - 31
Daughter: Libby - 26
Son: Michael - 23
Son: Samuel - 19

Pete and Chelsea Marshall (Chelsea is Squire's sister, and they own Courage Reins, which is housed at Three Rivers Ranch)

4 sons:
Paul - 26
Henry - 24
John - 21
Rich - 18

Reese and Carly Sanders: They're the admins for Courage Reins, Pete and Chelsea's equine therapy unit at Three Rivers Ranch. They have no children.

Garth and Juliette Ahlstrom (former foreman; vet technician)

Son: Jake - 23
Son: Carson - 21

. . .

Cal and Trina Hodgkins (he's the full-time vet at Three Rivers Ranch)
  Daughter: Sabrina - 34
  Daughter: Abby - 26
  Daughter: Olive - 21

Ethan and Brynn Greene (they own Bowman's Breeds, which is housed at Three Rivers Ranch)
  Daughter: Carolina - 23
  Son: Tyson - 21
  Son: Bryan - 19

Beau Peterson (foreman at Three Rivers Ranch), single

Bennett and Ellie Peterson (he's a cowboy, she works on the finances on the ranch with Kelly)
  Daughter: Joy - 9
  Son: Jaxon - 6

Tad and Sandy Jorgensen (he's a cowboy, she owns the pancake house in town)
  Son: Nathaniel (Nate) - 21
  Daughter: Helen - 18

. . .

Kenny and Taryn Stockton (he's a cowboy, she works for a local online newspaper in town)
Daughter: Joelle (Jo) - 20

Jon and Grace Carver (he's a cowboy, she helps Heidi run the bakery in town)

Andy and Lawrence Collins (he's a cowboy, she owns a clothing boutique in town)

Summer and Tanner Wolfe (he's a cowboy, she's a nurse at the hospital in town)

Gavin and Navy Redd - they own their own single-family ranch on the northeast side of Three Rivers

Boone and Nicole Carver (Squire's cousin) - they own and operate the full time veterinary clinic in town

. . .

Camila and Dylan Walker (he's a cowboy and an electrician, she owns a plumbing shop in town)

Seven Sons Ranch:

Momma & Daddy: Penny and Gideon Walker

1. RHETT & EVELYN WALKER

Son: Conrad - 22

Triplets: Austin, Elaine, and Easton - 18

2. JEREMIAH & WHITNEY WALKER

Son: Jonah Jeremiah (JJ) - 20

Daughter: Clara Jean - 18

Son: Jason - 16

Daughter: Emily - 14

Daughter: Hattie - 11

3. LIAM & CALLIE WALKER

Daughter: Denise - 26

Daughter: Ginger - 22

4. TRIPP & IVORY WALKER

Son: Oliver - 34 (and married to Aurora Glover)

Son: Isaac - 22

. . .

5. WYATT & MARCY WALKER
   Son: Warren - 19
   Son: Cole - 17
   Son: Harrison - 16
   Daughter: Rachel - 13

6. SKYLER & MALLERY WALKER
   Daughter: Camila - 19
   Son: Sawyer - 17
   Son: Gideon - 14

7. MICAH & SIMONE WALKER
   Son: Travis (Trap) - 18
   Daughter: Daisy - 16
   Son: Jensen - 12
   Daughter: Laurel - 10

Shiloh Ridge Ranch:
Lois & Stone (deceased) Glover, 7 children, in age-order: (Lois is now married to Donald Parker)
   1. Bear — Sammy, wife

   - Lincoln (26), adopted son
   - Stetson (Smiles, 16), son
   - Russell (Rock, 15), son

- Heather (13), daughter
- Sunnie (12), daughter

2. Cactus — Allison, ex-wife / Bryce, son (deceased) // — Willa, wife

- Mitch (27), adopted son
- Cameron (22), adopted son
- Kyle (20), adopted son
- Charlie (Chaz, 18), son
- Lynn (17), adopted daughter
- Melissa (14), daughter

3. Judge — June, wife

- Lucy Mae (32), step-daughter
- Birch (15), son
- Willow (12), daughter
- Linden (9), son

4. Preacher — Charlie, wife

- Betty (16), daughter
- Hank (13), son
- Daisy (10), daughter

5. Arizona — Duke Rhinehart, husband, living at the Rhinehart Ranch, just south of Shiloh Ridge

- Shiloh (16), daughter
- April (13), daughter
- Dwayne (11), son
- Dallas (8), son

6. Mister — Libby, wife

- Belle (13), son
- Marley (11), daughter
- Hazel (8), daughter
- Brantley (6), son

7. Bishop — Montana, wife

- Aurora (34), step-daughter and married to Oliver Osburn
- Robbie (20), son
- Georgia (14), daughter

Aurora and Oliver have 3 children, who are Bishop and Montana's grandchildren:

- Jewel (7), daughter
- Laramie (Lara, 4), daughter
- Mason (almost 2), son

Dawna & Bull (deceased) Glover, 5 children, in age-order:

1. Ranger — Oakley, wife

   - Wilder (17), son
   - Fawn (16), daughter

2. Ward — Dot, wife

   - Glory Rose (17), daughter
   - Silver (14), son
   - Flint (12), son

3. Ace — Holly Ann, wife

   - Gunnison (16), son
   - Pearl Jo (14), daughter
   - Ashton (11), son

4. Etta — August Winters, husband

   - Hailey (24), adopted daughter
   - Joey (14), son
   - Nash and Nellie (twins - 12), son and daughter

5. Ida — Brady Burton, husband

   - Johnny and Judy (twins - 17), son and daughter

- Riggs (12), son
- Sonora (9), daughter

Bull and Stone Glover were brothers, so their children are cousins. Ranger and Bear, for example, are cousins, and each the oldest sibling in their families.

Chapter One

Lincoln Glover straightened his tie, his eyes roaming from his throat to his eyes. A sigh slipped through his lips, and he turned away from his reflection. He'd let his hair grow out since the New Year, and now it hung almost to his collar despite his momma's frowns every time she saw him.

She'd brighten afterward, but the way she tucked his hair behind his ear and let her fingers linger there told him plenty. She still smiled at him, and still loved him, and Link simply needed something different in his life than every other cowboy he saw around him here in Three Rivers.

He left his bedroom and found Mitch decked out in his fancy clothes too. "Ready?" he asked, making the sign for his cousin.

Mitch put another bite of cold cereal in his mouth and nodded, a dribble of milk sliding down his chin. Link grinned at him and tossed him a paper towel. He hadn't eaten, because

Alex Baxter and Nicki Johnston were serving a full dinner at their wedding that night.

Link had been out on several double dates with Alex and Nicki, but his plus-one that night was Mitch.

He wished it was Misty Granger, but Link hadn't spoken to the woman who'd dominated his autumn and winter, but it turned out that he didn't know how to do casual dating. His parents had started asking about Misty, and Link wanted to bring her up to the ranch to meet them.

But apparently, that wasn't casual behavior, and Link had decided he wanted more than that. Misty still didn't, and while his heart had been smashed, flattened, and nearly ripped out between two ribs, Link had broken up with her.

If he could even break-up with someone he wasn't really dating.

Link turned away from Mitch and his thoughts and went to get a drink out of the fridge. After all, another June had arrived, and that meant the summer dances Link refused to attend, as well as the Texas heat.

So the drive from Shiloh Ridge Ranch to the apple orchards on the east side of Three Rivers, where Alex and Nicki were tying the knot, required a Gatorade in Link's favorite flavor. He twisted the lid and guzzled the cherry-flavored liquid before facing Mitch again.

His cousin stood and put his bowl in the sink, then picked up his jacket and shrugged into it. He'd dated Lily Ryders for a while, which for Mitch was three or four months. But they had a pretty big barrier in their communication, and Mitch had finally ended things with her. He hated typing or writing everything out, and if someone didn't know sign language, that was how he had to talk.

Link wouldn't be surprised if this was the last summer Mitch stayed on the ranch, truth be told. He'd been talking more and more about going back to Virginia and working at his deaf school, training hearing dogs, and trying to meet a woman who knew how to talk to him. Who he could talk to more easily.

Link wanted that for him, but he missed his cousin already. If Mitch moved out, another cowboy would move in, and then Link would have to navigate how to live with that person. He'd started thinking about where he should be in a more permanent way, and while he wanted his life to be here at Shiloh Ridge, he didn't want to live in the cowboy cabins forever.

He knew that if he went to Daddy, or Uncle Ward, or Uncle Preacher, or Uncle Bishop, and said, "I want a place of my own," they'd be meeting the next day to go over blueprints and where the house should be.

Link knew that, and he hadn't done it yet, because he wasn't sure he truly deserved it. He wasn't a Glover by birth. He had no Glover blood in his veins, though the lot of them treated him like he did.

Mitch handed Link his truck keys and led the way out of the cabin. Link followed him, ready to breathe in apple-scented air, and smile at the flickering candles, and congratulate his friends on their wedding.

Like his daddy said, he only had to wear the teddy bear skin for a couple of hours, and then he could relax the muscles in his face, come home, and try to figure out what to do this summer that would ward off the boredom.

Since he had to drive, he couldn't swipe on his phone, flirting with the idea of using Two Cents to find his next date. Uncle Ranger had added a Connections Center a few years ago, and now the app not only boasted the best places to eat in Three Rivers, or ranked the favored activities around town, but men and women could connect with each other over their votes and choices.

He scoffed lightly as he thought, *I should tell Uncle Ranger to put in a section for how serious someone wants to be when they're dating.*

He wouldn't. Absolutely would not, because he wouldn't even say anything to Mitch about it. Everyone knew he'd broken up with Misty, but Link had been pretty clammed up as to why.

With the radio on loud, he drove himself and Mitch off the ranch and down out of the gentle hills to the apple orchards. Plenty of other cars and trucks were arriving, as Alex owned a one-man family ranch that he'd been running himself since his sister Edith had married Finn Ackerman only a couple of months ago.

The cowboys on all the ranches—big or small—around Three Rivers pitched in and helped one another when needed, so Alex knew all the ranch owners, all the cowboys, and most people in Three Rivers that had anything to do with ranching.

Link parked and looked over to Mitch. *Maybe we'll meet some pretty women here*, he signed, his smile wide, and he got out of the truck before Link could respond. Link's response was, "Yeah, right," because he knew everyone in Three Rivers too.

He'd been back from his two-year college stint in Amarillo for six years now. Six years. Working the ranch. Running his momma's errands. Eating Sabbath Day lunch with his family. The summer bonfires here at the ranch. The dances. The Christmas traditions.

Link had lived all of it for *six years*, and the only blip in the monotony of it had been Misty Granger.

"Gotta move past her," he muttered to himself as he got out of the truck. He'd broken up with her five months ago, and he vowed not to let another one go by with him sighing like a lovesick schoolgirl while he flipped through the old photos on his phone. He could choose to act a different way. He could choose to delete those photos. He could choose to have the same attitude as Mitch—maybe he'd meet a pretty woman here tonight, sweep her off her feet, and be married by the holidays.

Link joined his cousin as they went under the welcoming arch and deeper into the orchards. Not really too deep, though, because the Apple Valley Orchards had a reception center specifically designed for big groups, and plenty of people got married here.

So the path was well-kept and lined with railings to keep people away from the apple trees, and Link found himself getting spit out into a tea-light-lit area with a tent roof wafting overhead. Fans blew air here, and misters kept things cool in the shade, and twinkling music filled the air, and Link looked around in wonder.

It almost felt like he'd stepped into another time and place, and he found himself smiling at the thought. Just like his video games with portals to other worlds, where he played as a character he got to design and name.

He could be anyone here, as he often thought about who he'd be in a group of people who didn't know him, didn't know the last name Glover, had never heard of him or his family.

"Howdy, fellas," a young woman said, and Link automatically signed it for Mitch. The woman glittered and grinned and giggled and she added, "Names?"

"Lincoln and Mitch Glover," Link said.

The woman couldn't be older than Link, and in fact, she was probably a few years younger. She looked down at her clipboard, then glanced back up. "You're this way, please." She turned and walked into the crowd, and Mitch once again led the way as he followed her. Link wished he could live his life that fearlessly, because if that woman said anything to Mitch, he wouldn't be able to communicate with her.

She led them to a table that seated eight but only had one couple sitting there, and Link smiled at John and Nina Malone. He owned both hardware stores in town, and he nodded over to Link and Mitch.

"You're here," the woman said. "You can sit anywhere, but the tables are full tonight, so we ask that you don't leave a single seat between couples." She smiled over to Mitch, who stood there with a smile on his face. "My brother and Nicki are so glad you could join them tonight."

Ah, so she was Alex's sister, and definitely one of the

younger ones. Alex and Edith had several siblings that Link knew of, but they all lived in Florida still. Of course they'd make the trip to Three Rivers for their brother's wedding, and Link pulled out a chair across from the Malones and sat down.

Mitch sat beside him, and Link had deliberately put his back to the rest of the party. He didn't want to look around at everyone walking in, holding glasses of champagne, and making small talk. He was just fine, sitting here and talking to Mitch.

Too young for you, Link said with a smile, and Mitch laughed.

You're right, he said. *She's pretty though.*

You think everyone is pretty.

Mitch didn't wipe away his grin, but he did shake his head. *Glass half full, brother.*

Sure, Link said. Then he leaned forward, and with his hands still moving so Mitch could keep up with the conversation, he asked, "How are you, Mister Malone? How are things in the paint shop?" He added a smile to his questions, because Momma would've.

John Malone smiled, his relief not hard to see and feel. "It's going great, Link." He glanced over to Mitch as Link signed what he'd said. "How're you boys up at Shiloh Ridge? Don't suppose you need more of that blue paint for that barn?" His eyes shone like bright lights on a dark night.

Link chuckled and shook his head. "Uncle Bishop just had it redone last year, Mister Malone. I don't reckon he'll do it again anytime soon."

Mitch tugged on his sleeve, and Link turned to look at him. *What about wrapping my truck? Could he do that?*

Link relayed the question to John, who looked right at Mitch as he said, "Not me, Mitchell. If you want to wrap your truck, you've got to take it to Ginny at the sign shop."

The sign shop? Mitch asked.

"Yep," John said with a slow nod. "Now, if you want me to paint your truck, I could get you in touch with Barry, a new mechanic in town who customizes in...." He looked over to his wife. "What did he say?"

They grinned at one another. "Tricking out vehicles," Nina Malone said as she lifted her wine glass to her lips.

"Tricking out vehicles," John said, and Link laughed as he signed it to Mitch. "Does that even make sense to you young cowboys?"

"Sure does," Link said with a grin, glad he'd decided not to sit here silently.

"Glad it does for someone." John chuckled as another couple arrived, and Link looked up at the pair of women. Mitch lurched to his feet, his hands smoothing down his tie and buttoning his jacket.

He clapped his hand on Link's shoulder as Alex's sister gave them the same spiel about where to sit, and they looked at the two chairs between Link and John, and then the two between Mitch and Nina.

"What about over there, Abby?" one said, and they moved to go around Link and Mitch. To Link, it felt like a complete stab in the fleshiest part of his heart, because they'd clearly chosen Mitch over him.

Nothing new, but still. Didn't mean it didn't hurt.

"Hi," Abby said as she sat next to Mitch. She had the dark hair he liked, and he positively beamed from every pore. He touched his chest and signed, and Link leaned forward a bit.

"He's Mitch," he said. "I'm Link." He looked over to the other woman, and they looked like sisters. Cousins. Something. They were probably relations of Alex's too, or maybe Nicki, though the Johnston's had been living in Three Rivers for years.

But Link knew better than most that people had aunts and uncles and cousins, and these two dark-haired women could be related to Nicki as cousins.

"You two are Abby, and...." He looked at the other woman, and she smiled as his fingers finished spelling out Abby's name.

"Julienne," she said. "Nicki's our aunt."

Aunt? Mitch asked. *How old are you?*

Link ducked his head, because he didn't want to ask that question out loud. "Mitch," he muttered as Abby tried to explain she didn't know what he'd said.

"He just wants to know how old you are," he said finally, lifting his head to save everyone from further embarrassment. He gave the women a smile. "He's looking for a date."

Mitch swung his attention back to Link in time to catch the last word, and he zipped his attention back to the women, a flush crawling up his neck. His hands moved quickly, but Link caught what he'd said.

Abby and Julienne glowed like the sun, moon, and stars, and Abby said, "I'm twenty-two, and she's twenty-four."

"How are you nieces for Nicki then?" Link asked, not bothering to sign their ages for Mitch. He could read lips. "Isn't she only about that old?"

"Nicki is thirty-four," Julienne said. "She's the youngest in her family, and our momma is almost fifty, so."

"She's our aunt," Abby finished.

"Thirty-four, wow," Link said. "I didn't realize she was that old."

Julienne unfolded her napkin and placed it in her lap, only looking up through her eyelashes at Link. "Is that old, cowboy?"

"Oh, no," Link said quickly, his own embarrassment rising now. "No, not at all." He shot a look over to Nana Malone, who gave him a smile. "Sorry, that came out too harsh."

"This is your table," a woman said, and Link mercifully looked away from the two women seated on the other side of Mitch. "Seems like these are your seats. My brother and Nicki are so glad you could join them tonight."

Link looked up and found another man standing there, this one not wearing a cowboy hat. And in Three Rivers, at a formal wedding, that said a whole lot. His eyes darted over to his date, and then he was the one lurching to his feet.

His thighs hit the table, and the dishes and silverware clinked together as it all moved. "Oof," he grunted, the yelp of Mrs. Malone filling his ears. His face flamed hot, but he couldn't look away from Ralf's date.

Misty Granger.

"Misty," he bellowed right as the music cut out. Of course.

She looked at him, and she wasn't the only one. Link felt dozens of eyes on him, and he prayed the Lord would suck him down into that portal he often fantasized about.

Chapter Two

M isty Granger touched Ralf's arm, and then they shifted together. Him to the right and her to the left, so that when they took their seats, she'd be right next to the best-looking cowboy in the state of Texas.

Probably the whole country. No, the continent.

Misty's thoughts sparked and flew up into the air like bits of paper had caught fire and then been picked up by a tornado. She smiled at Link as the feedback from a microphone filled the silent night.

Everyone cringed and groaned, Misty included, and she half-shrank into Link as the shrill screech faded and Alex's daddy chuckled nervously into the mic. "Sorry, everyone," he said. "If you'll take your seats, we're ready to begin."

Misty twitched her hand slightly, as if to pull out her chair, but Link lunged in front of her. "Let me," he said, and Misty ducked her head, her newly colored hair falling down between them.

"It's not as red," Link said, barely giving her room to sit down. "Your hair." The last words came out as a whisper, his breath drifting across her cheek and reminding her of when he'd take her into his arms and kiss her.

Misty's pulse throbbed through the big vein in her neck, making her hearing fuzzy and her throat so narrow. "Yes," she finally managed to say. "I got it done for the wedding."

"It's really blonde."

"She took out some of the red," she admitted. "Could you give me a couple more inches, Lincoln?"

He cleared his throat and backed up all the way, and his cousin grabbed onto his sleeve and practically pulled him back into his own chair. But he was a big, tall, broad-shouldered cowboy, and this table held eight chairs. If she relaxed her knees so they weren't so rigidly pressed together, her leg would touch Link's.

For some reason, that made every cell in her body vibrate. She'd held the cowboy's hand. They'd laughed together. Laid together and watched the stars come out. Hiked together. He'd brought her lunch at City Hall, where she'd been working, and they'd toured these very orchards together near the end of the season last year.

She'd kissed Link Glover plenty of times, and these past five, kissless months had been torture without him.

I don't want to be used.

Some of his last words to her, and Misty had never felt so

guilty. She'd also never cried over anyone...until Link. She wasn't sure what that meant, but she also still didn't have plans to stay in this small town in the Texas Panhandle, and she hadn't found the courage to reach out to him and apologize for "using him."

She hadn't thought at the time that she was, but as she'd had some time to reflect in his absence, she'd been able to see their relationship from his side. "Link," she started, but the wedding march started in that moment, and they all got to their feet again.

He'd grown his hair out, and Misty found she couldn't look away from him, though the bride and her father were walking down the aisle on her opposite side.

"Are you gonna stare at me all night?" Link murmured out of the side of his mouth.

"No." Misty linked her arm through his, marveling that he didn't shrug her off instantly, and turned to look at Nicki Johnston in her gorgeous wedding dress. As she moved, her shoes flashed with blue, and that made Misty smile. She did love a good wedding, but until she met Link, she'd never wanted to be the one with the glowing eyes, the painted lips, and the pure joy radiating from her.

She couldn't believe she was even thinking about it right now.

It was Link's cologne, infecting her mind and confusing her, twisting her thoughts and making her wonder if there were indeed good men in the world.

Of course there are, she thought. She and Link had been out on double dates with Alex and Nicki, and she'd seen how Alex treated his almost-wife. He absolutely adored her, and he'd never belittled her or spoken ill of her.

Link had treated Misty the same way, and when she'd started to feel him getting too close, slinking in too close, she'd had to remind him that they weren't serious. Misty couldn't *be* serious with anyone.

Especially not someone from this tiny town Misty had been planning to escape since the moment she'd arrived.

As Nicki reached Alex, he took her into his side and pressed his lips to the side of her face. Nicki's eyes drifted closed in bliss, and Misty found herself sighing. The love permeating the air seemed to scent the orchards with roses instead of blossoms, and baby powder and everything sweet and pure and good.

"Alex and Nicki would like their wedding party to come forward," the pastor said. "To act as witnesses to their union."

Link cleared his throat and moved his arms to button his suit coat before he moved away from her without a word. Mitch went with him, as did the two brunettes they'd been talking to before Misty and Ralf had arrived at the table.

Misty watched him walk away in those matte cowboy boots, every stitch of clothing on his body exactly right. She could admit she found him incredibly attractive, and something inside her absolutely needed to be next to the magnetism inside him.

"So you're not over him," Ralf whispered from over her shoulder, and she ducked her head, finally breaking her stare on Link. She said nothing, because she didn't have a defense and she'd been working to be honest in all things. With herself. With her friends. With her family. With God.

"All right." The pastor beamed out the same love and sunshine that Alex and Nicki possessed as she surveyed the guests. "The very best part of my job is performing ceremonies like this."

Willa Glover carried such a good spirit with her, and Misty could admit she'd attended a few of the woman's sermons simply because she liked the idea of a female pastor. She'd always been glad when she'd attended church with Willa at the pulpit, and she smiled at the woman now.

She said, "There's nothing more amazing than two people in love, willing to commit to each other—and God—that they're going to work together, sacrifice for each other, and build a family."

Misty let her words sink into her ears and really sit there. So much more existed inside the curves and dips of the letters, and Misty had never thought of marriage as something to work toward. Something to want. Something...good.

All the examples she'd had in her life had convinced her from age ten to never, ever trust her happiness to a man. By then, her mom had been married three times, and each husband had brought massive complications to her life, Misty's life, and her younger brother's life.

Danny currently sat in prison for his role in a bar fight, and Misty's heart suddenly felt too big for her chest. Everything hammered and throbbed through her, because neither of them had been protected by a mother or father, and Misty wasn't even sure she understood what a family looked like.

She held an ideal in her mind, and she simply didn't want to be disappointed. It had been when Link had wanted to start introducing her to his family that Misty had panicked and reminded him that they weren't serious.

But with his aunt officiating the ceremony, Alex and Nicki must know the Glovers. With the amount of people here in this massive outdoor ceremony center, surely the Glovers had been invited. That meant his parents could be here.

Misty glanced around, trying to determine which of the cowboys she saw could bear Link's last name. Before she knew it, cheering and whooping started, and she yanked her attention back to the altar, where Alex had his wide smile pressed to Nicki's.

They laughed and turned toward the crowd, and they stepped down off the stage where they'd been a few feet higher than everyone else. Their wedding party parted, and Misty started clapping along with everyone else as the bride and groom walked back down the aisle together.

"Ladies and gents," someone said into the microphone. "They're just going to mingle for a few minutes, and then we'll settle down to dinner."

Sure enough, Alex and Nicki came back down the aisle to the front tables to hug their friends and family members. Nicki stepped into her mother's arms, both of them emotional, and Misty's stomach clenched and swooped.

She didn't have that relationship with her mom. If Misty

were to ever get married, she wasn't even sure her mom would come. She'd never left New Orleans, where she currently lived in a tiny apartment that surely had mice and bugs for how unclean it had been the last time Misty had seen it.

As the crowd near the altar started to break up, Misty turned to Ralf and gave him a shaky smile. "That was nice."

"Sure was." He indicated her chair, and Misty sat. Only a few minutes later, salads and bread started arriving, and Misty focused on eating, even when Link and Mitch and the women returned to the table.

They all chatted excitedly with one another, and Misty didn't dare look over to Link. He wanted what Alex had just achieved; Misty knew that. He didn't date casually, and Misty suddenly didn't want to either.

She didn't know if she could just tell him she'd had a change of heart, maybe ask him out, and see if they could try again. Thankfully, it didn't take long to eat, and then the dancing was announced.

Misty looked over to Link before she could stop herself. But Mitch met her eyes, not the gorgeous cowboy she'd spent all of her free time with for a few months.

Wanna dance? he signed and then he pushed back from the table.

Link tilted his head slightly to look at her out of the corner of his eye, no smile in sight.

"Sure." Misty signed as she spoke, and she got to her feet too. She flashed Mitch a smile that felt fake and forced, but he wore an easy-going grin as he took her hand and led her away from the table. From Link.

They couldn't talk while they danced, and Misty's heart pounded. Too many eyes watched her, and when the song ended, Alex's father said, "We're going to have Alex and Nicki's first dance now."

The music changed dramatically, and surprise shot through Misty as a rambunctious country music song filled the apple orchard. The crowd cheered and parted, and Misty went with the others to the sidelines.

Smiling, she watched Alex and Nicki do a lively country line dance for several counts, their joy practically a being on the floor with them.

Cowboys and ladies clapped along, with an occasionally "Yeehaw!" thrown in, and Misty found herself enjoying this immensely. It felt like a perfect small-town, country-cowboy celebration, and like she *belonged* here.

These were her friends, and she'd rather be here than anywhere else. So she clapped with everyone else, and when a man said, "All right, ladies and gents, join 'em out there," the floor got flooded with those willing to dance, and the man with the mic continued to call the moves.

Misty loved a good country line dance as much as the next Texan, and she laughed as Ralf grabbed her arm and said, "Let's do this."

They joined the other dancers, and Misty finally felt herself relaxing completely. She'd been invited to this wedding. She could dance with everyone. With abandon.

And she did.

When the song ended, Misty's breath came in pants, and she'd lost Ralf somewhere. She found herself retreating to the sidelines again and someone said, "You must be Misty."

She turned toward a blonde woman who wore the prettiest flowered dress Misty had ever seen.

She took a big breath, trying to calm her beating heart and said, "Yes."

"Momma," Link said in the next moment, appearing at her side. He didn't look at her, but kept his eyes trained on his mother. Misty remembered her name to be Sammy—and her husband and Link's daddy, was Bear.

"Do you want to dance?"

The music had gone back to the subdued, flowery wedding music, and several cowboys and their women swayed back and forth on the dance floor.

"Not with you," his momma said with a smile. She tucked her arm into the tall, bearded, glaring cowboy at her side. "Daddy and I are going to take a breather after that line dance."

Link frowned, and he looked over to Misty. She stood there with him and his parents, no one talking, no introductions being made, for two breaths before he drew one and opened his mouth.

Before he could say anything, another blonde woman joined them. Breathlessly, she grabbed onto Link's arm. "Link, I need you."

"I—" he said, but she towed him away.

"Wonder what's got Hailey worked up." Link's daddy

glared around, as if his gaze alone would scare off anyone daring to hurt Hailey.

"Her ex is here," Sammy said.

Misty watched as Link took Hailey into his arms and they started dancing. She spoke with him rapidly, and Link simply wore his gruff cowboy face as he nodded a couple of times.

"She's his cousin," his momma said.

Misty turned back to his parents, her heartbeat flailing in her chest. Link hadn't looked over to her at all, and she glanced back to him.

Their eyes locked for a beat of time, and Misty employed every ounce of bravery she had as she tore her gaze from his and looked at his glowing mother and his grumpy-cat father. "I need some help with him," she said. Every cell in her body quivered. "I hurt him. I know that."

She took a breath and pressed her palms together. "I want to fix things with him. Maybe try again. How do I—?" She exhaled heavily, her lungs suddenly holding too much oxygen.

"How do I do that? Any ideas?"

Bear looked at his wife. Sammy looked back at Bear. Then they both looked at Misty, and she stood there in agony, waiting for one of them to give her the key to Link's heart.

Chapter Three

Link did not like what was taking place on the sidelines of the dance floor. In front of him, Hailey continued to talk a mile a minute, and even if Link hadn't been discombobulated by Misty's presence in his life—the two of them standing there with his parents—he wouldn't have been able to keep up with the words streaming from his cousin's mouth.

He glanced over to where Misty had been standing with his momma and daddy, and his heartbeat thumped hard at him when he found they'd dispersed. Well, a couple of them had, at least. Momma still stood there, looking radiant in a flowing, formal dress in flowers and blue—which matched her eyes and made her blonde hair seem lighter—and she cast a look in his direction.

Immediately, her eyes drifted back to the right, and Lincoln followed her gaze. His body lost all ability to function, and his feet came to a complete standstill.

For Daddy—a big, burly man named Bear—now swayed with Misty—the strawberry blonde who still had a tight grip on Link's heart.

"Blast it," he muttered, but he wasn't sure if it was because of what his daddy might be saying or if he'd finally admitted to himself that he wasn't over Misty.

As he stared, and as Hailey said, "What is it?" and turned to see what he was looking at, he realized neither Misty nor Daddy were speaking.

In fact, Daddy looked about two seconds away from going into fully Grizzly Mode. Link cast a frantic look back to his mother, and he found her taking the first step toward where Misty danced with Daddy.

"Hailey," he said as kindly as he could. "I'm real sorry about you and Scott. You'll have to come by and tell me more about it, okay? I need to—" He swallowed and looked briefly at his cousin. Then he simply walked away from her and toward Daddy and Misty, though Momma had now interrupted them.

Before Link could arrive and make proper introductions—what had gotten him in trouble with Misty in the first place—Mitch tapped on her shoulder and asked her to dance. She smiled, glanced at Link, and allowed his cousin to twirl her out of the situation.

"My goodness," Momma said, her fingers fluttering up by her neck. "That was interesting."

"Daddy," Link said as he arrived on the scene.

"I said nothing to her," Daddy said, his voice gruff but his eyes pleading. "I promise. I just wanted to get her away from your mother." They exchanged a glance, and while Link had grown up with them, he couldn't speak their language.

"What does that mean?" he demanded.

"Nothing," Momma said lightly. "Let's get off the dance floor, so we're not making a scene." She glanced around, but no one seemed to notice they even stood there. "Come with us, Link. Mitch can drive your truck back to the ranch."

Link hesitated, but something told him to go with his parents. "Let me tell Alex and Nicki congratulations and that I'm going." He met both of his parent's eyes and pulled his keys from his pocket. "I'll meet you at the main entrance. Five minutes." He gave his keys to his father, and looked to his mother for confirmation.

"Okay." Momma still looked worried, but she allowed Link to duck into the crowd and start weaving his way toward his friends. They broadcasted life out into the party, and Link grinned as he stepped up to Alex and took his hand.

"I have to go. Congratulations, brother." Link pulled Alex into a hug and clapped him on the back a couple of times. "Beautiful wedding," he said as he stepped back and looked at Nicki.

"We still want to double with you," Nicki said as she hugged him. "My nieces have already said they want to go out with you." She grinned as they separated. "Abby said you were the best-looking cowboy she's ever laid eyes on."

Link flushed as he laughed. Then he shook his head. "I always like getting together with you guys, but I don't want it to be a blind date. Too awkward for everyone."

"Can I give her your number?" Nicki asked as Alex pulled her close to his side. "Then you guys can just start talking."

"Does she live here?" Link asked. "I thought only your family was in Three Rivers."

"They're in Oklahoma City," she said.

"Only a couple hours," Alex said, grinning.

"Still long distance," Link said. He shook his head, unwilling to have this conversation right now. "No reason we can't talk, but yeah. Not sure how anything long distance is going to work out."

"You never know," Nicki said.

"I'll give you that," Link said, because he hadn't predicted that he'd be seated next to Misty for this wedding tonight. "Anyway, my folks are waiting. Congrats, you two. Enjoy Niagara Falls."

They said their good-byes, and Link headed for the exit. He didn't allow himself to look left or right, and he successfully made it away from the party and through the barn. Daddy waited in the truck at the entrance, while Momma waited just outside the door, and pure relief filled her face when she saw Link.

She smiled and let him step in front of her to open her door. "Thank you, baby."

He closed her door after she'd climbed into the passenger seat, and then Link got in the truck behind her. Daddy met his eyes in the rearview mirror, but Link looked away.

He just wanted to go home, and he didn't want to talk about Misty Granger quite yet. Thankfully, Daddy almost always let

Link gather his thoughts first, and while Momma definitely possessed less patience, she held her tongue as they drove through town. Once they hit the highway that led south out of town, Link started to relax.

His shoulders actually went down, and he focused on releasing his breath in a slow, controlled way. By the time they passed the turn for Seven Sons, Link felt like he could talk and his voice would come out normally.

"So, what did she say?" he asked, his tone quiet and yet plenty loud enough for his parents to hear.

They exchanged another glance, and Link wasn't surprised that Daddy answered. "She asked how to make things right with you," he said. "Said she knew she'd hurt you, and she missed you, and she just wanted to know how to make it right."

"How to get you back," Momma said quietly.

Link looked out his window, part confusion and part irritation pulling down his eyebrows into a cowboy frown. He'd enjoyed dating Misty; that wasn't a secret, nor was it a problem.

No, the problem was that she was now a year into her two-year assignment here in Three Rivers. She'd made sure he knew she wasn't a permanent resident of this small town in the Texas Panhandle—and that she had no intentions of staying here for even a single day past her job requirements.

Her temporary status in town had lingered in the back of his mind, but something had told him that if he could just get her to fall in love with him, she'd change her mind.

"Well, we've met her now," Momma said.

Link sighed and pulled his attention away from the

browned grass along the side of the highway. "It wasn't about that, Momma."

"It was, though," she said.

"It spoke to the seriousness of our relationship." Link pulled his hat from his head and ran his fingers through his hair. "Nothing's changed." He drew his shoulders up and back as he breathed in. "Right? Her feelings for me are irrelevant. They don't change the situation."

"Maybe she'll be more interested in becoming serious," Daddy said, but he was grasping at straws, and everyone in the truck knew it.

Link shook his head. "Nah, this is just her coming face-to-face with me and panicking." He knew Misty, and while she was a couple of years older than him and didn't pull punches, he knew she didn't always handle awkward and delicate situations all that well. "As soon as she's back home tonight, she'll realize what she's done, and ten to one, she'll text me and apologize. Say she lost her head for a second."

Heck, she'd done the same thing after their first kiss, months ago. Link had not liked that apology, nor the fact that she'd tried to dismiss away the deepening of their relationship. That terrified Misty to the core for some reason she had refused to share with Link.

He'd put up with such things too, because she had been honest and upfront with him from the beginning. She did not want anything serious, and spilling past trauma or telling him about her family history, her former dating life, or anything besides what was going on in that moment, indicated something more serious than what she wanted.

Kissing had been too, but she'd definitely kissed Link back plenty of times, and after they'd smoothed out her apology, he'd held her hand, kissed her, and yes, they'd started sharing deeper things with one another.

Link had fooled himself into believing they could fall in love, that he alone could change the trajectory of her life. He scoffed now, because such a thing was so laughable with a woman like Misty. She rode the wind, laughing as she did, and no one—certainly not a simple cowboy like Link—could bring her down to reality. And definitely not a reality in small-town Three Rivers.

"Link," Momma said as Daddy made the right turn off the highway and onto Shiloh Ridge Ranch. Uncle Preacher's house welcomed them on the left, with Uncle Mister's on the right. Cowboy cabins—full-up down here on the lower part of the ranch—and big sheds and barns rounded out this part of the ranch before Daddy started going up the hill toward the main part of their land.

"Maybe she won't do that," Momma said gently.

"It doesn't matter," Link said. "I want—" He stopped himself, feeling his own desperation and longing rise through him. He didn't want that to come out in his voice, though his parents knew how he felt about Misty. Everyone seemed to know.

"I want her," he said miserably as he mashed his cowboy hat

back on his head. "But she's not available, not in the way I want. I don't do casual; she doesn't do romances. We're incompatible."

Daddy said nothing, but he gripped the steering wheel and his shoulders rippled from left to right, indicating he'd like to speak.

"Maybe it'll just take another try," Momma said, forging ahead now and further annoying Link. "Daddy and I had to try three times. Look at Finn and Edith. They dated three times before they made things work too."

Link wanted to shout that neither of those situations were the same. Misty did. Not. Live. Here.

And worse, she didn't *want* to live here. She'd told him she disliked small towns, that she'd been living in Dallas-Fort Worth for the past decade, and she loved the vibrancy of the big city. She loved the fancy restaurants, and the sheer multitude of choices of such things in a place like Dallas.

He wasn't going to get into this again. He'd already gone over it all when he'd broken up with Misty and then slept at his parents' house for four nights. He couldn't go back to that. He simply wouldn't.

Daddy drove past the main homestead, Bull House, the Ranch House, and around the bend. Past Uncle Judge and Aunt June's place, and past Aunt Etta and Uncle August's. He turned into the driveway at the big house where Link had spent the last several years of his childhood, and he sighed. "I don't want to come in," he said.

"I can take you home." Daddy looked over to Momma, and they had a conversation without a word.

Then Momma twisted and looked at Link. "You are the best cowboy in the world, Lincoln."

He flashed her a smile that slid from his face quickly. "Okay, Momma."

"I mean it. I don't want you spiraling over this woman."

"Okay, Momma," he said in a quieter voice.

Momma looked at him with pure determination in her eyes. "I love you, my son. Promise me this isn't going to send you back to February."

"It's not going to send me back to February," he murmured. "I can just walk home, Daddy." He reached for the door handle and opened it. The Texas summer heat hit him, and Link changed his mind. He pulled the door closed. "Just kidding. It's hotter than Hades out there. You can drive me."

Daddy chuckled; Momma slid from the truck; Lincoln let her open the door and hug him tightly. "Come for dinner tomorrow," she pleaded. "I'll take the kids to Uncle Ranger's, and it'll just be quiet."

"I'm in," Daddy said, and that got Link to smile for real.

"Okay," he said.

"Bring Mitch if you want," Momma said. "He's quiet."

He was in some ways, and in others, he definitely wasn't. He wondered if Mitch had told anyone else he was considering leaving Shiloh Ridge again, but since Link didn't know, he didn't open his mouth and say anything.

"Okay." Momma stepped back and started to swing the door closed. "I love you, Link."

"Love you too, Momma." The door slammed, and Daddy

waited for Momma to make it to the front door before he started around the circular driveway and the road they'd just been on. He continued down another small jog, then turned left and headed along a road that split the ranch nearly in half from north to south.

The cowboy cabins where Link lived sat along this road, and out of the six of them, only four were full. The ranch had a few more cabins up in the hills just below the Top Cottage, but while they'd renovated them a few years ago, those usually only got lived in when the ranch brought in seasonal help around harvest time, for branding, or for planting.

Daddy pulled into the driveway at Link's cabin, which was the second one down the lane. He put the truck in park and exhaled. "Where you at tonight?"

"Checking fences and gates in sector four," Link said without thinking. Yes, he needed to go change out of his fancy wedding clothes and get back into his working cowboy jeans and plaid shirt. He'd saddle his horse and go check on their security to make sure they didn't lose domesticated animals to the wild things that lived beyond the borders of the ranch.

"I'll go with," Daddy said, and that was the same as him saying he'd support Link in whatever he decided. Even if he said he wanted to get back together with Misty. Even if he said he wanted to leave the ranch and go strike his way in the world. Yes, Bear Glover had always been exceptional at championing Link, and his emotions surged.

He opened the door and slid from the backseat while Daddy did the same up front. He met Link on the sidewalk, and they went into the cabin together. "Smells interesting in here," he said as he closed the door behind him, sealing in the air conditioning—and the leftover scent of whatever Cutter had burnt for dinner.

Daddy looked left and right, which wasn't big enough to do more than once. "We need to talk about you gettin' your own place."

Link didn't argue as he went down the hall to the bedroom he shared with Mitch. Usually only two cowboys shared a cabin, but he and Mitch had grown up together, and neither of them minded sharing with the other.

He pulled his tie loose as Daddy filled the doorway. "Link."

"I don't want to be alone," he muttered. He unbuttoned his shirt and shed it, then started working on his belt. "I don't have much, and certainly not enough to fill a house." He looked over his shoulder to his father. "I have no wife, no family. You could build me a house that's way too big or far too small. It's too soon. I don't need it."

He stepped out of his slacks and into his jeans, then reached for his shirt before he faced Daddy again. "Don't look at me like that."

"I'm worried about you."

"Why?" Link asked, because he'd really like to know. "Because you think I'm going to go back to Misty and get my heart broken again? Or because I'm not moving past her fast enough and going out with someone new? Or because I'm frozen, standing still, while everyone and everything moves forward around me?"

As he spoke, he realized he was afraid of everything he'd just said. He'd never held back with his daddy, and he saw no reason to now. "Because I'm worried about all three. But a house of my own won't fix any of 'em."

Daddy pulled Link into one of his big bear hugs, and Link sank into it. He let himself be small and weak and cradled, because he needed it. Bear Glover had always made Link feel so safe, and he found he needed that in this moment.

"I just want you to be happy."

"I'm not *un*happy," Link whispered. But he couldn't say he was happy either. He felt stuck, and with every passing day, he grew more frustrated in his current situation.

"I know you, son, and I saw you with her." He pulled back and leaned forward, his eyes searching Link's. "I'm real sorry it's not working out the way you want. If I could fix it for you, I would."

"I know." Link nodded and finished buttoning his shirt. He looked up, wishing he was brave and strong like his father. "I'm not going to get back together with her. I have more dignity than that. But I'm not ready to date someone else either. I still really like her, which sounds stupid, but I can't change that faster than I am."

"You're doing great," Daddy murmured.

"I do feel frozen," Link said. "But if there's anything you and Momma have taught me, it's to put my faith and trust in God, then forget myself and go to work. And that's what I'm trying to do, day by day, so I'm okay. Okay? I'm okay."

"Okay," Daddy said, agreeing with him maybe a little too quickly. "I'll tell Momma not to worry."

Lincoln scoffed and then chuckled. "That's like tellin' the sun not to shine, Daddy."

"I know." He grinned at him. "But I'll tell her all the same." He draped his arm around Link's shoulder and turned with him as he moved toward the door. "We're prayin' for you."

"Thank you," Link said. "Now, if you'd go get changed and help me ride the fences, I'd take your company."

"I thought you'd never ask." Daddy grinned at him and said, "Give me a half-hour, and September and I will come find you and Copper."

"Yes, sir," Link said. "Can we not talk about Misty?"

"Not another word for tonight," Daddy promised, and Link knew his father always kept his promises.

Link nodded and headed into the kitchen to fill his water bottle while Daddy went out the front door. He sighed as he leaned against the countertop, and he looked out the window to the ranch beyond. His backyard wasn't much to write home about, but he wasn't surprised to see Dusty and Rio, two ranch dogs, trotting across the fields from the stables. It was as if they knew he'd just gotten home and would be headed out to work soon.

He moved to open the back door and whistled for the dogs, who both broke into more of a run. Link filled a big bowl with cold water for them, and he chuckled as he scrubbed them along their ears and jowls.

"We're just ridin' fence tonight," he said. "Daddy's coming, okay?"

Neither dog confirmed, but Link drew comfort from their presence anyway. The ranch employed a dozen dogs, and somehow this blue heeler and this border collie had taken a shine to him. He didn't mind at all, and he suspected they'd started hanging around this cabin, because they liked Honor, Mitch's hearing dog.

Link didn't care, and because he gave them steak and chicken and other treats, both Dusty and Rio kept coming around. "Let's go saddle up," he said, and with the sun still hanging in the sky, and the dogs trotting alongside him, and Daddy riding up a bit later, Link let his mind linger on the gorgeous Misty Granger while he did his evening chores.

By the time he went to bed, he still hadn't heard from her—no apology, no lost head—and Link had no idea what to do next. Call her in the morning? Text her that they had no chance, that he wasn't interested?

His parents had taught him not to lie....

Frustrated, he rolled over, begging God to take her from his mind just for a few minutes, until he could fall asleep and find some rest from the gorgeous woman who'd dominated his life for the past year.

He'd figure out what to do, if anything, in the morning.

Chapter Four

Misty sighed as she laid down on the couch.

"Uh, oh," Janie said from where she stood in the kitchen, finishing up the wiping of the counter. Misty didn't mind sharing the small, two-bedroom-one-bath, apartment with her co-worker. She'd rather have a roommate than live alone, that was for sure.

"I know what that sigh is," she said. The water ran in the kitchen while Misty stared at the ceiling, her phone resting on her chest. She couldn't believe Link hadn't called or texted yet. At the same time, she didn't expect him to.

"All right." Janie exhaled as she lifted Misty's socked feet and sat underneath them. "Start talking."

"I miss him so much," she said, because she could admit she had started to fall in love with Lincoln Glover. She didn't know what to do about it, but she could admit she'd enjoyed dating him, she'd loved kissing him, and she missed him greatly.

"Did his parents say anything?" Janie asked.

Misty closed her eyes and shook her head. "No," she said. "He got squirreled away to dance with his cousin, and his parents said nothing."

"You said Sammy said you must be Misty."

"Yeah, that," she said. "Then they looked at each other, and the next thing I know, his daddy's asked me to dance."

"And he said nothing?"

"He's tighter-lipped than Link." Misty smiled then, because she'd often teased Link about how he never said more than what was necessary. He'd teased her back that she said plenty for the both of them.

Her chest felt absolutely hollow, and Misty feared taking a breath. Perhaps her ribs would shatter with the oxygen, or the air would super-cool her lungs to the point of freezing. Tears pressed behind her eyes, and she hadn't felt this helpless since she'd hugged her brother good-bye and then watched him get led away in handcuffs and shackles.

Alone. She'd done that *alone*, while her mother had stayed home, claiming she couldn't handle seeing Danny like that. Misty couldn't imagine *not* being there, but her mother had always chosen herself over her children, so Misty shouldn't have expected anything differently.

She hated going back to that place, because she'd worked so dang hard to pull herself out of that pit. She'd never felt lighter than she had when she'd driven across the Texas border and left New Orleans and Louisiana in her rearview mirror.

Drawing a deep breath, Misty yanked on the string that had started to unravel. It snapped, relieving her of any more memories. "Then Mitch arrived, and he spun me away, and the next thing I know, Link's gone."

"And nothing since," Janie said, not asking. "What are you going to do?"

"I don't know," Misty whispered. "All his mom would say before his daddy hustled me onto the dance floor was that I should talk to Link."

"Maybe you should."

"I don't even know what to say." Misty groaned and sat up. She started pulling the barrettes out of her hair. "I know what he's going to say, and you know what? I don't have answers for him."

"Okay, practice on me," Janie said. She shook her hair over her shoulders and straightened them.

"I'm not going to practice on you."

"Go on," she said with a smile. "Maybe it'll help you iron out your thoughts."

"Sure." She closed her eyes and ran her hands through her hair. She had colored it. She'd started doing yoga in the morning before work. Walking along the river in the evening. Anything different than she'd done when she was the Misty-with-Link. Because it hurt too much to be the Misty-without-Link.

"I miss you," she said, opening her eyes. "I'm sorry about last year, and I'd love to meet at the coffee truck and get coffee with you."

"Why?" Janie barked out, her voice lower. "So you can eat all my cookies?" A smile flashed on her face, but she shoved it away.

Misty almost rolled her eyes, but her heartbeat shuddered through her body. "I'll buy you another box of cookies."

"And then what, Misty?"

"Then, I don't know. We could go hiking like we used to, and you could show me that old car you've been working on with your momma, and I don't know. Just...something."

"We can't go back to who and what we were before," Janie said in her fake cowboy voice.

"I know," Misty said, but she honestly hadn't considered that. "But I want to." She wiped at her right eye, though she wasn't about to cry. "I could bring you lunch up on the ranch. I always said I would, but I never did."

"So what's changed?" Janie asked. "You're not planning to live here in Three Rivers are you?"

Misty pulled her eyes from the carpet then, and she looked at her best friend. She couldn't get herself to say *no, of course not*. But she wasn't planning on staying in Three Rivers once her restoration assignment ended.

And Link knew that.

No wonder she hadn't heard from him.

Janie wore a look of sympathy, and she shook her head. "I'm sorry, Misty."

"Me too." She got to her feet, because she thought she might cry, and she really wanted to do that alone. "I'm going to bed. Thanks for cleaning up dinner."

"Thanks for making it." Janie watched Misty as she went by, and Misty did her best not to run down the hall to her bedroom. She had the back bedroom, with a large window that overlooked the big grassy area behind the apartment building. Janie's window overlooked the balcony and parking lot, and Misty thanked the Lord that she had a better view as she moved to the glass and looked out.

Darkness had already covered Texas, and she couldn't stop herself from wondering what Link was doing right now. "He's in bed," she murmured to herself. Link was a cowboy, which he'd used as a reason for being in bed by nine p.m., but eventually, Misty had gotten him to admit that he simply liked getting up early. It was part of his personality, whether he wore a cowboy hat or not.

She and Janie had stayed at the wedding until the end, and then Misty had been too keyed up to simply change out of her party dress and into her pjs. So she'd cooked up a feast of red beans and rice, and now her stomach clenched around the rich Creole food.

She had no idea how she'd ever fall asleep, though her mind simply wanted to be shut off. She went through the motions of brushing her teeth and returned to her bedroom and snapped off the lamp.

The window called to her again, and Misty moved over to it. "Lord," she said to the glass, to the darkness beyond. She didn't regularly pray, though she had gone to church many times in the year she'd been living and working in Three Rivers.

She didn't know how to pray, though she'd listened to others do it loads of times. She almost felt like God had forgotten about her, or that He expected her to be perfect in her speech, in her gratitude, in what she wanted or needed.

And she didn't even know what to say.

"I know I only come to You when I'm sad or upset or hurt," she whispered. "I'm sorry I'm not better about that. I just...don't know what to do about Lincoln Glover." Pure pain flowed through her, and she hung her head as those tears came again.

"I hurt him, Lord, and I feel *so guilty* about it. I don't know how to fix it. Please, help me fix it." She felt completely out of words, and she turned away from the window without even saying amen.

She crawled into bed and hid under the covers the way she had as a child, a teenager, and a younger adult than she was now. Outside of the bedding, she wasn't safe. The world raged. But under the blanket, she could concoct a sense of safety, however false, that lasted long enough for her to fall asleep.

Misty jolted awake at the sound of a heinous buzzer. Then an alarm. Flashing lights strobed through her room as Misty sat up and threw her safety blanket off.

Then she smelled smoke.

"Janie!" she yelled as she took the quick steps to the door. But she hesitated, her brain screaming at her to *wait! Think!* The words sounded in her head as loudly as the fire alarm, as intensely as her heart hammered in her eardrums.

She turned and grabbed her phone from her nightstand and shoved her feet into a pair of sandals with furry stuff inside.

"Misty!" Janie called from the other side of the door, and then it got pushed open. Janie's dark eyes flashed with pure fear. "Our apartment is on fire."

"Fire?" Misty couldn't comprehend much over the buzzing alarm, but she stumbled into the hallway with Janie. There wasn't much smoke out here, but it still warned Misty strongly as she smelled it.

The kitchen definitely held more smoke than anywhere else, but not a stitch of light existed. "Our power's out," Misty said.

Someone banged on their front door as Janie turned them toward it, and both of them cried out. "You guys okay in there?" a man called, and Misty towed Janie toward the door now.

"No," she said as she hurried to unlock the door. It opened in too, and Misty half-expected a huge flame to roar inside with the introduction of more oxygen. "Something happened in our kitchen."

She pulled Janie outside and into the arms of their next-door neighbor, Seth. Misty panted as he hugged them both, and then he faced the apartment again.

That was when a horrible buzz filled the air, and Misty looked up to the porch light above her apartment. It wasn't on, and in that moment, it brightened and burst.

She screamed and threw her hands up to cover her face from the falling glass, and Seth swore as he pulled her and Janie down. "We've got to go," he said, and they all stumbled and crawled for a few feet.

Misty found her balance, and she followed Seth and Janie toward the stairwell as lights along the entire fourth floor disappeared. Just went out.

Another alarm started to wail, and Misty gripped her phone like her life depended on it. She thought of all the things she'd left inside her apartment. Her purse, with her wallet. All of her clothes. Her painting supplies. Her phone charger. Everything but the pale purple pajamas on her body and her phone.

"I'm calling nine-one-one," she said when they reached the third floor. She looked to her right, to the building beside the one where she lived, where Ralf had an apartment. Lights went out as if someone had dropped a curtain, as if a giant eyelid had closed over the whole building.

"The power is out in a lot of places," she murmured. Seth and Janie continued downstairs while Misty tapped to call Emergency Services. The moment someone answered, she said, "The fire alarm in my apartment went off, and the place was filled with smoke. We made it outside, but all the power is out. The electricity surged, and yeah. We need help."

"I see you're over in the Ivy Ridge subdivision," he said. "The apartment buildings there?"

"Yes, sir," she said.

"This is our fifth or sixth call. We've got fire, police, and medical on the way."

Relief filled Misty. "Okay," she said. "Thank you." Even as she spoke, she heard the sirens. She didn't want to be without

Janie for too long, so she hurried down the flights of stairs, glad Janie hadn't wandered too far from the door.

Misty gripped her hand while Seth went to start banging on more doors. She couldn't look away from the corner of the fourth floor, where smoke definitely lifted into the air silently. Ominously.

"Come on." Ralf appeared in front of Misty, suddenly there in the night. She realized then that it wasn't nearly as dark as it had been a few minutes ago. Police, fire engines, and ambulances had arrived, throwing red, blue, and white light around.

"We don't need to be here," he said.

"There was a fire in our apartment," Misty said. "Maybe we started all of this." Guilt and horror pulled through her, and she started to weep again. She let Ralf lead her away, and they huddled near her car until the cops came to talk to them.

"Name and apartment," one of the officers in the pair said.

Before any of them could speak, the other policeman there said, "We have to relocate everyone in this complex. An electrical fire started in Building A here, and it quickly spread throughout the area."

"We have two thousand people without power," the first officer said. "We're working to find temporary shelter for people tonight who don't have friends or family they can call and huddle up with." He looked at the three of them, and Misty hadn't felt this alone in a long, long time.

"But we want to make sure everyone is accounted for," the second officer said. "We'll go apartment by apartment if we have to, but we want to keep our people safe too."

"We're in Building A," Janie said, her voice so much stronger than Misty felt. Her brain had started buzzing about "a friend" she could call for somewhere to stay.

Link.

What would he do when she called him in the middle of the night, begging for a bed to sleep in until the sun came up?

And what about tomorrow night? she wondered.

Janie gave them the information they needed, then Ralf did, and Misty just stood there with them, shivering in the summer nighttime heat as she thought about the cowboy cabins Link had told her about.

We have several, he'd said once. *They're only full during the harvest. We might have a few extra cowboys on the ranch during branding or round-up.*

Shiloh Ridge Ranch had beds going un-slept in. She, Janie, and Ralf could make the drive and go back to bed. There'd be food and plenty of people to welcome them. Link had told her his family was huge, and that he wanted to introduce her to all of them, that they'd love her, welcome her, and try to feed her so much food, she'd never be hungry again.

They'd laughed about it; he'd broken up with her a week later, when she'd reminded him that meeting his family was anything but casual.

I guess I don't know how to do casual, he'd said. *I want more than that, and you don't, so it's time for us to be done.*

Done.

Done, done, done.

He'd left his beloved cookies on her dining room table when

he'd walked out, and Misty hadn't seen much of him since—until the wedding.

Finally, the officers left. The three of them stood there and looked at one another. They'd been dispatched here by the state of Texas to do a job. The state paid for their apartments, and surely Patty in the office down in Dallas could get them somewhere else to live fairly quickly.

But when?

"Well," Ralf said with a big sigh. "I guess we'll wait until they tell us where the shelters are tonight."

Misty held up her phone, her thoughts finally ready to come out of her mouth. "I can call Link, and we can stay at Shiloh Ridge Ranch until we get new apartments."

Janie blinked at her, her eyes wide as the summer moon. Ralf settled on his back leg and folded his arms, a silent challenge to see if Misty would really do such a thing.

She stood there and stared at her friends, the chaos around her so loud and so obnoxious. Misty thought of the peace and serenity waiting for her at Shiloh Ridge. Supposed, as she'd never been there, but Link had told her about the wide sky, the way he could talk to the wind and listen to it whisper back.

She didn't want to go to a group shelter, and she couldn't stay here. She had her phone and her car and Link's number, and Misty pressed her eyes closed.

Really, Lord? she asked silently. *Is this the answer to my prayer?*

She wasn't sure, but she couldn't stand there and wait for someone to save her. She'd saved herself from terrible situations before, and while she'd failed with her brother, she wouldn't fail her friends.

She tapped and it was surprisingly fast and easy to get to Link's name and make the call. But the cellphone felt like a two-ton boulder as she lifted it to her ear, and she started praying in earnest again that her ex-boyfriend would answer her middle-of-the-night call.

Chapter Five

L ink rolled over when his phone buzzed. He didn't silence it completely at night, because sometimes things happened on a ranch, and sometimes Uncle Ward or Uncle Preacher needed all cowboys on deck.

Irritation fired through him, because it had taken him forever to fall asleep. Misty lingered with him even now, and he felt like he'd been asleep for maybe five minutes.

"Holy stars in heaven," he said when he saw Misty's name on the screen. He sat up and threw his legs over the edge of the bed, and he didn't have to keep his voice down when he answered with, "Misty? What's goin' on?"

She wouldn't call him in the middle of the night for no reason, he knew that. Sure, she was a night owl and he was an early bird, but it was three-twelve in the morning. He glanced over to Mitch, who would only wake up if bright lights flashed in his face.

Still, Link got up and left the bedroom while Misty breathed into the receiver. "Can you talk?" His pulse rate spiked. "Where are you? I'll come get you."

"Say something," another woman said, and Link tilted his head as he tried to place the voice. Had to be Janie.

"Lincoln," Misty finally said, and Link would never get back to sleep now. He loved it when she called him by his whole name, and he pressed his eyes closed and let her pretty little voice say his name in perpetuity in his head. "We had an electrical fire in our apartment building."

"You're joking," he said.

"I wish." She heaved out a couple beats of laughter. "The cops are asking people to call family and friends to see if they might have somewhere we can stay. They're setting up other shelters—"

"Just ask him," a man said. Ralf. "Do I need to do it? We can explain later."

"I can do it," Misty griped. "Just leave me be." Scratching came through the line, and Link simply waited. He knew what Misty was going to ask, and he wanted to run down the lane to the first empty cabin and make sure it was ready for her and Janie to stay in tonight.

"We need somewhere to stay," she said. "The cops are talking to ranches and farms who might have extra cabins, as I guess that's something a lot of you guys have, not just Shiloh Ridge. But I thought—I don't want to go sleep in the high school gym tonight."

"I wouldn't think so," he said quietly. "I'll drop you my pin.

You've got your car?"

"Yes," she whispered. "I know how to get to Shiloh Ridge."

"It's a big place once you get here," he said. "My pin will lead you right to me, and I'll go two doors down and make sure the beds are ready for you." He drew in a deep breath, wondering if he needed to call Uncle Ward once he got off the phone with Misty. "You, Janie, and Ralf?"

"Yes," Misty said. "Janie and I can stay in the same room or bed or whatever."

"Not necessary," Link said. "Unless that's what you want."

"How many cabins have you got? There might be more people who need somewhere to stay."

Link definitely needed to get on the horn with Uncle Ward. "How many people are out of a bed tonight?"

"Hundreds," Misty whispered. "All six apartment buildings in my complex, Link. We had an electrical fire in my kitchen."

His heart seized, and in that moment, Link knew he'd do whatever he had to do in order to help Misty. Just because she didn't want to get serious with him didn't mean he wanted her hurt or scared or upset.

"Are you okay, Misty?" he asked.

She sniffled and said, "Yeah." She took a breath. "Yes, sir, cowboy. I'm not hurt physically."

"Then I'll get the two cabins on this lane ready for you, Janie, and Ralf, and I'll call my uncle and let him know there are others who could use our cabins."

"Thank you, Link."

"See ya real soon," he said, and the call ended. His exhaustion thumped at the base of his skull, but Link had been raised to help others if he could. And it sure seemed like he and the rest of the Glover Family could help a lot of people who'd been displaced tonight.

He stepped outside and sent a map pin to Misty, which she could use to navigate right to him once she got on the ranch. Then he went past the third and fourth cabins, which housed cowboys, to the fifth, which didn't.

The door was locked, but Link opened it with an app on his phone and left the door open to let out some of the mustiness that had gathered from unuse. He called Uncle Ward, who unsurprisingly answered on the third ring.

"Link, there better be something on fire."

"There was," Link said. "Not here, so don't panic. But Misty called, and there's been a fire at her apartment complex. They're relocating everyone—six buildings' worth of people— and she said the cops are trying to put people up on ranches and farms if they have extra room."

Uncle Ward didn't say anything, which gave Link time to switch on all the lights in the cabin where he stood. He walked down the hall to the first bedroom, which stood ready with a made bed and a bare desk. Bedroom two held the same items, and Link wandered back to the kitchen as Uncle Ward said, "I see the texts and alerts that have gone out."

He sounded exhausted, but he'd text down to town and let them know what they had available at Shiloh Ridge.

"I'm putting Misty and Janie in cabin five on my lane," Link said. "Ralf in cabin six, but there will be another bed there."

"Okay," Uncle Ward said. "That leaves a single on your lane and all five cabins up by the Top Cottage."

"And the Top Cottage," Link said. "No one's there." His aunt's sister and her family had lived there for a few months last year, but then Uncle Duke had offered them a job—with a house—at his ranch, and they'd moved across the ranch border to the Rhinehart Ranch.

"And Preach has a single down in his community," Uncle Ward said. "I'll call Brady."

"Sounds good," Link said. "I'm up, and I can come help."

"Get your friends set up, and then head over to True Blue. We'll operate from there."

"Yes, sir," Link said, and the call ended. He took his phone off silent and started tidying up the dusty cabin. The fridge held no food, but he couldn't do much about that, unless he wanted to call Momma and tell her about the three a.m. happenings of tonight.

He did not want to do that, as he'd have plenty of raised eyebrows and questioning glances and outright questions once Momma and Daddy learned that Misty was going to be living two doors down from Lincoln.

"Living isn't the right term," he said. "She might only be here for a single night." His hopes still soared, and Link didn't even know why. It wasn't like anything between him and Misty had changed. She'd get up and go to work at City Hall, and he'd move animals around the ranch while thinking about her restoring art and molding and architecture down in town.

She wasn't going to move here permanently. "She doesn't

want anything serious," he reminded himself as he got the air conditioning running. It should be reasonably cool by the time Misty made the forty-minute drive from her apartment to the ranch, and Link left the fifth cabin and headed for the sixth.

He'd become friends with Ralf and Janie over the months he'd dated Misty, and he found himself excited to see them again. Even at four in the morning.

He got everything ready in the second cabin, and then he went back to the fifth cabin and sat on the front steps. Uncle Ward had started a group text with him and Uncle Preacher, and the three of them alone were apparently going to manage anyone who came to the ranch tonight.

Should be twenty-six people showing up in the next hour or so, Uncle Ward said. *Some of those cabins by the Top Cottage have bunks, and because they're literally houses with kitchens and bathrooms, we've got families coming to stay with us.*

Charlie and I are getting the initial welcome center set up down here, Uncle Preacher said. *Then we'll send them up to you and Link at True Blue.*

I'm not sure when Misty and her friends are getting here, Link texted to his uncles. *I gave her my pin and told her to come right to me.*

We'll let her through, Uncle Preacher said.

I can hold down the fort until you get to me, Uncle Ward said. *I'll hold people here until you can show them to their cabins. It's dark up there, and they'll be with kids and pets and likely a little unsure.*

I'll be there as soon as I can, Link said, glad he had a reason not to linger with Misty. At the same time, he heard the tremor of uncertainty in her voice when she'd called, and he wanted to get her set up in her cabin and then curl himself around her and hold her until she fell asleep.

But again, nothing had changed between them. So she'd called him for help in an extreme emergency. It didn't mean she wanted to get back together, despite what she'd asked his parents at the wedding less than twelve hours ago.

"You're not getting back together," he told himself firmly. Once, then again. He wanted to get out his guitar and play away the minutes, but Mitch was the only deaf one living and sleeping on the ranch. So he sat on the front steps and fantasized over what life could be like if he could find a woman who loved Three Rivers, loved him, and wanted to build a serious life with him right here on this ranch.

Before Link knew it, the crunching of tires over Uncle Ward's immaculate gravel road sounded, and he looked to his right to find headlights carving a path through the darkness as a car turned the corner.

Misty's car.

Link got to his feet, his pulse pounding away the way it had when he'd turned from the coffee truck and seen her sitting with her friends at that metal table almost a year ago. He started down the road and waved her into the driveway at the fifth cabin.

Then three doors opened, and she got out along with Janie and Ralf. They looked around like they'd entered another dimension, and Link supposed they probably had.

"Welcome to Shiloh Ridge Ranch," he said. Misty looked at him first, and even in the middle of the night, with her in purple pajamas, her hair a mess, and a wild look in her expression, she was the most beautiful woman he'd ever laid eyes on.

So much of what he wanted with her wasn't casual, and he pulled on the reins of his thoughts as hard as he could.

He gave Ralf a quick smile as the man extended his hand toward him to shake. "Hey, brother," he said. "I've got you in the cabin one down." Link nodded to it. "Got the AC going. The bed is all made up. We'll be sending someone to stay with you, most likely. My uncle got in touch with the cops, and we're housing almost thirty people here until they can get back in their places."

"No problem," Ralf said. He spread his arms wide, and he held his phone in one palm. "This is what I've got." He grinned, as if this was a grand adventure. "They wouldn't let anyone go back into their unit to get anything. Said they weren't sure what was compromised."

Link couldn't even imagine how he'd feel if he'd been separated from literally everything he owned except his phone. "Well, there's approximately four thousand people who live here at Shiloh Ridge. Closer to dawn, I'll put out a call for food and clothing, and you'll have more than you can handle, I guarantee it."

He surveyed them again, wondering if his gaze lingered too long on Misty. Probably. "We'll put all the donations in True Blue. It's this barn by the main entrance of the ranch. Well, up the hill, once you get on the main part of the ranch." He hated babbling, and he felt like he was saying too much. "I'm sure Uncle Ward will send out a text."

He snapped his fingers. "Which reminds me. I need all of your numbers for him. He'll communicate with you about anything you need here." He looked over to Misty again, and she offered him the brightest ray of sunshine in the whole world when she gave him a closed-mouth smile.

"You know my number," Misty said.

"Sure," Link said as easily as he could, which meant the word choked him. He looked over to Janie, praying she'd save him. Thankfully, she did by rattling off her phone number. Ralf's joined hers in Link's note-taking app, and he'd make sure Uncle Ward had them so everyone could get the messages and updates they needed.

"You ladies are here," Link said, turning to open the door. "It's not much, but you'll have your own bedrooms, single bathroom, and a full kitchen." He entered the house. "Coupla couches. It's...." He didn't know how to finish, and he had no plans to walk Ralf through a cabin tour.

Foolishness hit him hard, and he turned just in time to get out of the way as Janie entered the cabin. She likewise only carried her phone, and she wore a pair of stretchy pants which widened down to the ankle, a pink tank top, and socks. No shoes.

Misty had her fuzzy sandals on, and that alone brought another ray of sunshine to his soul, as small as it was. She loved those sandals; he could still remember the day she'd worn them on their dinner date. She'd just gotten them, and she'd been

69

thrilled she could get such things mailed to her in Three Rivers.

They didn't really match her pale lavender pajamas, which flowed around her ankles in waves of silk. The sleeves reached her wrists, and Link wondered how she slept in such winter pjs.

"Thank you, Link," Janie said as she headed down the hall.

"Beds are made up," he said as the scent of Misty reached his nose. She smelled like fresh linen and flowers, and oh, how Link missed her. Everything inside him wanted to be close to her, as if she was made only of iron and his cells were a magnet.

Misty stood right next to him as if they went together as a pair. He itched to get closer but forced himself to step away, to put just a smidge more distance between them. "Extra blankets and pillows are in the top of each closet."

"Thank you, Link." She tipped up onto her feet and swept her lips across his cheek, branding him.

"Breakfast at my house," he said faintly. "I'm two doors down."

She smiled just as faintly as he'd spoken. "I know, cowboy. You just met us there."

"Right." He had to get out of this cabin. "Well, I have to go help my uncles with the families coming. Breakfast is usually around seven, but whenever is fine."

Link started backing up before he finished speaking, and he turned and left the cabin while Misty's eyes still lingered on him. He strode away from the fifth cabin as he went back toward his, and he finally took a full breath when he knew for certain the air wouldn't be perfumed with Misty's skin, her hair, all of her.

As he got in his truck and headed for True Blue to assist Ward with the placement of the families, Link prayed everyone —absolutely everyone—would be able to get back into their apartments quickly.

"Like, tomorrow, Lord," he said. "I can't live this close to her. I really can't."

His parents had taught him that God would never give him a challenge he couldn't handle, but Misty living two doors down? Link absolutely could *not* handle that and keep his heart, so he simply needed Misty to be able to move back into her apartment.

Tomorrow.

Chapter Six

Misty met Janie in the kitchen of the cowboy cabin, where she somehow had miraculous started brewing coffee. "You're wearing the same thing as last night," she said playfully. "You didn't go home since I last saw you?"

They grinned at one another, and Janie indicated the second mug sitting next to the coffee pot. "Your boyfriend stopped by with morning essentials."

"He's not my boyfriend," Misty said, giving Janie a look. No, they hadn't talked about how quickly Link had answered his phone last night. Nor Misty's inability to speak to him in front of her friends. Nor how Link had taken perfect care of all of them in the middle of the night—in his cowboy hat, of course.

She poured herself a cup of coffee and asked over her shoulder, "Are we working today?"

"Ralf said we didn't need to," Janie said. "He's calling Patty and Floyd as soon as the office is open in Dallas."

Misty stirred a spoonful of sugar into her coffee and faced her best friend. "Clothes?"

"Ward Glover texted and said there would be clothes, food, first aid supplies, and more at the family barn." Janie's eyes sparkled with delight. "He included a map." She hit the P hard, and she giggled afterward.

"Cowboys have a code," Misty said simply. When she'd first come to Three Rivers, she'd been dead set against dating. She still was, to be honest, but she could admit a cowboy really pulled at her heartstrings. Something about the hat, the boots, the drawl, and the way they took care of the things and people that mattered to them really spoke to the soft parts of her heart.

Misty just didn't have very many of those, as her fleshy heart had been hardened over the years of her life, as she saw man after man march through her life and leave nothing but harsh footprints and pain behind. Link had somehow snuck into the few soft parts of her heart she did have.

"So, we just need to follow the yellow brick road over to True Blue," Janie said. "I was waiting for you to wake up."

"I want to shower," Misty said.

"I'm sure they'll have your favorite shampoo sitting on a table in that barn," Janie said. "Because Link's been working on getting food, clothing, and supplies since you called him, and Misty, that man...he is nowhere near over you."

Misty took a sip of her coffee, something dangerous vibrating in her chest. "So what?" she finally asked. She joined Janie at the table and looked earnestly at her. "I mean that seriously. I'm not over him either, but so what? We have thirteen more months on this project, and then you and I both return to Dallas." She wanted to cry, but she held back her emotion. "Do you know how far Dallas is from Three Rivers?"

"Far," Janie said without missing a beat. Her dark eyes turned into hard marbles. "Do you know what you have waiting for you in Dallas?"

Misty opened her mouth to respond, but she swallowed the retort. Nothing. Nothing was what she had waiting for her in Dallas.

She swallowed and reached for her coffee again. She took a huge sip, which burned her tongue and the roof of her mouth. Now wanting to scream, she managed to get the hot liquid down before she coughed. "My job is in Dallas," she said.

"Oh, yes," Janie said with a hint of sarcasm in her voice. She still wore that look of steel, and Misty wouldn't get out of this conversation without several wounds, she knew that. "I also forgot how much money Link has, but then, I remembered I could do an Internet search." She picked up her phone. "So I did that, because not only did an incredibly sexy and rich and tall, dark, handsome cowboy bring me coffee and quiche this morning, he brought phone chargers."

Misty noted that her phone was indeed plugged in as Janie tapped on it. "He's not dark," she said, only because it was her only argument against what Janie had said. "He has blue eyes and sandy hair."

"And he's super rich." Janie turned her phone toward Misty. "That man would take care of you every minute of every day for the rest of your life. No job necessary."

Misty didn't even look at her friend's phone. They'd looked up the Glovers and Shiloh Ridge Ranch as part of their town research before they'd even come to Three Rivers. Then again after she'd started dating him. She knew this was the largest and most profitable ranch in the Panhandle. She knew Link was the oldest son of the oldest son here at Shiloh Ridge, and that meant he was in line to run this place at some point.

"I like my job," she said, a completely weak argument. "I don't even know why I'm arguing this. I don't want to be married. I don't want kids."

"Don't you?" Janie asked, and then she got to her feet. "Your non-boyfriend brought toothbrushes and paste. He said he knew you wouldn't even want to come over to the barn without break-fast and brushing your teeth."

She left the kitchen, calling, "So hurry up and eat. Then we need to go get clothes and supplies. Groceries in town. Check on our apartment. All of that."

Misty sat at the eat-in table with her too-hot coffee, her mind spinning. Her phone buzzed, and she reached to plug it into the charger Janie had been using. Link had texted with, *Did Janie give you your quiche?*

She mentioned it, Misty tapped out. *But I haven't seen it or eaten it yet.*

I put it in the oven on warm, he said.

Misty simply stared at the words, sure they couldn't be true. The only thing going through her mind was, *Why?*

So she tapped to call him. "Hey," he said easily. "It's quiche Lorraine, with bacon, not ham."

"Of course it is," she said, her flirty smile matching her tone. They'd gotten quiches at a tiny diner in Parma several months ago, and she'd made a big deal about the quiche Lorraine being better with bacon while the restaurant had made theirs with ham.

"Link, I just—thank you for everything, really. But I want to know why you're doing this."

"What do you mean?"

"I mean, you brought me a toothbrush. Coffee. My favorite breakfast food in the world—oh, and you put it in the oven so it would be warm when I woke up and finally dragged myself out of bed." She didn't mean to sound so frustrated, but in fact, she felt the same emotion pulling through her. "I wasn't nice to you. I used you. I hurt you, and you have no idea, because I was too weak to tell you, but I feel *so guilty* about that. I hate it. I hate that I made your life anything but wonderful, and I'm sorry."

She exhaled heavily. She hadn't realized how much the words had been choking her until they all came out. "I can breathe again. Your turn."

"I don't know what you want me to say," he said quietly.

"Coffee? Quiche? You told me you don't cook, so that didn't come from your kitchen, where you said breakfast would be." She knew where he'd gotten their quiches, and that was down in town, at the Ackerman Bakery. That was an eighty-minute round trip, and it was barely eight-fifteen.

"I took supplies to a lot of people this morning," he said. "So stop feeling like you're special."

"Okay," she said lightly. "I'm not special." Except she was, and they both knew it. He'd said exactly that to her before, and she'd fired back at him that she wasn't special. Then he'd hooked one leg over hers and rolled toward her. Kissed her. Told her she was incredibly special to him.

Then, they'd watched the stars awaken in the sky as they laughed and talked. Finally, they'd made their way out of the hills near midnight, and Misty had never felt so special—because Link didn't stay up late and he had for her.

"Janie and I are going down to town to check on our apartment."

"If you can't get in, there are clothes in True Blue," he said.

"Is that where you are?"

"No, ma'am," he said. "I was there until about an hour ago, when I started making deliveries. I'm in the stables now."

"You're going to work today?"

"The horses don't care that there was an electrical fire in your apartment last night," he said dryly. "They want their breakfast, and I'm actually twenty minutes late. Morning Sky huffed and gave me the side-eye and everything."

"Lincoln," she said quietly. "I care about that." *And you*, she thought, but she caught herself before saying it out loud. "I'm sorry I called you and woke you up."

"Why? You don't need to be sorry about that."

"I'll get a bunch of groceries and make lunch," she said, the idea popping into her head. "Can you come to my cabin for lunch?"

Link didn't answer right away, and that made Misty's heart shrink. She wanted to blurt out more about what she'd make, possibly to entice him with his favorite foods. Or maybe she should tell him that she wanted to apologize in person, as he hadn't even addressed the fact that she'd sorry-vomited all over this call.

"You can bring Morning Sky and finally show her to me," she said, going for what Link loved almost as much as food. Horses.

He chuckled then and said, "I do have to eat lunch."

"Yes, you do," she said decisively. "I'll text you when I get back and get started, so you know when it'll be ready."

"So you're not working today."

"Ralf called us all off," she said. "He's dealing with the office in Dallas, as they'll have to get us somewhere to live if we can't get back in our apartments."

"Mm." Something slammed on his end of the line. "Can I ask you for a favor?"

"Sure thing," she said.

"If you're cooking today, can you make a lot? Bring it to True Blue? We've got a lot of extra people to feed. If you stop by the stable on your way by, I can give you a credit card from the ranch. You won't have to pay for it."

Misty blinked, not sure how to answer. Her mind opened, and heavenly light flowed into it. "Of course I can do that," she said. "Your aunts and momma won't be cooking?"

"They are," he said. "We're doing shifts, though." His voice had turned guarded, and Misty cocked her head as she tried to hear what else he was trying to say.

"What aren't you saying?"

"Your part of town is still without power," he said. "Social media is saying no one is allowed into their apartments. We've got people living here who can't just go buy entire cartloads of groceries or new clothes for themselves and their families."

Misty's heart sank into her stomach. "How long do you think we'll all be living up here?"

"At least a week," Link said quietly. "So we'll be providing meals for a while, and if you're not working today, I'm sure the extra food will be appreciated."

"I'm sure," she echoed. "So yes. I'll bring something to the barn."

"Great. Hey, listen, I have to go. I'll see you later."

"Sure," she said, and he hung up quickly, the same way Link always had. He didn't super love talking on the phone, and when he was done, he was done.

Misty sat there and sifted through the conversation until Janie said, "You haven't even gotten your quiche out?"

She got to her feet and turned away from Janie. "I had to talk to Link for a minute." She opened the oven and found her quiche Lorraine waiting for her. "Link says we won't be able to get into the apartment."

An overwhelming sense of gratitude filled her, because she *could* stop by the department store and get a few things to wear. She *could* fill carts full of food and bring it up here to this cabin. She could fill her car with gas and drive it back and forth. She didn't have children to worry about.

"I've been chatting with Phoebe," Janie said. "She just went by, and they turned her away. So yeah." She sighed as she sat down. "We still need groceries, and I need a pair of shoes that actually fit."

Misty glanced at her feet and found a pair of flip flops that were at least a couple of inches too long. "Did Link bring those to you?" Then she opened a couple of drawers until she found a fork.

"He said he noticed I wasn't wearing shoes last night."

Misty grinned at her, glad when Janie smiled back. "Cowboys are observant," she said right before forking up the first bite of her breakfast.

Janie laughed and finger-combed her hair back into a ponytail. "Well, that one is." She gave Misty time to eat and brush her teeth, and as they left Shiloh Ridge, they made a plan to hit the grocery store in their pajamas, and then head to the department store after they opened.

Misty deliberately went right past the stables without stopping. She could afford to buy the groceries for her lunch meal that day, and she really didn't want to face Link in her silky violet pjs again.

She filled Janie in on the conversation she'd had with Link, and when they hit the highway, their sights sent on Wilde & Organic, Misty started to panic. She drew in a gaspy breath and gripped the steering wheel.

"What should I make for lunch?" she asked, plenty of fear in her tone. "Link's mom and all his aunts are like, amazing cooks." She looked over to Janie. "His uncles too. Why did I agree to do this?"

"You're an amazing cook too," Janie said. "But yes, to get

Link back, you better come up with the most amazing lunch today. Hmm, let's see...."

So much panic paraded through Misty that she didn't even argue that she wasn't cooking today to impress Link. Because she so was.

Now, she just needed her brain to come up with his favorite meal, and she needed the grocer to have all the right ingredients, and then she needed her hands to be skillful enough to pull off the dish.

"What to make, what to make," she mused, and Janie started naming off things Misty had made in the past that she'd enjoyed. None of them struck her right, and as Misty parked at Wilde & Organic, she prayed that the aisles of food would hold the perfect inspiration for the perfect lunch dish.

After all, she was going to apologize to Link again, whether he liked it or not, and that required the cowboy's favorite foods to be lined up behind her.

Chapter Seven

Link had been awake for nine and a half hours by the time he ducked out of the blistering sunshine and into the cooler back foyer of True Blue. He sighed and then drew in a long breath of the air-conditioned air here, noting the noise beyond him, around the corner of the wall that concealed him from the larger room of the barn.

He wanted to kick his boots off, grab a huge plate of food, and settle onto the couch. He'd eat and fall asleep, get back his energy, his equilibrium. Too bad that wasn't his reality and wouldn't be anytime soon.

The summertime chores on a ranch took a great many hands, and Link had turkeys and chickens to round up and move from one field to another this afternoon.

Laughter rang out from the other room, and Link ducked into the bathroom along the back wall to wash his hands and face. He'd have done it no matter what, but as he scrubbed the dirt and sweat from his hands, forearms, neck, and beard, he thought of Misty.

Surely she was already here. Link had passed her number to Uncle Ward, and then he'd told his uncle that Misty was willing to cook today. He assumed Uncle Ward had passed it to Uncle Bishop, who was leading out on the coordination of food assignments here on the ranch.

His heartbeat bumped erratically as he ripped off a paper towel and dried his neck and face, then his hands. With nothing left to do but go face the crowd in the barn, Link did just that. Several tables stood at the back of the hall, with the white plastic folding chairs Link had seen many times in his life.

In front of the kitchen window, three long tables held the food, with similar tables lining the walls at the front of the barn and down the wall from the main entrance. Those held clothing and shoes, clearly marked as men's, women's, and children's, with size placards. Link had worked this morning through the men's clothing that had come in from the cowboys who lived here on the ranch, but Link hadn't had a spare moment to go through his closet. He hadn't donated anything but time and energy to the efforts to help those who'd been displaced, but he didn't feel too guilty.

He surveyed the people in the barn, unsurprised to find his momma, Aunt Oakley, and Aunt Willa. Uncle Bishop and Aunt Etta ran the tables of food, also not shocking. Link never had to go very far to get a good meal and an even better hug.

He loved his Aunt Etta with every particle of his being that knew how to love, and he headed in her direction. She spotted him coming, and she dusted her hands on the apron tied around her waist.

"Hey, you," she said, her smile blooming big. "I haven't seen you all day."

"Been busy." Link stepped into her arms and let his much shorter aunt hug him tightly. "Smells good here." He pulled back and looked at the food-laden tables. "Looks like we have plenty to eat."

"Get some of what you want," she said. "Ward just sent out a last-call for lunch, and we're going to start boxing things up for families to take for dinner tonight."

"No dinner tonight," Bishop said as he came over to them. "We're doing breakfast in the morning, but lunch leftovers will be enough for dinner."

"That's what I said," Etta said to him. "Link hasn't eaten yet, though."

Bishop grinned at him, and Link smiled on back. "I'll hurry," he said.

"No need to hurry," his uncle said. "Ward said to come in the next thirty minutes. We won't start boxing until then."

"Seen my daddy today?" Link asked.

"He's been around," Etta said. "I think he ate early and went down to town."

Link didn't ask more questions, because he knew why his father would go to town: to get more groceries. More clothes. Whatever he had to get to help those who'd lost their places of refuge—their apartments—until they could go home.

That, and he'd just spotted Misty. She turned and looked at

him too, almost like she'd felt his eyes land on the side of her face. She got to her feet, and Link didn't see the pale purple pajamas now. Oh, no. She wore a form-fitting pair of jeans and a bright blue blouse without sleeves. The thick straps went right over her shoulders, where her hair fell down.

She'd bought some makeup, and she looked like Link's fantasy come to life. Her pink lips shone as she smiled at him, and her hips swayed as she walked toward him.

Link flushed, the heat rising through his body impossible to ignore. He focused on the food in front of him instead, and reached for a serving spoon in a pan of beef tips and mushroom gravy. One of his favorite foods, and not something he saw often around Shiloh Ridge.

He ladled it over his mountain of mashed potatoes, knowing Misty had to be standing right in front of him. He did look up, almost gasping at her beauty.

"Hey," she said. "Look who finally came in to eat."

"Yeah, I'm a little late," he said. "You found some clothes. Did you get into your apartment?"

She looked down at her blouse and blue jeans. "No, Janie and I hit up the department store in town. We're good for a few days, at least."

Link nodded and moved down to the sweet pea salad. "That's great," he said.

"We got groceries," she said. "Toiletries. The essentials, so we won't need you to bring us anything anymore."

Link nodded, though he hadn't minded taking supplies around to people, especially Misty. "Good," he said. His plate had filled easily, and he looked up, wondering where he'd sit. Misty gestured to him, and he went around the tables with more food and toward her.

She led him to a different table than where she'd been sitting before. "You got the beef tips," she said.

"I love them." He set his plate down and took the chair beside her, sure someone somewhere had started snapping pictures. They'd send them to his parents, and Link would have twenty questions to answer in the next sixty seconds. He looked over to Misty, everything tense inside him releasing. "You sure are pretty, Misty."

"Thank you, Link," she said.

He picked up his fork and mixed up a bite of beef, mushrooms, potato, and gravy. "One of my favorite foods." He lifted the forkful of food to her, feeling more and more foolish by the nanosecond. Why had he told her she was pretty? Why were they sitting at this table alone? Who was watching them?

"I made the beef tips," Misty said just as the deep rich flavor of the beef, gravy, and mushrooms tangled together on Link's tongue.

His eyebrows shot up, but he couldn't speak, because he'd just filled his mouth with food.

Misty ducked her head as if she didn't want him looking at her. "I texted your uncle for what you might like, but he never answered. So I reached way down deep into my soul, and I remember you ordering beef tips and mushroom gravy when we did that to-go order from that place in Amarillo. Remember that? Then we took the back way to Three Rivers and talked about all the funny ranch names as we drove by."

She grinned at him with full wattage, and Link chewed as fast as he could and swallowed. "You remember that?"

"Yes," she said simply. Then she reached up and tucked her hair behind her ear. "I mean, I had to reach way down deep into my memory, but it surfaced."

She'd said soul a minute ago. She'd reached way down deep into her *soul*, not her memory, but Link didn't clarify. "Thank you," he said. "It's delicious."

"I didn't make them for you," she said. "I was asked to bring something that would feed a lot of people, and I did. It's not like you're special."

Link tipped his head back and laughed. He didn't care if it was too loud. He didn't care who looked over to him. He did enjoy immensely the way Misty's higher-pitched voice joined his, and in that moment, Link didn't care if she broke his heart again.

He just wanted to spend more time with her. He hooked his fork over his shoulder, in the general direction of the back door. "I've got Morning Sky outside."

Misty's expression turned to one of surprise. "You do?"

"Yes, ma'am," he said. "We could go riding a little later tonight, if you're not busy."

"Mm, let's see," she said. "I'm going to be loaded up with leftovers from this luncheon, so I won't have to cook. Seems like my evening is wide open."

"Great," Link said. "Then I'll come by and get you about seven?"

Misty nodded, a flush coloring her cheeks. "Can I meet her before tonight?"

"Sure. I'll take you out as soon as I'm done eating," he said. He scooped up another bite of food. "Tell me what's going on with you, with the job, with your housing."

Misty blew out her breath and then she started talking. Link could listen to her talk about almost anything. Today, she said, "Ralf called the office, and Patty's doing her best to find us somewhere new. She's *such* a cute lady, and she acts like we're her kids, so she's insisting we find somewhere that isn't in that apartment complex again. Oh."

Link looked over to her, waiting for the second half of her "oh." She did that a lot—thought of something she'd forgotten but wanted to tell him, interrupted herself with "oh," and then she'd tell him a different story. He'd gotten used to her circling around from one thing to another, and he nodded at her to go ahead.

"We did go by the complex, just on the off-chance we could get in." She leaned closer to him, and Link found himself doing the same. The scent of oranges and cream from her hair tickled his nose, driving his desire for her even higher.

"But we couldn't, and they took our names and asked our apartment number, and you know what they told us?"

"I have no idea," Link said as he chased peas around his plate.

"The electrical fire started in my apartment." She swatted

his bicep, and Link looked at her. "The whole back wall of the kitchen burned, and the fire licked across the ceiling. Even if they were letting people in, our apartment is unlivable."

Link's pulse pounded a time or two. "I'm glad you're okay."

"The Lord definitely blessed us with working smoke alarms," Misty said.

"What about your belongings?" he asked. "Smoke ruins things."

"We don't have the status on that yet," she said. "But Janie and I were required to have renter's insurance, so things might be a little iffy for the next little bit, but eventually, I think life will be back to normal again." She perched her elbows on the table and cradled her face in her hands as she looked at him. "Enough about me. Tell me about you, your job, and your housing." She grinned at him.

Link grinned on back. "You never came to get the credit card. Steak's expensive."

"I can afford it," she said airily, and Link knew better than to push Misty when she spoke in that tone. He finished eating, and because he didn't need the Glover Family Circus making him and Misty the main attraction, he stood and picked up his plate.

"Let's go see Morning Sky," he said. He couldn't help glancing around as he took his plate over to the enormous trashcan, and he saw plenty of aunts and uncles looking at him. He wanted to take Misty's hand and shield her from every eye, but he remembered she'd been there without him for who knew how long.

So he nodded left and right at people, basically telling them they could ask questions later if they wanted to. He'd regret that, he was sure, but he made it to the corner, and all he had to do was turn it. Then he and Misty would be free.

"Oh, hey," someone said, and Link came to a complete stand-still before he could bash into his younger brother.

"Smiles," he said. The dark-haired, bright-eyed teen was smiling, of course.

"Hey, Link," he said. "Daddy just texted us. Said he wanted you to run down to the equipment shed and see if we have the oil that tractor takes. He said you'd know which one."

"Yeah," Link said with his heart suddenly weighing him down. "I know which one."

"I'd go." Smiles glanced over to Misty. "But—"

"It's fine," Link said as his phone chimed with his father's notification sound. "I'm sure that's Daddy right now."

"He said he'd be at the IFA for a bit." Smiles openly stared at Misty now. "So no rush."

"Smiles," Link said. "This is Misty Granger. Misty, my younger brother, Smiles."

"Smiles is such an interesting name," Misty said as she extended her hand to shake.

Smiles grinned and grinned. "My real name is Stetson. I just go by Smiles."

"Is your memory stirring again?" Link asked, his voice low and meant just for Misty's ears. "About the nicknames?"

She turned to face him, and if there wasn't a party raging behind them and Smiles standing there staring, Link could kiss her. "Yes," she said. "Now that you mention it, I do remember that."

"Thus, Smiles." Link turned and pulled his younger brother into a hug. "I'll go check on the oil. Thanks, brother."

"Yeah." Smiles stepped back, glanced at Misty again, dipped his hat, and then brushed by them. "I better eat before it gets all boxed up."

"Yep." Link went in the opposite direction, his hand automatically curling around Misty's and bringing her with him. She didn't pull her hand away, and in fact, she adjusted her hand in his so it fit perfectly.

Outside, the heat rushed at them, but Link pointed over to the glorious, red-coated horse that stood in the shade. "There she is. Morning Sky." The dogs who shadowed him had found a patch of shade near the horses too, and Link had more introductions to make.

Misty pulled in a breath. "She's beautiful." She looked at Link with glee in her expression. "Did you ride her here?"

"Nah," he said. "She came with Copper, the bay back in the bushes there."

"Oh, right. Copper's yours."

"That's right." Link pulled her closer. He wanted her to be his, but he didn't dare say so. Mitch would've. Maybe a lot of men would've. But Link didn't know how. "Hey, Sky."

The horse lifted her head at the sound of Link's voice, and both Dusty and Rio got to their feet and came closer. "Hey, guys." He grinned down at the dogs. "This here's Misty. Misty, these are the canines who seem to think I can't do anything without them right at my heels. The blue heeler is Dusty, and the collie is Rio."

Misty did drop his hand then as she dropped into a crouch. "Hey, you guys." She lavished love onto his pups, and Link wasn't surprised when Rio tried to lick her face. She giggled and dodged, and when she straightened, Link pulled her into his embrace.

"I have missed you so much," he whispered.

"I am so sorry about everything," Misty whispered back.

He pulled back enough to see her, the breeze playing with the long ends of his hair. "What are we doing?"

Before she could answer, at least five dogs started barking, including both of his. Link jumped back as Dusty and Rio darted past him and Misty and toward Uncle Cactus's dogs. He'd had a plethora of them over the years, and he currently had his German shepherd and both of his chocolate labs with him.

The barking ceased as the dogs formed a sniff-chain, tails wagging mightily. Link chuckled at them, and then raised his eyes to his grumpiest uncle.

"Did you know they're feeding everyone in there?" Cactus asked.

"Yes," Link said. "You didn't know?"

The growly frown on his uncle's face said that no, he didn't know. "Aunt Willa was helping to coordinate the schedule," Link said, his voice trailing off at the end.

"I've been helping Duke up at Rhinehart for a couple of days," Cactus said. He finally looked over to Misty. "I'm sorry. I didn't mean—"

"This is Misty, Uncle Cactus," he said. He took her hand in his. "My uncle Cactus, who is the most polite cowboy this side of the Rockies."

Cactus said nothing for a moment, and then it seemed like a light bulb illuminated his whole being. "Oh, Misty. Sure. Great to meet you."

"Likewise," she said as she shook his hand.

"They're boxing up lunch for dinner leftovers," Link said to his uncle.

"My word." Uncle Cactus continued to grumble as he marched away from Link and Misty, but Link only smiled after him.

"I think you've had enough introductions for one day," Link said. "And I have to get back to work."

"Okay," Misty said easily. "Horseback riding at seven."

"Yes," he said.

"You remember I've never ridden?" she asked, and she seemed a bit nervous.

He swept his lips along her cheek, wanting so much more. "I remember, beautiful. I'll see you later." And then he forced himself to walk away from her, whistle to his dogs, and lead his horses back to the stable.

Then he had to get down to the equipment shed and check on the oil for his daddy. "At least he wasn't on the ranch to meet

Misty today," he muttered to himself. But he'd have to formally introduce her to his parents soon enough, especially if she was going to be staying mere seconds down the lane from where they lived for much longer.

Chapter Eight

Misty could still hear Link's question as it echoed through her head, her body, her soul. *What are we doing?*

She didn't have an answer for him, but she did like talking to him. She liked that they had inside jokes, and she liked the way his big hand covered hers. He made her feel safe, and that meant everything to Misty. Absolutely everything.

He disappeared with a duo of horses, his pair of dogs trotting alongside them all, and the pure cowboy goodness of it made her heart so happy. When she couldn't see him any longer, she ducked her head and headed back toward the coolness of the barn.

Misty normally filled her days with work and her evenings with friends, movies, or painting. She wasn't sure if the cabin had anything good to watch, and all of her painting supplies were unreachable in her apartment.

She and Janie could go do something together, and they probably would. But right now, she could help clean up from lunch, and Misty returned to the charming blue barn where she'd spent the past couple of hours, waiting for Link to show up.

Cowboys had come in and out, eaten and gone back to work, and Misty had watched the door religiously. Women and children did the same, and while a couple of tables still remained in the hall, the others had been taken down and rolled away to some hidden closet or compartment.

Misty spotted Janie flirting with a cowboy probably a decade younger than her, and he certainly seemed game for whatever she wanted. She shook her head as she approached them, and Janie grabbed her arm and pulled her in. "Misty, have you met Brandon Rhinehart?"

"I just heard the name Rhinehart outside," Misty said. "Cactus has been up on your ranch for a couple of days?" She looked at the dark-haired, dark-eyed man, and saw all of Janie's hopes and dreams.

"Sure," Brandon said easily, and Misty knew instantly that he was far too young for her—and Janie was four years older than her. Someone called his name, and they all looked toward a lighter version of the cowboy in front of them.

He wore a scruffy beard that looked like he'd shaved this morning and it had grown in already. "Brandon," he said as he arrived. "I have to get back to the ranch. Daddy says there's a wildlife officer there. C'mon."

"All right," Brandon said as his brother finally acknowledged Misty and Janie.

"Hello," he said. "Sorry to interrupt."

"It's fine," Misty said. "We're just going to help clean up. Did you *boys* get leftovers for tonight?" She shot a look at Janie that meant a great deal, and the Rhineharts said that yes, they'd been loaded up with food for that evening.

As they departed, Misty fell to Janie's side and watched them. "He's a baby," she said.

"He's cute, though." Janie nudged her with her elbow. "Besides, it's not like Link is that much older than them." She turned toward the kitchen to go help, and Misty flowed with her.

"He absolutely is," Misty said as they reached the table where the leftovers were. She picked up a container and started filling it with potato salad.

"Please." She scoffed and passed the container to Janie so she could add some barbecue ribs. "He's barely twenty-six. Does he know you're *four* years older than him?" She leaned closer and whispered their age difference, as if it was truly scandalous.

"Yes," Misty said simply, pretending putting salad in a Tupperware required all of her attention. "Brandon is barely twenty."

"He is not. He's at least Link's age."

"He is not," Misty argued back. "He had a baby face."

"Who?" a woman asked, and Misty looked up from her task. A woman with deep, dark auburn hair stood there, her blazing eyes demanding an answer. She had to be a Glover, and Misty caught the glint of a diamond on her left hand as she picked up another container and ladled in some of Misty's beef tips and mushroom gravy.

"Uh, just Brandon Rhinehart," Misty said.

"Oh, sure." The woman smiled. "He's older than you think." She glanced over to Misty and Janie. "He just can't grow a beard." She laughed lightly, and she stood taller than most women Misty knew. She didn't carry an ounce of fat on her body, and she definitely could command a room. This whole barn, probably.

"He's my brother-in-law," she said. "I'm Arizona Rhinehart." She smiled at Janie and then Misty. "Are you guys staying for long? I heard they opened up Building C."

"Our apartment is the origin of the fire," Janie said.

"Are you a Glover?" Misty blurted out. She'd abandoned filling any containers, and she ignored Janie's thump on her hip.

Arizona blinked at her. "Yes," she said slowly. "I haven't carried that name for a while, but, yes."

"Once a Glover, always a Glover," another woman said, and Misty looked past Arizona to find Link's mother standing there. Her heart froze in her chest, just suddenly came to an icy, stuttering stop.

Arizona looked at her too. She swiveled her head back to Misty. "Have we met?"

"Oh, let me," Sammy said as she moved to Arizona's side. "Zona, this is Misty Granger. Misty, one of Link's aunts. I'm sure you've met millions of them today, but she's the most beautiful."

Arizona shook her head, her smile radiant. "Misty Granger —oh, you mean—" She drew in a breath and stuck her hand out. "Misty Granger. So nice to meet you."

Seeing the different reactions of Link's family members had been interesting, to say the least. They obviously all knew her name. Every single one of them, right down to an aunt who didn't live on this ranch anymore.

Arizona turned back to Sammy. "And don't let Oakley hear you say I'm the most beautiful."

Sammy only laughed, and they went back to dishing up leftovers. Misty exchanged a glance with Janie, and then she turned to Arizona. "So how old is Brandon?"

Arizona pinned her with a look. "For you? Or for you?" She looked over to Janie.

"She likes the dark-haired type," Misty said with a smile. "I'm more into blonds."

"Mm hm." Arizona finished with another container and got interrupted by a girl in her early teens. "Shiloh, baby, take this over to my bag. Daddy will want these beef tips."

Misty's pride and satisfaction grew inside her, but she hid her smile. "Your daughter?" she asked.

"Yes," Arizona said.

"You named her Shiloh?" Misty looked at her. "After this ranch?"

"Yes," Arizona said. "Names mean something to us." She smiled over to the teen, who'd been joined by another one. "My

other daughter's name is April Rivers, but she goes by Trouble."
She gave the girl a dark look, and as she put her hand on the
chest of a boy a couple of years older than her, Misty could
see why.

"Who's that?" she asked casually.

"Jason Walker," Arizona said without taking her eyes off the
teenagers. "He's a good boy, but April is a bit of a flirt."

"It's innocent," Sammy said.

"Sure," Arizona said, cutting her a look out of the corner of
her eye. "If that was Heather, you wouldn't be saying that."

"If that was Heather, Bear would ground her and never let
her leave the house." Sammy scoffed and glanced around.
"Where's Duke?"

"Still trying to get the BRD out of the herd," Arizona said.
"We've had Cactus up to Hidden Hills a couple of times, and
they're getting close." She looked back to her daughters and the
Walker boy, and another teen had joined them.

Misty hadn't grown up here, but she had in another small,
Southern town, and she knew everyone knew everyone else.
They knew each other's business, and they had opinions that
had to grow and change as the people they knew did.

"What's BRD?" Misty asked, drawing the attention of the
older women again.

"Bovine Respiratory Disease," Sammy answered. "Spreads
fast, but Duke caught it early."

"He did," Arizona murmured. She stepped away from the
table and over to the teens. "You guys start getting the rest of the
tables and chairs put away, please."

"Yes, Momma," April said, and she ducked away from the boys. Shiloh didn't seem interested in them at all, and she stuck by them as they started folding chairs and stacking them against the wall.

Arizona rolled her eyes as she came back to the table, which made Misty smile and Sammy laugh. "So," she said. "You and Link are getting back together?"

"Zona," Sammy barked.

"Who's getting back together?" another woman asked, and Misty had met this aunt already. Etta. She cut her eyes over to Misty. "Ah, I see."

"I'm glad someone does," Misty said, trying to control the pounding of her pulse. Too bad it did whatever it wanted, despite her efforts to calm herself. "I don't...know...."

"She and Link just started talking again," Janie said, finally piping up and saving Misty from herself. "I don't think they've talked about if they're back together or not." Janie plunked a full container on the table. "I mean, I'm her best friend, and I think she'd have told me if they had." She speared Misty with a look strong enough to make Misty put up one hand in surrender.

"We haven't talked about it," she said, though his words shouted in her head.

What are we doing?

She looked up and found eight eyes on her. She suddenly wanted to run, to hide, to shout that she had reasons for doing what she'd done with Link. The words stuffed down her throat, choking her, and she looked to Janie for help.

"So they're talking again," Janie said while Misty silently

suffered. She turned away from the scrutiny of the Glovers, refusing to allow herself to cry in front of them.

"Come with me, honey." Gentle yet firm hands guided her away from the table and down a nearby hallway. It led into the kitchen, where dishes clattered and voices chattered.

Misty knew Etta had led her away from the others, but she couldn't look at her. Didn't know what to say.

"We all love Lincoln beyond measure," Etta said quietly, carefully, slowly. "He was never happier than when he was with you, but none of us want to see him hurt again."

"I didn't mean to hurt him," Misty said as she twisted her hands together, her gaze locked on her fingers. "It's just, I have so many knots inside me, you know? Haven't you ever just—?" She sighed out her breath and looked up helplessly. "You think you know what to do, so you make these rules for yourself, but in reality, you don't know anything. That's how things have gone with me and Link."

Etta looked at her with all the compassion in the world, and Misty couldn't fathom it. "You are a sweet woman, Misty. I don't know the source of your turmoil, but I've experienced plenty of my own in my life. We all have."

"I have so many things to make right," Misty said. "What if he won't listen to me?"

Etta smiled kindly at her. "Oh, baby, Link is the best listener on the ranch. He lives with Mitch, didn't you know?"

Misty huffed out a laugh. "Mitch only talks with his hands."

"Yeah, and he talks *a lot*," Etta said. "Link has to watch *and* listen, and he's so, so good at it." She took Misty's hands and pulled them apart. "Do not walk away with him without making him listen, okay?"

"I don't know if I can explain everything."

"Maybe just try," Etta said with a final nod. "Okay? Just try, and let God fill your mouth with words." She dropped her hands and moved to the door of the kitchen and right through it. "August, baby," Misty heard her say. "How are things looking in here?"

Misty pressed her back against the wall and took in a deep breath. She looked up toward the ceiling, not sure God would give her the strength—or the words—she needed to tell Link the real reason why she'd wanted only a casual relationship with him in the first place.

"Why do some people get families like the Glovers?" she asked the Lord. "When I got something so different? So...so inferior? So much worse than this?" Tears did press into her eyes then, and Misty didn't know how to hold them back.

She didn't want to be mad at God, but it sure felt extremely unfair that she'd experienced such a wildly different childhood and young adulthood than Lincoln had. "How do I explain it in a way he'll understand?"

Have faith and take the first step.

Misty had heard those words spoken by a Glover—Pastor Glover—several weeks ago, and now it seemed like they'd been implanted in her ears right when she needed them the most.

"What if I don't have enough faith?" she asked.

Take the first step.

After another deep, cleansing breath, Misty pushed away

from the wall and faced the big room of the barn. She'd be seeing Link that evening, and she made a promise to herself and the Lord that she'd do her best to open her mouth and let Him fill it with what Link needed to hear.

* * *

The hours in the afternoon seemed to melt into seconds, and before Misty knew it, she stood in the cabin kitchen and pulled on a pair of boots she'd borrowed from the clothing tables in True Blue.

She stomped her heel down and stood. "How do I look?" She spun for Janie, who barely looked up from her phone.

"Like you're going for a stroll, not a horseback ride." She went back to her phone. "Don't you need to wear long pants to get on a horse?"

"Do you?" Misty panicked as she looked down the hall to her bedroom. "I don't have long pants. It's June. In Texas."

Knocking sounded on the door, and Misty yelped. "Just a minute," she yelled, but the door had already started to push in. Link followed it, his smile sliding from his face when he met Misty's eyes.

"What's wrong?" he asked, entering the house fully now and kicking the door closed behind him. He strode toward her and took her elbows into his hands as he scanned her to her feet and back to her face. "What's—what's this look on your face?"

"I don't have long pants," Misty said, just expecting him to understand what she meant.

A sexy furrow pulled between his eyes. "Okay."

"Janie says I need long pants to go horseback riding."

His face relaxed, and he chuckled low in his throat. "Ah, I see. Well, they are preferred." He glanced over to Janie, who lay on the couch watching them shamelessly. She didn't even blink as they both looked at her.

"Maybe we could just take a walk," Link said. "I've always wanted to show you the best view in town." He grinned at her, his eyebrows up, that left one always a tiny bit higher than the right.

Misty reached up and smoothed down the higher one, and Link closed his eyes softly. Misty knew then that his feelings for her hadn't changed; hers for him hadn't either, and she tucked her hand in his.

"A walk sounds good," she said. "Is it a talking spot? Or a sit-and-watch-the-sun-set spot?"

"We can talk there," he said.

"Good," Misty said. "Because I have a lot to tell you."

"Is that so?" He turned playful, but Misty's gut vibrated and boiled like she'd swallowed a whole box of baking soda and it was now reacting badly with the stomach acid.

She nodded in tight little bursts. "Yeah," she said. "So let's go before I throw up."

Chapter Nine

L ink waited while Misty said good-bye to Janie, who said, "Good luck, girl," before the woman he hadn't stopped thinking about for even a single second today joined him on the porch.

"You're sick?" he asked.

"No." Misty brushed by him and went down the steps, leaving Link confused and suddenly feeling like this walk to the spot that overlooked the town of Three Rivers was a very bad idea.

He loved the spot on the edge of the lawn of the Ranch House. He'd gone there often as he'd grown up, more and more as he'd approached graduation, with questions about what his future held.

He'd never taken a woman there, and he didn't go with others very often. Sometimes, Uncle Judge came out and handed him a cup of hot coffee or hot chocolate, but he never said anything. Just clapped Link on the shoulder, looked down at the quaint, perfect town of Three Rivers, and went back into the house.

Link followed Misty down the steps and caught up to her easily. "Hey, are you okay? We don't have to do anything tonight. I've been up since you called, and—"

"I have to do this tonight," she said, her legs making long strides though she wasn't a very tall woman. "If I don't do it tonight, I'll never do it, and I just can't stand you not knowing."

"Not knowing what?"

She kept on, and Link wasn't sure if he should just keep up and let this storm inside her blow out, or if he should stop her and make her talk to him right now. He'd never seen her like this when they were dating previously, and Link honestly didn't know if they were dating now.

This is a date, he told himself. They were out together, doing something meaningful to him. It was a date.

He opted for silence as they went down the road. "To your right," he said quietly, reaching for her hand when they came to the T in the road. "This here's my parents' house. I grew up there, for the most part."

Misty relaxed a little. "For the most part? What does that mean?"

"Well." He inhaled through his nose and breathed it all out through his mouth. "I lived in town for the first several years of my life. My momma was a mechanic. She owned that shop right on the southern edge of town. I'm sure you've seen it."

"Yes," Misty said. "Ralf took his truck there once."

"Right." Link hadn't told her about his parents—the man and woman he'd been born to. Their relationship had been casual, and despite him slipping and sliding toward falling in love with her, he hadn't told her too many intimate things.

"Wait. So Bear Glover isn't your father?" Misty looked at him with wide eyes.

"Not biologically, no," Link murmured.

"Where is your biological dad?" She spoke with a touch of harshness in her voice that Link didn't understand.

"I, uh, I'm not sure we should be talking about stuff like this," he said, his own heart turning hard. "I didn't tell you before, because it's not what casual couples talk about."

Misty came to a halt, and she pulled on Link's hand. "Stop and talk to me."

"I am talking to you." Link released her hand and took a couple more steps. He couldn't look at her, and he rolled his neck, trying to find his patience, his self-respect, his dignity. He sighed and finally faced her. "What do you want from me?"

She gazed at him, her emerald eyes firing with passion, with determination, with anger. She lifted her chin and said, "I want more than casual."

Link immediately shook his head. "No," he said, a harsh barking laugh coming out. "No, you can't say stuff like that if you don't mean it." He paced away from her, expecting her girlish laugh, the teasing quality in her tone that told him she was kidding.

It didn't come, and he turned toward her again, his head down, barely looking at her from beneath the brim of his cowboy hat. "You broke my heart, and I can't do it again. So you can't say that stuff if you don't mean it." He watched her fight with herself, and that didn't exactly comfort him. "Do you mean it?"

"I mean it." Misty sounded hoarse. "I have reasons for everything, and that's what I need to tell you. Tonight. If I don't, I'll chicken out, and then we won't be able to try again."

"Is that what we're doing?"

"I'd like to," she said, that chin coming up in defiance again. "Tell me you don't want a second chance, and I'll march right back to the cabin." She pointed back the way they'd come. "Right now."

"I can't say that," he said.

"Good." She eased closer to him. "So you tell me about your dad on the way to this looking spot, and then I'll somehow be brave enough to tell you why we couldn't be together last year."

Link would do anything to be with her again, as her boyfriend, so he drew on the strongest part of himself, said a silent prayer in his heart, and then said aloud, "My parents were killed in a car accident when I was only three years old."

"Lincoln Glover," Misty said, her voice full of air and shock. "No."

He nodded and tugged her along, as she'd stopped walking again. "Yes, Misty. I was born Lincoln Josephs. My aunt Sammy adopted me, because she became my legal guardian according to my parents' wills." He glanced over to her. "I don't really belong to the Glover family."

Their feet crunched down the road. "That's not what I

heard at the barn today," Misty finally said. "It was your mom who said, 'Once a Glover, always a Glover.'"

Link smiled, because that sounded like something his momma would say. "Bear Glover was sweet on my mom. I was eight when they started dating, and they got married pretty quick. We came to live up here then, and we actually lived in the big homestead at the top of the hill."

"I see," Misty said.

"Bear adopted me, and they changed my last name when I was a teenager, because I wanted the same last name as them. I wanted to graduate from high school with the Glover name on my diploma. But I'm not a Glover."

"Link, yes, you are."

She wasn't hearing him. Or rather, she *heard* him, but she wasn't *listening*. "I feel like I'm not, though," he said quietly. "I feel like a fraud sometimes. Daddy talks to me about taking over this place, or building me a house of my own here, and to him, of course I belong here." Link sighed out his breath, because he wasn't sure what he was trying to say.

"Anyway." He shook his head as they approached Etta's house. "This is my aunt Etta and uncle August's house. Hailey, that woman I danced with at the wedding? She's their daughter. They have a few other kids too." He told himself to stop talking, but he still said, "She's a twin, and she's got twins. Her twin sister, Aunt Ida, she's got twins too."

"There's a lot of people in your family," she said.

"Don't I know it," Link muttered.

"I have one brother," she said. "It's a little overwhelming being here, actually."

Link tightened his hold on her hand. "I'm sure it is." He cleared his throat and cut a look over to her. "Anyway, that's me. It's not this sordid tale or anything, but I'm not a Glover, at least by blood. I was a Josephs, and then a Benton, and *then* a Glover."

"Names are just names," she said.

"Names mean a lot in this family." Link looked up into the sky, noting that it had started to bruise a little bit. "The sunset is going to be amazing tonight."

They went past Etta's house and continued down the road toward the Ranch House. "This is where Uncle Judge and Aunt June live," Link said. "We call it the Ranch House. Judge is my daddy's brother. Etta is his cousin. It's all confusing, and most of the time, I barely know how they're related to me." He gave a light chuckle. "And that's more words than I think I've ever spoken on a date, so I'm going to stop now."

Misty didn't even challenge him on the labeling of this walk as a date, and that was when Link realized how serious she'd become. They really hadn't ever had a date like this before. Everything had been laughter and jokes, playfulness and teasing, kissing and flirting.

He led her across the side yard of the house to the benches that sat right on the edge of the grass, before the wildness of the ranch took over. The majority of the ranch sat up on a plateau, and Link smiled as he remembered the earthquake and landslide that had stranded them all up here one Christmas.

Link led Misty around the bench and let her sit down before he eased himself in next to her. "I'm exhausted," he said as he groaned. "Whenever I'm trying to find my way, I come here." He gazed down the hills to the town. "It's Three Rivers from a bird's eye view, and I love it. It allows me to see things the way I imagine God does—from a higher perspective."

"I love that." Misty linked her arm through Link's and leaned her head against his bicep. "Lincoln, I am so sorry for hurting you."

"You've apologized enough."

"You said I broke your heart."

"Yeah, well." He didn't have much more of a defense, and he didn't need to repeat the pathetic truth of his life.

She drew in a breath, and Link found himself praying for her. Begging the Lord to give her the right words, and asking Him to open Link's mind and heart to truly hear what Misty needed to tell him.

"I don't even know where to start," she said. "So I guess I'll just babble on until the words dry up."

Link smiled, but he didn't let any of it show where she could see it. For this was Serious Misty, and he was just getting to know her.

"I have one brother," she said. "He's younger than me, and my daddy left us when I was four and Danny was two. Before I turned ten, my momma had been married three more times." She spoke without much emotion in her voice, but Link felt the pain streaming from her. He could almost see it bleeding out of her, in great waves of red sand.

"Every man was a nightmare," she said. "The first one was cruel, and Danny and I never got enough to eat. The second one took all of our money, and we lost our house, because my mom thought he deserved just one more chance." She scoffed, the bitterness in her voice prevalent.

"The third left when he found out about us, because see, my mother didn't tell him she had two children until they'd gotten married. I learned that I couldn't count on anyone, not even my mother."

"I had no idea," Link whispered.

"Danny and I stayed in the apartment for eleven days before my mom came back," Misty said, and she sounded hollow now. Broken. Link lifted his arm and put it around her, drew her close, tried to tell her she was safe here with him.

"See, my mom had gone with Husband Number Three, because she loved him. Claimed he was The One, and he'd come around. He'd come back and take care of all of us. But he didn't. She came back, but the message had already been delivered. She didn't want me or Danny. We were a burden to her."

"Misty, you're not a burden to anyone."

"Mm." She fell silent, and Link didn't know what to do to fill this quiet. He watched the sunlight glint off the windows on the tall buildings downtown, his eyes adjusting to the light as it continued to fade.

"She changed after that," Misty said next. "She didn't take care of us, and I did everything around the house. Lunches, dinner. I did the best I could with Danny, but he turned to drugs and drinking. I couldn't save him; I could barely keep my own head above water. It was then that I made rules for myself, and they alone kept me from...floating away."

Link didn't want to imagine Misty out there in the ether, being pushed this way and that by any whim or wist of wind. "This is when you decided not to date."

"Yes," she said. "I vowed I would never, ever be dependent on a man for my happiness, to pay my bills, for anything."

Link started to feel hollow too, because all he wanted was to make Misty happy, pay for anything she wanted, be the man who would show her that having a partner in life made things easier, not harder.

"I'm real sorry about your mom."

She curled into his chest. "She's a hoarder. I haven't seen her in years. Barely speak to her." She sniffled and waved her hand in front of her. "And here you are, with family for days, and months, and years, and you talk to all of them. They love you and care about you, and I've got your aunts giving me advice on how to get you back."

She wiped her face, and Link had never seen her cry.

"I want to make this better for you," he murmured.

"You can't," she said.

"Do you think I'm like those men your momma married?"

"No." She wrapped her arms around him even tighter. "Small towns scare me, Lincoln. I felt so trapped growing up. There was no way out. Absolutely none."

"You made it out, sweetheart."

"Danny didn't. He's in prison down in the Coastal Bend."

Link pulled in a deep breath and looked up into the sky.

Dear Lord, he thought. *I have no idea how to get through this conversation. What do I say here?*

I'm sorry sounded so inadequate. It *was* inadequate.

Misty sat up straight, and Link pulled his arm back. "So you see, I couldn't have you be a serious boyfriend. It had to just be fun, because the thought of actually letting you see the messed up pieces of my life was too scary." She glanced over to him but didn't really look at him.

"I don't do romances," she said. "Because I barely have my life together."

"You're an incredible woman, Misty," he said. "You have an amazing and interesting job. You're a college graduate. A great friend. Your past doesn't define you."

"It definitely makes you into who you are today," she said.

"Yeah, and that person can change into anything she wants." He took her hand again. "Anyone she wants, at any time."

She squeezed his fingers. "You understand why I did what I did last year, though, right? It's really important to me that you understand. I never, ever thought my feelings for you would get so deep, and I certainly never meant to hurt you."

Misty faced him then, and pure agony lived on her face. "I am so, so sorry, and I need you to know that the very idea of being with you scares me. You're so good, Link. Your family is so big and so amazing. I don't like small towns, because I still feel a little trapped here." She swallowed, and Link just wanted to take all the scary things in her life and root them right out.

Just strip them away until she didn't have to think about them or worry over them any longer.

"I am an island," he said. "The only one in my family. I have no one who shares my blood." He lifted her hand to his lips. "You make me feel less alone. When I'm with you, I feel like maybe, just maybe, someone will see me the way they see Mitch or Smiles or my daddy. No one ever sees me, Misty, and you did. You do."

She cradled his face in her hand. "I see you, Lincoln."

"And I'm not like any other man you've ever known," he said with as much force as he dared. He needed her to know there were good men in the world, and that he was one of them. No, he wasn't perfect, but he wasn't here to use her, abandon her, or hurt her.

A tiny smile touched her face. "I know, because you let me dictate everything in our previous relationship."

"I'm weak is what you're saying," he said.

"No." She shook her head.

"Desperate, then."

"Link, you're wonderful."

He looked away, back to the town he loved so much. "Three Rivers has actually doubled in size in the past twenty years," he said after several long moments of silence between them.

"Oh, you're making that up."

Link chuckled. "I am not. Those high rises weren't there when I was a little boy." Heck, only five houses or cabins had existed on the ranch when he'd come to live here as an eight-year-old. Now they had over a dozen, with a new cabin community too.

"I think they're pretty."

"I don't hate them the way some of my uncles do," Link said. "So." He took a deep breath. "Are we really doing this?"

"I think so," she said.

"No," he said, hardly feeling like himself. "That doesn't work for me. I need you to look me in the eye and tell me we're dating again, and that it's okay for us to be serious."

Misty turned toward him, and he caught a flash of fear in her expression. He'd just asked her to break her rules, the ones she'd implemented to keep herself safe for all these years.

And as he pulled his hand away from hers, he had no idea what she'd say next.

Chapter Ten

Misty could scarcely believe she'd told Link all she had. Looking at him now, on the other side of the hard conversation, she only felt pride for being strong enough to face him, to tell him the truth.

Her hand echoed with coldness without his enclosing it, and she looked down at her fingers, his intense gaze way too heavy to hold. All she knew from men were flirtations. Some fun kissing, sure, but nothing more.

Pain, and lies, and hurt, and anger, and unkindness.

"Lincoln," she said quietly. "If we do this your way, and to be clear, I want to, it'll be the first serious relationship I've had."

"Okay," he said. "Me too."

That got her to look up. "What? You told me you'd dated throughout high school and college." He'd confessed he hadn't had much luck with women once he'd graduated and returned to Three Rivers, to the ranch, but he'd definitely had other girl-friends in the past.

"Yeah, sure," he said. "But they weren't serious. Never made it that far." He shifted on the bench and gazed down to the gorgeous town. As the darkness continued to gather, the lights came on, casting the buildings, houses, cars, and people in cheery, twinkling magic.

"In fact, even as casual as we were, I think our relationship is the most serious one I've had." His hands hung over his knees, between his legs, and he finally ducked his head to look at her. "I told you, no one sees me. Not with Mitch around. Not with Smiles. Not with all the other cowboy hats. It's like a sea of us, and I'm...insignificant."

"I saw you," she said, reaching for his hand and tugging it gently into her lap. She stroked her thumb over the back of his. "That night at the summer dance."

"You saw Mitch."

"You're wrong about that," she said. "I saw you, *and* I saw that cute blonde dancing with you. She liked you."

"Maybe," Link said.

"There are no maybe's for me," Misty said. She used her free hand to turn his head toward her. "I want to try again. I'm not going to apologize again for the first time, but I would over and over and over if you needed me to." She swallowed, her pulse like butterfly wings in her chest, tickling her ribs and making her throat scratchy.

"I want to try again, and I want it to be serious this time."

Link nodded, ever-so-serious. "Misty, I just—" He exhaled,

and Misty leaned closer, almost desperate to hear what came next. If given space, he'd continue, at least if the words plagued him enough.

"What?" she asked. "Say it."

He shook his head. "It's not something that can be said. It has to be shown." He leaned toward her, and Misty's lips tingled in anticipation of touching his. But he didn't kiss her on the mouth. Instead, he brushed his lips across her lower jaw, then dipped his mouth to her neck.

A thrill ran along her shoulders and down her arms. Being his felt fantastic, and phenomenal, and so...freeing.

She hadn't expected that. She'd thought belonging to someone else would cage her, trap her, suffocate her.

"Will you go out with me this weekend?" he asked.

"Maybe," she said, easily slipping back into the fun, flirtatious Misty she knew precisely how to be.

"Maybe?" He glanced at her, and she grinned at him. "What's a man gotta do to get a yes?"

"I wanted you to kiss me," she said, her eyes dropping to his mouth. "If you'd have kissed me, you'd have gotten a yes. But you didn't. So you get a maybe."

He chuckled and shook his head, his gaze dropping to the ground. "I'm not ready."

"We've kissed before."

"Have we?" He cut her a look out of the corner of his eye, and he'd folded himself onto the bench and still leaned over his legs, his jeans probably dirty from his long day of work around the ranch. He still smelled like sunshine and warmth and his sexy cologne, so maybe he'd changed. In the twilight, she couldn't really tell.

"I remember kissing you, so yeah, I think we've checked that box."

"It's not a box you check off," he said. "And that was before, when things were just for fun. This is different, and I'll not have you push me to do something I'm not ready to do." He gave her half a smile as he said the last part, and Misty wrapped her other hand around his too.

The wind blew by on this cliff, and Misty turned her face into it. "I won't," she said.

"Good." He straightened and slid his hand away from hers only to lift his arm around her. She curled into his chest, liking how close she could get to him this way. His lips touched her earlobe as he whispered, "I want to, sweetheart, but if we're tryin' again, this is like Date Zero, and no respectable cowboy kisses on Date Zero."

"Okay," she said. "So a cowboy could get a yes to a weekend date if he mentions the words 'deep dish pepperoni pizza' and 'Starlight Trail' in the same sentence."

He lifted his head and together, they looked out over the horizon. "Oh, so you're going to plan our first date now?"

"It's okay for me to say what I like and want."

"It sure is," he said. "But it's okay for a cowboy to plan something he *hopes* his girlfriend will like, even if it's not exactly and precisely what she *says* she wants."

"True."

"But only if he gets that yes," he said.

Misty tipped her head back and looked up at him. He didn't return her gaze, but she kissed his cheek, pure joy flowing through her. "Yes," she said. "I'd love to go out with you this weekend."

He brought her closer somehow, and Misty allowed the sense of safety Lincoln Glover had always given her flow over her, through her, around her, inside her.

It sure felt good, and she couldn't wait until the weekend. Then, she'd find out what Link had planned for their second first date.

* * *

Remember when we got a five-gallon container of mint chocolate chip ice cream and ate it on the tailgate of my truck?

Misty stared at Link's text, her blank memory of such an experience sending her stomach to the soles of her shoes. She'd just put a bite of her favorite salad from Jurassic Produce in her mouth, and she set down her plastic fork and looked across the table to Janie.

They'd been back at work for a couple of days now, and the weekend hadn't arrived yet. They hadn't been able to get back into their apartment yet, but someone—a police officer or a fireman or maybe a structural engineer—had gone into their place and packed up everything that could be taken out.

She had her own clothes now, but they'd lost everything in their kitchen, all the blankets in their living room, and any electronics that had been plugged in. Therefore, they didn't have computers, and their phone chargers had to be replaced.

"What?" Janie asked. "Link's texting."

"I don't—we never got a five-gallon container of ice cream and ate it with our legs dangling over his tailgate."

"Then what's he talking about?" Janie twirled the phone and read the next text that had come in. "Remember when we packed a weekend bag, got in the truck, and just drove until we found something interesting to see?"

Misty suddenly got the inside joke, and she grinned as she reached for her phone. Janie said, "You never did that. An overnight trip with Lincoln Glover? It actually sounds scandalous."

"It's a game of ours." Misty left her salad behind and took her phone with her. She stepped out the back door of City Hall as she tapped to call Link.

His phone only rang once before he said, "Yep." He never answered her calls with a hello, the way a normal person would. It was always, "Yep."

"Remember that time you let me bring you dinner, and we packed it into a saddlebag and rode out to the edge of the ranch on Copper and Morning Sky?"

He laughed, and Misty joined him. "Yeah," he said around his chuckles. "That was a great evening."

She sighed as she sank onto the top step, glad this side of City Hall hadn't been baked quite yet. The sun would come over the roof soon enough, though, and she'd lose her shade.

"Five gallons of ice cream? Do you know how much ice cream that is?"

"Enough for a summertime family bonfire," he said.

Misty tilted her head, trying to hear the words he hadn't said. "Are you in town?"

"Yes, ma'am."

"Do you have said ice cream right now?"

"I think you know the answer to that."

Misty got to her feet, sudden excitement shooting through her. "Talk to me about the weekend bag and driving until we see something interesting."

He laughed again, and it sure made her heart happy to hear him so upbeat again. She could admit that she too felt different this week than she had last week, and that the increase in her mood had everything to do with the cowboy on the line.

"That was me reminding you of how we used to talk," he said. "Because I thought you might not get it."

"I got it," she said, the small fib sitting wrong in her throat. "When you sent the text about taking a weekend trip together."

"Thus, why I sent it." He paused for a second, and Misty listened to someone honk on his end of the line. "Shoot. I did not see that guy. Sorry!"

She smiled at how he talked to a driver who surely couldn't hear him. "Now, listen," he said. "I don't want you thinkin' you're special or anything, but I got you something to go with your lunch. Can you run out and grab it? I don't dare leave the groceries in the car without the AC blasting directly on them."

"Oh, come on," she teased as she wove down the hall and

toward the big open rotunda where she, Janie, and Ralf had been working for the past year. "Your momma sent you to town with those insulated bags. Admit it."

"I actually own some of those insulated bags myself," he said.

"Stop bragging," she said, and they both laughed again. "I'm almost to the front doors."

"I'm at the stoplight."

"See you in a sec." Misty ended the call and heaved open the big, heavy doors. She took the extra few seconds to make sure they came all the way closed behind her, or she'd lose her head—and her job. Then she jogged down the thirty-four steps that led to the sidewalk.

She arrived about the time Link pulled up in his big truck, and she didn't even give him a second to swing down. Instead, Misty pulled on the door handle and catapulted herself into the passenger seat. "Hey."

"Hey, yourself." He grinned at her and twisted to reach into the backseat. Plenty of reusable grocery bags sat there, and yes, several insulated ones as well. "You sure look nice today."

Link grinned as he presented her with what looked like an ice cream sandwich. But it wasn't cold, and it was bright yellow.

"Lemon whoopie pie," he said. "With cream cheese frosting."

"You're joking."

"I saw them at the store and thought you might like one."

"Have you had them before?"

He shook his head as she pulled the flap back on the clear

plastic wrapper. She adored everything lemon, even going so far as to put the crystallized lemon packets in her water bottle throughout the day. At this point, she wasn't even sure how people drank regular, unflavored water.

The scent of lemon hit her nose, and she grinned. "Mm, smells good."

"Off to a good start then," he said.

She glanced over to him, found him smiling warmly, and returned her attention to the treat he'd brought her. "What kind did you get?"

"Peanut butter chocolate," he said.

Misty took a bite of the lemon cream cheese whoopie pie, the delicious tartness combining with the sweet and creamy frosting. "Mm, yes," she said around the treat.

"I don't get it, but I'm glad you like it."

She met his eye, and so much energy zipped around the truck. "It's good. It's lemon."

"Desserts should not be made with sour citrus," he said.

She laughed, because he loved everything chocolate. Chocolate and peanut butter. Chocolate and mint. Chocolate and coffee. But throw an orange in with some vanilla ice cream to make a creamsicle, and Link thought a crime had been committed.

"I love this," she said. "Thank you, Link."

"You bet," he said. "I do have to get the food back up to my momma. There's a bonfire and picnic dinner at the firepit tonight. I'm sure Uncle Ward will send out a text."

"We're invited?"

"Everyone on the ranch is invited, yes," he said.

"But it's not a date." She took another bite of the whoopie pie and let her eyebrows go up.

"No," he said. "Our first date is tomorrow night, so stop snooping to find out what we're doing. It's going to be great. You'll love it."

She swallowed her treat and said, "I'm sure I will, Link."

"Now go on," he said, extending another whoopie pie toward her. This one actually looked gray, and Misty stared at it. "It's cookies 'n cream. For Janie."

Misty took the treat from him and then gazed at him. "You're so good," she said, no trace of teasing in sight. She didn't deserve someone as good and kind and thoughtful as Link. Did she?

"If you want that mint chocolate chip, I know where I'll be about eight-thirty tonight." He gave her a nod toward the door. "I've gotta get going, sweetheart."

"Right." She reached for the door handle and spilled from his truck, her hands full of whoopie pies. "See you tonight."

"Can't wait," he said, and Misty slammed the door and stood on the sidewalk as Link drove away.

"Can't wait," Misty said as he turned the corner and disappeared. She couldn't wait to take the next step with him. A door had suddenly been thrown wide open, and all she had to do was walk through it.

She hadn't known it until now, but she'd been hiding inside a dark room for a long time, refusing to let in the light. Still, something made of fear trembled through her body, and Misty murmured, "Lord, please protect me as I take these scary first steps out of the darkness."

For she hadn't truly ever allowed a man into her life for any significant amount of time, for anything more than something frivolous and throw-away.

And this thing with Link was anything but that, and it scared her way, way down deep.

I am with you.

The words entered her mind and settled her nervous stomach. Misty closed her eyes and took a deep breath, unsure if she'd just thought the words herself, if they were a scripture she'd once known and had forgotten, or if God Himself had truly just spoken to her.

No matter what, she took her whoopie pies and made her way back to the break room, where Janie still sat with her now-eaten salad and her phone. "Link brought you dessert," Misty said.

Janie looked at the cookies 'n cream whoopie pie, and her face split into a grin. "He's the best," she said as she took it.

"Yes." Misty sat down and picked up her plastic fork. "He sure is." Now, she just had to figure out how to be with him in a real, serious way, or she felt certain there would be more than one broken heart at the end of all of this.

Chapter Eleven

L ink walked into Bull House to the sound of several voices all talking over one another. They usually held ranch meetings next door at the main homestead, in one of the wings up on the second floor, but Uncle Ward had invited everyone here today. His wife, Aunt Dot, had brought up a huge spread of pizza and baked pasta from her landscaping company.

Apparently, she'd just redone the asphalt at the Italian restaurant, and the owner had sent over enough food to feed a small army. Link wasn't going to say no to free pizza, even though he'd just come from grocery shopping in town and had grabbed a hamburger on the way home from City Hall.

He rounded the corner to find a half-dozen of his uncles standing around the oblong table, which did hold a metric ton of food.

"Link." Glory Rose, a tall, lanky fifteen-year-old, brightened when she saw him. "You've got to see this poll on Two

Cents." She whipped her phone from her back pocket, and Link smiled at her jean-clad legs, her red-and-white plaid shirt, and her cowgirl hat. She'd clearly just come in off the ranch from doing some chore, and Link pulled her into a side-hug.

"Hey," he said. "Where's your daddy got you today?"

"Workin' with Uncle Preacher down in the equipment shed," she said. "We haven't been through stuff down there in years. It's so gross."

"Good money, though," Link said.

"Yeah," Glory Rose said. She smiled up to him. "I'm going to have more than enough for that truck I want next summer."

"Yeah?" Link glanced over to Aunt Dot, who poured a glass of orange juice for Silver, Glory Rose's younger brother. He didn't see his other Ward Glover cousin, Flint, but he'd probably be along soon enough. He tended to the small animals on the ranch—when Aunt Dot and Uncle Ward could get him away from his sketch book.

"Is your momma gonna let you get it?"

"It's my money." Glory Rose lifted her chin and held up her phone. "Uncle Ranger just released the results of the Summertime Favorites list."

"Oh, boy," Link said. "Let's go." He peered at Glory Rose's phone while his uncles laughed about something, thinking he could find something for his first date with Misty tomorrow night.

No, he thought as he scanned the list of food trucks, events, outdoor activities, and restaurants that the townspeople in

Three Rivers had voted on as the places to be this summer. *You have a plan for your date tomorrow night.*

Dinner suddenly felt a little too simple to him, but Link didn't know what else to do. He wasn't going to replicate the things they'd done last summer and fall. This was a brand new start. Something fresh and new, and he needed them to be fresh and new too.

"There's Three Cakes," he said. "Aunt Holly will be happy about that."

"She's already planning a party." Aunt Dot appeared in front of Link and drew him into a hug. "How are you, baby?"

Link hugged his aunt back, because he loved her immensely. She was very, very good at making room for him in her life, in her husband's life, and here at Bull House. Uncle Ward and Uncle Preacher were both foremen for Shiloh Ridge, and everyone knew Link would most likely take over for one of them.

So he'd been working with them a lot in the past couple of years, and he'd most likely replace Uncle Ward, as he had an agricultural degree, and adored the rotational ranching Ward had been doing for decades.

"Good," Link said. "I'm sure you heard Misty and I got back together." He pulled back and met his aunt's eyes. "My momma isn't known for keeping secrets." He grinned at her while she smiled back.

Dot had dark hair and eyes for miles, and her genes had overpowered the lighter, blue-eyed genes in the Glover family. All of her children were dark, with Flint having a hint of red in his hair. Glory Rose sported freckles to go with her brunette locks, and Silver wore a thick pair of clear-framed glasses wherever he went.

"She can keep some secrets," Aunt Dot said. "I heard about Misty from Oakley, actually."

"I'm not upset if people know," Link said quickly. "She's coming to the bonfire tonight."

"As she should," Dot said. "Will you introduce me to her?"

Link's stomach turned into liquid lava. He swallowed. "Shoot. I suppose I'm gonna have to do that, aren't I?" All he'd wanted the last time he'd dated Misty was to take her around to every house and every family here and have her meet them. Start to get to know them the way he did.

But now, it felt like a massive boulder on his shoulders, a terrible burden to bear.

"I'd send a text to everyone if you don't want her to be overwhelmed," Dot said.

Link nodded, his jaw tight. But he didn't want to warn everyone away. "She met a few people earlier this week at the luncheon on Monday." Several other families had needed more meals, but Misty and Janie didn't. They worked in town and had gone grocery shopping, so Link hadn't seen them in True Blue again.

Ralf had come over last night for dinner, and Link had sat beside him and Smiles while they'd eaten. He'd seen Misty afterward, on the lane in front of their cabins, and he still wasn't sure how much longer she and Janie would be on the ranch.

The state was trying to find them another place to live, as

Janie and Misty couldn't go back to their apartment. Ralf had said last night that he should be back to his place over the weekend, as he lived in a different building, a separate apartment.

Link loved a routine, and he wasn't sure how having Misty so close would impact their second chance. Before, he *couldn't* physically see her every day. She lived too far away, and that made the times they could get together feel forbidden and special.

"It'll be fine, Link," Dot said. "We're better at meeting people than ever before." She smiled at him. "Come get something to eat."

"I ate on the way back from town."

"Take it home then," Dot said. "Cutter and Mitch would love it."

"Yeah, I'll take some."

Dot smiled at him. "Come on then."

Link followed her further into the kitchen, and he stepped into Uncle Ward's open arms. "Hey, son." Ward laughed, and Link's whole heart lifted. "Get everything in town?"

"Yep," he said. "I put the fire starters in the bonfire shed, and Bishop said he has a huge stack of newspapers, so I didn't get any of those."

"Okay." Ward lifted a box of all-meat pizza, and Link couldn't stop himself. He loved all-meat pizza, and he thought of Misty, and the margarita pizza, and then the veggie delight she'd ordered when they'd gone to a pizza parlor for a date.

So much about them didn't line up. Didn't mesh. The two of them shouldn't really be together, and yet Link was inexplicably attracted to her. He thought he and Misty got along real nicely, too, so he didn't dwell too long on the differences between them.

He leaned against the counter and took a bite of his second lunch while Aunt Dot picked up a box and started loading pizza slices into it. "Preach and I wanted to meet with you," Ward said.

Link moved his eyes to his uncle. "Yeah? About what?"

Ward glanced over to his older brother, Ranger, who'd also zeroed in on Link. Preacher, Mister, and Cactus had also come to Bull House that day. The conversation died, and Link could barely swallow his bite of sausage, ham, and pepperoni.

"Maybe we should wait until his daddy brings it up," Ranger said.

Link surveyed the crowd of cowboys, and said, "He's mentioned a few things. I'm not ready for my own house."

"Maybe not your family home," Uncle Cactus said. "But regular cowboys live with other cowboys in Cabin Row."

"And you're not really a regular cowboy," Uncle Preacher said.

"So I'm going to move...where?" Link asked.

"The Top Cottage," Ward said.

Surprise darted through Link. "The Top Cottage?" Surely they were joking. "It's not much bigger than the cabin I'm in."

"But it's not in Cabin Row," Preacher said. "It'd be all yours. The foreman's cabin."

"But I'm not the foreman."

"But it's time you were," Ward said.

Link met his eyes. "You're going to retire?"

"Not entirely," Ward said. "About how your daddy has." He grinned at Link and then around to everyone.

"I called it a junior foreman position," Ranger said. "Your own house to take care of, which would be a step up from where you are. Separate from the other cowhands. Better pay as you move into full-time training with Preacher and Ward."

Link nodded, because he wasn't sure what to say. *Mitch* rang through his head, but he didn't speak his cousin's name out loud.

"Daddy," a boy called, and all the cowboys turned toward the front door hallway. Flint came around the corner with a big golden retriever. "Uncle Duke needs help."

Everyone moved at the same time, even Link. He joined the flow of cowboy boots as they left the house, and outside, he found Duke with a rope around one cow on his left, and one on his right. The stubborn bovines wanted to go in opposite directions, and he looked at everyone with a hint of panic in his eyes.

"Cattle are loose," he said.

"It's summertime," Cactus growled. "They're free range."

"Not here," Preacher said, limping alongside Link as they let the others go to help Duke with the black cows in front of them.

Phones started chiming, Link's included, and he pulled it out in sync with Uncle Preacher. "It's my daddy."

"Cattle are out," Ranger boomed. "We've got to drive them back up into the hills. Let's saddle up, men." The crowd flowed toward the stables then, and Link hurried to saddle his beautiful bay. He worked with Copper every single day, and he trusted the equine completely.

Activity buzzed throughout the stables as everyone worked to get ready to head out, and Link wasn't the first to leave. He wasn't the last to arrive on the western fence on the ranch either, where his father rode atop his black and white Appaloosa. A pretty, confident, strong horse named Peppermint.

"They're comin' back here," he said. "Not sure why, and we've got to get a perimeter on them and get them back into the hills."

Cactus whistled through his teeth, and all of the ranch dogs —even Dusty and Rio—went to him. "C'mon, hounds," he said. "Round up." He actually led out on his pretty gray horse, and Link fell into line with Uncle Ward and Uncle Preacher.

"Thoughts?" Preacher asked.

Link kept his eyes on the horizon, no cattle in sight. He thought of Misty, then him and Misty living here on this ranch. His mind bucked against that, because he simply wasn't sure she'd ever accept a life with him here in the Texas Panhandle, in a small town of only twenty thousand, on a ranch thirty minutes from a grocery store.

Then, as the harsh sunlight shimmered against the far distance, a scene opened up for Link. One with Misty standing on the porch of a house Link couldn't fully imagine. A little girl with red hair stood at her side, waving, and she carried a blond-haired boy in her arms. Pure happiness accompanied the scene, and Link wanted the idyllic life with a wife and family, dogs and horses, cattle and this ranch, with every fiber of his being.

"I think I'm ready to be a junior foreman," he finally said, grateful his uncle hadn't pressured him to answer. Hadn't kept needling him with questions. Preacher had just said, *Thoughts?* and let Link think.

"I can take good care of the Top Cottage," he said next. He looked over to Ward, then Preacher.

"Tell us what's on your mind," Uncle Ward said.

Link took a breath. "I'm worried about Mitch."

"Mm," both Ward and Preacher said at the same time.

Link started to chuckle, and he shook his head. "Did you guys practice that?"

"No," Ward said with a chuckle. "Preach?" He looked past Link, who rode between them.

"Yeah, Mitch." Preacher sighed out a sigh that didn't sound super happy. "Mitch is worried about Mitch. I'm worried about Mitch. Everyone is worried about Mitch."

"Should I not be?" Link asked. "He's older than me, Preach. Why isn't he foreman?"

Preacher didn't need to answer. Mitch couldn't be foreman, because he couldn't speak to everyone the way Link could. He was an excellent cowboy and Link's absolute best friend in the world. He'd stopped going to church at some point last year, but Link loved him all the same.

"He's mentioned going back to Virginia a time or two," Link said casually. "I don't think he wants many people to know that." He looked ahead to where Cactus rode, the dogs fanned out alongside him.

"He'll always have a place here," Ward said. "And yeah, if he wants to be here, we'll make sure he's got a house, all of that."

"I think he'll be okay," Preacher said. "He knows who he is, and that's one of the most important things a man can have."

"Let me talk to him," Link said quietly. "Okay? I'll talk to him about it, and honestly, I wouldn't mind if he moved to the Top Cottage with me. It's two bedrooms, and that would still be a step up from us sharing." Which was how they lived now.

Cactus whistled again, and he motioned left in big sweeping motions.

"All right, boys," Daddy yelled. "Peel right and left, and let's get 'em back where they belong."

Link moved into position with his uncles, too much space between them now to keep talking. He grinned and grinned at the dozen or so dogs that could probably round up the cattle by themselves. One of them, probably a retriever named Lula, barked every so often. She loved to talk to the other dogs, but the heelers and collies simply ran and ran and ran.

He loved this life, here on Shiloh Ridge, and since most of the cattle were on the left, and he'd gone right, he had a few slow moments to pray, "Lord, am I being stupid starting something with Misty again?"

He wouldn't be leaving Shiloh Ridge, Three Rivers, or Texas. Misty wasn't here permanently. *But she said we could be serious*, he thought.

He listened, trying to hear the guidance of the Lord. Not

much came through, but Link experienced a tiny pinprick of peace in the very center of his heart. He wasn't sure what that meant, but God had never stayed silent when Link needed to do something. So maybe a relationship with Misty simply wasn't on the Lord's radar right now, because it wouldn't be a bad thing.

"Bless me to know how to become the man she deserves," he whispered. "I want to be everything for her. Her best friend. Her partner. Her Prince Charming."

And he'd do anything he had to do in order to make that happen.

The scent of smoke and flame met Link's nose the moment he left the cabin through the back door. Behind him, Mitch laughed in his strange, too-loud voice. Cutter spilled out of the cabin behind them too, while Link looked to his right, down to Misty's cabin.

He'd told her he'd meet her at the bonfire, because with the loose cattle, regular ranch chores had been delayed, and Link hadn't known when he'd be finished.

"Smells like Uncle Ward has the fire going." He signed as he said it, and Mitch nodded.

My momma made her chili for tonight, Mitch said. *I can't wait.*

Aunt Willa did make a mean pot of chili, and Link grinned as they crossed the grassy area behind their cabins to the trail between a couple of fields. Beyond that, the barns and stables lined the road, and Uncle Ward had built a beautiful family picnic spot on the ranch, sheltered from the winds and eyes of anyone who came to the ranch.

They continued talking and laughing as they made the fifteen-minute walk, and Link brought up the rear between two silos before the picnic area opened up. Dot kept the gravel immaculate, and the picnic tables had just been re-stained so they shone with lacquer.

His momma spread a bright blue tablecloth over one of them, and Aunt Oakley helped her straighten it and clip the corners in place. They moved to another one, where a flowery pink tablecloth covered that picnic table.

Aunt Etta and Uncle Bishop worked with Aunt Holly at the food table, setting out pan after pan of something baked. Four large pots of what Link assumed was chili stood down the table too, with stacks of bowls beside them.

Children ran and played, as there were still some younger kids in the Glover family. Heck, Link's own baby sister had just turned twelve. Sunnie held one end of a jump rope while Hazel, one of Uncle Mister and Aunt Libby's girls, jumped over it. Pearl Jo, Ace and Holly's daughter, held the other end of the rope, with other cousins waiting for their turn.

The youngest Glover—a little boy named Brantley—had just turned six, and he was Mister and Libby's youngest. Aurora and Oliver Walker had three children now, and their youngest was only eighteen months.

So the age-range at Shiloh Ridge literally went from one to

eighty-three, as Grandmother Lois had reached that age on her last birthday. Link expected to see her at the bonfire tonight too, though she didn't live at Shiloh Ridge anymore. She came up for family things all the time, and sure enough, he saw her arrive with Aunt Ida and Uncle Brady and their four children.

Their twins, Johnny and Judy, were seventeen now, almost seniors in high school, and they came over to Link, Cutter, and Mitch. Link often hung out with the older teens in the family, and he fist-bumped Johnny, who asked, "Did you see what's for dinner?"

"I know Aunt Willa made chili," Link said.

"And Auntie Etta and Uncle Bishop made cinnamon rolls to dip in it," Judy said.

Link's mouth started to water. "Oh, boy," he said. "That's a winner." Then he laid eyes on Misty and Janie, who'd arrived from the homestead side of the picnic area. Perhaps they'd just gotten back to the ranch from their job down in town and had parked there instead of going home.

Link's stomach did a flip and a flop and growled at him for the long afternoon without feeding it. And his mouth watered even more, this time for the gorgeous woman who'd just found him and had smiled.

Mitch's hands moved, but Link couldn't tear his eyes from Misty. "Give me a second," he said to his friends and cousins, and then he headed Misty's way.

Chapter Twelve

"Hey, beautiful," Link said, and Misty could get used to being greeted like that every single day.

"Hey, Link," Janie said before Misty could respond. "Oh, were you not talking to me?" She grinned at Misty and then Link, who took a moment to blink.

Then he said, "Of course I meant you, Janie."

She trilled out a laugh and took him by the elbow, turning him back to the group of Glovers who'd already assembled at the bonfire. "Tell me which of these cowboys are old enough for me. With the hats and the jeans and the boots, y'all start to look my age."

"Sure," Link said. "Do you guys want to go around and meet everyone?" He cut a look over to Misty, who suddenly wanted to ball her hands into fists and shove them in her pockets.

"Are your parents here?" she asked. Janie released him, and Link reached for Misty's hand.

"I've seen my momma. She was putting tablecloths on the tables a few minutes ago." He nodded to his right. "She's standin' right there with Uncle Ace."

"We didn't meet an Ace at lunch the other day," Misty said.

"He's gluten-free, so he probably didn't come."

"Yeah, these cinnamon rolls look totally made for him, then." Misty squeezed his hand, glad when he grinned at her.

"Well, my aunt Holly is a chef, so I guarantee she made a pan of them gluten-free for him. She's his wife."

"Who's whose wife?"

"Speak of the wife," Link said as a tall brunette stepped in front of them and slid a tray of condiments on the table. "I was just telling these fine ladies about how you're the best gluten-free chef in the world, and that you'd for-sure made a pan of gluten-free cinnamon rolls for Uncle Ace."

The woman—obviously Holly—smiled. "Two pans, actually. Have you seen how much chili we have here tonight?" She looked down the twenty feet of folding tables and back to Link.

Misty looked up at him too, which allowed her to see him swallow. "I'm—"

"Don't you dare," he hissed out of the side of his mouth. Misty pretended to zip her lips, which only made Holly smile wider. "Aunt Holly, this is my girlfriend, Misty. Misty, this is Aunt Holly. She and her husband Ace live right next to the cemetery."

"It's so great to meet you," Holly said as she leaned in and pressed a quick peck to Misty's cheek. "Link has said a lot about you."

"Not true," Link said quickly.

Misty laughed lightly. "Oh, Link doesn't talk a whole lot, ever, so I doubt that."

"I've heard your name," Holly said as someone yelled. They all looked that way, and Misty saw yet another Glover arriving with his family.

"That's Bishop and Montana," Link murmured. "He's the only one with grandkids."

"He barely looks older than me," Misty said, shocked at the youthful exuberance on the man bringing over even more cinnamon rolls. "Are we really eating chili with cinnamon rolls?"

"Is there a better way to eat chili?"

"It's June sixteenth," Misty said. "I didn't know Texans ate hot things in the summer."

Link simply blinked at her. "Chili is an all-weather food," he said, deadly serious.

"What about that one?" Janie asked, and Misty wanted to roll her eyes. Janie had definitely dated more than her, but she had a sister back in Dallas who was probably going to get divorced, and there was no way she'd stay in Three Rivers past their assignment.

Misty didn't have anything or anyone truly tethering her to Dallas—only the stubborn streak inside her which insisted she live in a big city.

"That's Russ," Link said. "And he's probably fifteen years older than you."

"That's okay," Janie said, and she moved toward the dark-haired cowboy who stood with a couple of other men who looked to be in their forties.

"She's going to be the death of me," Misty said as her friend walked away.

"My daddy just got here," Link said. He stepped in front of her. "I don't really see how I can just ignore them tonight. You've met Momma already. Can we just do the formal intros and be done with it?"

"Link." She reached up and brushed her fingers along the longer curls of hair that hung down from his cowboy hat. "Of course." She smiled at him, and he returned the gesture, but it wasn't the brightness she'd seen previously.

His nerves definitely shone through, but he turned and faced his parents. "Let's do this."

"It's just your parents," she said. "I met them at the wedding."

"Sort of," he muttered. "And it's a big deal to me, Misty." He looked at her as they kept walking toward the group of adults—not just his parents—who'd gathered on the fringes of the bonfire's heat. "It's why we broke up last time. This is what I wanted to do, and we're doing it before we even go out."

"You've got to stop worrying about when things happen," she said. "There's no timeline for how a relationship is supposed to go." Plus, they'd been out before. He wasn't a complete stranger the way he'd been when he'd sat down at the table outside the coffee truck.

Several of the Glovers saw Link and Misty approaching,

and they seemed to stop talking mid-sentence. "Stop staring," someone hissed, but Misty didn't see anyone's mouth move.

"Hey," Link said. "Everyone, I wanted to introduce you to Misty Granger. She's staying in Cabin Five for a bit, until things with her apartment get sorted." He smiled down at her, and Misty caught sight of a glimmer of the Link she got when they were alone. "We're seeing each other again."

"It's so great to be here," Misty said, really meaning it. "This place is so nice. Link's told me a lot about it, but there's nothing like seeing it."

"We'll start closest to you," Link said. "This here's Aunt Willa. I think you probably met her on Monday."

"We did," Willa said. "From a distance." She wore a warm smile, and Misty's heartbeat cartwheeled through her chest.

"I love your sermons," Misty said, a bit star-struck to be standing here with her. "You always seem to strike something in my soul that needs to be awakened."

No one said anything, and Misty looked down the row. "And Cactus," she said. "We met outside by the horses."

He simply glared back at her, and Misty wondered if he ever smiled. Willa nudged him and said, "Say hello. It's not her fault you didn't get your way with the desserts."

"Hello, Misty," Cactus said, and there appeared a smile. His bright blue eyes crinkled, and oh, he was charming and charismatic when he brought that thing out.

"Beside him is my aunt Ida," Link said. "Her husband is a cop, but I'm not sure where he is." Link looked around while Misty shook hands with Ida.

"You're Etta's twin," Misty said.

Next to her, Link's daddy chuckled. "She loves being introduced that way."

"I didn't introduce her that way," Link said and Misty followed up immediately with, "I didn't mean it like that. I just meant—" She looked at Link for help, because she'd already made a blunder here.

"I met Etta the other day, at the luncheon, and you look like her. I was just verbalizing the mental connection I'd made. I'm sorry."

A beat of silence filled the entire world, and then several people started laughing. Misty wasn't sure if she should join them or burst into tears, and she squeezed Link's hand hard. He hadn't burst into laughter, but he definitely wore a happy grin. A golden retriever grin.

"Hey, relax," he said. He lifted his arm around her and pulled her closer. "Ida doesn't care at all. She knows she's Etta's twin, and she knows Etta meets most people before her."

"Why's that?" Misty asked.

"Because she lives down in town, and Etta lives up here." Link glanced to his father, and he said, "Daddy, this is Misty. Misty, my father, Bear Glover." He didn't stumble over any of the words, but Misty thought of him as a little, tiny boy. Three years old. Without a mother or a father.

How much could he remember? Anything?

She remembered too much of her childhood, and she determined she'd ask Link later as she stepped toward his daddy. "Link has told me all the best things about you," she said as he gave her a quick Texas-style greeting. A fast hug and a quick peck on the cheek.

"Then you guys must not talk much about me," Bear said, his smile healthy and happy on his face.

"Daddy," Link said, shaking his head. "And you've met my momma, but Momma, this is Misty. Misty, my momma."

She took a moment to watch the love as it rolled across Link's features, and then she focused on Sammy.

"You don't have to call me Momma," she said, her gaze still on Link too. "My name is Sammy."

Link's cowboy boots shuffled along the gravel, but he didn't speak.

"Sammy, it's great to formally meet you," Misty said as she stepped in to greet his mother.

"The cabin's okay?" Sammy asked. "No one's lived there in a while."

"It's awesome," Misty said, smiling at everyone. "I don't know how long we'll be here, but Link says it's okay."

"It's fine," Bear said. "No one else is using it."

"The state is trying to find us somewhere, but there's not much for rent right now. My whole building can't go back."

"You can stay here as long as you want," Sammy said. "It's just a long drive to work every day, I imagine."

"Yeah," Misty said, because she wasn't going to argue about that. Getting up earlier had been a challenge, as she wasn't much of a morning person, but she and Janie could at least carpool and split the cost for gas.

Before Misty could think of something else to say, the gravel made a skating, grinding sound, and someone slid into the back of Misty's legs. She took a step forward as a child started to cry.

Without thinking, she dropped into a crouch and pulled the little girl onto her lap. "Hey, it's okay."

The blonde girl kept crying, and she looked up at Misty. She smoothed back her hair as she smiled at her. "You're okay. It was just a small tumble. Let me see, okay?" Misty brushed away the gravel that had stuck to the girl's knees, catching a bit of blood.

"It's nothing, see. I bet we can grab a bandage and it'll be fine." She wiped the girl's tears, only then realizing that more than one person had started to stare at her.

"Lara." A woman who couldn't be older than Misty arrived.

"I falled, Mama."

Misty transferred the girl to her mother's lap. "It's not bleeding too badly."

The woman looked at her with a small smile. "She has a couple of left feet." She got up with the help of Link. "Thanks, Link. Come on, Lara. Auntie Etta will have a Band-Aid."

Misty accepted Link's hand too, and he pulled her up as well. She hadn't gone home from City Hall before stopping by this bonfire, because she and Janie had been late getting away from the work.

"That's Aurora," Link said. "She's my uncle Bishop's daughter."

"Ah, yes," Misty said, though the family tree was starting to splinter in her head. "Uncle Bishop." She looked at him, and he seemed to get the hint, because he waved good-bye to his family.

He turned as he said, "Excuse us for a minute."

Misty wasn't sure why she'd suddenly become so overwhelmed, only that she had. "Sorry," she said.

"It's fine," he said. "I know it's a lot."

Everywhere Misty looked, she saw more people. She wanted to escape back to her cabin, but she wouldn't pull Link from his family bonfire. "Did your aunts make this just for you?" she asked as they left the blazing fire behind.

"What do you mean?" He swung her hand easily between them.

"I mean, you've told me about the famed chili with cinnamon rolls. I thought I'd never see it."

He chuckled and shook his head. "Coincidence."

"You didn't ask them to make it to show me?"

"No, ma'am." He nodded to someone on their right. "Do you want to sneak away and eat somewhere else?"

"Yes," Misty said with a long sigh. Immediately, her stomach clenched. "I mean, it's fine."

"I know we're a lot," he murmured. "I was hoping to introduce you just to my family, and we'd expand from there, but...."

"Electrical fire," she said, because she'd been using that as a reason for a lot of things this week.

"Electrical fire," he said. "As soon as we pray, we'll just dish up some food and head back to my cabin. Or yours. Or something. We can come back in a couple of hours, when it's dark and the marshmallows and Starburst come out."

Misty smiled at him. "I can do this."

"But you don't have to." He pressed a kiss to her temple.

"Okay? It's fine. We've had a crazy day on the ranch today, and I'm fine to get away from the chaos for a bit."

"Okay," she said, because she wasn't going to argue with him over this.

Behind her, someone emitted a shrill whistle, and a couple more people joined in. Misty and Link turned back to the group, but he didn't take her closer. Ward had gotten up on a chair, and he lifted both hands above his head.

"Everyone's not here yet, but we're gonna get started anyway. We'll pray, and then there's dinner, desserts, and roasting later. Please keep an eye on your kids with the fire and everything, and thanks for comin'."

He got down and another man that Misty was pretty sure was Link's uncle Judge got up on the chair. He pressed his cowboy hat to his chest and waited several moments while the other cowboys did the same.

Misty quickly crossed her arms and bowed her head, something she'd never felt before seeping through her.

"Dear Lord," Judge said, and tears crowded into Misty's eyes. She knew instantly what this ranch had that she didn't. That she sorely lacked.

Family.

As Judge prayed with gratitude for the hands which had made dinner tonight, for the people who had come to join them, and for the land they'd been entrusted with, Misty fought a great battle with herself and her emotions.

"Bless the food," he said, and Misty started to feel more stable. "Bless any who are here who have a special need at this time, like a place to call home or a health issue. We're grateful for family, for each other, and for the bounty in our lives. Amen."

"Amen," rang through the air, but Misty couldn't get her voice to work. She spun away from the Glovers and all of their guests and walked away.

"Misty," Link said after her, but she couldn't stop. Of course, he wasn't going to just let her rush off, and she heard his footsteps behind her. "Sweetheart."

She ducked into the shade cast by the silo, a sob wrenching out of her throat. Link caught her then, and she faced him as he said, "Hey, hey, hey. What's wrong?"

"Nothing." She grabbed onto him and sank into his arms, his chest.

"It's something," he murmured.

Misty couldn't articulate too much, so she simply wrapped her arms around Link and held on. His family, his reality, literally everything about him was so different from her and hers. She couldn't help thinking as she stood there in his embrace that he could rescue her from her shell of a life and provide one that was truly worth living.

Chapter Thirteen

L ink stepped into his bedroom, a towel around his waist, and found Mitch lying in his bed. "Hey," he said with a wave. "You okay?" He seemed maybe a bit pale, but Link wasn't sure

Fine, Mitch said as he sat up. *Going out with Misty?*

Link nodded and started getting dressed. He faced Mitch and signed. "What are you doing tonight?"

Mitch shrugged and got to his feet. *Probably going to my parents'. Something.*

"No summer dance?" Link smiled at Mitch and pulled his polo over his head.

Mitch shook his head. *Link.* He finger-spelled his name quickly, but Link caught it. Sometimes Mitch dropped the last two letters and combined them into a sort of swooping K, and that had become the sign for Link's name.

Link stilled, because Mitch wasn't his usual self. "What?" He didn't sign, but Mitch could read lips.

I'm not happy here, he ducked his head, but his hands kept moving. *I'm going to talk to my parents about going back to Virginia. I've been talking to the director there, and she says I can come back any time.*

"Mitch," Link said, but the man had his gaze down. Link stepped over to him, needing a belt to keep his pants up. But he could finish getting dressed after this conversation. "Hey, brother."

He grabbed onto Mitch's shoulder, and that got his cousin to look up. "I'll miss you," Link said. "But you have to do what makes you happy. I know it's not here. Not right now."

He backed up as Mitch started to sign. *What if I'm not happy there either?*

Link didn't spend a lot of time giving anyone advice, least of all Mitch. He'd been making the drive to church alone for a while, but he couldn't change what he felt or what he believed. So he said, "Maybe it's time to just put your head down, work hard, and let God guide you."

Mitch nodded, sniffed, and wiped his eyes as he looked away. *I'll miss you*, he said, his face and fingers and entire being full of emotion. Link imagined his voice if Mitch could use it, and it would be torn, ragged, and anguished.

He grabbed onto him and hauled him into his chest. "I love you, brother," he whispered, though Mitch wouldn't be able to hear him. Somehow, Mitch knew he'd spoken, because he nodded and pressed this hand in the *I love you* sign against Link's back.

They separated, and Mitch drew a deep breath and signed, *Have fun on your second first date.*

Link smiled and reached for his belt. He didn't want to go through all of his reservations about starting something with Misty he couldn't finish, so he simply ran his hands through his hair while Mitch left the bedroom they shared.

"It would be nice to have my own place," he said quietly, not that Mitch would overhear. At the same time, if he lived in the Top Cottage, he wouldn't have had this conversation with his cousin. His best friend.

He settled a cowboy hat on his head as he left the bedroom, and he grabbed his keys from the hook in the kitchen. No one had cooked tonight, and he didn't see Cutter anywhere. Mitch had already left, and Link exited through the front door.

He'd gone halfway toward his truck before he remembered he wasn't driving down to the Ivy Ridge apartment complex to pick up Misty. He did an about-face and started down the lane toward her cabin.

Before he could go up the steps and knock on the door—these cabins didn't have doorbells—Misty came outside. She wore a pair of dark blue shorts that went halfway down her thigh and a tank top with fluttering sleeves and a blue, white, and green floral print.

"Aren't you the prettiest thing on the ranch tonight?" Link came to a complete halt as she skipped down the steps. She wore a bright smile to go with her stunning radiance, and Link didn't care if he was starting something he couldn't finish.

Everything inside him wanted to be with this person, be next to this woman, have Misty in his life for as long as possible.

"You look amazing," she said as she moved right into his personal space. She slid her hand up his chest to his collar, where she gripped the fabric in her fingers. "Smell great, too."

"Thank you," he said. Misty had always been great at complimenting him, and she made him feel so good about himself.

His hands went around her easily, holding her against him. She smiled up at him, and Link lost his mind for a moment. With his ranch dogs watching, he leaned down and touched his mouth to Misty's.

She drew in a breath through her nose and kissed him back, which only made Link happier than ever. He kissed her and kissed her, only remembering he stood out in the open when someone catcalled loud enough for the sound to penetrate the high he found himself floating on.

He pulled back and filled his lungs with air. "Remember that time I kissed you before the first date?"

"Yeah," she whispered back. She ran her hands through his hair, which sent a tingling sensation through his whole body. "Remember when we had the most amazing first date ever?"

"Hmm." He leaned his forehead against hers, breathed in the clean, fresh scent of her skin, and straightened. "Okay, let's go then." Link took her hand and led her back down the road to his truck.

"Hungry?" he asked.

"Around here, no one goes without food," she said. "But somehow, yes, I'm hungry."

"Great," he said. "Because I think you're going to love this place we're going."

"Where are we going?"

"Okay, so remember how we were going to eat at every little place around town?" He glanced over to her as he drove, barely catching her nod. "I'm not sure if we'll ever accomplish that, but—"

"Positive thoughts," she said.

He didn't bring up that they only had another year, and they couldn't possibly get through all the eateries in Three Rivers by then.

He cast her a smile. "I'm pretty sure we were somewhere in the Cs," Link said. "And you were excited about trying Castleton, so...."

"Castleton?" Misty made a little shriek and gripped his forearm. "Link, they have the cornbread cookies this week."

"They do?" Link grinned at her.

Misty half-rolled her eyes at him. "You knew that."

"I may have looked it up."

"You're my favorite person," Misty said, and Link dang near slammed on the brakes. The mood in the truck sobered, and he shifted in his seat.

"Do you mean that?"

"Yes." She slid her hand down his arm to his, and Link laced his fingers through hers. "Don't go thinking you're special or anything, though. I only have like, three people in my life that I even like. It's not like your family, where you have a hundred people I have to weed through to get to the top."

Link laughed, because one, his family wasn't quite to one hundred yet, though if he brought in all the cowboys at the surrounding ranches, the way they did for big parties, weddings, or when someone needed help, that number could definitely go into three digits.

Two, Misty had been number one in his life almost since the moment he'd met her. He lifted her hand to his lips and pressed his smile there. "I don't think I'm special," he said.

"Good," she said.

He pulled into the lot at Castleton and went around the truck to open Misty's door. Being with her felt easy and fun, and since he'd made a reservation, they sat in a booth with a window view only a few minutes later.

The hostess handed them menus, and since Link hadn't been here before, he actually needed to look at his. Misty had ordered to-go from here before, so she glanced around. "This place is nice," she said.

"It has a good vibe," he agreed.

"How are you two tonight?"

Link looked up at the waitress, who shone with starlight. "Great," he said.

"Drinks?"

He looked across the table to Misty, and she'd picked up the drink menu. "Mm, yes, I'll take the Sour Cranberry." She set down the menu and looked up at the waitress. "And what are the chances of having dessert first?" She smiled over to Link.

"I can bring you whatever you want," she said.

"He wants a Diet Coke with lemon," Misty said. "The Sour Cranberry for me. And we're going to need a four-pack of the cornbread cookies to start with. The sooner the better."

"Wow," Link said as the waitress nodded and smiled her way away from the table. "A four-pack?" He laughed while Misty simply picked up her menu again. "I suppose I should've told you I have dessert plans too."

She peered over the top of the menu. "Dessert plans? When you knew they had cornbread cookies this week? You know they only have these for one week every year. One. Week, Link."

"And you forgot about them, because of the electrical fire."

"That blasted electrical fire." Misty giggled and shook her head. "But it did make me forget about the cookies." She sighed and gazed at him the way she'd kissed him. Like she really did like him.

He wanted to ask her about next summer, but something inside him seized. The words dried right up, and he reached for the straw as the waitress returned with their drinks and cookies.

Misty clapped her hands and pulled her mocktail and the box of cookies closer to her. "What's for dessert? I need to know so I can judge how many of these to eat."

"Coffee and cookies," he said.

"Americano and chocolate," she said, giving him a coy smile. "My favorite."

He nodded to the cornbread cookie already in her hand. "Really?"

She looked at it and then him. "They're tied."

"It's okay if the cornbread cookies are number one," he said.

She nudged the box toward him. "Try one."

He looked at them, the pale yellow cookies with a scoop of frosting right in the middle. It looked like honey had been drizzled over the top of them, and he did love honey. Still, he hesitated. "What if I don't like them?"

"Then there's more for me." Misty took her first bite of the cornbread cookie, her eyes falling closed in bliss. She'd put makeup on tonight when she didn't for work, and Link liked the darkness around her eyes and the flush in her cheeks. She groaned, and that only made him laugh.

They'd had a couple of serious conversations now. He'd introduced her to his parents. They'd snuck away from the bonfire last night, where she'd then told him how amazing it was to be surrounded by so much family, so many people who cared about each other.

So her joke tonight about the largeness of his family was in good fun. Yes, they could be a lot, but for a woman like Misty, they might just be exactly what she needed. Link had never viewed his enormous, loud, sometimes obnoxious family like that, but as Misty had talked over chili and cinnamon rolls last night, Link had felt how special they were.

He picked up a cookie. "Here goes nothing." He bit into the cookie, realizing he should've spread the frosting out a little bit, because he hardly got any. The texture surprised him—this thing had actual cornmeal in it.

It wasn't too sweet at all, and while his momma's cornbread had kernels of real corn, this didn't. It was almost like a sugar cookie with cornmeal, that delicious vanilla frosting, and honey.

He studied the cookie as he chewed, only switching his gaze to Misty when she asked, "Well?"

He swallowed and said, "I think that rivals cinnamon rolls dipped in chili." He grinned at her while she giggled, then took another bite. "Yeah, this is great."

"See? I knew you'd like them." She lifted her cookie to take another bite too, but paused. "And hey, I think this is the first thing we both like."

Link shook his head. "That can't be true. Remember when we went on the starlight hike? We both liked that."

"Food-wise, though," she said.

"It can't be," he said. "You ate like, six cinnamon rolls last night."

"But independent of the chili," she said. "I just couldn't bring myself to dunk it."

"Next time," he said like there really would be a next time. He wanted there to be a lot of next time's with Misty. The next time he held her hand. The next serious conversation they had. The next time he kissed her.

"Hey, so I think I'm going to be moving soon," he said.

Misty froze mid-chew. "What?" she asked around her mouth of cookie appetizer.

He grinned at her. "Is your heart beating hard?"

She stared back at him, those long, painted-black eyelashes blinking.

"If I'm not special, why do you care where I live?" he teased.

Misty thawed back to normal activity. "We're going there?" She set down the second half of her cookie. "Already?"

"I kissed you before we even got out of your driveway," he said. "So yeah. I'm going there already."

Misty sighed like he was insufferable, and she reached up to push her hair back off her face. "Fine, Mister Glover. You're special enough for me to care where you live."

He leaned back in the booth and folded his arms, waiting for her to continue. When she didn't, he said, "This is when you tell me something I won't like."

"You aren't really moving soon," she fired back.

"I am," he said. "I'm getting a promotion on the ranch too. I'm going to be the junior foreman, and he gets his own house. I'm moving into the Top Cottage over the Fourth of July weekend."

"Dang," she said without missing a beat. "I was hoping we'd take our get-in-the-truck-and-drive road trip over the Fourth of July weekend. Now you're moving?" She wrinkled her nose. "That's a terrible time to move."

Link had started up their game to see what she'd tell him, but she'd just twisted it all up. "You'd go on a road trip with me?"

"Maybe," she said.

"What's a cowboy got to do to get a yes to that question?"

Misty broke off a piece of her cookie and gave him a calculating look as she popped it into her mouth. "If I'm not special, why do you care if we go on a road trip together or not?"

Link grinned at her, though they both knew she'd just cheated in their little game. "Fine, Misty," he said quietly as the waitress arrived at the end of the table to take their orders. He hadn't even looked at the menu yet, and he picked it up as he added, "You're special enough for me to want to lock myself in a truck with you and drive for a while."

"Do you guys need another couple of minutes?" the waitress asked.

Link put down his menu. "Nope. She's gonna order for both of us."

Panic paraded across Misty's face, but she recovered quickly as she picked up the menu. "I want the French dip, please, with the French fries. And he'll have...." The pause lengthened, and just when Link figured he better open up his menu and save her, she said, "The crispy chicken sandwich. With fries."

The waitress nodded and left, and Misty looked past the cookies to Link. "Can't go wrong with a crispy chicken sandwich," she said.

"We'll see." He told himself not to get too keyed up over the fact that she knew him well enough to order for him. He could think about it later, after the date had ended and he'd gone to bed.

He'd been so bored in his life before, simply working the ranch every day, hour after hour, month after month. Misty had been the one bright ray in his life, and now that she was back, Link felt like he'd embarked on the greatest journey of his life.

Thank you, Lord, he thought. *For helping me talk to this woman. For opening a door and giving me the courage to walk through it.*

"So," he said. "I have to head up into the hills tomorrow to make sure Jed and Jimmer are okay with the dogs and the herd. We're takin' them some more supplies. But...Sunday? You and me and a pew in church?"

Misty took a moment to answer, and then she said, "All right."

"All right," Link said, glad to have another time and place to see her again. "Now tell me: if you could only go on one road trip in your whole life, where would you go?"

She chuckled and shook her head. "I don't know."

"Oh, come on. Name somewhere."

"*You* name somewhere," she said.

"Road trip," he said, his mind working fast. "I think I'd head north, to the Rocky Mountains. Have you ever seen them?"

"No, sir," she said.

"Me either." Link reached for his cola and squeezed the lemon into it. "Yeah, I think that would be a good adventure, and you like adventures."

She smiled at him and slid to the end of the bench seat. Alarm pulled through Link, but she just took the two steps to his side of the table and sat next to him. "I do like adventure," she said. "But Link, you don't have to do everything I like."

"I know," he said. "That's why we're getting coffee and cookies after this."

She smiled in that soft, gorgeous way she had, shook her

head, and matched her mouth to his right there in the restaurant. Sure, he'd kissed her in public too, but only family could see them on the ranch.

Here, *anyone* could see them, but Link found he didn't care. With every stroke of her mouth against his, Link fell further and further in love with her.

How long will this last? burned through his blood, but Link ignored it by tasting that cornbread cookie on his girlfriend's lips.

Chapter Fourteen

Mitch Glover hurried into the library, his hearing dog right at his side, bypassing the checkout counter without even looking over to see if Kaytee Larsen stood there. Sure, he'd had a crush on her for a few weeks after meeting her a few months ago before one of his calls to his friends back in Virginia.

He loved her dark hair, her sparkling eyes, and those soft-as-pillows lips. She hadn't seemed to mind that all of their conversation had to be typed, but Mitch did. He wanted someone he could truly talk with, and that meant he needed someone who could speak sign language—or he had to learn to hear and speak, an avenue he'd started thinking about more and more.

In the Texas Panhandle, in a town of barely twenty thousand, the people who could communicate with him all lived at Shiloh Ridge. And they'd all learned to sign simply so they could talk to him. With him. Because they loved him.

Now that Link was back together with Misty, Mitch could easily see and feel the gaping holes in his life. His parents loved him, and Mitch knew his daddy would do anything for him. *Absolutely anything*, Cactus Glover had said last week when Mitch had gone to talk to his parents about returning to Whispering Paws, the deaf education school he'd worked at after he'd graduated from high school.

He'd worked on the dog-training side of the academy, but they'd been asking him to come back and teach for nine months now. They wanted someone who knew specialized signs for ranches and farms, and seeing as how Mitch had been living and working at Shiloh Ridge since he was ten years old, he knew a lot of that vocabulary. All of those signs.

The thought of living so far from Texas had his heart tied in a knot, but every time he thought about staying here, he just knew it wasn't right. He didn't talk to God as much these days as he had in the past, but it sure seemed like the Lord still cared about him. Still wanted to guide Mitch where he was supposed to go.

So he slid into the chair at an open computer and started clicking around like crazy while Honor found a spot at his feet. Mitch possessed quick and nimble fingers, as he'd spent his whole life talking with them. Either through a computer, a phone, or sign language, and Mitch did his best to take good care of his hands.

The video conference window came up, and he made sure the volume was down. Phil, the director of Whispering Paws, could speak and sign, and he did both on calls. No one else needed to hear this conversation, though they could read the captions over his shoulder if they really wanted to.

Mitch, Phil said with a smile. *You made it.*

Sorry I'm a little late, he said. *Things on the ranch are a little unpredictable in the summer.*

Mitch ignored the look from the man next to him. He was used to people looking at him a little strangely, but they usually went back to their business fast enough.

It's fine, it's fine. Phil waved away Mitch's apology. *We miss you here. You're so good with the dogs, and we do have a gaping hole in our curriculum where you'd fit nicely.*

Mitch smiled and nodded, his cowboy hat ducking low to cover his face. He wouldn't be able to see Phil if he started signing, and of course, he couldn't hear. But sitting here, on this day in late June, Mitch wasn't sure he could say what he'd come here to say.

He looked up and found Phil waiting for him. Of course he would be. Phil knew not to talk to a deaf person without making eye contact first. *So what can I do for you today, Mitch?*

He took a deep breath and blew it out. *I've talked to my folks, and we all agree that it's time for me to come back to Whispering Paws.*

Lowering his hands, he nodded. Just once. Like, *that's that. What do you think? Will you hire me, or have you just been saying things?*

Mitch didn't like that. He didn't understand people who talked and talked and didn't mean what they said.

Phil looked straight at him, seemingly into his soul. Then a smile broke out onto his face as he started cheering with his hands. *We'll take you whenever you can get here, Mitch. When do you think you'll be here?*

August, Mitch said, making the three-letter sign quickly. *I've got to get packed up, drive across the country, all of that. It should be in time for the new semester, and for me to get settled. Get back into a routine of working with the dogs. All of that.*

He shifted in his seat and glanced down at Honor, who looked back at him.

When Mitch looked back at Phil, he asked, *You've still got Honor?*

She's right here with me, Mitch said. *I don't go anywhere alone, and sometimes I wish I could.*

Here, you can, he said, smiling.

Mitch smiled back at Phil. *Nah. My daddy says that's not safe.* And he knew it wasn't, even at a place like Whispering Paws. He couldn't hear anything. If something went wrong, and Mitch wasn't actively looking at it, the only way he'd know was through Honor.

I don't mind having a dog with me, he said. *She's a good friend.* He reached down and patted Honor, whose eyes closed in apparent bliss.

I'll get the paperwork emailed over, Phil said.

I wanted to talk about housing, Mitch said, shifting in his seat again.

Our professors are eligible for on-campus housing, Phil said. *I'll have Martha send you the information packet on it.*

Is there room for me there? Mitch asked.

Absolutely, but you don't have to live on-campus. We have teachers and staff who find a place in town. We can assist with whatever you need. We know people in the community who can sign or who our employees have rented from before.

Mitch nodded, and he wasn't sure why the housing in Willowbrook was concerning him so much, only that it was. Last time he'd gone, he'd simply taken a dorm in the canine trainers wing without a second thought.

This time, he wasn't sure where he'd fit at Whispering Paws. He wasn't a student, so he wouldn't live in the student dorms. He hadn't last time either. He'd only worked with the dogs in the training facility, and he'd lived in a room with another trainer.

I'll look for the email, he said. *Thanks, Phil.*

I'm just so excited you're coming, Phil said. *I'm going to be the most popular guy in our meeting tomorrow.* He laughed, though Mitch couldn't hear him.

Mitch grinned back, and he let Phil end the video conference. He leaned back in his chair as the screen went back to black, a sigh leaking from his mouth. Honor put her paw on his leg, and he looked at her. The golden retriever looked over to something else, and that was his cue to do the same.

He did, and he jumped to his feet when he saw Kaytee. *Hey,* he said. He pulled his hands up his body. *What's up?*

She'd done her hair up today, the start of twin braids happening on either side of her head. She wore enough makeup to make his throat go a little dry, and she wore a dark blue polo with the library logo across the chest and a pair of jeans. Her bright white sneakers made him smile, as did her bright grin.

Kaytee was a couple of years younger than him, but still within an acceptable age for dating. She held out her hand, and Mitch tugged his phone out of his pocket and handed it to her. She started typing while he stood there awkwardly.

He hated this part of things. He just wanted to see someone and start talking to them. This was why he didn't go shopping anywhere he might need to talk to someone.

Kaytee turned his phone back to him, and he read the screen. *What are you doing this weekend? A bunch of us are meeting for a picnic in the park and then watching the fireworks from Mount Cross.*

He looked up at her. *Maybe*, he signed. Kaytee didn't know sign language, but they'd gone out a few times, and he could generally get the gist across for simple things. He took his phone and let his fingers fly as he answered her below her text in his notes app.

Maybe. My cousin is moving out this weekend, and I'm helping him with that. If we get done in time, I could come.

He gave her the phone and watched her face light up. So she still liked him. Mitch could read facial expressions and body language extremely well, and the interest in Kaytee's expression sure wasn't hard to find, even as she looked down to type him another message.

If it's Link, he could come too, Kaytee said, and Mitch nodded.

She kept the phone and typed some more. *Would you come*

pick me up? If you can come, that is. Text me and let me know. We aren't meeting for dinner until seven.

Mitch read her message as he took the phone back. He looked up at her while keeping his head down. He liked Kaytee just fine. She was incredibly pretty. He'd kissed her before, and they'd been out a few times. He'd stopped texting her when he'd decided to move back to Virginia, but he hadn't told her that.

I'll text you, he typed out. *But Kaytee, I'm moving to back to Virginia and Whispering Paws at the beginning of August.* He read over the message once, and then again, and then gave her the phone.

She read it quickly, and she looked up with a measure of surprise in her eyes. "Oh," she said. "That's too bad." Then she moved into his chest, her hand with the phone sliding around his waist and slipping his phone into his back pocket. She kissed his cheek, then moved her mouth to his.

Surprised, but knowing what to do, Mitch kissed her back. Probably a mistake, but she'd surprised him. He loved Link, but he wasn't a whole lot like him. Link wanted serious and long-term, and while Mitch did too—eventually—he didn't mind having more of a summer fling.

Moving Link out of the cowboy cabin where he'd been living for the past few years took about thirty minutes, and most of that was the drive up to the Top Cottage. He didn't own his own bed, dresser, couch, nothing.

So moving turned out to be furniture assembly and positioning those pieces where a suddenly indecisive version of Link wanted them. Plenty of people had come to help, and Mitch did recognize the passive, stands-back man Link became when his daddy and uncles showed up to get a job done.

Mitch knew, because he did the same thing. He didn't know how to be like Uncle Bear or his own daddy, so full of life, confidence, and experience. Mitch supposed that was why he, Link, and the other Glovers coming up worked alongside their fathers and uncles, but he still always felt vastly inferior to those older than him and everyone who could hear when he couldn't.

Finally, everyone left but Mitch, and he stood in a new, updated interior of the Top Cottage. Link's new house. He faced his cousin and started talking. *How are you feeling?*

Weird, Link signed back, and he looked a little disheveled, a little uncertain. *I've never lived alone before.*

It's nice, Mitch said as he looked around again. *Really big. New everything.*

The Glovers certainly had resources to furnish a house on a moment's notice, put together a huge spread of food for whoever needed it, and more. They'd done just that for the victims of the electrical outage and fire down in town, and only Janie and Misty still lived at Shiloh Ridge. Everyone else had either been able to get back into their apartments or find other housing.

He looked back to Link, who said, *It's too nice. I feel kind of awkward here. Like, where do my dirty boots go? Why do I have that empty bedroom?* His chest rose and fell, and Mitch imagined the frustrated sound his cousin might make.

You'll get used to it, Mitch said.

Enough about it, Link said. *Tell me what you decided to do at Whispering Paws.*

Mitch made his own version of a frustrated sigh. *I'm not sure yet. Daddy and I are flying there next week to actually look at places, at the faculty lodging. Talk about feeling stupid. Why can't I just decide?*

Everything had become harder after Mitch had decided to leave Three Rivers. He felt like things should be easier, but nothing was.

Link clapped one hand on Mitch's shoulder, and they stood nearly toe-to-toe, looking at one another. "You'll figure it out," Link said without his hands. "Because you're smart, and you're capable, and you're Mitchell Glover." He grinned, and Mitch's emotions pitched left and right and up and down. He couldn't leave Link here at Shiloh Ridge. What had he been thinking?

"Don't ever forget that," Link said. "You're my best friend, my brother, and *Mitchell Glover*." He brought his fist to his chest in the same way their daddies and uncles did. In a display of family and camaraderie. "That means something."

Mitch nodded and said, *Yeah, it does*, wishing he could use his voice to get a point across, the way Link did. *Thanks, Link.* He pulled him into a hug and held on tight. They stood there for a few seconds, and then Link stepped back and ran one hand through his hair.

Well, he signed. *Should we head to town for that picnic and the fireworks?*

Mitch grinned and said, *Yeah, we should. I'll let you go pick up Misty.*

She's coming here, Link said. *So you better head out.* He grinned. *We'll come pick you up in twenty minutes.*

Mitch nodded, and with his emotions still a bit raw, he left through the front door. Link had been at his side for seventeen years now. He translated for him whenever Mitch didn't understand. He described the music in movies, so Mitch could imagine the big horns and trumpets that played during the biggest moments of the plot. During the emotional reunions. All of it.

He'd never have a friend as good as Link, Mitch knew that, and he smiled and saluted to Misty as she pulled up in her SUV. Link would want to show her around the house and talk about how it was too big, with too many nice things in it, by himself.

So Mitch headed back to the bedroom he'd once shared with Link, and with every turn of the wheels, he felt more and more confident that he was ready for the next phase of his life too.

In Willowbrook, Virginia, at Whispering Paws.

Chapter Fifteen

D awson Rhinehart pushed the shirt off his eyes as his alarm sounded. Yes, even at five o'clock in the morning, he needed something to block the sunlight from waking him even earlier than that.

His eyes felt like someone had spent the night rubbing sand in them. He sat up and pulled his arms up over his head, his ribs on the right side pulling in a not-quite-comfortable way. He'd been battling cattle all summer, and they only had one more round of antibiotics to get through the last group of cattle to eradicate the BRD on the ranch.

Respiratory diseases weren't trivial, not on a cattle ranch in Texas. Especially when it bordered the largest cattle operation in the Panhandle. His oldest brother, Duke, ran the ranch, and he'd been down to the hospital twice this year alone from accidents on their family land.

He worked the ranch with his wife, Arizona, and Dawson

loved going to their house for dinner. They had four children who adored Dawson, and he'd see all of them out on the ranch somewhere today. Their parents made them all work in the summer, and Dawson remembered really looking forward to school starting again, because then he didn't have to work in the hot sunshine for twelve hours every day. Seven days a week. All holidays.

At the same time, Dawson loved nothing more than working the family ranch. In his mind, he just called it the Rhinehart Ranch, as did plenty of others. But on the books, they did business as Hidden Hills Ranch. They weren't as fancy as Shiloh Ridge next door, with big arches and fancy houses.

Dawson currently lived with his younger brother Brandon, and he wasn't surprised to hear the shower in the cabin start while he still tried to stretch out the discomfort in his right side. He gained his feet and walked out of his room, stretching out his arms and legs. He wouldn't shower until he finished his run anyway, and by then, Brandon would be finished, with breakfast on the table.

They had a good routine going, and while that sometimes drove Dawson nuts, he also liked the predictability of his life.

Back in his bedroom, he dressed in his running shorts and shoes, then pulled a tank top over his head. He'd probably lose it at some point, because the sun baked Texas in July, no matter the time of day.

Dawson liked to check his calendar for the day before his run, because then his thoughts would set his intention and mindset for the day, something he'd learned to do in high school to avoid panicking when something came up he hadn't anticipated.

He'd been through quite a bit of cognitive behavior therapy in an attempt to get his thoughts to bring up the good things about him instead of the bad, and a morning run with his schedule in his head had helped immensely.

"Oh, my triple date is tonight," he muttered when he saw the event on the calendar. He was going out with Finn and Edith Ackerman and Alex and Nicki Baxter. Yes, they were both married couples, but Dawson was the same age as Finn and Edith, and he got along well with them.

Alex was Edith's younger brother, and he'd only been married for about a month now. Dawson didn't have a serious or steady girlfriend, but he'd asked Galatia Haws to go to dinner with him and his friends. He'd met her through Brandon, who'd met her when he'd gone to pick up his girlfriend at her office in one of the downtown high rises.

He'd taken her out a couple of times now, but he hadn't kissed her. He was still deciding if he even wanted to kiss her. If he did, that would take their relationship to another level, and Dawson wasn't sure if he wanted to go to the *I-have-to-talk-to-her-in-person-to-break-up* stage.

Right now, he could text her—or just *not* text her about another date—and that would end things.

Besides the date, he'd be meeting with Duke and also Cactus Glover to administer the last round of antibiotics, and then he had soil samples to collect from their far western fields, and then he'd get to escape to the office to handle some administrative tasks here on the ranch. All in all, he'd probably eat lunch at Zona's house, laugh with his nieces and nephews, and stop by the homestead to visit his parents before his date tonight.

All nice, normal things Dawson did on a regular basis.

He ran; he ate breakfast with Brandon; he showered. Seven o'clock still hadn't struck, but he left the cabin with his brother to get their nastiest chores done before the heat really burned them.

He fed horses, swept stalls, and then finally saddled his equine so he could ride out to where the last group of cattle waited for their final dose of antibiotics. His long sleeves and cowboy hat kept the sun off his skin, thus avoiding a burn, and he wasn't surprised to find Duke and Cactus at the temporary fencing that had created a paddock for the remaining cattle.

"Morning," he said to his brother, who was really his half-brother. They only shared their daddy's genes, but Duke gave him a nod and said, "Morning, Daws."

Cactus said nothing, because if there was someone grumpier than Duke, it was Cactus Glover. He handed out the supplies and they all went over the fences and into the thick of the cattle. No wonder Dawson's ribs and shoulders hurt him almost all the time.

As he went about his job, his mind wandered down a road it shouldn't. A path he didn't even explore during his morning runs.

Continuing his education and doing something a little less physically taxing. Something where he wasn't body-slammed by thousand-pound cows into fences or the ground. Something where he didn't have to lift hay bales or haul feed bags or shovel mud out of stalls in the winter.

Something a little more white collar and a little less cowboy.

The problem was, Dawson had already been to college. He'd earned a degree in ranch management, in fact. When he wasn't helping with the chores and things like making sure their herd stayed healthy, he managed most of the back-end affairs on the ranch.

Forms, paperwork, and accounting took up most of his afternoons, but at least he got to work indoors. Still, in his most uncomfortable moments, Dawson wondered if he was old enough to be feeling so...rusty.

About halfway through the antibiotic dosing, Duke's phone rang. He stepped out of the fence to answer it, and he paced away from the contained herd while Cactus and Dawson continued to work. Duke never stood still to talk on the phone. Heck, Duke never stood still. He ran on high energy all the time, and just thinking about him exhausted Dawson.

"Dawson," Duke barked.

He straightened and found his older brother perched on the top rung of the temporary fence. "Yeah?"

"I thought you talked to that wildlife officer about the owls."

Dawson's face scrunched up as he tried to remember such a conversation. "What?"

"A few weeks ago," Duke said as he frowned at his phone. "Her name is Caroline Thompson, and she said the paperwork for the endangered owls on our ranch never got filed." He lifted his eyes. "We have endangered owls on our ranch?"

"No." Dawson stood among all the bovines, his mind sparking at him. "And I met with a guy named Ryan Murphy. He said they'd had sightings of burrowing owls here, due to our large population of prairie dogs. It was nothing."

"Well, it's not nothing to Caroline Thompson. You need to call her and figure out what form she needs. Then file it."

Irritation sparked through Dawson. If he'd needed to file a form, he would've. The last wildlife officer who'd been out to the ranch had said no such thing. "Yes, sir," he said as he turned his back on his brother to return to work.

* * *

After lunch—which his sister-in-law Zona did feed him—Dawson went to work in the detached office next to the main barn. He'd built it himself with the help of his daddy, and while it wasn't huge, it suited him perfectly.

A big desk waited for him, with a view of the ranch beyond the only window in the building. Four filing cabinets flanked the desk, two on each side, and Dawson knew every file in every folder in the drawers. He'd hung a whiteboard on the right-hand wall, where he kept track of deadlines and dates, websites where he needed to file various taxes and forms, and his own notes from his thoughts.

He closed the door behind him and reached to flip the air conditioning up higher. He kept it on seventy-five when he wasn't working in the office, and seventy when he was. It wouldn't take long to cool down, but it did run continuously most afternoons.

By some miracle Dawson didn't understand, his father didn't complain about the cost of air conditioning the small office.

He settled at his desk and looked at the list from yesterday. He made sure to keep a meticulous to-do list, and he paged back in his desk planner until he found the day he'd met with the Wildlife Officer Ryan.

It had been the same day of the electrical fire—well, the day after. They'd all gone down to Shiloh Ridge Ranch, where they'd hosted a big luncheon for the people who'd been displaced, and Dawson had taken the call from there.

He'd pulled his brother away from talking with Link's girl-friend and Misty's best friend, and they'd come back to the ranch to talk to the man. Only Dawson had met with him, but he'd taken notes.

Sightings of burrowing owls in prairie dog colonies. Watch for them and report them to the Texas Parks and Wildlife Department if seen. That was it.

"And I haven't seen any owls," he said, flipping back to today, a little over a month later. In fact, Dawson hated the prairie dogs that holed up the farmland here on the ranch, and he'd consulted with Daddy and Duke over the years about means of removing them from Hidden Hills.

Duke had forwarded the text from Caroline Thompson, a woman Dawson had never heard of nor met, but he'd deal with her after he finished today's to-do list. He added her to the bottom of it and went back to the top to get through the tasks that needed doing today.

After setting his phone to play classical music through the Bluetooth speaker on his desk, he pulled the ledger with the ranch's finances toward him. Duke had turned in receipts for payroll, the water bill, and more, and he needed to get everything entered for June so they had an accurate picture of their money for July.

They weren't all billionaires like the Glovers, after all.

Hidden Hills did well for its size—it produced enough to support him, Brandon, and Duke, as well as a tidy retirement amount for Dawson's parents. They all worked hard around this place, and with some of Arizona's money, they'd expanded the ranch on the western edge and added three hundred more cattle to their herd.

Duke partnered with the Glovers in everything, from when they drove the cattle into the hills, to splitting the manpower required to watch over them there, to the round up, branding, planting, harvest, all of it.

Dawson lost himself inside the pretty music notes and a series of numbers, and before he knew it, someone had opened the door behind him. It took him a moment to pull himself from the computer screen and what dominated his thoughts, so he hadn't turned around before a woman demanded, "Why have you been ignoring my messages?"

He turned then, blinking at the person who'd interrupted

his peace. Who was letting in all the hot air and releasing all the cool air conditioning.

A blonde woman stood there in a pair of sexy khaki shorts with a matching shirt with buttons running up the front. She wore the insignia of Texas above her breast pocket and a pure tornado in her expression.

"I—who are you?" he asked as he stood up. He didn't want to be attracted to her, but plenty of fizz fired through him as she took another step toward him.

"Caroline Thompson," she spat at him. "We spoke on the phone this morning."

Dawson returned her glare, the only thing on his mind how stunningly gorgeous her blue eyes were. He'd forgotten his own name. What he'd been doing. Why he hated being interrupted, and how the heat of a Texas July bothered him.

Something nagged in his mind, and his eyebrows drew down. "We talked this morning? Are you sure?"

She scoffed, which only made his heart beat faster. He couldn't wait to find out who she was, if she was single, and if she might go out with him.

Chapter Sixteen

Caroline Thompson glared at the handsome cowboy who wouldn't look away from her. He could be categorized as all-brown, from his hair to his eyes to his skin. He wore a full beard that somehow made him feel more like a con-man to Caroline than the cowboy hat suggested.

She shook her head, trying to dislodge the thoughts. She hadn't come here to flirt or find a date. The very idea made her ribs constrict against her lungs.

She wasn't authorized to make an arrest, unfortunately.

No, she'd come to stop the Rhineharts from destroying the habitat of the burrowing owls here in the Texas Panhandle.

"I spoke to you this morning, Mister Rhinehart. And I've left several messages in the past—"

"Can you close the door?" He nodded behind her. "You're letting out all the AC, and it's expensive." He spoke in a calm, even voice, but definitely one that wouldn't be disobeyed.

Caroline huffed and reached behind her to close the door. But that only sealed her in this room that smelled of leather, sweat, and pure masculine cowboy. *Stop it*, she told herself. *This man is married.*

Her eyes drifted to his left hand, but she didn't see a wedding band. Didn't matter. Most cowboys didn't wear their wedding rings, as they worked so much with their hands, and they could get lost easily.

Not only was Duke Rhinehart married, he'd been far more responsive over the phone than he currently was standing in front of her. Younger than she'd thought too, and her mind blanked for a moment while she tried to remember why she'd driven to this ranch forty-five minutes out of her way.

She suddenly remembered she'd eaten garlicky and oily Chinese food for lunch, and she wanted to back out of this cabin. She had gum in the truck, and she could freshen up and come back to give this cowboy a piece of her mind.

"I haven't gotten any messages from you," he said, and he lifted his phone and extended it toward her to take.

She did, for some reason she couldn't name. "I...don't—" Caroline looked at the phone, but she wasn't sure what she expected to find. "Messages are easily deletable," she said.

"Is deletable a word?" he asked, a cute smile appearing on his mouth. And not cute in like a cute-cute way, but cute in the way that said he knew he was being sassy.

"Of course it is," she said. "I just said it."

"Well, I didn't get them, so I couldn't have deleted them," he said. "Tell me what you need, and I'll see what I can do."

"We've had numerous sightings of burrowing owls in the area," she said. "They've migrated into this region, and Texas just put them on their threatened list." She really didn't want to explain all of this again. "I sent you all of this already, along with the forms you were supposed to submit by June thirtieth. Plus, I've yet to receive any of your documentation as to whether you've sighted any burrowing owls."

The cowboy stood there, and Caroline wondered if she'd have to repeat herself again. The very idea made steam start to rise through her whole body.

"I think you're confused," he finally said. He twisted back to his computer and clicked a couple of times. "I don't have any emails from anyone like you."

"Like me?"

He faced her again, something sparking dangerously in his earth-colored eyes. "You're wearing a uniform as a state officer," he said. "I've got nothing from someone in any Texas State Department."

"That is just not true, Duke. You've even responded—"

"I'm not Duke."

Caroline blinked faster and faster until she told herself to stop doing such a thing. Perhaps this Rhinehart wasn't married. "I...thought you were Duke."

She couldn't believe she'd already wondered if he was single. She didn't even know his name yet.

"He's my older brother," the cowboy said, and he sure exuded confidence. Or maybe he just hadn't stomped into someone's barn-office and started making assumptions and throwing accusations. "I'm Dawson Rhinehart, and I do believe you spoke to Duke this morning. I have it on my to-do list to call you today."

She didn't know what to say, so she simply stood there, willing her shoulders to go down and her muscles to relax. He seemed to be waiting for the same thing, because the moment she finally got the tension out of her neck, he said, "We don't have owls here on the ranch."

"I'm sure you do," she said.

"You're sure of it?" His eyebrows went up. "How would you be *sure* of it?"

"They've been populating this area for several months now. You've reported prairie dogs as pests in the past, and I'd be shocked if there are no burrowing owls in those abandoned dens."

"We don't just leave the prairie dog dens," he said. "That would be like inviting them to move back in, and we spend a great deal of time and energy—and money, Miss Thompson—to get them out."

His word sounded final, which only drove Caroline's ire higher. "You have to stop doing that immediately."

"Doing what?"

"Removing the natural habitat of a threatened animal," she said.

"Which we don't have here," he said.

"You still can't fill in the prairie dog dens." She indicated the door behind her, meaning her truck. "I have the paperwork in my truck."

"I'd love to see it," he said. "I'm sure you sent everything to Duke, but he doesn't look at his email more than once a week. Everything needs to go through me moving forward."

"Noted," she said coolly. "Now, if you'll give me your phone number and email address, I'll get you everything you need." She folded her arms and leaned her weight on her back foot. "Again."

* * *

Caroline felt like she'd been carrying a half-dozen horses on her back since she'd left her house that morning. She hadn't felt this tired since she'd had walking pneumonia several years ago, and she just wanted to eat, shower, and take to her bed.

She put her box of files on the kitchen table and moved over to the freezer. She had plenty of dinners there, and she tried not to feel pathetic as she looked at her selections for that night. Lasagna. Chicken parmesan. Chicken pot pie. Some more chicken.

"I'm so sick of poultry," she said as she reached for a bowl of beef and Spanish rice.

She eyed the files she'd brought home for the weekend while her dinner rotated in the microwave, and she decided to do things a little bit out of order. She went down the hall to her bathroom and stripped out of her gross half-khaki, half-mustard-colored uniform.

Caroline had thick, blonde hair in need of a trim, so she pulled it up and hid it beneath a shower cap, unwilling to deal with it tonight. She'd sent all of the material to Dawson Rhinehart that she'd sent to his older brother, and he'd already responded and confirmed receipt of them.

She had his phone number, and she tried to think of a reason she'd need to call or text him while she scrubbed away the awfulness of today. For the most part, Caroline loved her job, but her office here in the Panhandle had been extraordinarily busy this summer.

"I just need a break," she muttered to the sudsy water as it went down the drain.

What she really needed was someone to spend evenings with. She had a couple of friends from her office, but they all had boyfriends or husbands. Caroline had played the third wheel—or sometimes the fifth or seventh wheel—and she'd grown tired of it.

She finished showering and dressed in a pair of pajama shorts with ice cream cones all over them and an oversized sweatshirt with the Texas star on the front of it. Back in the kitchen, she refilled Gondola's water bowl and opened a can of her favorite cat food.

Her feline rewarded her with her presence then, meowing once as Caroline took too long to empty the contents of the can into Gondola's food bowl. She did love her cat, but they weren't the same as dogs, always eager to see her when she got home.

But her job didn't allow her to bring a dog with her to work, and she couldn't stomach leaving the canine home alone all day long. Cats seemed to like that, and so Caroline pretended

Gondola was overjoyed and thrilled to see her when she got home from work.

"She is," she told herself. "Because she wants her dinner."

The microwave had stopped heating a while ago, and she hit the minute button to get things hot again. As her Spanish rice rotated, she looked at her phone, praying for a miracle that Dawson had needed something and texted her for help.

She didn't have any messages, not even from her mom or sister. That wasn't super unusual, except for her older sister had been going through some things in her marriage, and she usually sent an update several times each day. Caroline read or listened to them as she was able, because sometimes she didn't want to hear about Bella's drama when she'd been through her own and had no prospects for a second chance at love, marriage, or family.

"A lot of that is by your choice," she said to her silent device. And it was.

Caroline had made a lot of choices to be where she was right now, and she didn't know how to undo the past to have a different present.

"But you could have a different future with different choices," she murmured. And then she started typing out a message to Dawson, a prayer running constantly in her head that she wasn't about to make a fool of herself.

Again.

Chapter Seventeen

Finn Ackerman stepped into the farmhouse he shared with his wife, Edith, and called, "I'm back." Since they both worked from home—right here on their small one-man ranch—he never said, "I'm home."

When she came in from her she-shed, she said the same thing he'd just called. *I'm back.*

Finn stepped over the kitchen sink to wash up. He'd shower before the birthday party tonight, but he had to get the muck off his hands to even do that. Over the running water, he heard Edith call, "In the bedroom! Come back here when you get a sec."

"Okay!" He finished rinsing the soap off and grabbed a kitchen towel to dry his hands. Behind him on the island countertop sat a birthday cake and dozens of small, brightly wrapped presents, and he smiled at the pile of them. He'd celebrated his thirty-second birthday with his family a couple of nights ago, on the actual day. Tonight, he and Edith were hosting some of their friends for dinner and games, something they'd never done on their small ranch yet.

It felt like a big milestone for him, and he couldn't wait to see Link and Misty, Alex and Nicki, Dawson and Brandon Rhinehart, and Henry.

Fine, Alex and Henry were technically family, but they were the same age as Finn and Edith, and they didn't work with them. It wasn't a couples' event, and Finn would've invited Mitch Glover too, if the cowboy hadn't moved to Virginia literally a day ago.

He tossed the towel back onto the stove and headed for the master bedroom in the back of the house. "Hey, sweetheart, the horses want you to come out and see their new stalls." He went through the open door, but didn't see Edith getting dressed.

They had a teeny tiny master closet, mostly filled with her clothes, but only one person could stand in it at a time, and they didn't get dressed in there.

"Edith?" He kept going and found her standing in the bathroom. She lowered the mascara wand and looked at him.

Finn knew instantly that she'd been crying. One, she'd already done her makeup for tonight's party. She'd sent him a picture an hour ago. Two, her eyes held a little bit of puffiness around them, which she'd tried to hide with a watery smile.

Oh, and the tears leaking down both sides of her face totally clued him in. "Hey, what's wrong?" he asked. She hadn't sounded upset a minute ago when she'd called to him. He immediately took her into his arms, not caring if she smudged black on his shirt. It would wash out.

"Why are you crying? What's going on?"

Her dachshunds, along with Gumbo, sat on the floor with her, seemingly unconcerned.

"I want that mini dachshund," she whispered in a tinny voice.

"Okay," he said. "No problem."

"Silvy has two left, and I just need to call her."

"I'll call her," Finn said. "It's fine. Are you really crying over a third dog?"

"No." She sniffled and pulled back. "Now I have to do my makeup for a third time, and your mama's gonna be here in ten minutes."

"My mama?" Finn peered at her, but Edith seemed to have other places to look. "Why is she coming over? We need to leave to get the food in about thirty minutes. Right?"

Edith nodded and reached for the washcloth she'd obviously already used to clean her face and start again. She ran the water in her bathroom sink and nodded over to his sink while she wetted her washcloth. "Look over there."

Finn looked, but he didn't see anything of note. His razor. A cup he used after he brushed his teeth. And something he didn't recognize. He looked at Edith, but she had her face buried in the washcloth.

He walked around her, moving closer. All at once, he realized what she'd laid there for him to see.

A pregnancy test.

He picked it up, his pulse suddenly hacking through his body the way a lumberjack chopped at a tree trunk. "Is this...?"

The test held two lines, and it was dummy-proof, because it had the results printed right on the stick. Two lines = pregnant.

His brain caught up with his eyes, and he huffed out his breath. "You're pregnant." Shock and delight mixed into a delicious cocktail in his veins, and he turned to face his wife, his best friend, his everything.

"You're pregnant," he said again, his voice louder and more excited.

Edith looked at him, her smile wide but her tears still flowing down her face. "I'm pregnant."

Finn laughed and reached for his wife. He swung her around while she laughed too, and when they both settled back on their feet, he pressed his smile to hers. "I love you. I love you. I love you."

He pulled back, keeping one hand on her back while his other moved to her flat belly. "We're going to have a baby."

"We're going to have a baby," Edith repeated in just as reverent a whisper. She looked up at him, and Finn pulled her into his chest.

"We can do this." He and Edith had decided to try for a baby right away, and they'd only been married for three months. "How far along do you think you are? I want to go to your first doctor's appointment with you."

"Maybe five or six weeks," she said. "And Finny." She stepped back and picked up the washcloth again. "I don't know who to go see here. I'm going to ask your mom about it."

"Oh-ho." Finn shook his head. "You tell my mama about the baby, and she'll be over here doing your chores every morning." He shook his head. "I don't think that's a good idea. Ask JoJo. She just had a baby."

"You don't get it, do you, Shortstop?"

"Obviously I don't." Finn settled his weight onto one foot. "Telling my mama is a bad idea, Edith."

"Telling your mama is how we bond even more," Edith said. "I could totally ask JoJo. I probably still will. But I really think your mom will be so excited and so helpful." She glanced over to him, her raw, makeup-less face so beautiful, so open, and so vulnerable. "My mom isn't here. I'm going to need help after the baby is born, and that's going to come from your mom."

She drew a breath. "I won't tell her tonight if you don't want me to, but I'd like to, and I want to ask her about a good doctor."

"She hasn't had a baby in ages," he said.

"She knows everyone in town." Edith started applying her makeup again, and since she didn't wear a lot, she could definitely get it done before his mama showed up.

Finn turned away from her, his brain whirring now. His beautiful wife was so good, always looking out for others even when she should be celebrated. *Lord,* he thought, starting a back-and-forth conversation with himself. *Does it really matter if my mama knows?*

She would like it.

No, she'll love it.

And she always wants to be included, as much as we want to include her.

He sighed and turned back to Edith. "All right. You're right."

She smiled at him. "Wish I had my video rolling for that one."

"I say you're right all the time."

She smiled and kept working on her face.

"Finn," his mama called from the front of the house. "Edith. I'm walking in."

"Go say hello," Edith said. "I'll be out in five minutes, and we'll tell her together."

"All right," he said. "I want to pick out of the two mini dachshunds."

Edith met his eyes in the mirror, clear surprise there. She blinked; it disappeared. "Fine."

Finn grinned at her and kissed the side of her neck. "I can't believe you're going to make me a father." He turned before his own emotions could rear up and choke him, and he jogged through the bedroom saying, "Mama, I'm comin'."

His mother had brought something, of course. "Cupcakes for tonight," she said.

"Edith made a cake, Mama." He stepped into her and hugged her, fighting for control again.

"Then cupcakes for breakfast. You're within a week of your birthday."

As if he couldn't have cupcakes any day of the year, whenever he wanted. He was an adult after all. A hard-working, tax-paying adult who owned his own ranch.

"Thank you," he murmured.

His mama wasn't one to miss things, and she pulled out of his embrace and looked at him with her shrewd eagle-eyes. "What's going on?"

"Nothing." Finn ducked his head and side-stepped her. "We have friends coming over in a little bit. We have to go get the food soon."

"I know," his mama said. "I'm not going to ruin your game night."

Finn didn't know what to say that wasn't *Edith's pregnant!* so he opened the fridge and looked inside. "Want something to drink?" he asked, a prayer starting deep in his soul.

"Kelly," Edith said. "Thank you for stopping by."

Finn turned to watch his wife hug his mother, and Edith's smile stayed stitched in place as her eyes closed. She moved back, immediately reaching for him, and Finn instantly went to her side. They joined hands, and his mama took them both in.

"You guys...you know what? I'm not going to ask."

Edith looked at Finn, and so many conversations were had. *Should we really tell her?*

Her: I want to tell her.

Him: Then tell her.

Her: I love you.

Him: I love you.

Edith turned to his mom and said, "I wanted to ask you something, but you have to promise me you won't tell a single soul."

Mama looked at Finn, who shrugged one shoulder. "I mean,

maybe Daddy. I don't think Mama can keep a secret from Daddy."

"It would be very difficult," Mama said.

"Squire can know," Edith said. "But not a single soul more."

"Is this a good thing or a bad thing?" Mama asked. "Because I'm starting to get really nervous."

Finn let his smile show then, and Edith said, "Kelly." Her voice broke, and Mama's whole face fell. "I'm going to have a baby, and I need—help."

Mama rushed at them, saying, "Oh, oh, oh." She gathered both Finn and Edith into her arms while she laughed. "Of course, my sweet girl. I'll help you. Yes, of course I will." She stepped back and looked at them both with pure joy streaming from her face.

"A baby. How wonderful." She kissed Edith's cheek and then Finn's. "Now, tell me what you need, and I'll get it done." She practically vibrated with enthusiasm, and Finn chuckled as he stepped over to the cupcakes she'd brought.

"I need a good doctor," Edith said with a sniffle. She hadn't cried again, though her voice had gotten tied in knots for a second there. "That's where I want to start."

"Of course, of course." Mama pulled out her phone and paused. "Well, I'll—let me do some discreet...investigating on who's amazing, and I'll let you know."

"Thank you," Edith said.

Mama took Edith over to the couch as she said, "Now, come tell me what you want for the nursery, the name, all of it."

Finn stood there in the kitchen, a delicious chocolate

caramel cupcake in his hand, feeling like this wasn't going to end well. "Mama, we have to go get the food for tonight."

"Yes, yes," his mama said. "Five minutes, Finny. I promise I won't ruin your party."

Finn had the distinct feeling he'd be making the drive to town by himself to pick up the food for his own birthday party, but he didn't say anything. He simply wanted Edith to be happy, and it was true that her mom didn't live here. He hadn't realized how untethered she'd felt until she'd told him during the wedding planning, and he'd told her to ask his mom.

Heaven knows she'll love it, he'd said.

And she had. Edith had too, and Finn reminded himself he wanted them to have a strong friendship, as they both seemed to really need it.

Edith also seemed to know exactly what Finn needed, because ten minutes later, she said, "We have to go get the food, Kelly. Thank you so much." She hugged her and they both stood from the couch. Edith met his eyes, and Finn opened the drawer where he kept his keys and wallet.

"Ready, baby?" Edith melted into his side and pressed a kiss to his jaw.

"If you are." He grinned at her as his mama left ahead of them, and then he and Edith followed, getting into her SUV to make the drive to town.

He started the car and then looked over to her. "I am so in love with you. I can't wait to witness every change. I will do anything to make sure you're comfortable and taken care of."

"I know, baby." She cradled his face in the palm of her hand. "And I love you for it."

He started to back away from the house, and they settled into their normal positions. Edith started swiping on her phone, and when he reached the end of the dirt road and stopped to turn onto the highway, she held up her device.

"Look at these dachshunds," she said. "And pick one, so I can text Silvy."

Finn took her phone with a hooked eyebrow in her direction. But Edith didn't back down. She'd been talking about getting a third dog since his birthday last year, so he couldn't say he wasn't prepared for it.

"I like that brown spotty one."

"That's called a chocolate dappled," Edith informed him, taking her phone back. "And it's a boy. The other one is a girl."

"She's all beige," he said. "Kinda boring." He grinned at her. "But whatever you want is fine with me."

"That's actually a pretty rare coloring," she said. "It's an Isabella, where the brown has faded out to milky color. I think she's beautiful." She didn't look away from her phone. "So...boy or girl?"

"This is when you get to pick," he said, thinking of their baby. He wasn't sure how he felt about having a boy or a girl first. And he didn't care. He'd love that baby with his whole heart, no matter what.

"I want to name him Oscar," she said. "I think it fits with Otto and Frankie." She looked up from her phone. "Don't you?"

Finn knew better than to have an opinion here, so he just

laughed as he made the turn onto the highway. "Sure," he said. "Fits great."

"Then we have to get the boy," she said, her fingers flying across her phone, presumably to text her friend about which dachshund she wanted.

"Happy birthday," he said, because finding out they were having a baby and making his wife happy with a new puppy? That really was the best birthday gift Finn could've gotten.

Chapter Eighteen

"Mister Glover?"

Link looked over his shoulder at the very familiar voice. It wasn't Misty's, but he'd spent enough time with her best friend to recognize her voice. Sure enough, Janie entered the storage shed where Link was working with Ward, cataloging the oil filters, box fans, and other mechanical equipment they had here.

Misty followed her, and his throat narrowed. He hadn't seen her for several days, since they'd gone to Finn's birthday party and she'd gotten sick a couple of days later. She hadn't been to work in a few days as she quarantined at home, but she'd texted him that morning to say she finally felt like the antibiotics were working.

They had a date planned for later that evening in his new house. *Dinner and a movie*, he'd told her. *Staying in.*

She'd said she'd bring dinner, and he could pick the movie.

He'd agreed, because while he could put together simple meals, he didn't want to show Misty that his culinary skills didn't really extend past scrambling eggs and frying bacon quite yet.

"Roberta says that none of the checks we've sent the ranch have been cashed." Janie looked over to Misty as she came to her side. "We've got rent for June, July, and August."

Link turned fully to watch this unfold. No one who'd been misplaced after the fire had paid rent, and he wasn't surprised at all to hear the checks from the state had gone uncashed.

Ward looked at them for a long moment, his chin dipping as he looked at the envelope in Janie's hand. "We aren't taking rent for refugees."

Janie sighed, and Misty took the envelope from her. "We're not refugees. Patty transferred departments, and Roberta is new. She's just getting into the swing of things." She shook the envelope.

Uncle Ward folded his arms. Link stifled a snicker.

"There aren't many furnished apartments in town," Janie said. "Roberta wanted us to ask if we could keep living here, but there's a budget for rent."

"None of our people pay rent," Ward said.

"But they work here," Misty argued, a cute little frown appearing between her eyes. "Their boarding is part of their pay."

Ward sighed. "Misty, you're dating Link, right?"

Link's smile dried right on up. He took one step toward his uncle and the women, then decided to see where this went.

Misty exchanged a look with Janie. "Yes, sir."

He hadn't exactly told Misty about his financial situation, but she'd admitted that their department did research on the towns and areas where they worked. She'd known about his family before she'd even come to Three Rivers.

"Then you should know we don't need the money," Ward said. "I won't take it. Tell your office to save its budget. Whatever. It's an empty cowboy cabin, and we don't charge rent for them."

Both Misty and Janie frowned at each other and then Uncle Ward. "You won't take it?" Janie asked.

Ward sighed and took the envelope from Misty. "How much is it?" He pulled the check out. "Oh, nine hundred bucks." He peered over the slip of paper to them. "Every single one of us here has a million times that."

He stuffed the check back in the envelope, folded it in half, and shoved it in his back pocket. "Okay, I took it."

"One million times that?" Misty asked, and Link got himself moving then.

"Hey," he said, drawing her attention away from his uncle. "I thought I heard your voice." He glanced over to Janie. "Hey, Janie."

"Link." A fast smile catapulted across her mouth before disappearing again.

He kissed Misty in a peck on the lips. "What are you doin' here?" He shot a look to Uncle Ward, who turned back to the shelving unit he'd been inventorying.

"Trying to pay rent," Misty said crossly. "Your uncle won't take it."

"I took it," Uncle Ward said.

"You won't cash it," Janie said.

Uncle Ward shrugged, and Link decided to get the women out of here. "You guys are done early today," he said, turning Misty toward the exit.

"Weekend," they said together, and he managed to get them out of the shed. Outside, the sun burned brightly, but a breeze kicked up, actually making it easier to breathe than inside.

"Listen," he said.

"Is what he said true?" Misty demanded. "Every one of you here has a million times nine hundred dollars?" She stopped walking and faced him. Her freckles made him smile, but Link knew he couldn't side-step this question.

"You know Shiloh Ridge does well," he said.

"Yes," she said slowly. "But there's a difference between rich and like, *rich*."

Link swallowed, trying to find the right words. "It's generational wealth."

Janie gasped. "I knew it. You guys are like the Hiltons."

He laughed then and shook his head. "Sure, the Hiltons of the Texas Panhandle." He tried not to look at Misty, but he couldn't stop himself. She wore an expression like he'd picked up a two-by-four and hit her with it.

"Generational wealth," she repeated in a soft tone that hardly sounded like her. "Link, how much do you pay in rent?"

He set his sights on the nearby stable and started walking that way. Both women fell into step with him. "I don't pay rent," he said. "Anymore. I mean, I used to. But yeah, not anymore."

"Who does pay rent here?" Misty asked.

"No one," he said. "Only family members who are required to live as hired hands, for the first year." He hung his head as if he should be ashamed of himself for not having to pay rent. A tiny part of him—the sliver that whispered he wasn't a true Glover—did feel guilty about that. If his mom and dad hadn't been killed in that accident, and Sammy hadn't married Bear Glover, his life would be drastically different.

But his parents *had* died. Sammy *had* adopted him. She'd married Bear. This was his life, and as he took the next step, he felt like he was finally moving into it.

"The other hired hands get room and board as part of their salary," he said. "So right now, we don't have anyone paying rent. Gunn, Smiles, Robbie, and Wilder will soon enough—if they choose to work the ranch."

"Does anyone choose not to?" Misty asked.

Link shook his head. "Not in a while, no. Uncle Ward toured with a band for a bit. Uncle Mister went into the rodeo. But they came back."

Neither Janie nor Misty said anything, and Link didn't know what else to add either. "I went to college," he said. "Got my agricultural science degree. Came back. It was then that I lived like a regular hired hand for a year. On their salary. That kind of thing. It's what we do here, so we Glovers know what it's like to try to make ends meet."

They went past the stables and toward the Ranch House before Misty said, "Did you hear that, Janie? What I heard was all of the Glovers are so rich, they never have to think about making ends meet."

"I heard that too," Janie said. "For generations. With their *generational* money."

Link didn't like their tone, and he stopped. "You knew I had money," he said quietly, wishing he and Misty could talk about this alone. "I told you that the first time we went out."

Misty looked up at him, something salty in her expression. "I didn't realize how much, I guess."

"Why does it matter?" He glanced over to Janie, who gazed back at him. "The state should be happy they don't have to pay for rent. Uncle Ward's right. Have them save it for something else."

"That's not really how state budgets work," Misty said.

Irritation lit through him like someone had ignited a trail of gunpowder leading to a stick of dynamite. "Okay," he said. "Well, I have to get back to work. I'll still see you later? My place, probably close to seven?"

She nodded, and Link turned and walked away from the pair of them. Before he'd even made it back to the shed, his phone chimed Misty's notification tone at him. He automatically pulled his phone out, as his pulse had zipped through his body in a Pavlovian way.

It matters because money is really powerful, Link. Are you saying YOU have a lot of money, or the RANCH has a lot of money? They're two different things.

Why is money powerful? he asked as he walked, praying he didn't ram into anyone or trip over anything.

He made it back to the air conditioning of the shed before Misty messaged again. *Because, with money, you don't have to worry. You can go on vacation any time you want. Take a day off if you want. Pay for anything you need without many sleepless nights.*

As Link read, he heard all the things she really meant. He could feel all the things she'd been through—not able to take time off. Not being able to pay for things without losing sleep. Available for a fun vacation.

He thought of that road trip they'd joked about. Maybe it wasn't really a joke. He'd never thought to ask her if she'd ever been on vacation, but given what he knew about her past and her family, now he wondered if she ever had.

And if she hadn't, where would she like to go? Link would take her there.

With money, you can relocate without worrying about finding another job. With money, you can literally do anything, Link. Money is important and powerful, even if we don't like that concept as Christians.

He felt properly chastised, but he didn't want to admit it. *Where would you go on vacation if money wasn't an issue?* he asked instead.

I don't know, Link. Her frustration came through loud and clear, and Link looked up from his phone.

Would you relocate to Three Rivers if money wasn't an issue? he typed out. He didn't send the text, because he didn't have to. He knew the answer to that, and for the first time in the last month, Link's heart lifted on a tiny balloon of hope.

He had money. If she fell in love with him and married him, she wouldn't have to work ever again. He had plenty to take care of her. To relocate her. All of it.

So he erased that text and typed instead, *Remember that time you found out I was really rich? Me, not the ranch. Like, millions-of-dollars-rich. And remember how, after you knew that, we started planning our future together? You wanted a bigger house than the Top Cottage—one where you could have a whole room just for painting—and I just wanted you to move to Three Rivers permanently so we could be together. Remember that?*

With a booming heartbeat banging against the back of his tongue, Link read over the text, hesitating. "Should I send this, Lord?"

It sure would lay out a lot between them. He wasn't sure who he was trying to hide from. He'd just kissed her—super chastely, sure—in front of his uncle. Everyone knew they were dating. He felt moony-eyed and soft in the bone whenever he got lucky enough to be with Misty. She *had* to know that. See it. Feel it.

So he made a bold decision and sent the text.

Chapter Nineteen

Misty waited until she and Janie returned to their cabin before she showed her best friend the text. "How do I respond to that?" She paced away from her phone, glad to be out of the heat. She'd been sick for about a week, and she sank onto the couch, feeling as weak now as she had been while in the throes of her sinus infection.

Being sick in the summer was the worst curse God could give her—oh, besides the mega-rich cowboy who'd just asked her to move to Three Rivers permanently to be with him.

"I told you already," Janie said. "He's in love with you."

"He's not," Misty said with a sigh. "Link says stuff like that out loud, Janie. When he's in love with me, he'll tell me."

"Are you sure he won't just send a text that says, *Remember that time I told you I loved you for the first time?*"

Misty smiled through her irritation. She and Link did have some games they played with one another. He knew he was special to her; that game was designed to say so without saying so. And this one about how they said the things they wanted to happen like they'd already happened?

She loved it. She loved thinking about what she wanted with Link and trying to project or manifest those things into existence. She'd been praying too, specifically to know what to do about Link. What to do about her job. What to do with her life.

She was thirty years old, and she'd thought she had everything figured out already.

No dating.

An amazing job she loved.

Good friends.

A big city.

Lincoln Glover had ruined it all. He'd ruined *her*.

"Can I have my phone, please?" She held out her hand, and Janie brought over her device.

"What are you going to say?"

"I'm going to tell him he's not special because he has millions of dollars in the bank." Misty typed out exactly that and sent it. *I don't want you thinking you're special because you have a lot of money.*

I don't think that, he said. *Just like you're not special because you have a great job and a fun life in Dallas.*

The little bit of air she'd managed to take into her lungs went right back out again. It was as if Link held all the oxygen molecules in the world, and she could only get them from him. He'd become very important to her. Very important indeed.

"You're thinking of moving here to be with him, aren't you?" Janie asked in a tiny, timid whisper.

Misty couldn't speak, so she simply nodded. Her phone chimed again, and she couldn't stop herself from looking at it.

I want you to be mine, Link said. *I want to be yours. I know we're still in the early stages, and I can be patient. I guess I'm just fishing for the same thing I wanted when we started seeing each other again a couple of months ago—is this still serious for you? And if so, does that mean you'll consider moving here permanently?*

Another text came in as she re-read the first one.

I don't need you to tell me you'll move here for certain. I just need to know it's a possibility. And I'm going to stop now, because I hate that we're texting about this and not talking face-to-face. We can talk more about it tonight at my place.

Misty read both messages again, then read them out loud to Janie. Her face glowed like she'd set up a rim light to make a video. "That cowboy is in love with you," she said again. "And you have to decide if you're willing to love him back...or not."

"He's asking a lot of me," Misty whispered miserably. "He's asking me to rearrange my whole life to be here, to be with him."

"Yeah, to be *his*," Janie said with a sigh. "It's so romantic." She got to her feet and turned toward the hall. "Hey, I have a date with that guy Stephen tonight. Misty." She faced her again. "Think of your Future Self. Would she want you to give up your job and apartment in the city to be here and belong with that sexy, tall, gorgeous, rich cowboy? What's the sacrifice, really?"

With a kind smile, she left the living room, left Misty to her own thoughts and feelings. *What's the sacrifice, really?*

Every single thing Misty had put in place over the past two decades, that was the sacrifice. She'd have to burn her whole life to the ground and trust that she could rise from the ashes a better, different person than she'd been before. And what if Link didn't like that woman? What if she wasn't who he really wanted?

What if he abandoned her like everyone else had?

* * *

Link sat on the front porch at the Top Cottage, his guitar across his lap, when Misty arrived for dinner. He'd said he'd come pick her up, but she felt silly having him do that. Their eyes met through the windshield, and Link lifted his chin in a very cowboy nod of hello.

Misty smiled and ducked her head, her hair falling down between them. She'd let it grow out this summer without dying it again, and the strawberry had definitely remixed with the blonde. When she and Link spent time outside together, he lightly tapped all over her face with a glorious smile on his face.

He'd started lighting kisses across her freckles too, claiming he absolutely loved them. Meanwhile, Misty kept trying to cover them up with foundation, and he kept telling her how amazingly gorgeous they were.

She reached for the food she'd driven to town to get for tonight's dinner, her heartbeat thumping like a bass beat in a dance club. If her life had a soundtrack, right now it would be playing a medley of tense stringed instruments, and everyone would be on-edge, waiting to see what would happen next.

"Can't prolong this anymore," she muttered to herself as she picked up the authentic Texas barbecue, with all the sides she knew Link loved, and got out of her car. She hadn't answered his texts, because he'd been right. She didn't want to have a conversation about their future with typed letters.

She wanted to see his face and hear his voice when he said things like, *I want you to be mine.*

She shivered just imagining him saying that to her. Had her mother ever had someone say that to her? Did she feel this same sort of string of excitement bubbling through her? Had she hoped for a future filled with love, happiness, and joy?

Children, and family dinners, and slow Sunday afternoons after church? Misty couldn't even believe she'd thought about church on Sundays, but she had. "I love church on Sundays," she murmured to herself as she started down the sidewalk that led to the wide, spanning porch at the Top Cottage.

Link hummed along with the music his fingers made, and because Misty had sat beside him during a Sabbath Day meeting, she knew what his singing voice sounded like. Deep, rich, and dripping with honey.

He stopped as she got closer, but his fingers continued to pick over the strings of his guitar. "Hey." He didn't smile or make any move to get up and take her into his arms.

Misty set down the bags of food, seeing as how Link wasn't in a hurry to eat, and settled onto the step beside him. The bridge of the guitar stuck out across her chest, but she leaned into Link's strong arm and shoulder anyway.

"Hey," she finally said back.

He didn't play loud, and it set the stage for this new scene she'd entered. "I didn't mean to make things awkward between us," he said. "I sincerely thought you knew I had a lot of money."

"I suppose I did," Misty whispered. "I guess I'd never given it to *you*. It was always the ranch that was rich."

Link nodded. "Just another thing for me to work through about not really being a Glover."

"I hate that for you." She cuddled into his side, glad when he finally stopped playing and set his guitar aside. He stared out toward the road she'd driven down, to the trees on the other side of it. His hands hung down between his knees, the way they had that evening they'd sat overlooking the town of Three Rivers, talking about her fractured past.

"You're a Glover through and through," she said. "They don't just give anyone a junior foreman position, you know."

"I'm not special because I'm the junior foreman," he said.

"No." Misty drew in a deep breath, about to take their game into a brand-new direction. "But you're special because you're a Glover."

He put his arm around her and pulled her against him. "Thank you for saying that."

Misty felt the world open up, the way one of those pop-up cards did. She'd been living as a flattened version of herself, but with Lincoln Glover, all the flaps and pieces could expand into something intricate and beautiful.

"You're special to me," he murmured.

Misty's emotions swirled and surged. Her throat felt like one of those tiny coffee-stirring straws. "I don't know how to talk the way you do."

"You just open your mouth," he said. "And let God fill it with the right words." He kneaded her closer and pressed a kiss to her hair. "No one has ever told me I'm good at talking."

"Better than me."

"You've always done just fine with me, Misty," he said. "It's just the two of us here. I'm not going to judge anything you say."

She laced all ten of her fingers through just a single hand of his and squeezed. "I'm falling in love with you," she murmured.

"I'm going to take that to mean things are still serious."

"They are for me."

"Good," he said. He nodded toward the food. "Smells good. Should we go inside and eat?"

She nodded, and Link somehow knew what she wanted though they both faced the landscape opposite the cabin. He stood and took her hand in his to pull her up. His eyes hooked into hers, and while Misty wanted to look away, she couldn't.

"I'm just going to open my mouth, and I don't know what will come out."

"Oh, this sounds like a new game for us," she said.

Link gave her half a smile that stayed for half a second. "The Lord's been telling me to be patient for quite some time now. It's perfectly exhausting, if I'm being honest. I don't want to be patient. I *feel* things for you Misty, that I've not felt for anyone, ever, before. I'm hungry for you. I want you here without an end date, because if I'm not in love with you, I'm really dang close."

Misty nodded, tears squeezing out of the corners of her eyes.

"I'm not going to ask you to move here," he said.

"You already have." Maybe not in those words, but Misty knew what Link wanted.

"I don't think you're ready for any of this," he said. "I don't feel ready either, so maybe God has been telling me the right thing, and I've just made a huge mistake by opening my big mouth."

Misty smiled at him. "Again, nothing anyone has ever said about you."

He smiled more fully this time. "I feel out of words, so it must be a good time to stop." Link bent and picked up the bag with their dinner. "Let's go inside."

Misty went with him, her mind whirring around all he'd said. They didn't speak as he pulled the Styrofoam containers out and got down plates. Misty removed silverware from the drawer, and she took the plate he'd prepared for her.

"You've been standing there like you've been taxidermied," Link said. "I'm done for now, okay? I apologize for bringing it all up."

Misty looked at him, feeling a bit more life come into her limbs. "You don't need to apologize," she said. "I just think you're right." She followed him over to the couch, where he set down his plate of food so he could use the remote to start their movie.

"I'm right about what?" he asked.

"I'm not ready for this yet," she said as she sat down on the other end of the couch. He looked over to her again, and Misty decided to be as brave as him.

She opened her mouth and allowed God to fill it.

"Link, there's so much I still need to do in order to be with someone as amazing as you."

"I'm not amazing."

"I mean, your hair's a little long, but otherwise, you're about perfect."

"Stop it." He stabbed a piece of brisket and glared at her now. "I'm impatient, and stubborn, and ungrateful for all I've been given." He looked back to the TV. "I know I'm not special."

Misty wanted to argue with him, but she just forked up a cheese cube from the pea salad.

"Are we ready?" he asked.

"I have one more thing to say."

He gestured with the remote, and it felt like an ocean existed between them, though it was a single couch cushion and nothing more.

"Two things."

"Misty."

She grinned at his irritated tone for a reason she didn't understand. "First, I could cut your hair. I'm pretty good at it. I've done Ralf's while we've been here in Three Rivers."

Link grunted, his mouth full of his dinner. Misty wasn't sure why he'd decided to grow out his hair, or what it meant to him, but she catalogued that as something she could ask him later.

"Second, I am *seriously* considering moving here," she said next. "Permanently."

He looked at her again, and she smiled over to him. "I don't want you to think you're special or anything. If I choose to move here, it'll be for me. Not for you."

"I don't think I'm special," he whispered.

"Good," she said. "Now, can we watch the movie? And can I sit beside you, or are you going to shun me for the whole date?"

"No," he said. "You can't sit by me."

Hurt stung through Misty, reverberating like a gong in waves that blistered her stomach, her ribs, her fingers and toes.

Then Link slid over and handed her his plate as he practically crawled into her lap. "I'm going to sit by you."

Chapter Twenty

The next time Misty came to Link's house, she held up a black bag to go with her grin, her brightly colored tank top, and her denim shorts. "Ready for this?"

Link would do anything for her, and he backed up as he said, "If you are."

"I've been watching a couple of videos online."

"Oh, well, now I'm reassured that you know how to cut my hair." He grinned at her and took the bag of hair-cutting supplies from her. "Hey, am I allowed to say it's great to see you?"

"Of course you are, Mister Glover." Misty grinned at him like their serious conversation from a couple of weeks ago hadn't changed anything in their relationship. Maybe for her it hadn't. For him, well, Link wasn't sure how things had shifted yet, because they hadn't quite settled.

He felt like he'd been thrown back in time twelve months,

when he'd sat down outside the coffee truck with Misty and asked her for her number the first time.

"You're looking at me like that again," Misty said, stepping out of his arms.

"Like what?"

"I don't know." She brushed her hair over her ear and took her scissor kit over to the table. She opened it and added, "Come on, now. I'm not going to do anything that can't be fixed."

Link followed her over to the table and pulled a chair out. "All right," he said. "I trust you."

"Do you?"

"Yeah." He looked back to her, over his shoulder. "Hey, remember when we went to church together and then went to the End of Summer picnic? And we danced and laughed and maybe even saw some summer fireflies?"

"Fireflies?" Misty asked. "Really?"

"It's been a bit rainy and cooler," Link said. "They like that, and I—ahem—read an article that said there have been a lot of them in the Amarillo area lately."

"Then, yes," Misty said as she snapped on the clippers. "I totally remember going to church with you and then attending the End of Summer picnic where we saw a whole herd of fireflies."

Link burst out laughing, glad he could still do that with her. She giggled with him, which also helped him settle. He said, "You forgot the dancing."

"I never forget dancing," she said as the first tendrils of his long hair started to fall to the floor.

"Fireflies don't come in herds."

"They come in something."

"It's called a *glow*."

"You're making that up."

"I am not," Link said.

"That's so...perfect," she said, the smile he couldn't see sitting in her tone.

"I mean, it could be a swarm, but I liked glow better as a kid."

"Did you have a lot of questions about fireflies then?" Her teasing tone wasn't lost on him, but Link nodded slightly.

"After my parents died, my momma told me I could always feel their love in the sweet light of a glow of fireflies." He gave himself a little shake. "I didn't remember that until now. And with the article...." He trailed off, not sure why these memories, this part of his life, had come forward now.

"That's amazing," Misty said quietly. She kept working on his hair, and Link did his best not to shiver at every touch of her delicate fingers along his neck, his scalp.

To distract himself, he prayed. *Dear God in Heaven*, he started. He wasn't sure how to continue, and all of his prayers in the past fortnight had been similar. He could start, but he wasn't sure where he was going. He wasn't sure what he deserved, and he wasn't sure what God would grant and what He wouldn't.

So, because his parents had taught him to express thanks for what he had and spend less time asking God for what he wanted.

I'm trying to forget myself, he thought. Misty's touch faded away as Link escaped into his own mind. *I really am. I want to be a good man, and I'm trying to put my head down and work every day. I'm grateful for this life I have. For this ranch, and so many good men to teach me.*

He closed his eyes, the images of his parents, his siblings, his aunts and uncles filling his mind, overwhelming him.

I'm grateful to be a Glover, he prayed. *Bless me to be the best one I can, and—* He cut off the thoughts, because he'd just asked for something, and he wanted this prayer to be outward focused.

It wasn't about what he wanted or needed. It was about what he'd already been given.

I'm grateful for the time I have with Misty Granger, he prayed. *Several weeks ago, I told You I'd take whatever time I could get with her, and I've lost sight of that. I'm trying to get back to it, so thank You for putting her in my life.*

Thank You for good parents, and an amazing horse, and the two dogs who follow me everywhere.

A smile touched his soul and worked its way to the outside. To his face, where he let it show.

"What are you thinking about?" Misty asked. "I see that smile."

"All the things I'm grateful for," he murmured. "Don't go thinkin' you're on the list."

"I would never," she said as she moved around his right side and in front of him.

Link opened his eyes and looked up at her. He felt like he was seeing her again for the first time. He reached toward her, expecting to get burned by her glorious light. She was simply so angelic, and Link had liked her from the very moment she'd twirled into him at that summer dance over a year ago.

She lowered her scissors. "What?"

"I don't know." He caught her fingers with his and tugged her onto his lap. "Is it okay if we don't know everything?"

"I think that's the very definition of life, Link." She stroked his hair back. "Isn't it?"

"Yeah, maybe." He cradled her face in his hands. "After this, can we go get coffee?"

She gave him a small smile. "I'd like that." Misty looked up to his hair. "But you won't want to go like this." She started to get off his lap, but Link's grip on her tightened.

"Kiss me so I know the past couple of weeks haven't broken us," he said. "I honestly didn't mean to push you anywhere you didn't want to be. I didn't—don't know where I am, either." He took a deep breath and looked up from the neckline of her tank top.

"You've been worrying," she said. "When I told you not to worry."

"Yeah," he admitted. "It's hard for me, with Mitch gone. I don't have anyone to talk things through with, and the quiet here can drive a cowboy insane."

"You can talk things through with me."

"Not when the things I need clarity on are you."

She smiled. "I suppose it's nice to have Janie to bounce things around with."

"I'm sure." He wasn't super-keen on her talking about him

to Janie, but he wasn't surprised. "Do you and Janie live together in Dallas?"

She gave half a laugh. "No, sir. I have my own place there. We just got paired for this assignment."

"Tell me about your last assignment."

"Can I cut your hair while I do it?"

Link released her, noting she hadn't kissed him. He had kissed her in the past couple of weeks, and he really wished he could do what she'd asked of him—to stop worrying.

"I worked on this really great old church in the Texas Hill Country," she said. "The state bought it a few decades ago, and it needed a lot of structural work."

"Lots of art in a church."

"Yeah," she said. "I went for that, and the structural conservationist was this guy named Porky Dillard."

"That was not his name."

Misty giggled. "I swear to you, it was." She took a breath, her scissors snip, snip, snipping away. "Anyway, our lead manager—like what Ralf does—was this woman named Clarice Terry. She didn't like me much, and I managed to live with her for sixteen months."

"So how much time do you actually spend in Dallas?"

"I'm usually there for a solid year or so between assignments," she said. "We do trainings, take a couple of classes, and work on small projects in the area." Before he could ask her something else, her phone rang. "Oh. It's Janie. Just a sec, baby."

She moved away to take the call, and Link searched his memory to see if she'd ever called him *baby* before. Nothing came to mind, and Link turned to watch her wander into his kitchen as she talked to her best friend.

Misty spun back to him, her eyes wide. Link got to his feet, a dart of worry spiking through him. "What?"

"I'll tell him," she said. "Thanks, Janie." She hung up, her smile growing into laughter. "Link, guess what?"

"Seems like something you're excited about," he said as he arrived in front of her. He strung his first finger through the belt loop on her waist, wanting to be close to her.

She blinked at him. "Roberta found us a house in town." She bounced on the balls of her feet. "Isn't that great?"

He grinned at her. "Yeah, that's fantastic."

Her smile cleared. "I mean, we've loved living here too, Link. It's just a long—"

"Way to town," he said. "I know. When can you move in?"

"This weekend." She laughed and danced back over to the table. "Come on, baby. Let's finish your hair and go celebrate with cookies and coffee."

Link grinned at her. "Yah," he said. "Let's do that." He returned to his seat, still feeling a little bit lost. But Misty had told him not to worry, and she had admitted that she was falling in love with him, and she had said she was seriously considering moving here.

Either he trusted what she told him, or he didn't, and as she finished up his hair and they left the ranch to get cookies and coffee, Link took strength from the summer sunset. God had painted the sky with colors Link loved.

It reminded him that *he* was loved, and not only by God.

You're special because you're a Glover.

Misty had told him that, and it had sunk into his brain and refused to let go.

"Can we go by the house first?" she asked, and Link glanced over to her.

"For sure."

"Great." She looked at her phone. "Turn right up here then."

He wanted to give her the dream house, the dream family, the dream life. Now, he just had to figure out how to do that—and how to be her dream man. Oh, and sooner rather than later would be nice.

* * *

"It's just me," Link called as he walked in the front door of his parents' house. The scent of marshmallows hung in the air, and Link knew what that meant.

"Link," Sunnie said as she came rushing out of the kitchen. "We just made rice crispy squares. Come see."

"There better be some with coconut," he said. "That recipe of Auntie Etta's is my favorite." He grinned at his younger sister and followed her into the kitchen. His momma worked there, pressing down another batch of marshmallowed rice cereal into a sheet pan.

"There you are," Momma said with a warmth in her tone only mothers could achieve. "Your daddy is still out on the tractor, and Smiles is picking up Heather from the pool."

"We got done early in the southern fields," Link said. And he hadn't gone home to shower first. He squirmed as he sat down, and though Momma wasn't even looking fully at him, she paused in her work and did exactly that.

"What's going on?" she asked.

Link opened his mouth to say *nothing*, but the word wouldn't come out. "Mom, how did you know to marry Daddy?"

Sunnie opened the microwave, seemingly oblivious to the conversation. Momma cast a glance over to her and then went back to pressing the treats into the pan. "I knew, because I didn't want to go to bed alone for another night." She turned to help Sunnie with the bowl. "Just stir it as best you can, hon. Then it goes back in for another minute."

Link let her look right at him as she faced him again. They'd talked about Misty before, but not much since Link had started seeing her again this summer. "Of course, I had to wait a few more months before I didn't have to go to bed alone." She smiled at him. "You and Misty are getting along?"

"Yeah, seem to be," he said. "I mean, it's not like we have every single thing in common or anything."

"No one does."

"What? *Everyone* does," he said.

"Link." She flinched as Sunnie slammed the microwave. After casting a glare over her shoulder at the girl, she sighed. "Of course they don't."

"You and Daddy do."

"Me and Daddy absolutely do not," she said. "He wants to

go to every high school football game, and Smiles won't even start." She folded her arms and gave him a glare. "I am not doing that."

Link grinned, the idea of his momma sitting through every football game because Smiles was on the third string team grew into something hilarious. He started to laugh, and Momma gestured to him.

"Exactly," she said. She returned her attention to helping Sunnie stir in the cereal, as well as a bunch of chips in a variety of chocolates. White, semi-sweet, dark, and milk.

"What are the rice crispy squares for?" Link asked.

Momma glanced at him. "End of Summer picnic in a couple of days." She helped Sunnie butter up her hands so she could press this batch into a cookie sheet. "Link, if there's anything I've learned since coming to Shiloh Ridge, it's that every relationship will look and feel different."

He frowned. "What do you mean?"

"I mean, I'm friends with all of my sisters-in-law, right? But not a single one of them looks or feels the same. I'm closer to some than others, but at the same time, I love them all. I'd call your aunt Oakley for anything, but when I want help with a recipe, I head down the road to Etta's. If I need to know how to hang a new light fixture, I call Montana. If I need to complain about Daddy, I call Zona."

"Or Uncle Cactus," Link said with a smile.

Momma grinned back at him. "I try not to do it at all, but sometimes that man forgets he's not twenty-five years old."

"My boots are a mess," Daddy called, interrupting the conversation.

Momma looked toward the back door and sighed. "Or the fact that he can take his boots off outside if they're a mess."

"Hey, Link's here." Daddy spoke with pure warmth too. "There's a couple of muddy spots out there." He leaned in and kissed Momma on the cheek. "Mm, you smell nice."

"It's marshmallows," she said with a grin. "You left your boots by the back door?"

"Yeah," he said. "I might have tracked a little on the rug there." He looked over to Link. "What are you doin' here?"

"Actually, I wanted to ask you guys if you'd have me and Misty for dinner one night."

"Yes," Momma said instantly. "When?"

"Hold on," Daddy said. "You sure you want that?"

"She's moving off the ranch," Link said. "Tomorrow. And I don't know, I feel like I might...like it might put a bunch of distance between us. Like, the physical distance will cause other kinds of distance too."

Momma looked at Daddy, who looked back at her. "We managed to make it work," she said.

"Yeah, and Uncle Preacher got in a car accident trying to bridge the distance between him and Charlie," Link said. "I don't know. I need to stop worrying so much, I think. I just don't know how."

He looked at his parents, desperate for them to tell him how to stop worrying. Neither of them said anything.

"When I'm worried about something," Sunnie said. "Momma helps me make a plan. Then it's easier to see how things are going to go." She looked at Link with wide, bright blue eyes. "So, like, just make a plan with Misty, and it'll be fine."

Momma grinned from ear to ear. "Yeah, Link. Make a plan with Misty."

Link loved his younger sister, and she did make things sound so simple. "A plan," he mused. Yeah, he just needed to make a plan to keep Misty close even when she lived further from him.

Chapter Twenty-One

Mitch's phone flashed as it rang, lighting up his room—
and painting the backs of his eyelids with the bright
light. He wasn't really asleep, but he hadn't gotten out of bed
yet. He wasn't in Three Rivers, on the ranch, anymore, and he
didn't have to be up by five-thirty and out on the ranch by six to
beat the heat.

Here, he got to wake up at a normal hour, and work in a
regularly air conditioned building, and be done at a decent hour
that didn't leave his shoulders bunched with tension and
exhaustion. Here, at Whispering Paws, Mitch already had
friends he could talk to. Really talk to.

Too bad he was terribly lonely, despite having made this
choice, this move across over a thousand miles, and had plenty
of what he'd thought he wanted.

You do want it, he told himself as the bright light filled the
room again. *You are happy here.* He reached for his phone and

tapped to answer the video call from Link. He'd left Three Rivers two weeks ago, and Link had called four times now. Mitch wasn't sure who was lonelier—him or Link.

Hey, Link said, the word appearing at the bottom of the video on Mitch's phone. He signed the greeting as well.

Mitch waved, his version of *Hey*.

I caught you in bed. Link smiled at him. *Lucky.* He ducked down and heaved up a golden retriever. *Honor says hi*, he signed with one hand. Then he waved one of Honor's paws. *How's the new dog?*

Mitch grinned and grinned at the dog he'd left behind in Texas. He'd bought the dog outright, and he didn't have to put her back into hearing service. He'd made the trip to Willowbrook with his daddy and Honor, and his father had driven the dog home again once Mitch had his small, century-old house set up the way he wanted it.

He'd gotten a new hearing dog to train, and as he sat up on the edge of the bed, his dog—a pretty, burnished red cockapoo— jumped down to the ground, his smile absolutely adorable.

He's learning, Mitch said. *Here he is. His name's Beacon.* He turned his phone, so the camera showed the curly-haired dog. When he faced the phone back to him, Link had dropped Honor back to the ground. His phone sat propped up on his dining room table, and he had a plate of sausage and eggs in front of him.

I'm calling to see how the first day was, he signed. *You said you'd call, and you didn't.* Link kept his gaze down, and Mitch appreciated that. He wasn't trying to be accusatory, which was why he'd dropped eye contact.

Mitch knew Link though, and his heart grew two sizes, banging against his ribcage. When Link looked back up, Mitch started talking. *First day was really great, actually. I'm teaching college, Link. I was scared out of my mind when I walked into that first class.*

He tipped his head back and let laughter come out of his mouth. Ninety percent of the people who lived and worked at Whispering Paws were either completely deaf, legally deaf, or hard of hearing. Had he opted to live on campus, he wouldn't have had to worry about disturbing his neighbor by laughing too loudly too early in the morning.

The advanced students are first thing in the morning, he said. *So the day got easier from there.*

I can't imagine there's a sign you don't know, Link said. *Especially ranch vocabulary.*

Probably not, Mitch agreed. *It was still terrifying.*

But you did it. Link smiled at him. *And it's the weekend now. What are you doing?*

Training Beacon, he said. *He's got lessons every afternoon, and a long session on the weekend. You?*

Misty's moving today, Link said. *Back to town.*

Mitch watched his best friend and cousin, trying to read how Link felt about his girlfriend moving off the ranch after being there for months. Link, as usual, gave nothing away. Mitch longed to be more like that. More level-headed. Less smiley. Less "happy hands" and blurting out whatever came into his head.

When he couldn't decipher his cousin's mood, he asked, *How do you feel about that?*

It's time, Link said.

Are things still serious?

Link nodded. *Pretty serious, yeah. I've—we've talked about her moving here permanently after her job with the state finishes up.*

Mitch was surprised and unsurprised at the same time. *Definitely sounds serious then.*

Maybe more for me than her, Link said. *But I'm trying to be patient.*

Mitch smiled, but it didn't hold a whole heap of happiness. *Ah, our favorite word.*

Link's smile opened his mouth, which indicated that he was probably laughing. He once again dropped his head as he signed, *Right? I'm sick of hearing it.* He looked up at Mitch again. *Too bad it's the only message I'm getting from God. It's like it's on repeat.*

Mitch's stomach growled, and he ignored it. *At least you get something from God.* He couldn't believe he'd said the words, but his hands dropped back to his lap, the signs out. Done.

Link blinked, but his gaze didn't waver one bit. *Do you think you're in the right place, Mitch?*

Yeah, Mitch said. *Yep. I do.*

Then you are, Link said. He didn't ask anything more. He didn't start lecturing Mitch about his lack of a testimony in Jesus

Christ. He simply sat with him for another moment, and then said, *I miss you around here.*

I miss you too, Mitch said. *You don't talk to my parents, do you?*

Sure, Link said. *I do. Not about you, though. They haven't said anything to me about you. Why?*

No reason, Mitch said, though he hadn't talked to his parents as much as Link since moving here. He reasoned he was twenty-eight years old, and he didn't have to call his mommy every day to check in. He hadn't done that when he lived at Shiloh Ridge, and just because Willowbrook and Whispering Pines was further from her didn't mean he had to start now.

Call your momma once a week.

The thought entered his mind, in the voice he imagined his daddy to have. That had been Daddy's parting advice to Mitch when he'd finally loaded up Honor to make the drive back to Texas. *Call your momma once a week.*

Mitch had called her once, so he wasn't exactly behind yet—if he called today or tomorrow.

Are you coming home for the Angel Tree? Link asked next. *I know it's not for another couple of months, but I think it'll probably be the next time I see you in person.*

Yeah, Mitch said. *I've got airplane tickets already.*

You're going to fly? Link's eyebrows went up. *That'll be a new experience for you.*

Mitch grinned. *Yeah, one I'm kind of excited about.*

Why?

Because it's what normal people do.

Once again, he found himself having said something he hadn't anticipated saying. And his hands weren't done yet. *I just want to feel normal, Link. And here, I feel so much more normal than I do at Shiloh Ridge.*

But at the same time, I'm so homesick I just walk around the grocery store, comparing it to Wilde & Organic. He drew in a big breath and blew it out. *Nothing makes sense.*

Everything is still new, Link said. *And we both know I'm way better at adjusting to new things than you.* He maintained a perfectly straight face as he said it, and Mitch wasn't sure if he was joking or not.

His hands flew into motion again, protesting against his inability to change, and Link fully laughed now, his boxy shoulders vibrating as he did. Mitch stopped talking, his own smile gracing his face.

Is Misty gonna come to the Angel Tree? Mitch asked when they'd both stopped chuckling.

Link's smile slipped away to nothing, and he looked away from his almost-empty plate. *I don't know.*

You wanted to ask her last year, Mitch said. *Surely you will this year.*

I'm going to talk to her about it, Link said. *Oh, she's here. Want to say hello?*

Misty could speak a little sign language, and she crammed into the same frame as Link to ask him how Virginia was. Mitch liked seeing the two of them together, and he sure did notice the softness that came over Link when he looked at her.

He chitchatted with Misty for a minute, and then she

turned to go into Link's kitchen to pour herself a cup of coffee. *I miss you, brother*, he signed. *I'll call again soon.*

Yeah, Mitch said. *I miss you too, Link.*

The video went black very soon after that, and Mitch got to his feet and pulled on a shirt. At his feet, Beacon got up and trotted toward the bedroom door. Then the dog came back to him and sat.

Mitch made the training sign that said, *Show me*, and Beacon led the way out of the bedroom and down the hall. Mitch had two bedrooms and a single bath in this house, with a big, open area for a living room and dining room. The kitchen sat at the back of the house, along one wall, and Daddy had bought a portable island to give some delineation between the kitchen and the living room.

Beacon went past the black leather couches and to the door. He put his front paws up on it, then turned back to Mitch and sat. Mitch patted the dog and continued to the door to open it. Sure enough, a woman stood there in a dark blue uniform.

I need you to sign for this, she said, and Mitch imagined her voice to be pitched up a little, with a slightly Southern twang. Her dark hair had been braided half back, with the rest spilling over her slight shoulders.

Mitch smiled at her and reached for the electronic pen. He signed his name on the tablet and took the envelope she extended toward him. She smiled too, and in that brief moment when the package transferred hands, a spark jumped between them.

In a normal situation, Mitch would've asked for her

number. At the very least, he'd have said something flirty and fun. He'd seen other men do it plenty of times. He normally wasn't too self-conscious of his inability to communicate with hearing people, but something inside him had flipped.

He simply ducked his head in thanks, backed up a step, and closed the door between them, all while the dark-eyed beauty made eyes at him that said she'd have given him her phone number.

It's that kind of thing that Link doesn't understand, he told himself as he peeled back the tab to open the envelope. Asking a pretty woman for her number should be easy, and Mitch couldn't even do that. Not without a big explanation about how he was deaf, and then too many texts back and forth to get the information he wanted.

He'd put himself on a female fast besides. He made his own breakfast and just as he'd sat down to eat, his phone lit up with a text.

Link: *I think you're an amazing man, Mitch. I don't want to lecture you at all. It's the last thing I want. Your momma said something at church last week that has been in my mind a lot this week.*

Mitch was sure she had. His mother was an excellent preacher, because she actually lived her religion. She made mistakes and worked to fix them. Then, she told people about it, and they felt this great connection to her.

He did too, but he also sometimes felt like she had something to say to him she just hadn't found a way to say yet. She'd once told him that if he felt like he had to hide something from her, it probably wasn't a good thing to be doing. He just needed some space. He needed to figure out how to be who he was, because he wasn't going to suddenly be able to hear when the sun rose in the morning.

Link: *She said to remember the long view. That our day-to-day challenges can sometimes feel so overwhelming, and they can make us think or only be able to see short-term. So I know you're frustrated right now. Still settling into something that feels new and scary and big. I just want you to know that I love you, and I know God loves you, and I hope you can have the longest view possible right now.*

Mitch's heartbeat pulsed through his body, because he believed every word Link had spoken, and he had to acknowledge that God loved him. He had not been forgotten.

He simply hoped God would have a long view on his life too, and that He could potentially forgive this little bump where Mitch had doubted everything in his life, including his belief that God was aware of him, cared about him, and wanted to guide him.

Chapter Twenty-Two

Misty drew a deep breath and smoothed her hands down the front of her body to get her dress to lay where she wanted it. Everything in her life seemed to be coming up daisies and sunshine, and she wanted it to keep going that way.

A knock sounded on the door, and she turned away from her reflection. "It's Link," she called to Janie, but her roommate made it to the door first. Janie squealed and stepped outside without even acknowledging Misty.

"I guess it's not Link," she said, but Janie hadn't said she had a date this fine Sabbath morning. She hurried to the window and pushed the gauzy curtain aside to find out who Janie was going out with. She sucked in a breath at the baby face she found smiling at Janie as he opened the passenger door to his truck so she could climb in wearing her own sundress.

"Brandon Rhinehart." Misty straightened and turned in a

circle, looking for her phone. "I can't believe she didn't tell me she was going out with Brandon Rhinehart." She started typing in all caps, shouting at Janie for hiding such a thing from her. She'd never withheld a single thing from her about Link. Well, at least not the trivial stuff.

Janie hadn't answered before Link knocked on the door, and seeing as how Misty had been pacing in the living room of her new rental, she only had to spin and open the door. "Did you know Janie is going out with Brandon Rhinehart?"

Link blinked at her, then his smile took over his face. This morning, he wore a pair of sunglasses with his sexy cowboy hat, and he might as well have been a bodyguard in those things. They gave him a sense of mystery and intrigue, as if Misty needed another reason to like him.

"No, ma'am," he said. "I tend to talk more to Dawson than Brandon." He stepped up into the house. "She didn't tell you?"

"She did not." Misty huffed out her breath and shoved her phone in her dress pocket.

"That's kind of odd, isn't it?" Link asked.

"It is," Misty said." And you know what else? It hurts. I have this pinching inside, like someone has reached through my ribs and is squeezing my lungs."

"I'm sorry, sweetheart." Link didn't make fun of her for her feelings. He simply gathered her into his arms and held her while something stomped and stormed through her. "You sure look pretty today," he murmured. "I really like you in flowers."

"Thank you." Misty stuffed everything that had spilled out back into its rightful place. She backed away from Link. "I'm ready." She swiped at her eyes, but she hadn't shed any tears, so her makeup should be fine.

Link took her hand and led her out to the passenger door of his truck, and he drove them over to the church. "Aunt Willa's speaking about having the long view again today," he said. "I had my nephew over for breakfast this morning, and he told me so." He flashed her a smile. "Should be good."

"Yes," Misty agreed. "It should be."

"Hey, I wanted to ask you." Link kept his eyes out the windshield, not that she'd have been able to see them anyway. "My family does this big thing every year. For Christmas." He glanced over to her then, and the only indication she had of his nerves was the way both hands gripped the steering wheel, almost to the point of his knuckles being white.

He wore a pristine white shirt too, with a brilliant tie in orange and gray paisley, and she marveled that he could be so put together in his Sunday best one moment, and in blue jeans and cowboy boots at another.

Misty reached over and took his nearest hand off the wheel and into hers. "You're nervous."

"This is a big celebration in the Glover family," he said. "For Shiloh Ridge. We put up a family tree every year at the homestead—the one where Ranger and Oakley live. We decorate it with my great-grandmother's homemade ornaments, and it stands for a couple of months, reminding anyone who comes to the ranch about our heritage."

He swallowed, and Misty thought about her own family traditions. Had they even had any? If so, she couldn't remember them. Once she'd realized that she couldn't count on her mother to protect her and Danny, she'd done the best she could. She'd helped him dye eggs at Easter, and she'd hidden them around the house while her mother was passed out drunk.

She made pancakes every Saturday morning. For Christmas, she'd hung the stockings for her and Danny, and she'd filled them with whatever she could trade for at school. Tears pricked her eyes at the awful memories, and especially at how her feeble attempts to make a normal life for her brother had failed so spectacularly.

"I want you to come this year," he said. "We have a big family meal. We vote on our investments during our annual ranch meeting. Then we decorate the tree. Eat dessert. It's really amazing, and I'd really like you there."

Misty pulled herself out of her past and looked at Link in her present. A great, booming voice in her head told her that this man could also be her future, and that made her throat dry and her palms sweaty.

"I'd love to come, Link," she said softly.

He blew his breath out, as if he'd been holding it since he'd awakened that morning. "Great. It's the last Sunday of October."

"You decorate a Christmas tree in October?"

"Yes," he said simply. "It's our Angel Tree."

"An angel tree," she murmured. "It sounds nice. Like you have people watching over you."

"We do," he said. "Our family members who've passed. You —they could watch over you too."

She smiled at him, the movement of her mouth a little too wobbly for her liking. "I'd like that, Link."

He pulled their joined hands back to his lap and raised her wrist to kiss it. "Great," he said. "Now I can really enjoy the sermon and the picnic."

"You forgot the dancing."

"I never forget about dancing with you," he said.

She grinned into the sunshine pouring into the truck. "Remember that time when you held me as the sun went down? And we danced to the sweetest, slowest song as a whole, glowing herd of fireflies came out. Remember that?" She whispered the last two words, because she really needed some of her dismal, gray, miserable memories to be replaced with more vibrant, colorful, and meaningful ones.

"Yeah," Link said wistfully, as if they'd already lived through tonight's picnic, dance, and firefly sighting. "That was such a great night."

"Link," she said, an idea flowing into her mind. "Would you ever want to meet my mom and my brother?"

"Of course I would," he said. Just like that. Without missing a beat. Without asking her another single thing. Just, *of course I would*, like she didn't even need to ask.

"Why?" she asked, twisting to look at him now.

"Because they're part of you," he said slowly. "I know you didn't have a happy childhood, and I know you've put distance between them and you. But they still shaped you, and yes, if you wanted me to meet them, and it was important to you, then of course I want to meet them."

"They might think you're special," she said. "I've never introduced them to anyone in my life. Not even a girlfriend."

"They might," he said. "It's a risk." He grinned at her, but she couldn't quite get herself to return it.

"Hey," he said, sobering. "It's okay if they think I'm special, because they'll only have to look at us once to know that I think you're the special-est in the whole world."

Misty's eyes watered then, but she didn't let any tears out. "I don't think you used the word *special-est* right in that sentence."

His big hand around hers tightened. "You don't, huh? Well, good thing there are no Grammar Police in this truck." He pulled into the church parking lot and jogged around the front of the truck to open her door for her.

He took her into his arms and asked, "Can I have my pre-church kiss, please? You were mad at your house, and I missed out."

She didn't tease him, or smile at him, or do anything flirty. She simply eased herself into his arms, a place she'd always fit, and pressed her lips to his. The fire in his touch licked through her body, and Misty didn't mind the way it burned some of the bridges she'd been afraid to knock down.

She'd once worried that Link would force her to burn everything she knew about herself, her family, her life, to the ground. Now, she was willingly lighting matches and tossing more fuel onto the dirtiest, dustiest corners of her existence.

Now, she was falling in love with this gentle giant of a cowboy.

Now, she was seriously considering becoming a permanent resident of Three Rivers—and a Glover.

* * *

Misty sure did like Pastor Glover's sermons. She had a way of standing at the pulpit and inviting everyone along on the same journey she was on. Today, she'd limped a little more as she'd taken her place behind the mic, and Misty had already silently begged Jesus to help her through this sermon.

She'd started talking about having what she called "a long view" last week, and this week, she'd expounded more on that.

"It's having eternal perspective," Willa said. "When Jesus Christ came to the earth, do you think He only saw the few decades He'd live here?" She shook her head. "No. He had the long view. The bigger picture."

She surveyed the congregation, but Misty couldn't look away from her. Willa smiled then seemed to look right at the rows of Glovers, who all sat front and center in the chapel. Today—and on other Sundays—Misty sat with them. Link's family had always been welcoming, with smiles and secret looks to one another. But they never made her feel like there wasn't room for her on the benches they normally filled themselves, just like they'd never acted like there wasn't room for her and Janie up at Shiloh Ridge.

"Life is a series of good and bad," Willa said. "Ups and downs and some strong curves that can leave you reeling, breathless, wondering if you're doing the right thing or not."

"My cousin Mitch should hear this," Link murmured in Misty's ear.

She leaned in close to hear him, then turned her mouth toward him. "Maybe she could send him her notes."

"She doesn't speak from notes."

No wonder she was so good, and Misty focused on her again. "Maybe we could send him some notes," she whispered.

Link nodded, and Misty stayed cuddled close to his chest. She liked how warm and strong he made her feel. How loved and cherished. No one before him had ever given her such a sense of safety and security—not that she'd let anyone try.

"But one hairpin curve is not what life is entirely," Willa said now. "One sudden drop doesn't mean you get to stay down forever. And yes, I know it can feel like all God has dealt you is bad cards. A losing hand. A curve here, and another there, and then a steep drop-off, and then an impossible hike back to the top. Oh, do I know that."

She stopped there, and the last note in her voice spoke of hurt and pain and difficult past times. Misty didn't know all of them in Willa's life, but in that moment, she realized that everyone—absolutely everyone—needed the master physician at some point. Probably a lot of points. Continually.

"There is no better friend than the Lord Jesus Christ," Willa said, and Misty pulled in a sharp breath. The words could've come from her in that moment, as the realizations continued to spiral through her. "He has suffered for all you're going through. For all I'm going through. For all I've been through; for all you've been through. For each one of us. Not only the things we've done wrong and need to repent for, but for the pain."

Again, that tone of understanding, of pure agony, rang in Willa's voice on the last word. She paused again, and Misty understood she needed a moment to solidify her emotions. Misty's felt like wobbling gelatin that had sat too close to a boiling hot burner. The fire flickered too close, and she was about to lose all composure and let everything she felt blubber from her.

She took another breath, trying to hitch things back where they belonged.

"For the disease and discomforts in your physical body," Willa said now, her voice quiet. "For the emotional and mental hurt others inflict upon you. For the burdens you carry." She seemed to look right at Misty then, and her head cocked. She too had reddish-blonde hair, and perhaps that was why Misty had always felt such a strong connection to her.

Either way, Willa smiled softly then. "Jesus has already carried those burdens, my friends. Perhaps it's time you set them down. Put them at His feet, where they belong. Don't carry them with you anymore." She drew a breath and switched her gaze to somewhere else in the church.

Misty felt utterly exposed, like every eye from every congregant had suddenly zeroed in on her. She even glanced around as if to throw off their gazes. No one had looked her way.

But she felt perfectly seen by God.

"Have the long view," Willa said. "Expand your perspective. If you don't know how, kneel down tonight, and ask God to help you see the bigger picture, and where you belong inside it. For my brothers and sisters, we all belong inside the family of God."

She might as well have invited Misty to move to Three Rivers permanently, marry Link, and become a Glover. That alone would provide such a sense of safety and belonging—two things Misty had given up on over two decades ago. But to belong to the family of God too?

It felt incomprehensible, and yet, perfectly right at the same time.

Her mind took off on a different path then, and Misty started discarding some of the bigger loads she'd been carrying for so long. It was never her responsibility to make sure her mother was comforted, or got to work on time, or paid the rent. She'd done those things, but she didn't have to carry the guilt that she hadn't done it well enough.

She shouldn't have had to raise her brother. While she had, she'd done the best job she could've possibly done as a ten-year-old. She didn't have to shoulder the responsibility of his incarceration any longer.

Perhaps she'd gone too far in the opposite direction by refusing to date, assuming all men would be as horrible as the previous ones she'd had in her life. But she didn't even have to keep packing those feelings, or that worry, guilt, or shame.

She truly could lay all of it down, for Jesus had already carried these troubles, trials, and turmoils for her.

By the time they rose to their feet to sing the closing hymn, Misty did so without thousands of pounds of her past burdening her. Link looked over to her and blinked. "Hey, are you all right?"

"Why?" she asked as the organ and piano began to play together. "Do I not look all right?"

"You look...different," he said.

Misty smiled at him, experiencing a true miracle—one where her Lord and Savior had done what He'd always promised to do. He'd walked with her. "I feel different."

Then she faced the front and sang along with everyone as they lifted their voices in praises—for the good, the bad, the evil, the pain, the heartache, the mental anguish, and the absolute saving power of God the Father and his son Jesus Christ.

She grinned as she stepped into Link's arms afterward, the congregation breaking ranks and streaming up and down the aisles. "All right, baby," she said, noting how his face lit up with her term of endearment. Today was a day of revelations, because Misty realized in that moment how very much Link needed to be told how amazing he was.

Her memory fired at her, reminding her that he often felt overlooked in his family, and she had the power to make him feel seen. Make him feel appreciated. Make him feel loved.

"You promised me an amazing dance."

"That I did," he whispered as he pulled her close and hugged her. "Let's hope we don't melt before those fireflies swarm us."

Chapter Twenty-Three

L ink could hold Misty in his arms forever and never tire of it. The world seemed to sway slightly left, then back to the right, with the two of them, and he never wanted to let go. Around them, others danced too, some light conversation floating on the air with the hint of the breeze here in the gardens outside the church.

They'd eaten with his family. Laughed and talked and watched the skits the junior Sunday School children had put together. As the afternoon had started to become evening, the food had been switched out to desserts, and the dance floor had gotten marked off with electric lampposts and strings of lights.

If Link's obsessive studying of fireflies the past few days had taught him anything, the glowing insects should be coming out soon. *Please, please, dear Lord*, he thought. He couldn't make the fireflies appear, but he believed God could—and Link really needed the fireflies to make tonight absolutely perfect.

For Misty, but maybe a little bit for himself too. Maybe his parents really did exist in the glow of a firefly, and maybe they were watching as he fell in love with Misty Granger.

The song ended, but Misty didn't make any minute moves to step out of his arms. Another frilly, music-only song came on, and while others around them shuffled on and off the floor, Link and Misty simply stayed.

He closed his eyes and lost himself in the scent of her skin, her hair, her very presence in his life. A more magical day probably hadn't existed, despite her initial frustration when she'd learned Janie had a date and hadn't told her.

Link allowed himself to sink all the way into love with Misty, though it did send a string of fear threading through him. He'd never been in love before, and he didn't want to have to figure out how to recover from having loved and lost.

But being in love felt absolutely amazing, and Link wanted to bask in this feeling for as long as he possibly could.

He opened his eyes, and the flitting of tiny specks of light in the twilight made his breath stick against the back of his tongue. Something like electric emotion zipped through him.

He felt the love of so many then, including the parents he hadn't ever truly known, and he sat with it for a few moments.

"Hey, sweetheart," he then murmured, easing Misty out of his embrace. "Look."

She fell to his side as the fireflies continued to drift and lilt through the air, more and more arriving with every passing second.

"Wow." Misty breathed the word out of her mouth as she

tilted her head back to look up into the sky. Link did the same thing, basking in the glory of dozens and dozens of pinpricks of light filling the navy space around them.

Link smiled, because God had answered his prayers. And because his childhood memories of Momma telling him his parents' love existed in the light of a firefly, and he could feel it now as strongly as he had back then.

And because the beauty of this slow, summer Texas evening —filled with fireflies—reminded Link of how amazing life could be. Alarms might sound early. The sun might burn the land and crops and a cowboy's skin. Not everything went his way all the time.

But that didn't mean life wasn't grand. It didn't mean God hadn't touched every particle of this earth, or that He wasn't in control of what happened in a small town in the Texas Panhandle. In Link's life, personally.

Looking up into the sky, he felt the vastness of the universe above him, around him. It seemed impossible that God could know him, this simple, singular man in such a remote place. But Link knew without a doubt that he'd been engraved in the palms of the Lord's hands.

He'd texted Mitch only yesterday that God loved him, and Link knew it as clearly as he knew his own name.

"This is the best night of my life," Misty murmured.

"It's gorgeous," Link said. They weren't the only people admiring the fireflies, but because they weren't dancing any longer, Link gently guided Misty out of the way. He grabbed a couple of treats for them from the dessert table and led her away from the crowds, from the lights.

They found a bench further into the darkness, where the fireflies continued to dance around them. He sighed and put his arm around Misty. "Cookie dough brownie or coconut rice crispy square?"

"Brownie," Misty said, and Link silently rejoiced. He handed her the treat of her choice and took a bite of the toasted coconut, marshmallow, and cereal.

"These are my favorite thing," he said. "My momma and aunts make a whole bunch of different kinds, and I love the toasted coconut."

"I probably could've guessed that," she said. "Seems like you ordered that mango cheesecake on one of our dates, and it has that coconut macaroon crust."

"From Beyond Elegance," he said. "I'd go there again *just* for that cheesecake." He grinned at her, and Misty turned toward him and leaned closer.

He took the opportunity to capture her lips with his in a gentle yet firm declaration that he wanted to kiss her every day too. Over and over again. He slid one hand along her neck and cupped her ear in his palm to keep her there, so he could continue to kiss her.

"Will you come to dinner at my parents'?" he asked. "Just us and them—and my younger siblings, of course."

"Yes," Misty said.

"I mean, I know you've met them, but this is—it would be—"

Link cleared his throat. "My parents want to start to get to know you too is all."

"Link." Misty leaned into his chest and smiled up at him. "I already said yes."

"Okay," he said. "Great. I don't know when yet. I'll talk to my momma."

Misty put her feet up on the bench and leaned her back into his chest while they finished their treats.

"One more dance?" he asked after she'd eaten her last bite of brownie. "Then I'm feeling a little beat, and I have to check on the horses in one of the stables tonight still." Work on a ranch never stopped, after all. Even in perfect summer weather, with a glow of fireflies, and the most beautiful woman in the world.

"One more dance." Misty stood and extended her hand to him. Link grabbed onto her and pulled her down onto his lap instead of joining her on his feet.

"Maybe one more kiss first," he whispered. And then he kissed the woman he was most certainly in love with—just one more time.

* * *

Link set down a perfectly white plate on his side of the table, which he normally only shared with Smiles. But this made the third place setting on the ten-foot table, which his father had asked Uncle Bishop to custom make just for their family, for the space they had in their dining room.

"Smiles, there's still no ice in these cups," Momma said.

269

Smiles had collapsed onto the couch with his phone, and he looked up to their mother.

"Link, silverware is on the counter."

"Got it," he told his mother.

"Heather, are you done with the napkins?" Momma worked in the kitchen, stirring something vigorously in a pot.

"I hope when I bring a boy home, things aren't this tense," Heather said from where she sat at the counter, folding cloth napkins into animals.

Link glanced over to her, a smile lifting a corner of his mouth. "If you bring a boy home before you turn twenty, Daddy will flip his lid."

Heather grinned at him. "Trust me, I know."

"Look at these butter sculptures I did." Sunnie put a plate of butter shaped like a rose on the table near where Link set down the last plate.

He took in the petals, shaped and molded out of butter. "Wow, Sunnie," he said. "That's amazing. Thank you so much."

"You said Misty likes to cook," his youngest sister said. "Momma said not to talk too much, but do you think I could ask her about her favorite recipe?"

"Of course you can," Link said. "There's no rules for dinner tonight, Sunnie. It's just a normal dinner."

"Momma's lectured all of us relentlessly," Smiles said as he dropped a few ice cubes into Daddy's cup at the head of the table. "So it's not normal, Link."

Link looked over to his mother in the kitchen. "She has?"

"You know how she is," Heather said. "If she's breathing, she's thinking of a lecture."

"That's not fair," Link said, though his mother did like to lecture.

"What's not fair?" Daddy appeared at the end of the table with him and Smiles, and Heather went on her way, putting an elephant on her place, and then a swan on Sunnie's.

"Nothing," Smiles said. "Unless you count all of us out here working on setting the table while Rock naps."

"Rock has a cold," Link said at the same time as his father. "Smiles, it's fine."

Daddy looked at both of them. "I just woke him up. He's showering and coming down. I'm sure Momma has a job for him."

"I'm sure," Smiles said with his sunny smile, which somehow made it seem like he wasn't being sassy. Link—or Rock himself—likely would've gotten his mouth washed out with soap had he said the exact same thing Smiles just had.

Daddy frowned and met Link's gaze. "What's going on?"

"Momma's lectured everyone about tonight?" Link murmured, though the silverware waited for him. "Sunnie wants to know what she can and can't talk about. Like...this is just supposed to be a normal dinner where y'all can get to know her a little better."

"I know," Daddy said. "That's what this is."

"Bear," Momma snapped over her shoulder. "There you are. This turkey isn't going to carve itself."

Link's eyebrows went up in sync with his father's. "Oh, boy."

"I see what you mean." Daddy started down the length of the table and toward the kitchen. "I'll talk to her."

"Misty will be here in like, two minutes," Link reminded him.

Daddy just waved his hand, and Link sighed as he went to get the silverware off the counter. He turned back and faced his siblings, all of them doing something to make the dining room table beautiful and ready for dinner.

"Hey, guys," he said as Rock came into the room. "Rock, c'mere." He waited for his younger brother to join the others. "It's—don't worry about Momma, okay? She's just nervous, because I've never brought anyone home for dinner, but it's not that big of a deal. Right? You've all met Misty before."

"Are you going to marry her?" Sunnie asked.

"I don't know," Link said honestly. "Maybe. Yeah, maybe. I sure do like her, and I want her to feel like she knows everyone before anything like that."

"I like her," Heather said.

"I'll thank God for that in my prayers tonight," Link said dryly. He opened his arms and gathered his four younger siblings into his chest. "I love you guys," he whispered. "This is for me, mostly. For Misty too, but mostly me. You can still be you. You can talk to her about anything, and you just have to act normal, all right?"

"All right," Smiles said, speaking for everyone. "You don't worry either, Link."

He stepped back as something crashed in the kitchen. The five of them faced their parents as a plume of steam rose from the sink. "Sure," Link said. "I'm not worried about anything."

"I got it," Daddy said at the exact moment the doorbell rang.

"That's me," Link said. "Smiles, Sunnie, could you go see if Momma needs anything?"

"On it," Sunnie said, already dashing toward the kitchen.

Link turned his back on the chaos, and took in a deep lungful of air. "Lord, it's just dinner. Can I not just get a couple of hours of non-Glover...ness?" He pulled open the door and crowded out onto the porch with Misty.

"Oh." She backed up, her hands sliding up his chest. "What's—?"

When the door clicked closed behind him, Link released his breath. "There's a little bit of tension in the house is all," he said.

"I can smell something delicious all the way out here," she said with a smile.

Link drank in her dark skinny jeans with her hair falling down over a dark green shirt. Her makeup sat flawlessly on her face, along with her smile, and the easy way she seemed immune to the stress pouring out of the house.

Honor stood behind her, and Link smiled at the pair of them. "You bring me so much happiness," he said.

Misty wrapped her arms up around the back of his neck. "Same, Link."

"My momma made a mini version of Thanksgiving dinner." Link wrapped her in his arms and danced with her, the way he had a couple of weeks ago at the End of Summer picnic. "She's apparently been lecturing my siblings about what they can talk about with you. My brother is sick. And when I came out here, my daddy had just dropped the potatoes in the sink. So."

He grinned at her, and she smiled back. He let his eyes drift closed as he brought her closer, and when he kissed her, Link suddenly didn't care about whatever happened tonight. He didn't carry on, because Daddy had a security camera pointed at the front porch, and he didn't need Momma ripping open the front door and demanding to know what they were doing.

"Come on," he said. "Welcome to the Glover family." He gave her a wry smile and stepped into the house ahead of her. With his hand in hers, he led her inside, calling, "Everyone, Misty's here."

"She's here," Daddy said.

"I heard she's here," Momma bickered back. "Kids, leave that. Just leave it. Misty's here."

The six of them spilled out of the kitchen and lined up at the end of the table, and Link started laughing and shaking his head as he walked toward them. He stopped at the edge of the couch while Daddy fixed his collar and Momma smoothed down her apron.

"Misty," he said. "You've met everyone before, but apparently we're going to make this a formal affair." He raised his eyebrows.

"Of course we're not," Momma said. "Come on in, Misty." She stepped out of line and over to Misty. Link let go of her hand and Momma took it. "You remember Smiles and Rock, Heather and Sunnie."

"Definitely," Misty said. "Sunnie, you're the chef, right?"

Sunnie's chest and shoulders expanded as she glowed with pride. "Yes, ma'am. I helped with the rolls and the green beans tonight."

"I can't wait to have them." Misty hugged Heather and said something about her hair, and then she properly shook Smiles's and Rock's hands. When she arrived in front of Daddy, Link simply watched as she took his tall, broad-shouldered, some-times grumpy father into her arms.

"Good to see you again, Bear."

"You too," he said easily, his eyes coming up and finding Link's. Link grinned, because Daddy could be tamed pretty easily. "Come sit down. Sammy put you by Link, of course." He stepped back and looked down the row of his children. "Every-one, sit."

And there was a bit of the grizzly Link knew and loved.

Link moved forward and glided his hand along Misty's lower back. "We're over here, sweetheart." He took her around the table and pulled her chair out for her. She glanced up at him as she sat, and Link took his place beside her while everyone else went back into the kitchen.

Momma talked in hushed, hurried tones, and then they all brought over a bowl or a tray or a serving utensil. The food got placed down the length of the table, and everyone sat.

All eyes, including Link's, moved to their daddy, and he brought his hands up and clasped them in front of him. "I love having dinner with my family." He smiled with all the force of a loving, caring father—which was exactly who Bear Glover was.

Link grinned at him. "Thanks for having me and Misty." Out of sight, he took her hand in his, and she beamed over to him.

"You two are welcome here anytime," Momma said.

"Okay, Rock, you feelin' well enough to pray?" Daddy looked at Rock, whose expression didn't move. His nickname was so apt, because he never really let much bother him, and he remained stoic through stressful situations.

"Yes, sir," he said, his eyes flicking over to Misty. "I'm not contagious anymore."

"Link told me," she said with a nod and a smile.

Rock nodded once and bowed his head. Link had grown up with Rock, so he knew the boy didn't waste any breath or any time when it was his turn to pray. So he quickly bowed his head, but Misty was a little slower.

Link grinned as Rock said, "Dear Lord, we're real glad to be together for dinner tonight as a family. Thank You for giving us families, and bless those that feel alone that Thou will send someone to them. Someone to remind them that they don't have to be alone, that Thou is aware of them, that we all have a place to belong."

He paused for only long enough to take a quick breath. "We're grateful for the food, for good parents, for this life in Texas, and for each other. Bind our hearts, and bless us to forgive each other. Amen."

"Amen," Link murmured while a few other of his family members said it much louder. He'd barely released Misty's hand, and Smiles had barely dove for the platter with the turkey on it before Sunnie said, "Misty, do you have a favorite recipe?"

Link hid his smile and reached for the bacony green beans, which had been placed in front of him. He didn't mind the questions, and he didn't mind if Daddy was a little polar-bear tonight, or grizzly, or teddy.

If Misty stayed around for much longer, she'd see all of his daddy's personalities. She'd realize that Momma sometimes snapped at the kids, and sometimes overcooked their poultry, and sometimes did everything exactly, exactly right.

She'd become Heather's and Sunnie's best friends, and Smiles would charm her with his positivity and optimism. Even Rock would claim her as part of the family by quietly confiding in her when he needed help with something and didn't want anyone else to know.

Link looked across the table to his brother, and their eyes met. He nodded at him, saying he sure was glad to see him, and Rock nodded back, saying, *I'm glad you're here, Link.*

Dishes moved around the table while Misty talked about a stuffed hamburger recipe she used to make in Dallas. Once the green beans made it back to him, Link picked up his freshly baked roll and started slathering on butter and jam. "You got everything, baby?" he asked, looking over to Misty.

She'd heaped food on her plate, and her eyes shone like stars and diamonds combined. Link couldn't help thinking of fireflies when he looked at her, and he grinned at her. "Looks like it."

She nudged him with her shoulder. "Don't make fun of me. I'm hungry."

"I can see that." He chuckled and looked to his momma.

She smiled at him, but she didn't start asking questions the way Link expected her to. "Thanks for dinner, Momma."

"Yes, thank you," Misty said, switching her smile over to Momma. "I've never seen anything like this."

"Oh, surely you have," Momma said.

"No, really," Misty said. "My mother didn't cook."

Link ducked his head, glancing at her as he went back to his food.

"But for special occasions, surely you had something like this."

"Momma." Link shook his head, and Misty looked over to him.

"It's okay, Link," she said.

He gestured with his fork, hoping this wouldn't be a disaster.

Misty took a moment, wherein everyone at the table didn't make a peep. Shockingly. "Uh, when I say my mother didn't cook, I mean it. Not even for Thanksgiving or Christmas or Easter." She cleared her throat. "We didn't exactly have special occasions." She glanced at Link's siblings sitting across from them, and both Sunnie and Heather seemed completely stunned.

"In fact," Misty said. "It was a special occasion when we had food in the house."

Link wanted to jump in front of her to shield her from all the stares of his family members. They simply had never experienced such a thing, and yes, it was horrible and not something Link liked thinking about.

"It's okay," Misty finally said into the stretching silence. "I didn't mean to kill the mood."

Chapter Twenty-Four

S ammy Glover swore her heart had stopped beating. She first looked at Bear for help, but he simply raised his eyebrows. She had pressed the issue about cooking, but how could she have known? Misty talked about cooking like she loved it, and most people learned to cook from their momma's or grandmother's.

"I'm so sorry, honey," she said when Link didn't offer any help either. To his credit, he had tried to warn her. She covered Misty's hand with hers. "I apologize for bringing it up."

"It's okay," Misty said. "My fault. I'll keep the conversation lighter." She glanced over to Link. "You said it would be lively."

"It usually is," he grumbled. "Heather, didn't you have a story from the pool today?"

"Oh, dove tails," she said. "You would not believe what people try to take into the pool with them." From there, his sister let her mouth run, telling a story about a package of chocolate cakes that had gotten loose from a child and looked like something terrible.

Everyone laughed, and the mood lightened. Until Daddy asked, "Do you have brothers and sisters, Misty?"

Sammy tensed again, but Misty easily said, "Yeah, just one brother, though. Nothing like this." She smiled around at everyone. "You guys don't know how lucky you are." She sure seemed to radiate light, and Sammy sure did like her for Link.

She was bright and fun and outgoing while he tended to stand on sidelines and observe. Together, they'd be a perfect team, and as Sammy watched her son, she could see he'd fallen. He was completely smitten with Misty, though he'd probably tell her as much if she asked.

Misty grinned at him, touched him, and seemed perfectly at-ease with him too. They knew each other, and she appeared to be just as into the relationship as Link. Thankfully.

Misty didn't name her brother or tell them where he was or what he was doing, and Sammy sure wasn't going to ask. Bear had gotten the memo too, because he didn't follow up with the most logical question either.

She couldn't comprehend not even having Thanksgiving dinner, or something special for Christmas. Even a grilled ham and cheese sandwich on Easter.

What about her birthday? Sammy thought, the question growing inside her. Everyone deserved something amazing and special on their birthday, even if the item was trivial. It meant someone, somewhere, had been thinking about them.

"When's your birthday, Misty?" she asked, trying to sound casual.

Both Misty and Link looked at her, and Link didn't jump in to answer for his girlfriend.

"Momma celebrates her birthday early," Smiles said.

That brought another drape over the table, but Sammy smiled at her son. "I do," she said. "My sister and her husband died close to my birthday, and I didn't want to be thinking about that when I should be celebrating." She casually stabbed another piece of turkey and swiped it through her pile of mashed potatoes and gravy.

"Mine's in March," Misty said.

"Oh, same as Link," Sammy said.

They both nodded, and Sammy would ask him what day later. Perhaps they could stage a big party for the two of them in True Blue.

"Momma," Link said, already shaking his head. "It's not necessary."

"What?" Sammy asked innocently. "You'll be twenty-seven in a few months. That's a big milestone."

"Is it?" he challenged. "Maybe I missed all the hype around *twenty-seventh* birthdays." He looked over to his father. "What did you do for your twenty-seventh birthday, Daddy?"

Bear smiled, of all things. "I worked the ranch." He took a big bite of his roll and said nothing more.

Sammy wanted to roll her eyes. "How old will you be in March, Misty?"

"Thirty-one, ma'am."

Sammy's heart fell to the soles of her shoes, especially when Link said, "Also not a milestone, Momma."

"Still, March is a big month for us," she said. She gestured between her and Bear. "We got married in March. So did Oakley and Ranger."

"On the same day," Bear said.

"So we could just have a big family celebration."

"I like parties," Misty said, and Sammy practically lunged at her to hug her.

"There you go. She likes parties, so we'll have a party."

"It's months away, Momma," Link said, glaring at her out of the corner of his eye.

Sammy knew how to win this and get out of it at the same time. "So we'll just wait and see." She smiled at Misty and looked over to Rock. "Rock, we get three sentences on what you did in your rodeo prep class this morning."

He looked at her like she'd just said speaking three sentences would torture him, but she didn't budge an inch. If she didn't give him a stipulation, he'd say nothing.

"Then can I tell everyone about the new girl in my health class?" Smiles asked. Sammy would get *two* whole conversations from him, and she nodded at him while also telling him with her eyes to stay quiet until Rock had his turn.

"Is this a new girl you like or just a new girl?" Daddy asked.

"It's Smiles," Heather said with a snort. "What do you think?"

Smiles didn't deny that he was a bit of a flirt, or that he

seemed to like every female who smiled back at him. In fact, he just smiled while his siblings teased him—everyone but Rock.

Sammy let it go on for a few moments, and then she said, "All right, all right. Rock, your turn."

He put another big bite of bread in his mouth, but they'd all learned to wait for him. If they didn't, he'd get out of talking, and Sammy would have to nag him again the same way she had Smiles about filling the cups with ice before dinner.

Sammy knew all of her children and the things they did to avoid what they didn't like to do. So she waited, and finally Rock said, "It's just the beginning, and we've started with a first aid unit."

That was one sentence, and Sammy waited patiently for a second, her love for her family expanding and filling her whole heart. She glanced at Misty, and she easily absorbed her into her heart too, which caused her to instantly start praying that all would work out between her and Link.

Her beautiful son, who Sammy knew only wanted someone to see him and love him and choose him.

Chapter Twenty-Five

M isty helped load one of two dishwashers with the glasses from tonight's meal. Growing up, she hadn't even had a single dishwasher, let alone two. In fact, she hadn't even had a dishwasher until she'd graduated from college and gotten an apartment with one of her friends from the single design class she'd taken.

Sammy whipped everyone into shape, and everyone—even Link—had a job to clear the table, put leftovers away, and clean up the dishes, pots and pans, and countertops in the kitchen. Misty went back to the table to get the bottles of jam they'd had for their rolls. Homemade strawberry, peach, and raspberry.

Misty had been in college before she'd realized that jams and jellies could even be homemade. And that scalloped potatoes didn't *have* to come from a box. And that cake recipes existed, not just cake mixes.

As she stretched for the big mason jar of peach jam, her shoe flexed, and she looked down as her shoelace broke. "Shoot."

She'd known her little runners might not last much longer, but she'd expected the soles to wear through before the lace broke.

Sammy came up beside her. "You okay?"

"My shoelace broke."

Link's mother looked down too. "They're white. I've got some you can have." She started to walk away, and Misty looked up from her broken lace to Sammy's retreating back.

"You have some?" She scrambled to follow her out of the kitchen. About halfway down the hall, Sammy slid open a door to reveal a set of shelves laden with household items.

Boxes of toothpaste. Several packages of toothbrushes. Stick after stick of deodorant, both men's and women's. Bottles of mouthwash. Painkillers. Cleaning supplies.

Sammy started rummaging through things, moving aside big packages of batteries—not cheap—feminine hygiene products, washcloths, laundry and dishwashing pods, a whole case of dish soap, body lotion—

"Here you go." She smiled as she came up with a package of white shoelaces.

Misty stared at them, managing to take them before she made it into a thing Sammy would notice. Behind them, Link's little sisters started squabbling, and Sammy headed back in that direction without sliding the door closed.

She lowered the laces and took in the inventory in the

closet. She didn't hear Link coming down the hall until he slid his hand along the waistband of her jeans. "You okay, love?" He leaned in, the tip of his nose tracing a line down the side of her throat.

"Look at this," she said. "Look at all this *stuff*."

Link looked into the closet, but he didn't seem surprised. "We live pretty far from town, and my momma hates being out of something important."

Misty held up the shoelaces. "Like this?"

"Not having shoelaces on a ranch is terrible," he said.

She turned away from the closet. "Can you please close that?"

He did, but he blocked her escape down the hall. "Talk to me about this," he said in a low voice.

Misty kept her focus on the floor, which shone with a golden gloss. High-end. Everything about this house screamed money, and Misty hadn't minded until this moment.

"When I was a Freshman in college," she started. "I needed more deodorant, and my roommate was at the store, so she said she'd get me some. I said I'd pay her back." She swallowed, so much stinging and streaming through her. "I never did."

Link folded her into his arms. "Okay."

"I never paid her back, because I couldn't afford a two-dollar stick of deodorant, and your mother has probably twenty of them in there."

"Sweetheart, I'll pay for whatever you want," he said. "Whatever you need, be it deodorant or hair dye or those fingertip bandages. Okay? It's just a closet of supplies."

"Yeah." She wrapped her arms around him and hung on. "It feels like it means something."

"It does," he whispered in her ear. "It means you don't ever have to live like you did in college again. It means I'll take care of you, though I know you're *not* that broke Freshman anymore and you don't *need* me to take care of you." He pulled back and gazed down at her. "It's all I want to do—to take care of you. To make sure you never have to have this look on your face again."

"Okay," she said. "Okay, look away."

"Look away?"

She flashed him a smile. "Yeah, look away."

"All right," he said dubiously as he turned his head. He even closed his eyes, and Misty fell for him a little bit more right there in the hallway at his parents' house.

She gave herself a tiny physical shake and a great big mental one. She ran her hands down her face and fixed the collar on her shirt. Since she couldn't see her own face, she wasn't entirely sure what she'd looked like, but she fixed a normal-feeling smile to her face, and said, "Okay, look again."

Link turned toward her, his eyes coming open. He grinned when he saw her face, and he started to chuckle.

"I have a different look on my face, don't I?" she asked.

"Yeah." He wrapped her up in a bear hug. "Yeah, you sure do."

"Okay, now I'm going to look in the closet again," she said. "And I'm not going to let it freak me out."

"You don't have to do that."

"I think I do." She turned to look at the closed door.

"Growing up, me and Danny never had anything in a cabinet or cupboard. Not a box of granola bars or an extra can of pork and beans, and certainly not any household supplies." She took a deep breath and swallowed. "Okay, I'm ready this time. I think I was just so surprised that I let it get to me."

"Ready?" Link reached for the divot in the door to open it.

Misty nodded. "Ready."

He slid open the door, and the aisles of a grocery store looked back at her. Nothing had changed, but Misty simply reached out and picked up a women's razor. "It's smart to have extras of these around. I always run out at the worst time."

"Take it," Link said.

Misty looked up to him. "Are you serious? No, I don't need to take one of your momma's razors."

Link reached past her with his long arm and picked up a package. "Really? This pack of twelve—plus a bonus one—will get her by, I think."

Laughter started to bubble way down deep in her stomach, and she let it rise and soar through her until the giggles came out of her mouth. It was still a lot of supplies, and Misty had never seen anything like it.

"Link," Sammy said. "Misty, we've got dessert on the back deck."

"Okay, Momma," Link said over his shoulder. He put the razors back on their shelf and pulled the door closed. "All right, love?"

"Yeah," she said. "I just needed a second look to know that

it's just normal. I mean, for you guys, it's normal." She slipped her hand into his. "Now, what's for dessert?"

* * *

A few days later, Misty went out into the kitchen to find Janie sitting at the dining room table, smiling at her phone. "Texting Brandon?" She moved over to the coffee pot to pour herself a cup. She'd talked to Janie about her date with Brandon, and her best friend swore up and down she'd told Misty.

Misty had been pretty preoccupied with Link and all they had going on, and she'd decided it was possible Janie had said something and she'd forgotten. They'd gone back to normal, but as Misty stirred sugar into her coffee while Janie giggled at her phone, she wondered how much longer they'd live in this reality.

"Look at his cat," she said, twirling her phone toward Misty. She hadn't gotten dressed yet, so she sat in her pajama shorts and top, her smile so genuine.

Misty sat down opposite her and picked up her phone. "Oh, it's an orange tabby."

"He says he's a real diva. Was supposed to be a barn cat, but he won't even walk on grass."

Misty grinned at her friend and pushed the phone back toward her. "He's cute." She took a sip of her coffee. "Brandon is too. You and him...is it turning into anything?"

Janie shrugged one shoulder, her eyes on her phone. "I don't really know. He's...I actually think he's not real serious about stuff like this. Too bad you didn't meet him last summer." Janie's voice held a note of sadness, though, so Misty didn't laugh or agree.

"If he's not the one," she said instead. "Maybe...."

Janie looked up. "I just don't know if I'll ever meet someone like Link."

"Oh, sure you will." Misty waved her comment away. "This town is full of cowboys like Link."

Janie shook her head, her dark eyes serious. "No, Misty. He's special."

Misty didn't want to argue with her, because Link had crossed the threshold to special a long time ago. "I don't know if he's special, or if he's just—I don't know. Something."

"He's just right for you," Janie said with a sigh. "I don't know if Brandon is just right for me. There were definitely sparks in the beginning, but it feels a little like they've fizzled out."

"So are you going to go see his cat?"

Janie shook her head. "He's never invited me up to his ranch."

"It's probably for the best," Misty said. "It's even further than Shiloh Ridge."

"Yeah, but for the right cowboy...is any distance too far?" Janie sighed again as she got to her feet. "I'm going to get dressed."

Misty watched her head for the hallway. "I'll put together our parfaits."

"Thanks."

Misty took another slow sip of her coffee before she got up to put blueberries and strawberries in vanilla Greek yogurt. Labor Day had come and gone, but the Texas sun was just as relentless up in the Panhandle as it was in the Dallas-Fort Worth area.

Link had moved into harvest season, which she remembered from last year. He worked from sun-up to sun-down, and sometimes overnight too. Other cowboys on the ranch were prepping for Market Day. According to him, everyone participated in the round-up, which included him.

They'd go up into the hills and drive their cattle back to the ranch. Winter crops would get planted. Another short birthing season, for calves they'd sell in the spring, which apparently yielded higher profits.

All of that would be done in the next couple of months, and Link had said by the time they made it to the last weekend of October, everyone in the family—and on the ranch—was ready for their family celebration.

Misty had moved onto the huge painting that sat behind the City Council whenever they sat in session, and the intricacy of working with old golden picture frames and paint covered in a hundred years of grime left her bleary-eyed and tired in the evenings.

She'd still seen Link almost every day, but she anticipated seeing him less this month and maybe next. For some reason, she felt a little more hollow and a little more lonely, and she'd spent all evening with him just last night.

She got up and made two yogurt parfaits before Janie came

back into the kitchen, and as they headed out to her car to get to work, Misty said, "I'm thinking of going to Danny's parole hearing." She looked over to Janie, whose eyes had gone wide. "What do you think?"

"I think—when is it?"

"Next month," she said thoughtfully. "He just emailed me about it, and he thinks he might be able to get out this time."

"Does he want you to speak to the parole board?"

"He didn't ask me to, no," Misty said. She had in the past, and it had taken a lot from her. Plus, Danny hadn't been granted parole in any of his three previous hearings, and she didn't expect him to get it this time either.

But maybe.... "I'm just thinking about it," she said. "I don't have to decide right now." She opened the passenger door and got in the car.

Janie reached over her shoulder and pulled on her seatbelt. "What will you do if he gets out?"

Misty raked her hand through her hair, considering the question. "I don't know," she finally said.

"He might want to move up here with you."

"I've never said I'm moving here."

"Not out loud," Janie said, and then she let the subject drop. Misty appreciated that, and she had plenty of time to think through what her best friend had said as they drove to work and started on their individual projects.

Did she want to return to Southern Texas to see her brother and attend his parole hearing? He hadn't asked, and Misty would have to decipher what he wanted without Danny coming right out and saying it.

What would she do if he got released? She felt a sense of responsibility for him, and she currently lived a long way from the Coastal Bend and Dallas.

And the real question that needed answering: Was Misty going to make her move to Three Rivers permanent?

Chapter Twenty-Six

U nder the cover of darkness, Link entered his house, shed his boots, and started unbuttoning his shirt. Every article of clothing came off as he moved from the front door to his master bathroom, where he turned on the shower as hot as it would go.

It took up to a minute for the hot water to come in if he didn't do so, and he was in no mood to wait. In fact, he grabbed his toothbrush and turned back to the shower without giving it another second to warm up.

The night still held heat, though Link had been mowing in an air-conditioned cab. He remembered his father taking the overnight harvest shifts growing up, and now, as the junior foreman, he'd taken them over.

He'd only been working from six p.m. until the job was done for the past week, and as he stepped into the stream of water, he wondered if he'd ever get the itch of mown hay shards off his skin. Or the scent of alfalfa and dirt out of his nose, and the taste of it out of everything he ate.

Such was the harvest on a ranch the size of Shiloh Ridge, and Link would be glad when it concluded. Of course, as soon as this monumental task completed, another began—replanting of fields with winter wheat, a short breeding season, and then the round-up.

Link longed for a crisp morning in the saddle, and he tipped his head back into the water now that it was hot and let the night's work melt off him. He adjusted the water so it wouldn't scald him, and he showered in a slow, calculated way that only prolonged the time until he'd crawl into bed.

Misty had been bringing him an early dinner when she could, but she'd been caught up with some drama at work that had prevented her from leaving early, getting food, and making the drive out to him before he had to meet Uncle Ward and Uncle Preacher at the mechanical shed for a report on the daily work that had been done.

He met his father at breakfast to give the update on the work he did at night, and since Daddy never let anyone work solo on the ranch, Link had been laboring alongside three other cowboys.

After he'd showered and pulled on a pair of pajama pants, he sank onto his comforter and closed his eyes. Just for a minute.

He woke to his alarm and the first rays of sunlight coming through a gap in his black-out curtains. Link groaned as he got to his feet. He fumbled to find a shirt, and he slid on a pair of sneakers to go meet his father.

"There you are," Momma said when Link walked into the house. "Bear, he's here!"

"I'm not late." Link took in the breakfast dishes on the bar. "Smiles is gone already?"

"He had an early-morning conditioning session," Momma said. "The girls are getting ready, and Rock's out doing morning chores in the family stable." She set a steaming plate of scrambled eggs with shredded cheddar cheese melting into them on the bar, and Link didn't hesitate to sit down and take the fork she offered.

She grinned at him. "Thank you for doing the overnight mowing, baby."

Link had already filled his mouth with food, so he simply nodded and waved his fork like it wasn't a big deal. It wasn't, not really. It was a few weeks of a different schedule, and Link could catch up on sleep come October.

"How's Misty?" Momma asked as Link swallowed, her timing impeccable.

"Busy," he said. "We don't see each other as much as we did in the summer."

"But it's still going well?"

"I think so," Link said.

"Hey, good morning," Daddy said.

"I've got eggs," Momma said. She brought over another plate while Daddy clapped his hand on Link's shoulder.

"How'd it go last night?"

"Finished the western fields," Link said. "I'd say we're eighty percent done with mowing."

"A few more days," Daddy said. "We're baling down on the Kinder side."

"Mm."

Momma put breakfast in front of Daddy, along with a plate of sausage links. Link immediately reached for one of those, glad he had such a good mother to feed him. Of course, his thoughts went to Misty, and he glanced over to his father, then looked at Momma.

"Misty doesn't have much family," he said carefully, keeping his eyes on his mother. "I imagine if we get married— and I'm not saying we are—it'll happen here. I just—how long will that take to plan?"

Momma exchanged a glance with Daddy, and Link dipped his head so he wouldn't have to see them. "Depends," Momma said. "On what you want. Catering, her dress, the flowers, that kind of thing."

Link hummed again and got up. "Can I make toast?"

"Sure." Momma twisted and then turned to watch him go by her and into the kitchen. "You could just ask Misty what she wants. Catering and flowers are pretty easy. You have a venue, and I know she loves Willa, so as long as she's available—and why wouldn't she be?—it'll probably come down to when she wants to get married, and how long it'll take her to get a dress."

Link set four pieces of bread in the toaster and pushed down the levers. "Does it matter when you get married? Like, what's the benefit of—I don't even know."

"It doesn't matter," Daddy said.

Momma scoffed. "It matters to women," she said. "She

might want to get married in a field of bluebonnets, for example, and they only bloom for a few weeks here in the Panhandle."

Link turned back to his parents. "So I'll ask her." He didn't think Misty would have a month she wanted to get married. Or a vision for what that looked like. She'd told him she'd never dated seriously before, because she did not want to get married. Ever.

Still, he should probably ask her, so he could make sure she got everything she didn't even know she wanted.

Thankfully, Daddy moved the conversation to something else before Link's toast popped up, and then Rock came in, grumbling about his horse needing new shoes, and the girls came downstairs, giggling and gabbing about something.

Link finished his breakfast without having to talk much, and then he retreated back to the Top Cottage to sleep. He dreamt of his wedding, and yes, there were plenty of spring flowers in bloom. He'd never given much thought to the ceremony or what it would entail, but he did stand in True Blue, with his family surrounding him as a woman in a pretty, lacy dress, the veil concealing her face, walked toward him.

He thought he caught a hint of reddish-blonde hair, but then the dream morphed into something else—the unending fields of alfalfa in the headlights of the tractor where he towed the bar mower.

Link's first clue that someone had arrived at his house was the way Honor lifted her head from his thigh. She looked toward the door, and right as someone knocked, she alerted him by putting her paw up on his stomach.

"Yeah, I can hear," Link told her with a smile. "Come on. Let's see who it is." Before he could get up from where he'd sprawled on the couch, the door creaked open.

Misty said, "It's just me, baby. Can I come in?"

Link hurried to stand now, and he faced her with the couch between them, wearing only a pair of basketball shorts and nothing else. "Hey." Surprise ran up his spine and down his arms. "I didn't know you were coming."

She stared at him, a couple of brown cardboard containers of food in her hands. "Uh." Her eyes skittered all over his chest, from left to right and down. She yanked them back up, and heat filled Link's whole body.

"Uh, let me find a shirt," he said. He took a step and tripped over Honor, stumbling forward as he grunted and griped at the dog. He'd thrown a shirt over the recliner at some point, and he snatched it up and pulled it over his head. "What did you bring for dinner?"

Misty startled as if she'd just been unfrozen in a game of freeze-tag, and she walked into his kitchen as he did the same. "It's nothing special. Just those waffles we tried a couple of weeks ago."

"I love those," he said. "Did you get me the—ah, yes. The Nuts About Berries." He grinned at the big, puffy waffle with Nutella spread, raspberries, and strawberries, all topped with whipped cream. "Thanks, love." He leaned down and kissed the side of her neck. "Work going okay?"

"Yeah," she said in a higher-pitched voice. She snuggled into his side, but Link definitely felt like something wasn't quite right.

"Did you text me?" he asked. "I couldn't sleep, so I came out here and laid down. Dozed a little more."

"I didn't text," she said. "I figured if I got here by five, you'd be here."

"Mm." He got out forks and handed her one. She opened her container, and he wasn't surprised to find a waffle with lemon curd covering it, then whipped cream with a few delicately placed raspberries in it.

"Can we share?" she asked.

"Of course we can," he said, taking his waffle over to the table. "Want some juice? I have milk too, or that peach lemonade you like. Sweet tea from Aunt Holly." He moved over to the fridge and opened it. Misty didn't respond, and Link reconsidered why she'd fallen into a trance earlier.

He'd thought it was because he hadn't been wearing a shirt, but now, he wasn't so sure. He got out the orange juice—medium pulp—because he knew Misty liked it, and he pulled down two glasses from the cupboard.

After he poured her a glass of orange juice, he plunked the heavy-bottomed glass in front of her. She blinked rapidly, and he asked, "What's going on?"

"I—well, I wanted to talk to you about something."

"You're as nervous as a long-tailed cat in a room full of

rocking chairs." He grinned at her. "As my grandmother would say." He cut a bite of his waffle and speared it on the end of his fork. "It's just me, Misty. Say what you want."

"I'm afraid you won't like it."

Link swallowed, then put the dessert waffle in his mouth. *Wait*, he told himself. He wasn't going to ask her if she was about to break-up with him. Surely she wouldn't bring waffles to end their relationship. He couldn't imagine her ending it at all. He'd gotten no hint or sign of that.

So he waited.

Misty hadn't taken a bite of her waffle by the time Link had eaten half of his, and he said, "Misty, baby. Just tell me."

"My brother is up for parole," she said. "First Monday in October. I want to go to the hearing."

Link looked at her. "Okay." He gave her a small smile. "That's what you're worried about?"

"I'm afraid," she said again, her voice much tinnier and higher than usual. "That if I leave...I don't know. I don't want to leave Three Rivers." She shook her head. "Or you." She stabbed off a bite of her waffle and stared at it. "It doesn't make sense. But I'm nervous."

"You're going to come back," he said. "You have a job here."

She looked at him with those gorgeous green eyes. "Link, we both know it's not the job I'm worried about."

"What are you worried about? That I'm going to find some other stunning blonde to fall in love with?"

She wiped at the tear as it started to creep out of her eye. "No, I'm worried that Danny will need me. That he won't want to come up here, or he won't be able to. That you won't like him. That everything is about to get so complicated, when it's been so easy."

Link listened to her, but he couldn't imagine anything she'd just said. Still, he didn't jump right in to refute her. After a few moments, he said, "Sweetheart, I will—" He cleared his throat. "I'm not going anywhere. If you have to take care of some things down near the coast, or in Dallas, or wherever, that's fine. I'd go with you, if you wanted."

He kept his head bent, studying the texture of the waffle in front of him. "I don't have to like your brother to love you. And being with you has been both complicated and easy, and I've loved every moment of it. So whatever is next for us is just that: the next thing we have to conquer."

Misty sniffled, and Link looked over to her. "When we do things together, we're stronger." He covered her hand with his. "You're not alone anymore, sweetheart. I'm right here, and I'm not going anywhere."

She nodded and wiped her face. "Okay, go back to eating your waffle. Give me a minute."

Link hid his smile as he did that, looking away so he could look again when she said he could. He'd give Misty whatever she wanted. A minute, an hour, a whole day. "I'll miss you while you're gone, but I don't want you thinkin' you're special or anything."

Misty's laughter filled his house, and Link had to have that every day for the rest of his life. He chuckled with her, glad she settled into eating beside him. He had more questions for her, but he figured now probably wasn't the best time to ask her about her ideal wedding.

"Remember when I left town for a little bit? And you missed me so much, because I am special, and I called you all the time, because you're special? Remember that?"

"Mm."

"And when I got back, you threw me this big party with all my favorite things."

"Those sour watermelon candies you like," he said.

"Yeah, those," she said, "And you had your aunt make cinnamon rolls, and remember how I was brave enough to dip them in the chili once I got back?"

"Yeah," he said. "And remember how much you loved it? Now you won't eat chili without a cinnamon roll." He caught her smile as she nodded, her wavy hair bobbing as she did.

"And coconut rice crispy squares."

"Brownies with a caramel swirl."

Misty leaned her head against his bicep, and Link loved the softness between them. He loved spending time with her, dreaming about a future thing that hadn't happened yet.

He simply loved her.

Chapter Twenty-Seven

Misty zipped her suitcase closed and took a deep breath. Today would be a very long travel day, but for maybe the first time ever, she felt strong enough to go. Strong enough to face her past without wallowing in it. Strong enough to embrace the future, no matter how uncertain it seemed.

Janie had to work today, and Link had already texted her his farewells before heading up into the hills to do the round-up. He'd be gone all week too, and Misty couldn't help feeling like her absence from Three Rivers was meant to be. She wouldn't be able to see or talk to Link anyway.

At the same time, she desperately wanted to be able to call him tonight when she arrived in Beaumont. She had a hotel there, and then she'd attend Danny's parole hearing in the morning. She wasn't sure if she should be praying for his release or not. If he had to stay in jail, Misty could simply repack her suitcase, change her flight, and be back in Three Rivers on Tuesday.

If he got out, though, Misty had planned to spend the whole week away, doing whatever she needed to do to get Danny settled. "As if that can happen in a week," she muttered to herself as she heaved her suitcase to the floor and extended the handle.

She drove herself to Amarillo. She boarded the plane. She put headphones in and distracted herself with games on her phone as the aircraft climbed to its cruising altitude. After landing in Houston, Misty collected her luggage and waited in line for her rental car.

She had a couple of hours of driving ahead of her, but Misty stopped to get something to eat first. Her stomach clenched around every bite of food, and she tapped out messages to Link she didn't send. He wouldn't get them anyway.

Looking around the fast-casual restaurant, Misty felt far from home. Such a thing made sense, of course, since she wasn't from Houston and hadn't spent a great deal of time here. She looked at other people like her—some younger, some older, some exactly her age—and she felt like a foreigner among her own people.

She wasn't even sure why. All she knew was she wanted to get back to Three Rivers. When she'd first rolled into town, she'd started planning when she'd leave. Small towns just weren't for her.

Perhaps she'd lived there too long now, or perhaps the wide highways and busy traffic had always bothered her, and she'd never admitted it to herself. Either way, Houston felt like one giant ball of noise and filth, and relief coursed through her when she put the city in her rearview mirror.

She took a few deep breaths. In, then out. In through her nose, where she held it, then slowly blew it out. "You don't have to see him today," she reminded herself. And it wasn't that she didn't want to see Danny. She did. She wanted to wrap him in her arms and promise him she'd get him out.

But she couldn't promise that. She'd failed him on so many levels, and she just wanted him to know she hadn't forgotten him. She'd tried her best. She still loved him.

The following morning, she arrived at the Beaumont facility where Danny had been incarcerated for the past four years. She stared at the bland building, having been here once before.

She kneaded the steering wheel, her courage failing her. Then, she simply went into some sort of robot mode. She opened the door, got out of the rental car, and headed for the building.

The parole room sat just past the check-in desk, and Misty waited her turn to be allowed in. She passed over ID, waited some more, and then got shown into the room with several others. She didn't recognize anyone, not even Danny's lawyer.

More waiting.

Misty's lungs felt like someone had doused them in gasoline and set them on fire. Finally, the door in the corner opened and her brother walked in. She sucked in a breath, the burning intensifying with the addition of oxygen.

So much in her life had been cleaned up and cleaned out.

But seeing her brother threw her right back to her life in that tiny apartment. The two of them alone, the cupboards bare, huddled together on a mattress on the ground, where they slept once the light faded.

She took a breath and steeled herself against the memories. Danny's eyes met hers, and she lifted a hand in a wave. Pure light entered his face, and Misty told herself over and over not to cry. She might get to hug him before they took him away again, and she nodded at him, hoping that would give him some strength.

He looked clean and well, which was more than she could say the night she'd gone to see him in jail after the bar fight. He seemed well-fed, healthy, and of good spirits as he sat at the table in front of her.

A man in a suit joined him, and they waited for the parole board to come in. Misty had not volunteered to speak for her brother, and she simply sat at rapt attention while they read the report from his behavior in the last year.

His lawyer spoke. Danny ran through his time here, what he'd been working on, how he'd improved. Then someone said, "Mister Granger, do you have anyone to speak for you?"

Danny turned to look at her, his eyes begging her to say something. Misty had no idea what she'd say. Last time, she'd had something prepared, and she'd been so disappointed he hadn't been released.

Her robot-body took over, and she stood. "I have something to say."

Every eye came to her, but she managed to move up to the

microphone. "I am Misty Granger," she said. "Danny's sister." She swallowed and thought of Link standing beside her. If any of the Glovers ever got in trouble, this room would not be able to hold them all.

"I have stayed in touch with my brother," she said. "Via email and phone calls. According to his report, he is excelling here. He has friends, performs his duties, and is fully reformed."

She took a breath. "He is the strongest person I know, because he has been dealt a horribly terrible hand of cards, and instead of giving up and walking away, he's done the best he could." Her emotions clogged and choked her, but she swallowed them back. Again, and then again.

"I raised him the best I could from the age of ten, and while I didn't do a perfect job, or even a good job, I tried. That's all any of us can do: Try. Humans have the extraordinary ability to change, and that's something I've only learned in the past few months, sir."

She gestured to her brother. "He is not perfect, but he is good. He got into a bad situation, but I'm older now, and so is he. Together, we're stronger. Together, we'll be brave enough to leave the past behind us and build a better, brighter future."

Misty's legs started to feel weak, and she added one last thing. "He has served two-thirds of his sentence, and I believe he is worthy to be released on parole." With that, she returned to her seat, a little too scared to look at her brother. Danny reached out and touched her hand, and she squeezed it as she went by.

The parole board read through another report, and then the

man sitting in the middle of the row said, "Thank you, Mister Granger. We have reviewed your case, your progress, and the statements provided. Does anyone here have further questions?"

Misty felt like a heavy drape had been thrown over the room. She could barely get a breath as the moment lengthened. No one said anything, and the parole board chairman said, "After careful consideration, we have decided to grant you parole, Mister Granger."

He continued to speak, but Misty's hearing seemed to disappear. Only white noise existed, and she only clued back in when Danny said, "Yes, I understand. Thank you for this opportunity."

"You have the power to change your future," the chairman said. "This hearing is adjourned. You must meet with your parole officer to sign the terms of your parole before you can be released. We wish you the best in your reintegration into society."

The hearing broke up then, and Misty stood on trembling legs while Danny turned toward her, his arms outstretched. "I love you," she whispered fiercely as he enveloped her in a hug.

"I love you too," Danny said in her ear. "You'll wait for me?"

"Right outside," she promised. He got led away with his lawyer and his parole officer, and Misty stood there and watched.

"Ma'am?" someone asked. "We need this room for the next hearing."

"Of course," she said, finally getting herself to move.

Outside in her car, she started typing out messages to Link, and this time she sent them, one after the other.

Her mind raced and ran ahead of her, and she just kept typing and typing until everything had been vomited out.

Only then did she slow down and go back to what she'd said. She'd told him about her travel. About her brother. About the hearing. How she'd be here for the full week now that she knew he'd need her to help him get settled.

Then she'd said, *I'm going to try to get him to come back to Three Rivers with me.*

He'll need a job, of course. And Link, I know this is really crazy, but I'm wondering if you have somewhere for him at Shiloh Ridge.

Or maybe you know of a ranch where he could work. He just needs a chance, and I have found so many second chances, love, and acceptance from your family, and from the town of Three Rivers.

You don't have to answer right now.

Just think about it, and I'll see you when I get back next week.

Misty wanted to write out three little words that would change everything, but she didn't dare. She'd already said too much as it was.

She waited for a long time before Danny came outside with a single Duffel bag slung over his shoulder. Misty popped the trunk and jumped from the car. She started to laugh, and Danny dropped his bag in the parking lot and ran toward her.

She hugged him, so desperate for his fresh start. "I have so much to tell you," she said.

"Yeah, you do," he agreed. "Because you didn't even tell me you were coming." He grinned at her, and she ran her palm down the side of his face.

"You're free," she said. "And we get to make our lives into anything we want, Danny. Anything at all."

"I'm going to need help for a bit," he said.

"Of course."

"Maybe I can crash in your place in Dallas." He released her and picked up his bag. He tossed it in the trunk and looked at her again. "I mean, you're not living there right now, right?"

She shook her head, but she couldn't get herself to move back to the driver's seat. "Danny," she said. "I don't think you should go back to Dallas."

He laughed. "Why not? Where else would I go?" He headed for the passenger door, and Misty's heartbeat pulsed through her whole body, but she followed him and got behind the wheel.

Dear Lord, she thought, something she didn't normally do. *I can't let him go back to Dallas. I need to get him up to Three Rivers. Please help me. Help me open my mouth and give me the words he needs to hear.*

Chapter Twenty-Eight

Henry Marshall finished shoeing the tall black beauty and bent to gather his tools. In moments like this, he wished his daddy could see him, see how hard he worked, and see that he was more than a twenty-five-year-old flirt.

He did like going out in the evenings, and no, he hadn't had a serious girlfriend for years. That didn't mean he was a bad person, or a player, or that he couldn't run his own farrier business. With the number of ranches and farms and horses surrounding Three Rivers—and the scarcity of farriers—Henry was actually very sure he could.

He was also very surprised he wanted to stick around Three Rivers, the small Texas Panhandle town where he'd grown up. But after a few years away, Henry had realized that having a family was better than not having one. When he wasn't in Three Rivers, he missed out on family events, seeing his cousins and aunt and uncle.

His farrier training was nearly over, and then he'd complete a twelve-month apprenticeship at a participating facility. "Gotta find one of those," he muttered to himself as he arranged his tools in his leather flap-bag and folded it all up.

Then he turned back to the horse named Blackeye who'd just gotten new shoes, and he took the equine out of the crossties that had held him in place and made him behave while Henry got his job done. His mind buzzed over his apprenticeship assignment.

His training took place in Amarillo, and he'd been living on-site since he'd started. They encouraged people to find their own apprenticeships and then get the paperwork signed. They'd had the greatest success that way, but it created a problem for Henry.

He didn't want to ask his daddy or his uncle if he could apprenticeship at Three Rivers Ranch. He didn't want to use their connections to find a farm or ranch in Three Rivers either.

No, Henry craved adventure, and he wanted to carve his own way in the world. He didn't want his father's friends reporting on him, talking about him to his daddy, any of it. That meant he'd been trying to find a ranch with enough horses to keep him busy for twelve months. It had to be a certain size to maintain that, and he'd have to talk to the owner or foreman, explain how the apprenticeship worked, beg for a place to stay, and get them to sign the paperwork.

He'd put his name on the placement list with his training program, but they didn't guarantee spots. If he didn't get one,

Henry would have to delay his graduation until he found a place and could complete the apprenticeship.

And that only got him to the exams he needed to take. Sometimes farriers stayed on in an apprenticeship for a few more years, and since Henry wanted to work with horses as a career, he imagined himself with specializations, advanced training, and continual professional development.

So maybe he'd do a longer apprenticeship, or several of them.

"And does someone with their head in the clouds do that?" he asked as he led Blackeye back to his stall. Then, he gathered his tools and went to find the man who'd sign his form and earn him his hours.

With that finished, Henry loaded his tools in the back of his truck and got behind the wheel. With the engine running and the AC blowing, he sat there, a sigh falling from his mouth. "You've got to move past the things your daddy has told you," he said. "He believes in you."

His momma and daddy were paying for his farrier school, after all. His father had said he'd be glad to have Henry at Courage Reins once he became certified.

His shoulders and back ached while he tried to get himself to get the truck in gear and leave the boarding facility that allowed the farrier students to come work on their horses. His stomach grumbled for food, and that got Henry to move.

He headed back toward the city, and he stopped by the fancy grocery store to go through their salad and hot bar. He could fill two containers with food—and Henry liked his cold food to stay separate from the hot—and head back to his dorm room.

Another wave of exhaustion pulled at his neck, and he rotated his right shoulder. His dominant side always worked too hard, and he paid the price of that every evening. He could have his roommate rub some icy hot on it when he returned that night.

"Can't believe you live with a roommate," he grumbled next. Something inside him fired salt through him today, and he wasn't even sure why. But he'd gone to a couple of years of college before he'd dropped out, wandered—lost and wondering why it was so easy for everyone around him to know what to do with their lives when he had no clue—worked, and finally found his calling as a farrier.

He went into the grocery store, the scent of herbs and lemon greeting him. He veered right and picked up one of the large containers to fill with salads and fruits and other chilled items. He smiled to himself as he thought about taking a picture and sending it to his mother.

See? I eat veggies, he'd tell her, and she'd send back several emojis cheering him on. Clapping hands. A New Year's Eve popper. A birthday toy horn that looked like it was blowing. He could see them all now.

"What are you smiling at?" someone asked, and Henry looked up.

A stunning blonde stood on the opposite side of the bar, a small container in her hand. "You know you're looking at broccoli, right? Nothing to smile about there, cowboy."

"Angel White," Henry said, the name sort of biting out of his mouth. "What are you doin' here? Doesn't your family grow all their own produce?" He took a peek at her container, which definitely had lettuce, grape tomatoes, and green peas in it.

"My mother isn't feeling well," Angel said with a hint of falseness in her voice. "So I'm getting her some of her favorite things."

"Fair enough," he said, a twinge of guilt pulling through him for giving her attitude. "Being sick in the summer is the worst."

"It's October," she reminded him.

"It's still hot."

"Cooling off now, though."

Henry hummed, because he didn't want to argue about the weather. "How's your daddy?"

"Good," she said, and her gaze came back to his. Looking through the sneezeguard, his eyes hooked onto hers too. She looked like she had something to say, and a pretty pink flush stained her cheeks.

"What?" Henry asked.

"You're a farrier, right?" she asked.

"Kind of." He moved down the bar and put on a couple of healthy spoonfuls of croutons. He loved them drenched in ranch dressing, and his mouth watered, telling him to wrap up this conversation so he could eat.

"How are you *kind of* something?" Angel stepped down her side of the buffet too.

"Because I haven't graduated," he said. "I don't have my certification yet."

"But you know farriers."

"Yes," he said slowly, watching her take his favorite thing on this buffet—the mayo-based potato salad. He took that, the sweet pea salad, and the frog eye salad. He didn't mind if they got a little ranchy with his lettuce and veggies, and the cold food stayed with the cold food in the same container.

"Any who do have their certification?" she asked.

"Why don't you just come out and say what you want from me?" he said. "It'll be faster."

She gave him a blue-eyed glare that sent bolts of lightning through his bloodstream. He had to learn how to breathe all over again every time he looked at Angel White, and he wasn't even sure why. They'd met once or twice over the past year while he'd been in his farrier training, as her father taught one of their courses.

She handled horses expertly, and Henry told himself that was why he liked her. He could tell himself a lot of things if it kept him out of trouble, and he needed to stay on the right track here.

He'd had schoolboy crushes on plenty of women. One date usually fixed that, but he hadn't asked Angel to dinner yet. Part of him was worried that the way he had to reinvent himself every time she looked at him would go away if they went out. So if they didn't....

"We're down a farrier," she said. "We need someone—quick."

"Your father is the most connected man in the Texas

Panhandle when it comes to horses, husbandry, and farriers." Henry watched her. "He's having trouble getting someone?"

Angel blew out her breath with a noise of frustration. "He doesn't think we need someone, but he can't keep up. I've seen him after he works all day in the shop, and he simply can't keep on the way he is."

Henry ladled ranch dressing over his lettuce and veggies. "Call the school. I'm sure James would announce it in class."

"Daddy won't take a student."

"We'll have new apprentices ready in January," Henry said. "If you can hang on for a couple more months." He closed the top flap on his cold container and moved the ten feet to the end of the hot one. He picked up another container and glanced over his shoulder to Angel.

She wore a pair of long jeans in the lightest color denim came in and could still be called blue. A white—snowy white— pair of sneakers sat on her feet, and she wore a purple blouse that made her eyes seem violet when she looked at him too.

Henry ducked his head and started down the hot bar. The grocery store homemade everything here in-house, and he loved their beef short ribs, the brisket, and the barbecue chicken tenders. He'd only gotten one protein before the soft, feminine scent of Angel met his nose.

She moved to his side, her small container closed over the things she'd gotten for her mother. "Listen, could you talk to James for me?"

"Sure," Henry said. "Apprentices in January will satisfy your daddy?"

"Should," she said. "And if James needs to place people, Daddy won't turn them away."

"And he won't have to pay them," Henry said.

"He pays his apprentices," Angel said. "It's not a huge amount, because they live for free. But they have to eat, don't they?"

"Yeah, farriers have to eat," Henry agreed.

"Are you taking dinner to your dorm?" she asked.

He paused in adding the baked beans to his container. "No, but thanks for suggesting I'm a hog." He cut her a grin and moved down to the scalloped potatoes. Since he'd never met a potato he didn't like, he took some of those. Only a single spoonful though, because he'd yet to get to the brisket and sticky chicken fingers.

"I wasn't suggesting anything of the sort," Angel said.

Henry chuckled and nodded good-naturedly. "Should I have James contact you or your daddy for the apprenticeship placements?"

"Daddy," she said. "And it would be best if he made it sound like he didn't have anywhere else to send them. Then Daddy won't be able to say no."

"I'll talk to him," Henry promised. "But Angel, I won't lie to him about it."

"Of course not," she said.

He took enough brisket to feed the men living on the third floor with him, but Angel didn't comment on it. "Got myself in a spot of trouble when not telling the truth," he said. "Now, I don't do that anymore. Makes life easier."

"I agree," she murmured.

"Angel," another man said, and she spun away from Henry. Another cowboy stood there—not her brother or her father—and she squealed in a way that would've made Henry's heart rejoice had she been prancing over to him and throwing her arms around his neck while he chuckled.

As it was, sharp jealousy tore through him as he studiously moved down the buffet to the poultry. He took his barbecue chicken tenders and added a slice of smoked turkey for good measure. He couldn't cook in his dorm, but he and his roommate did have a half-sized fridge and a microwave.

So he'd eat well in the morning too and not have to think about food again until lunchtime tomorrow. As Angel and her boyfriend walked away hand-in-hand, Henry sure wished he could stop thinking about her by lunchtime tomorrow.

"Or right now," he said darkly, not even the delicious food in front of him enough to distract him from watching the woman who sparked something deep inside him disappear around the corner with another man.

Chapter Twenty-Nine

D awson entered the diner, his thoughts only on pancakes and bacon. He should be sitting in a pew with his brothers and parents, but the call of something good to eat had gotten the better of him.

Unfortunately, a lot of other people had the same idea he had, and the diner didn't have a spare table or seat anywhere.

"Just you, Dawson?" Sandy asked.

"Yes, ma'am," he said.

"Might be a bit," she said. "We've got some bigger parties and couples." She looked at her list and wrote his name down. Then she grabbed a couple of menus and called someone's name.

Dawson did everything as a single, and he'd never been overlooked because he wasn't part of a party or a couple. But looking around, he definitely felt out of place and like he wouldn't get a table until Sandy had served everyone else.

His first thought was to go somewhere else, but he edged against the wall and waited. He busied himself with his phone, only looking up when names got called. Two tables, then three, and then Sandy called, "Caroline."

Dawson found the blonde easily enough as she stepped around another cowboy. He wasn't sure if his increased pulse was because of her beauty or because he'd never filed any paperwork, and the moment she saw him, she'd start lecturing. He certainly didn't need a public dressing-down in the local diner, in front of people he knew.

Caroline stepped over to Sandy and said, "My friend had to leave. It's just me."

Sandy frowned. "Just you?" It was clear she didn't want to serve singles today, though Dawson had never had any trouble before. "It's a table for two." She glanced at all the others waiting, clearly torn about what to do.

Before he could stop himself, he pushed away from the wall and took the few steps to Caroline's side. "There you are," he said above the din in the diner. "Sorry I didn't see you before."

Caroline looked at him like he'd spoken Japanese, and even Sandy's mouth had dropped open a little.

"You can cross me off, Sandy," he said. "I'm with her, and we'll take that table you've got for two."

Sandy recovered first, and she snapped her mouth shut and waved the two menus in her hand. "All right. This way."

Dawson waited for Caroline to go ahead of him, but she simply stood there staring at him. "Do you want to eat breakfast, or not?" he murmured. "Come on." He moved in front of her and reached back to take her hand.

Her skin against his sent a pulse of warmth through his body, which he tried to ignore. This was insane. The woman didn't even like him. His pancakes would probably taste like poison with her sitting across the table from him, glaring and throwing thinly veiled insults at him.

Sandy led them to a table against the wall, and Dawson sat down. "Thanks," he said as he picked up a menu. Caroline sat too, and Sandy had already left.

"She wouldn't have seated you without me," Dawson said. He studied the menu he had memorized like his life depended on having his eyes on the breakfast choices printed before him. "We don't have to talk. I'm just hungry."

Caroline made a noise of disbelief. "We don't have to talk?"

He glanced at her. "No."

"Well." She huffed, but Dawson went back to his menu. She wore a burgundy cardigan though it wasn't anywhere near cold enough to wear such a thing this Sunday morning. He'd only met her once, but Dawson found himself wondering if she had a thing for sweaters.

Why do you care? he asked himself.

He didn't, and he looked up as a waitress arrived. "Ah, howdy, Marianne."

A smile split her face. "Dawson Rhinehart." She laughed like they were best friends for life. "Haven't seen you in a while."

He glanced over to Caroline and then looked at Marianne again. "Been busy with harvest and Market Day and all that," he said. Then he allowed himself to smile at the woman who was probably only five or six years older than him. "I mean, I'm playing hooky from church just for some pancakes."

She laughed, and Dawson joined his chuckles to the sound of it. "You and a whole lot of other people," she said. "You want water and orange juice now, with milk when the food comes?"

"You haven't lost your memory," he said.

"I should hope not," Marianne joked. "I'm only thirty-six." She grinned over to Caroline. "What about you, honey? Something to drink before I take your orders?"

"Diet Coke, please," she said through tight lips and partially gritted teeth.

Dawson's heartbeat skipped over itself, and not in a good way. More of a *what-have-I-done?* way. *Dear Lord,* he thought as Caroline then asked a question about the hashbrowns here. *Don't let this be too big of a mistake. I just wanted pancakes.*

Marianne left to get their drinks, and Dawson looked over to Caroline. "You've never been here?"

"I've only been in Three Rivers for a few months," she said. "I got assigned up here out of the Amarillo office, and the burrowing owl issue is recent. There are three of us here to deal with it."

Dawson nodded, hating that they'd gotten to the owls already. His unfiled paperwork was surely only one breath behind. "The hashbrowns are good."

Caroline actually looked like he'd attacked her favorite band or insulted her sweater. "They're home fries," she said. "I want shredded, crispy hashbrowns. With cheese."

He found himself smiling at her, albeit briefly. "My mom makes them like that," he said. "They're really good."

"With the cheese too?"

"Sometimes," he said coolly, not liking her challenging tone. "Are you a cheese aficionado, then?"

"A what?"

Dawson's smile had slipped, disappeared, and hidden. Burrowed down into his body the way he imagined those silly owls did into the ground. He didn't want to talk this morning. He just wanted pancakes and some of the candied bacon with chili flakes.

Then, he'd head back to the church to pick up his brother, and they'd go on home to the ranch, where the work didn't stop just because it was the Sabbath. He pulled up the latest news articles on his phone, and Caroline got the hint that he did not want to socialize. She remained quiet and absorbed in her device too, which suited Dawson just fine.

He hadn't dated in a while, and he wasn't going to start with someone who made assumptions and chewed him out for no reason. They put in their orders, and since the diner had fast cooks, especially when busy, their food came quickly.

He'd just buttered his buttermilk pancakes and poured syrup over them and his chocolate chip stack when Caroline asked, "Are you ever going to file your paperwork to protect the endangered habitat on your ranch?"

Looking up from his food, he glared at her. "We don't have burrowing owls on our property."

"It's not about the animals," she said. "Yet."

"We cleared the dens before it was legally required to keep them," he informed her coolly. "Did you not get my email?"

"Did you get mine?" she shot back. "It clearly stated I needed the paperwork anyway."

He'd gotten it, but he pressed his teeth together instead of admitting so. "We've been busy." He indicated the diner beyond them. "You heard me tell Marianne about the harvest and the roundup."

"Yes," she said with a bite of attitude he did not appreciate.

"I just want to enjoy my breakfast," he said.

"That's all I wanted too," she said.

He studied her, trying to find a way past her displeasure. "She wouldn't have seated you without me. I did us both a favor."

"If you say so." She looked down at her breakfast—she'd gotten the All American, which was two eggs, two sausage links, two bacon strips, two buttermilk pancakes, and hashbrowns. "These aren't the potatoes I want."

Oops, home fries.

Dawson ducked his head before she could see his smile, and he tucked into his pancakes before the syrup could make them too soggy. As he swallowed, down went the insane words scratching through his head.

Do you have a boyfriend?

No? Perfect.

Would you maybe want to go out with me sometime?

I'll file the paperwork.

No, he definitely couldn't say any of those things, and he thanked God that he'd managed to keep them dormant, so he wouldn't make a fool of himself when she laughed and rejected him outright.

Chapter Thirty

L ink checked his phone again, but Misty hadn't responded. He'd been back on the ranch, back in service, for a few hours now. Once the cattle had been put to pasture, he'd helped put away the horses, and he'd come home to shower off the week's worth of work, dust, grime, and sweat.

Their family feast to celebrate the conclusion of the round-up would be at the firepit in another half-hour, and Link's stomach told him he would not miss it. But he missed Misty something fierce, and he needed to hear from her.

She'd sent a lot of texts, which he'd gotten in a flurry of notification noises and in a seemingly random order. He'd managed to piece together the events of this week as he made assumptions about which texts had come when.

He'd answered her and said, *I'm back, and I can't wait to hear your voice. Call me when you can.*

She hadn't called. Or even texted again.

Link didn't know how to breathe without her. Every moment where he hadn't heard from her made him into someone else. A different version of himself that would do anything to hear her voice and make her happy. A new cowboy in this moment, and then the next, who would know exactly how to tell her he loved her, and of course there was a place for her brother at Shiloh Ridge.

He hadn't spoken to his father, Uncle Ward, or Uncle Preacher about it, but Link still knew it to be true. Danny had been in jail for his role in a bar fight—armed assault—but Link believed in repentance. He believed in second chances—and he knew his family did too.

The problem was, Misty had messaged among all her other texts that Danny didn't want to leave Dallas.

So they'd gone to Dallas. To her apartment there. Link didn't want to think of her there alone, readjusting to the life she'd had there once...without him.

He once again became a different man, because that was what love did to a cowboy. Once he knew who he wanted to spend his life with, that love drove him to do better, be better, make quicker decisions, speak up, love her with all he had.

Link paced in his kitchen, his hand curled around his phone. Love for Misty made him feel bolder, braver, and better. He raised his phone and tapped to dial her. It was evening, and surely she wasn't working in Dallas tonight.

Her line rang once, twice, three times, and then she said, "Link, hi."

Relief rang through him. "Misty," he said. "Hey, baby, how are you?"

"Good," she said softly, and he imagined her to be hiding in a closet or around a corner. "Listen, it's not a great time to talk."

"Are you safe?"

"What? Yes, of course."

"I miss you," he said. "I expected you back here by tonight." He spoke gently, hoping she wouldn't think he was accusing her.

"Danny doesn't want to come," she said. "I changed my flight to Sunday, in the hopes I can convince him."

Link didn't want to tell her to leave him behind. He didn't understand all of the family dynamics with Misty and her brother, but he knew Misty felt a great obligation to Danny. She still carried guilt for what his life had become, and Link couldn't imagine what it would take for her to move past that.

He only knew he didn't want her doing it alone.

"I'll be there in the morning," he said. When Misty said nothing, he continued with, "Give me your address, sweetheart, and I'll bring breakfast for you and your brother."

"Lincoln," she said, using his full name.

"I—" He cut himself off before he could tell her he loved her over the phone. "Don't tell me no," he whispered. "Just give me your address and tell me if Danny likes quiche as much as you do."

He ignored the nervous tremble in his stomach that told him he'd never been on an airplane before. He'd never booked a flight. He had no idea if he could actually get from Amarillo to Dallas in the next fourteen hours or not.

"Danny's a garbage disposal," Misty whispered. "He'll eat anything."

"Great," Link said, keeping his voice low too. "I'll see you both tomorrow."

"You don't need to do this."

"Yes," he said. "I do. And you wanted me to meet Danny, right?"

"Right," she said.

"Well, then, I'll see you both tomorrow."

"Thank you, Link," Misty whispered, and he did his best not to coo good-bye to her. Then he turned in a full circle, trying to get his mind wrapped around what he'd just said he'd do.

Then he grabbed his jacket—the evenings could get a little chilly if there was a breeze at all. He'd made it out the door before he realized he needed to take some clothes with him. So he backtracked to his bedroom and tossed a few things into a backpack—another pair of jeans, two T-shirts, extra socks and underwear, a stick of deodorant, and his toothbrush—before leaving again.

Down at the firepit, he expected to find Uncle Ward there, getting the fire ready for roasting marshmallows and Starburst later. Link wasn't expecting to be the first man there, but he also hadn't anticipated being the last.

He probably wasn't, but it felt like it as he pulled up and jogged down the gravel path. He found his aunts setting up food, and his uncles putting out more chairs. They'd invited everyone on the ranch to tonight's dinner, because so many of them had been working for five straight days.

"Uncle Preacher," he said, breathless as he reached his uncle. Uncle Ward stood dozens of yards away, but Link would have to check with him too. He didn't have *time* to deal with any of this, as a sense of urgency to get a ticket and get to the airport came over him.

"Hey, Link." Preacher grinned for a moment, then quickly took in the look on Link's face. Whatever he was showing caused his uncle to sober instantly. "What's wrong?"

"I—I need the weekend off."

To Preacher's credit, he didn't refuse, and he didn't even question. "Okay," he said. "We're already operating on a vacation schedule after the round-up. You go do what you need to do."

"What do you need to do?"

Link nearly sagged to his knees in relief at the sound of his father's voice. He turned toward his father and said, "Daddy, I need your help." He took a breath and swallowed his nerves. He thought of Misty, and he became that new man—exactly the person she needed him to be. "I need to get to Dallas by morning, and I have no idea how to buy an airplane ticket."

Daddy blinked and asked, "What now?"

Link expected him to have all the answers, and he simply stared at him.

"The boy needs to get to Dallas," Preacher said. He turned and looked around. "Ah, there's Charlie." He waved his hand above his head. "Charlie!"

She came toward them, and she handed the casserole dish she carried to Hank, her and Preacher's twelve-year-old son. "Take that over to Aunt Holly, baby." She arrived, looked at everyone, and tucked her hands in her back pockets. "Why was I summoned?"

Preacher gestured to Link, and he should've known better than to expect his uncle would say what he needed. He cleared his throat and said, "I need to get to Dallas by morning. Can you help me book an airplane ticket?"

Charlie didn't waste a moment before she pulled out her phone. "Sure, we can do it from your device."

"We can?" Link asked.

His aunt only moved her eyes to look at him. "Yes," she said slowly. "Now, get your phone out and download this app."

Link scrambled to do what she said, and ten minutes later, he'd kissed his momma and all of his siblings, had his backpack riding shotgun, and was headed for the Amarillo airport.

* * *

Link woke in a strange bed, which wasn't all that unusual as of late. It only took him a moment to remember he'd flown to Dallas last night. He'd booked a hotel while waiting to board his flight, and now he had to figure out how to get breakfast and get to Misty's.

He got up and stretched his shoulders as he walked over to the window. Looking out, Link got assaulted by the vastness and busyness of the city. It didn't sit right in his gut, and it made his soul wince, but as he turned away, he steeled himself. This version of himself could do city life—because Misty needed him to.

Aunt Charlie had sent him a rideshare app and an app where he could order food and either pick it up or have it delivered. He'd found a great place to get breakfast, and he ordered the food, then called for a ride and left his hotel room. The driver waited while he ran into a fast-casual restaurant for his order, and then they started their journey toward Misty's apartment.

Link sat in the backseat, feeling a little foolish being driven around like he was someone important. At least no one had commented on his cowboy hat, and he reminded himself he was still in Texas. It only *felt* like a foreign land.

He texted Misty and then silenced and shoved his phone under his leg.

Remember when I met your brother? And it was so amazing, because we got along so well from the very first moment. And remember how he agreed to come work with me at Shiloh Ridge? That was so great, and we had the best weekend ever in Dallas.

Now he just needed the text to come true.

The driver pulled up to a nice apartment complex, away from the tumultuous freeway noise. Emerald green grass surrounded the building, which had stone and stucco on it. Link wasn't sure what he'd been expecting, but not something that looked...cute. Livable. Like Misty belonged here.

He shoved aside the second thoughts, the insecurities, and said, "Thanks, brother," before he collected his paper bag filled with breakfast and headed for the second floor. He wondered what he looked like as he strode across the sidewalk and took the stairs up to the next level.

He went to the appointed number and knocked, his heart pounding as loudly as his fist had on the wood.

"Coming!" sounded from inside, and Link dang near bolted. *Misty is here*, he told himself. *Misty is here. Misty is here. Lord, I'm here, and Misty is here, and please make this okay. Is this okay?*

He'd been so desperate to get to Misty, he hadn't stopped to consider if it was the right thing to do.

The humidity here seemed more oppressive than in the Panhandle, but as Link breathed in and waited, he settled. This was right. This was the man he needed to be right now, and he ducked his head and considered knocking again.

Then the door opened, and he looked up—right into the eyes that followed him into his dreams. The eyes he never wanted to see disappointment in. The eyes he could communicate with without saying a word.

"Hey," he said softly.

Misty came out onto the walkway, immediately lifting her arms up to encircle his neck. He dropped their breakfast and took her into his arms and let her shiver in his arms for several seconds. She wasn't crying; the lack of sniffling told him that. But she definitely needed him.

And he was here.

She stepped back. "I got your text."

"It is so good to see you," he said. She wore her hair up in a ponytail, but it still shimmered with a hint of red gold.

"Mm, you too." She touched her lips to his, and Link wondered if he could tell her he loved her standing outside an apartment he never wanted her to return to, in Dallas, which was seemingly so far from Three Rivers.

From home.

"You ready for this?" she whispered against his lips.

"Misty, I'm in love with you." He kept his eyes closed, so he could breathe in the scent of her without any other distractions. He could feel her in his arms, the perfect shape of her that filled the empty places inside him with exactness. The earth swayed with them once again, and he kept his eyes closed as she traced her hand down the side of his face.

"I love you too, Link," she whispered.

He dared to open his eyes then, because no better words had ever been spoken. He gazed at her, looking and looking and looking, learning how to breathe as a man who was loved, and reforming himself into the Lincoln Glover she needed by the moment.

Love really was such a powerful thing. The greatest impetus of change Link knew of.

She smiled and said, "Come meet Danny."

And he let her open the door, take his hand, and lead him inside her apartment to meet her brother.

Chapter Thirty-One

M isty gripped Link's hand as she led him into her apartment. She'd literally never thought he'd be in this place. She'd never intended to bring him to her apartment in Dallas. As she took a step closer to the kitchen, where Danny had started smearing cream cheese on his toasted bagel, she realized how foolish she'd been.

Of course Link would've come with her to help her move from Dallas to Three Rivers. He'd have seen the apartment then.

"This is a nice place," Link said, his voice tinged with admiration.

"It's usually cleaner," Misty muttered. In a louder voice, she said, "Danny, I want you to meet my boyfriend, Lincoln Glover."

Her brother lifted his bagel and took a bite as he turned, which was such a classic alpha-dog move. Misty wanted to roll her eyes, but she managed to refrain. He wouldn't say hello first. He'd juggle his food before he could shake Link's hand. He'd take the extra seconds to size up Link as if he might be found wanting.

"Hey, brother," Link said easily, his voice carrying the smile on his face. "It's great to meet you." He didn't move to shake his hand, and he looked between Misty and Danny. "I see the resemblance. You guys have the best eyes in the world." He pressed a kiss to Misty's temple, and she leaned into his touch, having missed it so much.

Her feelings streamed through her in bright colors, and Misty couldn't make sense of all of them. She did decide right then and there that she didn't care if Danny liked Link or not. *She* liked him—she liked him a whole lot—and Danny didn't get to influence her decisions when it came to where she lived, where she worked, or who she was with.

"Thanks, Link," she said. She met her brother's eye, and he finally swallowed his first bite of breakfast, though she'd told him Link was bringing them food.

"It's great to meet you," Danny said. "Misty's talked of hardly anything else this week." He gave her a knowing look, but Misty stood up strong against it. She didn't have anything to hide from Link or Danny.

"I brought you a bagel," Link said, lifting the bag of food. "But that one looks better, so maybe I'll eat it." He released her hand and started pulling out containers. "For my beautiful girl," he said, handing her a round tinfoil container with a cardboard cover over it.

He took out another one and looked at Danny. Link didn't seem nervous at all, but Misty knew he had to be. She knew him well enough to see the jump in his jaw and the way he hesitated, albeit slightly. "I got you a quiche too, my friend. Misty said you liked bacon and Swiss."

Danny stepped over and took it. "I do," he said. "Thanks."

"Here's that bagel too." Link tossed it to him, as it had been wrapped in white paper and basically resembled a baseball. "I'm not kidding when I said I'd eat it if you don't want it."

"I want it," Danny said.

"He's not used to having unlimited access to food," Misty said, giving her brother a look he ignored. "And Link isn't used to not having platters and platters of food." She grinned at him, and Link ducked that adorable cowboy hat and chuckled.

"Nice hat," Danny said, and Misty pulled in a breath.

But Link just said, "Thanks, brother. It's one I really like." He reached up and adjusted it on his head. "There's this famous rodeo star that lives in Three Rivers now that he's retired. My family is real close with his, and it's one of his signature hats."

"Wyatt Walker," Misty said, because she knew this now.

"Wyatt Walker," Link confirmed. "I think I'm gonna call it my traveling hat, and I'll wear it when I travel."

"Which means you'll never wear it again," she quipped.

"Hey." He laughed and pulled out another white-wrapped package. "I might. You never know. Maybe we'll go somewhere amazing for Thanksgiving, just the two of us."

Misty gaped at him, forgetting about Danny completely.

"The day you leave Shiloh Ridge at Thanksgiving is the day I die."

He laughed again and leaned toward her. "I sure do like your pretty accent. Di-ie. It's one syllable, sweetheart."

She'd made it two, and she let her eyes drift closed as he kissed her briefly.

"You two are sickly sweet," Danny said in a dry tone.

Misty pulled back and moved around him to get silverware out of the kitchen. "Danny, I'm not staying in Dallas."

"I figured," he said.

She wasn't sure how to tell him he couldn't stay here either. That she didn't want him living in her apartment, especially if the way he cleaned up after himself was any indication of future behavior. He'd told her that everything in prison was so strict, that he just wanted to toss his shoes and shed his socks, and he'd get to them later. That he wouldn't live like this forever.

Misty honestly wasn't sure she believed him. Of course, he'd told her so many things in the past that hadn't been true, so his track record with her wasn't great.

"There's a spot for you at Shiloh Ridge," Link said. "Poor Cutter's livin' alone these days, and that man needs someone to keep him in line." He grinned at Danny while Misty stared.

Danny scoffed—just like Misty wanted to—and then he just stared at Link. Her boyfriend casually took a bite of his sausage, egg, and cheese sandwich as if he hadn't a care in the world.

"You mean that?" Danny had stopped eating completely, and Misty hadn't started yet. Tension choked her, but Link took another bite as he looked between them.

He nodded, reached for a napkin, and swallowed. "Yeah, of course," he said. "Why wouldn't I mean...that?"

"Misty told you I was in prison, right?" Danny asked, glaring over to Misty now.

"Of course I told him that."

Danny focused on Link again. "And your daddy knows? All your family? They want me there?"

"Shiloh Ridge always needs good men," Link said.

"So you haven't spoken to them about it." Danny scoffed again and started to laugh in an unkind way. "Right." He rolled his eyes and his head in Misty's direction.

"Be nice," she hissed at him.

"This is why I don't want to go to Three Rivers," he said bitterly. "You say it'll be fine, but it won't be. Every job I get from now until forever is going to make me disclose that I'm an ex-con."

"Well, it won't be different here," Misty shot back at him. "And no one here is offering you anywhere to live, work, and be anonymous." She gestured to Link, who had stopped eating. "We're offering you all of that. It's a good thing, Danny. Don't make it into a bad thing just because you're scared."

Danny pressed his teeth together, his lips flat-lining over them. He took his food and stormed out of the kitchen and dining area and into the living room. Misty's adrenaline fell, and she let the breath out of her lungs too.

She looked helplessly at Link, who suddenly did wear an expression of uncertainty. Then, he grabbed his food and followed Danny into the living room. He sat down on the other end of the couch, leaving the middle cushion for Misty, should she choose to join them.

With her lungs pinched as they were, she decided to stay at the dining room table to eat. She'd just taken her first bite of quiche Lorraine when Link looked over to Danny. "You own any boots?"

"No," Danny said.

"A hat?"

Danny looked at him, pure irritation in his eyes. "What do you think, cowboy?"

"I think you can borrow one of mine until we can get you set up with your own," Link said without missing a beat. "The boots I can't help you with, because I think my giant feet will be like you wearing skis." He chuckled and went back to his sandwich.

Danny looked over to Misty, who likewise stared right back at him. She'd been nervous about Link meeting Danny, though realistically, she shouldn't have been. Link didn't pick up any more small talk, and the three of them ate in silence from their positions in the apartment.

Misty could only get down a few more bites, and then she got up and put the cardboard cover over her quiche. She slid it into the fridge and joined the men in the living room. "Danny, I haven't seen Link in a week, and I'm going to take him out to see my favorite things in Dallas." She grinned and extended both of her hands to Link.

He blinked at her, pure surprise emanating from him. "We're going around the city?"

"Yes, sir," she said. "You can keep your hat on, so don't worry."

"All right." He set his food on the side table and took both of her hands. He stood and wrapped his arms around her. "He can come, love. I don't care."

"Nope," she said, stepping out of his arms. "Danny, we're going back to Three Rivers tomorrow night. You can't stay in my apartment alone, so you'll need to find somewhere to live in the next twenty-four hours—and that includes an amazing, furnished-and-ready cowboy cabin at Shiloh Ridge."

"Misty."

"I'm just saying it's an option." His only option right now, but that didn't need to be said out loud, so Misty didn't say it.

"They won't have any airplane tickets left," he grumbled. "Not one we can afford, at least."

Misty looked at Link, and Link looked at Misty. She knew he'd pay whatever required if Danny wanted to go to Three Rivers with them, and neither of them had to say a word.

"Ready, love?" he asked, taking her hand.

"Ready," she said, and she let Link lead her out of her own apartment. She hadn't anticipated him being the one to convince Danny to come to Three Rivers, but as the door closed behind him, she was fairly sure he'd done just that.

* * *

"You're going to have to stop kissing me," Link murmured just before he touched his mouth to Misty's and kissed her again.

They'd been doing that for a while, and Misty did need to get back to her apartment—and her brother.

"I don't want to," Misty said, but Link broke the kiss and leaned his forehead against hers.

"I don't want to go another week without seeing you," he whispered.

"But you will," she said. "Next spring, when you drive the cattle up into the hills. And next fall, when you bring them back."

Link smiled, and Misty enjoyed the close-up beauty of it.

"But I'll hate every minute of it."

"You love being a cowboy."

He sighed. "Yeah." He pulled away and touched his keycard to the sensor on his hotel room door. "Hey, Misty?"

She toyed with her keys, not wanting to make the drive back to her place in the dark. "Yeah?"

"I love you, too."

Her smile spread across her face, and she turned back and threw her arms around him. Kissing him, she said, "I love you, too." She pulled away, suddenly feeling more serious. "Thank you for your help with Danny."

"Do you really think he'll come to Three Rivers?"

She nodded. "If I remember him from a few years ago, then yes. He's going to come with us."

"All right," he said. "I'll call my daddy tonight and make sure everyone knows."

"Will it really be okay?" Her worry rose again, and Misty just wanted Link to hold her and tell her everything would be fine. She also didn't want to share him with Danny, and that selfishness made a stitch of guilt weave through her.

"I didn't say anything that was untrue," Link said. "The ranch always needs good men, and Cutter really does need a roommate to be happy. I think it'll be fine, love."

"I guess we'll find out," she said, stepping back. Fear accompanied her a few steps away, and then she spun back to Link. "Baby, what if he's not a good man? What if he hates Cutter, or Cutter hates him?"

The last scenario was the most likely, if Misty was being honest. She wrung her hands around and around while Link considered her. "What if you have to fire him?"

He took a breath and closed the gap between them. He played with her fingers, gently pulling them apart and calming them. "My daddy used to say this: we'll cross any bridges that need to be crossed when we get to them."

Misty nodded, though her stomach still stormed and buzzed and stung with biting ants.

"Hey," Link said. "Does it feel right to have him in Three Rivers or not?" He put his hand under her chin and made her look up at him. "When you prayed about it? When you thought of it? Did it feel right or not?"

"Yeah," she whispered. "It feels like the perfect solution." She'd get to rekindle her relationship with her brother, show him how amazing small-town living could be, and help him get reintroduced to society in an easy, cowboy way. He'd have to work hard, but Misty believed in him—and she'd be nearby to help.

And the Glovers...they seemed to connect with every person they came in contact with, and Misty couldn't imagine they wouldn't take her broken brother under their collective wing and heal him...the way they'd healed her.

"Okay, then," Link said softly but with plenty of surety. "Then he's coming to Three Rivers, and we'll handle whatever comes up."

"Together," she said.

"Yeah, sweetheart." He grinned at her and kissed her again. "Together."

Misty did love that word when it was in reference to Link, and she managed to make the drive home without allowing the sadness to overcome her. At home, she found Danny asleep on the couch, and she paused as she looked down at him.

Love filled her, along with a peaceful purifying feeling that she truly had done her best with him. Now, it was up to him to take advantage of this second chance at his life. She brushed her fingers across his forehead and murmured, "I love you, Danny."

She went into her bedroom, a steady prayer coursing through her mind, body, and soul. *Please bless my brother to know how much he's loved. Please bless my brother to know how much he's loved—by me, by the Glovers, and by You.*

Chapter Thirty-Two

L ink pulled up to the homestead, taking one of the only remaining spots left in the gravel area out front. "This is the homestead," he said. "My uncle Ranger and aunt Oakley live here."

"But they don't run the ranch," Danny said, peering at the huge house. "Seems odd that they live in the biggest house."

"There are a lot of big houses here," Misty said from the passenger seat of Link's truck. He'd followed her and Danny to the house she shared with Janie, and then they'd all piled into his truck to make the final leg of their trip to Shiloh Ridge Ranch.

"My daddy and Ranger are the oldest brothers in their family lines," Link said. He watched the windows and didn't see any movement. "They lived here, in opposite wings, at first. Before Daddy met Momma. I lived in this house when they were first married. And when Smiles came along. Then Uncle

Ranger and Aunt Oakley started havin' kids too, and Aunt Etta was living in the downstairs suite, and it was just a lot of people in a big house."

He smiled over to Misty and back to Danny. "My folks built a new house, and Etta got married. She and August got a new house too, so now, Ranger and Oakley live here alone. They host all the big parties that aren't at True Blue or the firepit, and I don't know. This house feels like home to me too." He blew out his breath, and reached for the door. He didn't really spend this much time traveling and talking, and the quiet emptiness of his house sounded pretty amazing about now.

However, Link had spent an hour on the phone last night, with only the first ten minutes of it with his daddy. Then, they'd done a group call with Uncle Ward, Uncle Ranger, Uncle Cactus, and Uncle Preacher. All of them would be here tonight, and probably more. Link hadn't put a limit on it, and the Glovers never really passed up an opportunity to get together and eat.

"Time to rip off the Band-Aid," Link said. "Because my mother has some sort of radar that tells her when I'm nearby, and she knows we've been sitting out here for a few minutes." He flashed a smile all around and reached for the door handle.

"It's not radar," Misty said, "Every building on this ranch has cameras."

Danny chuckled as he spilled from the backseat, and Link led the way through the fenceposts and onto the sidewalk. To his surprise, no one opened the front door before he reached it, and he pushed into the homestead and called, "We're here."

He reached for Misty, and thankfully, she knew when to ground him. Her fingers slid between his, and they went under the arch and the carved mention of the Glover family name and into the kitchen.

So many eyes looked back at him, and he couldn't even imagine how they made Danny's skin itch and burn.

"Son." Of course Daddy would be the first to greet him. He'd probably been hovering next to the fridge for the last half-hour. He grabbed onto Link and pulled him into a hug. Link didn't believe for a moment that Daddy wasn't already sizing up Danny, but he'd be kind about it.

He had a very good first-impression-meter, and Link had been praying that Danny could pass it for the entire drive from Amarillo.

"Daddy," Link whispered. "Thank you."

"I love you." Daddy pulled back and looked at Misty. "Hey, Misty-girl." He hugged her too, and Link nearly lost his composure watching his father hug his girlfriend. His eyes filled with tears as God whispered to him that everything was handled.

I've got this, he heard as his mom tapped him on the shoulder. "Hey," she said as he faced her. He grabbed onto her and held her tight, not sure if he should tell her everything in his mind and heart right now or just let it all play out.

"Introduce us," she whispered, and Link stepped back.

"Daddy," he said, doing a quick swipe at his eyes. "Momma, this is Danny Granger, Misty's brother." He indicated the man, giving him a quick nod and even quicker smile. "Danny, these are my parents, Bear and Sammy Glover."

"It's so great to meet you, sir," Danny said, all proper and polite. "Ma'am." He shook hands and looked at Misty.

"Link's aunt and uncle," Misty said, "Ranger and Oakley."

"Great to meet you." Danny shook their hands too. "You live here. It's such a beautiful home."

"Thank you," Oakley said. "Our foremen." She indicated Uncle Ward and Uncle Preacher. "They'll be over what you do here on the ranch. Ward and Preacher Glover."

"Thank you," Danny said, stepping past Ranger and Oakley. "I am gonna work real hard here, I promise you that."

Link watched him pump Uncle Ward's hand and then Uncle Preacher's. Neither of them said a single word, and neither of their faces moved an inch. Link turned his head away to hide his smile, because his uncles were putting on a show, plain and simple.

And when Uncle Cactus stepped next to them and said, "We have a rule on this ranch, son," Link dang near burst out laughing.

Danny looked at his tall, broad uncle and said, "Oh."

"This is Cactus," Daddy said, and they'd so rehearsed this. "He's the second son behind me."

"Why's he here?" Misty asked, folding her arms and giving Cactus a shrewd smile.

"Because someone has to keep Bear from doing something senile in his old age," Cactus said without missing a beat. Link did let his laughter loose then, as did several others.

As Link sobered, he said, "Hiring Danny is going to be the

least senile thing any of us does." He gave the man a grin as wide as the sky. "Trust me."

"I'm here," someone called from the front door, and it sounded like Aunt Etta. Sure enough, she walked into the kitchen a moment later, carrying a big pot of something. Her husband, August, came right behind her, as did all three of their children. Hailey belonged to them too, but she didn't live at home anymore, so Link wasn't shocked not to see her.

Their oldest son, Joey, carried a huge tray of rolls that had been perfectly baked and browned, and Link's stomach roared for bread, butter, and strawberry jam. The twins, Nash and Nellie, carried a bowl each, and Uncle August set down cardboard bowls, plastic utensils, and a bag of bottles and containers.

"What do we have here?" Misty asked as she moved over to the island to help unpack the food.

"Misty," Nellie said, right in her face. "Momma made chicken pot pie stew. You are gonna *love it*." The ten-year-old lived life with a certain enthusiasm that Link could barely maintain

"I'm in love with it already," she said kindly. "Etta, this is my brother, Danny."

Etta threw her hot pads on the counter with wild abandon and stepped right over to Danny. She already wore a big smile to go with her bright blue eyes, and she gripped him by the shoulders. "Look at you."

Someone in the room stifled a laugh, and someone else cleared their throat. Link wasn't sure what to do. His heart hammered at him a couple of times, but the way Momma and

Aunt Oakley just stood there when they could've intervened had rendered him silent and still too.

"What a handsome man you are," Aunt Etta said. "Yep, I think you're going to do just fine here." She released him and stepped back. "My kids." She indicated them and then her husband, introducing them all around.

"Nice to meet you," Danny said, looking a little shell-shocked. In fact, his lips had barely moved when he'd spoken.

"Let's eat," Aunt Etta said. "Unless we're missing people still." She lifted the lid off her pot of chicken pot pie stew. "Are we?"

"No," Daddy said. "We're all here."

"Enough to start," Uncle Ward said. "Dot and the kids are headed over, but we can start without 'em."

"Then let's start," Momma said. "I think I just heard Link's stomach growl from here." She gave him a lopsided grin, and Link only smiled. A certain nervousness continued to run through him, though his family had been accepting and welcoming of Danny.

He prayed that having Misty's brother here wouldn't cause any problems, that he'd never have to reprimand or fire the man, and that everyone would be happy here at the ranch.

* * *

"And you just put the tack back where we got it," Link said several days later. "And—"

"We brush down the horses and put them away," Danny said. "I can do it."

Link looked over to him. He'd done every task asked of him since he'd come to the ranch. Sure, Link had found him icing his back and his shoulder in the evenings, because ranch work wasn't a walk in the park. But he showed up on time in the morning, he listened, and he worked hard.

Link hadn't heard a word of complaint, and even Cutter had texted Link to say that Danny was welcome company in the evenings.

"I can do it," Danny said. "Really, Link. If I need help, I'll grab someone." He moved to take the saddle over to the shelf. "Lord knows there's a cowboy every five feet around here."

Link grinned at him and said, "Okay. I have to go down to Preacher's for a meeting."

"Yeah, that's why I said I got this." Danny took his saddle from him, and Link met his eye. "What should I do after this?"

"Nothing." Link gave him a quick smile. "Go home. We're done for today."

"It's four-fifteen." Danny looked like he'd been told they'd open Christmas presents next.

Link chuckled and clapped him on the shoulder. "Yep, and the job is done, which means you're done."

Danny's smile spread across his face, and it made Link so happy. "Hey, could I ask a favor?"

"Sure thing." As Link spoke, he heard how much he sounded like his father.

"I don't have travel restrictions here," Danny said, his feet shifting. That could've been from the weight of Link's saddle. "And I'd love to go get pizza tonight."

"Sure, did you get the Two Cents app? Anything on their pizza list is going to be amazing."

"I got it," he said. "What I don't have is a way to get to town to pick up the pizza."

Everything clicked in Link's head. "We've got extra trucks here. I'll text Ranger that you're gonna come by and get the keys to one. Okay?"

Relief filled Danny's face. "Thank you, Link." He sort of tried to reach out to shake his hand, but he held a saddle, and the whole thing became awkward. Link ended up taking the saddle back before Danny could drop it, and he put it away before turning back to Misty's brother.

"Listen, Danny," he started.

"I'm okay, Link," he said quietly. He looked up, and those Granger green eyes stared straight into Link's. "I just want to really thank you for giving me this chance."

"I didn't do anything," Link said.

"You love my sister," Danny said. Just like that. Just right out loud as if it was common knowledge. As if everyone knew it. "And without that, I know you wouldn't have vouched for me and spoken up for me and let me come here." He swallowed and coughed a little cough. "So you did do something, and I really appreciate it."

Link's own throat worked as he tried to get it to perform its natural function. He nodded, and Danny nodded on back. Then Link headed out to get to his foremen meeting with his uncles. He sat in the cab of his truck and texted Misty really quick, though he was already a few minutes late getting down to Preacher's.

Your brother is great, he said. *Just wanted you to know.*

Really? she sent back instantly. *You're not just making that up?*

I would never make something like that up, Link texted. *He's doing well up here.*

Are you busy later? she asked.

Meeting now, he said. *Then I'm free. Probably close to six-thirty or so.* That would give him time to get home and shower. *I can pick you up for pizza?*

Can't wait, Misty said.

To which Link responded, *I love you.*

Chapter Thirty-Three

Misty scooped up a spoonful of ice cream and ate it slowly. As she licked mint chocolate chip off the back of her spoon, she looked over to Janie. "I'm not going back to Dallas."

Janie's eyes were the only thing that moved. "I'm shocked," she said in a totally not-shocked tone.

"You're the first person I've said it out loud to."

"You haven't even told Link?"

Misty shook her head and stirred together the melted part of her ice cream with the still-frozen parts. "I'm going to go back to Dallas over Thanksgiving and move out of my apartment there. Put it up for sale. Then...I'll keep letting the state pay for my housing here, and once our project is done...." She shrugged, the rest of the story already there in black and white.

"Maybe you'll be married by the time our project is done," Janie said.

Misty grinned, but she didn't confirm or deny anything. She wasn't sure about that, because while she and Link said "I love you" pretty freely these days, they hadn't talked about marriage or children at all. Misty's chest tightened mightily at the thought of being a mother, but at least it didn't send her running the way it had previously.

"I won't get married before our project finishes," she promised.

"It won't matter even if you do," Janie said. She sniffled and wiped her eyes. "Because even if you did, you'd move up to Shiloh Ridge. It's not like Link would come live here and cramp my single lifestyle."

Misty half-laughed as tears streamed down her face. "I'm just so—ugh. Who thought any of this would happen to me?" She covered her face with her hands and wiped at her eyes. "You're the one who's dated all these years. I haven't had a second date in a decade."

Every hole in her face had decided to leak then, and she didn't know how to get it to stop. "Maybe we can just prolong the project forever," she whispered. "Then I won't ever have to tell you good-bye."

"It'll take a lot more than you marrying some rich cowboy for us to stop being friends." Janie let herself cry too. "And I get to be your Maid of Honor. None of his siblings or cousins or any of his millions of aunts."

Misty tipped her head back and laughed. "He does have a lot of aunts, doesn't he?"

The moment sobered, and they went back to eating their ice

cream at their little table-for-two in the house on a quiet street in quaint, perfect, small-town Three Rivers.

* * *

"I'm so nervous." Misty smoothed both hands over her stomach, unconcerned about her dress and how it lay but super concerned she might actually throw up.

Link had just come down the hallway from his bedroom, and he currently brushed his teeth. "Ain't no thing," he said around the brush and toothpaste.

"How can you say that?" Misty wasn't going to be able to enjoy a bite of food tonight. Which made no sense, because she'd spent plenty of time with Link's family.

Tonight felt different, though.

Because tonight *was* different.

The last Sunday of October had come, and that meant it was the annual Glover family dinner, meeting, party, and Angel Tree decorating event.

Link turned and went back down the hall to his bathroom, leaving Misty alone in her panic. She took a breath and moved over to the window. "Lord," she prayed. "I don't know if I can do this."

The feeling in her stomach to run, to hide, faded to nothing as she looked at the trees beyond Link's porch. She went outside, clear to the corner of the porch and gazed into the landscape. It smelled like earth and pine and sky, and Misty drew in another long breath of it.

"I am strong," she whispered to herself. "I am invincible." Her thought patterns started to change with those few simple words. "I am unstoppable. My future is wide open. I'm a nice person, and Link's family loves me. *He* loves me."

It still baffled her that someone as amazing as him could love her, but Misty didn't doubt it. Not for a second.

"I am not going to stand in my own way." She shook her head. "Not tonight."

The door opened, and Link joined her outside. He didn't say anything as he crossed over to her. When he arrived, he simply put his arm around her and took a deep breath of her hair. "I like this dress," he murmured.

She wore a red, green, black, and white plaid dress that hugged her straight up and down. It fell to her knee with little ripples or fabric. She'd paired it with a pair of black ballet flats, and she wore a white cardigan over her shoulders. She felt like the heroine in a romcom movie, the kind that goes to London to marry a man they've never met. She had the cutest clothes and the funniest things would happen, and in the end, she'd have the man of her dreams.

Or in her case, the cowboy of her dreams.

"Remember the first time you came to my family's Angel Tree celebration?" Link asked softly. "And Uncle Bishop had made those banana cream tarts, and we snuck a couple out the door and took a walk. Remember that?"

"Mm," she said, picturing the scene as he started to paint it with his luxurious voice.

"And the sky was so amazing that night, because it had

those wispy clouds, and they hold so much color from the sunset."

"Really beautiful." She relaxed back into his chest.

"And I asked you about having kids, and you said...." He paused there, but every muscle in Misty's body had just jumped to attention. He had to feel that, and Misty moved away from him and leaned into the railing while her heartbeat flailed in her chest.

I am strong, she thought, and as she did, she remembered that strength did not come from forgetting the past, but from the courage to remember it—and still move forward.

"I don't know how good I'll be with kids," she admitted. Her voice felt stuffed way down in her pancreas. "I'm a little scared of being a mom."

"I think you'd be a great mom," Link whispered.

I am invincible.

She was strong enough to heal, to forgive, and to begin fresh. With every step she took with Link, she was coming home—not just to a place, but to herself.

"I'd try," she said. "I think I'll do better than my mom. But... I'll need a lot of help."

"I think we'd have to tie my momma in the stable to keep her away from any of our babies." He chuckled, and she finally turned to look at him.

"How many babies are we talking?" she asked.

"I don't know, love." He drew her back into his chest. "There's no set number. Sometimes the Lord blesses you with a lot of things, and one of them isn't children. Sometimes it is. I guess we'll have to see."

"Do you want kids right away? Or like...is there an acceptable waiting period in your family?"

"Rory and Ollie were married for six or seven years before they had their first baby," Link said. "I'm not in a hurry, Misty. We're young. Daddy started having baby after baby the moment he and Momma got married, because he was already forty-six years old."

She nodded and relaxed into the warmth of his arms. "Okay." A beat went by, and she added, "Remember when we were first married, and it was just us for a few years? And we needed that time to discover more about each other, and learn how to live together, and I needed to be shown how to be a Glover, and you were so patient with me." She swallowed, her future blooming in front of her. "Remember that?"

"Yeah, my love," he whispered. "I remember that."

* * *

Misty's nerves did not get in her way during dinner. She and Link did steal some banana cream tarts before dinner started, but they ate them on the front porch of the homestead, no hard conversations between them.

Dinner was lively, of course, with tables spilling out onto the deck and into the wing under the stairs to accommodate everyone. Then, the Glovers had their meeting, and Misty marveled at how they talked openly about money, about where to invest it, about how they'd done at market, all of it.

That broke up, and the crowd surged toward the foyer of the house, with children of various ages clamoring over one another about this ornament or that one. Misty had not seen a tree when she and Link had arrived, but as they joined the throng of Glovers in the foyer, she found Arizona and June removing a pure white tree from a box.

"Settle down," Ranger called, and when that did nothing, he put his fingers in his mouth and whistled. "Enough. Quiet."

That got everyone to do what he asked, and he nodded over to Bear. "I've asked Mother to talk about our Angel Tree this year," Bear said, his eyes roaming the crowd. Misty had eaten with Mitch, who'd come home specifically for this, and Link's cousin Hailey, so she hadn't seen too much of Bear and Sammy yet tonight.

They'd hugged her hello, of course, but with the sheer number of Glovers, it was hard to stick by too many people. Link's hand in hers reminded her of how they'd stayed so close all evening.

"Sometimes we talk about it, and sometimes we don't," Bear said. "But we have some new people with us tonight, and some of our littles are more grown, so they can understand it's more than just getting the toy soldier ornament." He looked pointedly at some of the smaller children in the front of the crowd, those gathered closest to the tree. "Mother?"

Misty had met Lois Glover—oops, she was remarried to Don Parker now—tonight for the first time. She'd held Misty close without saying a word, and that had somehow stitched their hearts together already.

Now, she emerged from the crowd and indicated the twelve-foot-tall tree as Zona and June continued to put it together, pulling out the branches and arranging them just so.

"This is our Angel Tree," she said. "My mother-in-law handmade all of the ornaments with white thread and red accents. She starched them into specific shapes, and I swear, I never saw her make anything else with a crochet needle."

She paused to smile, and Misty fell in love with the soothing sound of her voice.

"Every year, we put up our Angel Tree on the last Sunday of October. We each have special ornaments that mean something to us. Either they were made for us...." She glanced around. "Or they chose us. No matter what, there are more than enough ornaments to go around. Hang one, or hang ten, but please make room for everyone."

"What do the ornaments mean, Grandmother?" one little girl up front asked.

Lois put both hands on her knees and bent down. "Well, my Jewel, they represent the Glovers that have gone before us. Our grandmothers and grandfathers. Our fathers and uncles. All the great Glovers who built this ranch and now entrust it to us. Every time you come to the homestead in the next couple of months, you'll feel them." She put one fist over her heart and straightened. "Right here."

As if on cue, as if they'd rehearsed it, all the adult Glovers—

every last one of them right down to Link—lifted their right fist and pressed it over their heart.

Misty's tears streamed down her face, and she reached for her brother's hand. Danny lived here and worked this ranch, and while none of the other hired help had come, he had a special connection through her.

She found him gazing around at everyone with that Glover last name, pure awe on his face. He even said, "Wow."

Their eyes met, and Misty tried to smile. It didn't quite work, because she felt all the same amazing, wonderful things he did. "This is what family feels like, Danny."

She'd tried so hard to give him this, but there was no way it could be replicated. Absolutely no way. She'd known Lincoln Glover was special the moment she'd met him, years ago on a dance floor in town.

It was as if every scene with him in it zipped and played across her line of sight, and she fell in love with him again and again and again

"Yeah," Danny whispered. "That's right. This is what family feels like."

The Glovers lowered their fists, and Zona cleared her throat. "Thank you, Mother. I'm going to spread the boxes out a little." She picked one up and handed it to Oakley. "Put that in the kitchen, would you, Oak?"

She faced them all again. "Then, we'll have more room to look for the ornaments we want. It's not a race." She glared at the kids and pre-teens near the front. "Do you hear me? Where are my kids?" She glanced around. "It's *not* a race."

"Who wants Aunt Zona mad at them?" Bishop asked, his fun-loving personality joining hers up front. "No one? All right, then. We walk with the ornaments. We share with each other. We ask for help if you need to reach a higher branch. We speak in quiet voices, like church-quiet. This is an honor for our family, our ancestors."

"An honor," Misty whispered.

Link kneaded her closer and bent down. "You don't have to do it, but you're welcome to look through the boxes and find something. Most of us say a little tribute to our person when we hang our ornament."

"You do that?" she asked. "For who?"

"My momma and daddy," he said. "For Bear. And maybe this year, for you." He gave her a smile. "All the really important people who aren't here with me, and for those who've rescued me who are."

Misty teared up again, but she brushed at her eyes. She didn't want to miss a moment of this, and Bishop had finished with the rules.

"There's no order," Zona said. "Come on, everyone. Let's get the tree decorated."

People moved then, but it was with a hushed reverence they all seemed to understand. They'd all done this before, but it wasn't hard to let the prevailing feeling of love, peace, joy, and solemnity seep into her soul as she stepped over to a box that had been placed on the stairs, only a few feet behind her.

Simply gazing into it, she could feel the work and love and spirit of every stitch she saw. She could only imagine Link's great-grandmother making these, thinking of her posterity who might use them, but might not. Had she imagined this? Had she ever witnessed it while alive?

Hands dipped into the box and took ornaments out, all while soft voices talked. Link picked up a fairly large ornament —about the size of his fist—of an old-fashioned truck.

"This one's for my daddy," he said. "He loved old trucks, and my momma drove one of his for a long time after he died." He met her eyes, plenty of shining stars in his expression. "You okay here for a second while I hang this?"

"Yes," Misty murmured. The crowd around their box thinned, and Misty found herself standing next to it with Danny. He reached inside and pulled out an ornament, with a steel gray hook coming from the top of it.

"Misty," he breathed. "Look at this."

He held what looked to be nothing more than a leafless tree, with only a few branches flowing up. It almost looked like a Halloween decoration more than anything she'd hang on a Christmas tree.

But Danny gazed at her with pure wonder streaming from him. "It looks just like that tree we had in front of the house." He looked at it and then her. "Remember? And I said I was going to climb it and jump off from the highest branch and fly away from there." He could barely be heard by the end of his sentence, and Misty's memory overflowed.

"I remember," she said.

"This is mine," he said, pulling it closer to his body. "I'm going to hang this one." He left her standing at the box, and Misty bent down to get a better look at what remained.

She found snowflakes and stars, what looked like a wreath but had been smashed and disfigured on one side, and a couple of misshapen horses. She left that box and moved to the next one over, part of her wondering if she'd find anything that would speak to her soul. She couldn't even imagine what that might be.

A hole? A zero? How did one stitch loneliness and forced isolation with white thread and red accents?

She found nothing that called to her in the second or third boxes, and she looked up to realize quite a few people had finished already. They'd moved back into the kitchen for dessert, and the foyer wasn't empty, but it wasn't nearly as full either.

Link stood with his parents, the three of them talking quietly about something. He glanced her way and raised his eyebrows, but she shook her head. With a bit of desperation pounding along her temples, she moved over to another box.

"These are the oldest ones," Zona said lovingly as she dropped into a crouch beside Misty. She didn't wear a dress, and Misty realized she hadn't needed to either. Maybe next year, she wouldn't. She smiled at Misty. "I always want to go through the ornaments in order, but I've stopped trying to suggest it."

"They're so beautiful," Misty said. "Even more so with the natural light on them." She took out an ornament shaped and pressed just so—a duck. "They make me smile."

"They make me smile too," Zona said. "Have you found one for yourself?"

Misty shook her head. "I—what do you hang?"

"Grandmother made something for everyone," Zona said instead of answering Misty. "We'll find you something." She took out another ornament, this one a feather. Then a rocking chair. Misty shook her head. A fox, a badly smashed cardinal, a set of holly berries.

Etta joined them, saying, "Still looking, Misty?"

"I don't think there will be anything," she said sadly. "I...I just don't have many good memories of anyone in my life. Well, besides Danny and now Link."

"We'll find something," Etta told her. She pulled over another box and started sorting through the leftover ornaments.

Sammy got down and began to help too. "I always hang one for my sister and brother-in-law," she said. "And believe it or not, my first year here, I found a rocking horse for Patrick. He'd built one for Link when he was a baby, and oh, that boy loved riding his rocking horse." She smiled with all the tender love of a parent, and Misty sure hoped she could feel that way about her babies.

"And for my sister, I found a cardinal. Simple, and I've learned that Priscilla made many birds and cardinals over the years. But my sister loved birdwatching, and that ornament spoke to my heart. It reminded me that God knew me and loved me, and I hang one of the birds for Link's momma every year."

"So maybe God doesn't love me or know me," Misty said without thinking.

All three women stared at her, and Etta reacted first. "That's just not true, my darling girl. He knows you. He loves you. There's something here for you. I just know it."

"I found a racecar my first Christmas here," Oakley said as she joined them. "If you can believe that."

Out came crescent moons, and pine trees, and sun hats. None of them called to Misty.

She moved to the last box—her last hope. She just needed to keep looking. She'd look again and again, and she'd find something. Surely Etta wouldn't lie to her. They'd all found something just for them. Everyone had. Why shouldn't she?

So, she looked down, and there, nestled among several other ornaments, sat a little log cabin.

Her hand gravitated toward it like it had a magnet on it and she'd suddenly been fitted with an iron fist. She lifted it with a soft, "Oh, my goodness. It's the cabin I lived in here on the ranch. The one Link prepped for me the night of the fire."

The whole world slowed, for surely that cabin wasn't as old as this ornament. She took in the spaces for windows, and the darling little chimney on the roof, the near perfect corners, the round logs going up the sides. She looked at Oakley, Etta, Zona, and Sammy.

"It's my home." Tears rolled down her face, and Misty let the women sweep her into their arms and hold her tight.

"That's right, Misty," Sammy whispered. "You've come home."

Chapter Thirty-Four

L ink pulled up to Misty's house and found her suitcase on the porch, but not her. He took it to his truck and put it in the back with his bag. His nerves for this road trip fired at him as he walked back to her front door and knocked.

He'd been teasing her about going away for Thanksgiving, but he'd never dreamed they'd actually do it. And they weren't, not really.

They were going to Dallas to move her out of her apartment, clean it, and list it for sale. She wasn't going back there, and she saw no reason to pay for it when she wasn't going to use it again.

They'd technically be back in Three Rivers, at Shiloh Ridge, on Wednesday, the day before Thanksgiving. They'd be here for the stuffing, the homemade croutons, the turkey and mashed potatoes and gravy. All of it. So they weren't really missing anything except work.

Link wasn't upset about that, as he hardly ever took any days off work. He knocked again, this time calling, "Misty," as he opened the door.

"She's quietly freaking out," Janie said, only her eyes moving from the magazine she held as she lay on the couch. "Down the hall, first room on the right."

Link's frown flattened out, and he nodded to Janie. "Thank you, Janie. Are you still coming up to the ranch for Thanksgiving?"

She smiled and said, "Of course. Are you still coming to our Friendsgiving on Friday?"

"Of course," he said in the exact same way she had. He flashed her a smile and went down the hall to Misty's bedroom. He hadn't spent any time here, but he only had to stand in the doorway to see how quintessentially Misty her space was.

Floral curtains. A pristinely made bed. Her charging cord draped over the nightstand so she wouldn't have to bend to retrieve it. Two notebooks on her nightstand. Closet doors closed.

"Hey," Link said, and Misty turned from the window, where she'd been looking out. "I put your bag in the truck."

The tension in Misty's face dissolved away. "Thanks." She came toward him, each step reminding him how much he loved her. Today, she wore long pants somewhere between dark blue and dark purple, with wide legs that swayed with each step. Her blouse was blue, green, and purple, perfectly matched to the pants.

"You're not wearing shoes," he said.

"They're in the kitchen." She ran her hands up his chest. "We should go so we're on schedule, right?"

"We have no schedule, love." He grinned at her and leaned down to kiss her. "We can stop when you want, where you want. It's three hundred and fifty miles, give or take, and we can do that about five hours, straight through."

And the clock hadn't even struck ten yet. They weren't attending church today, and Link honestly didn't care when they arrived in Dallas. Misty would stay at her apartment, and Link, being a creature of habit, had booked the same hotel he'd stayed in last month when he'd made his first trip to the Dallas-Fort Worth area.

"I can't believe we're going away together," Misty murmured, her lips still against his.

"Next time we do it," he said. "We should actually go on vacation. The beach. The mountains. Something that isn't a chore."

"I'm in, cowboy."

He pulled away and took her hand as he fell back a step. "Come on, then. Let's get your shoes and get on the road."

She slid on her sandals with ease, and then she hugged Janie before they left the house. Link helped her up into the passenger seat; they buckled in; he set the course on his phone; and just like that, they left Three Rivers in the rear view mirror.

Misty hadn't said anything yet, and Link certainly wasn't one to chatter on if there wasn't anything to be said. But he glanced over to Misty. "So we haven't really talked about getting married."

She lifted her eyes from her phone, then tucked it under her thigh. "No, we haven't."

"Is that something you'd like to do?" He wasn't sure what he'd do if she said no. *What a dumb question*, he told himself. "I mean, I'm not going to rush you into it. My momma said you probably have some idea of when you'd like to get married, and I should ask you about it."

She grinned at him flirtily and leaned her head back against the rest. "Is that what your momma said?"

"Yes," he said. "So have you? Given any thought to a wedding? You know, if you'd like it to be in a field of bluebonnets or with, I don't know, hay bales and stalks of dried corn, or...." He trailed off when she started laughing.

Flustered, Link gripped the steering wheel and shifted in his seat. "If you haven't thought about it, then we can throw a dart at a calendar and get married on whatever date it lands on."

"Oh, we wouldn't throw a dart," she said, still laughing. "You'd throw a horseshoe."

Link smiled then. "Yeah, okay. Whatever you want to throw."

Misty's laughter quieted. "A marriage isn't all about one person, Link."

"No, it's not."

"So when would *you* like to get married?"

His heart nearly jumped out of his throat. "Just to be clear, we're talking about me and you getting married, right?"

"Yes, cowboy," she drawled out. "I mean, you're not special, but yes, me and you. Getting married."

"Well, if I'm marrying you, I'd like to get married as soon as possible."

Misty looked away, the boring, brown landscape beyond her window suddenly so enthralling. "That's so sweet, Link." She pulled in a breath that sounded a lot like a sniffle, and Link reached over and took her hand.

"Misty, I'm in love with you. Now that I know it and you know it and we're talking about marriage and kids and how to build a house of our own at Shiloh Ridge, every night I go home alone is awful." He couldn't believe it, but his momma had been right. "I don't want to sleep alone. I don't want to wake up alone. I want to see your face when I walk in after a long day on horseback, and I want to make you breakfast for dinner when you've been painting so long you can't even see colors anymore."

She nodded, truly sniffling now. "Okay," she said.

"That wasn't a proposal," he said. "And by the way, you don't say 'okay' when a man asks you to marry him." He chuckled, glad when she attempted a laugh too. "I'm just saying, when we get married is going to depend on you, because I'd stop by the closest courthouse I could find and get it done."

She shook her head, her smile so beautiful. "Link, there's a seventy-two-hour waiting period of marriages in Texas."

"Okay, well, we could still get it done by Thanksgiving." He grinned at her, knowing full-well she wouldn't do that. "And, uh, what about your mom? Are you going to tell her? Invite her? Maybe she'd like to come see the ranch? Meet me?"

Link forced himself to stop talking, and he wished he'd stopped to get something to drink. He could rectify that in

Pampa, as they had a little convenience store right off the highway.

"So many questions," she murmured.

"I don't need all the answers," he said. "Really, I don't. Just —you know how I have a lot going on in my head sometimes." He flashed her a smile, hoping to smooth things over a little.

"I love what goes on in your head," she said, squeezing his hand. "Let's start with the wedding. Link." She sighed and reached to tuck her hair behind her ear. "I didn't make plans to get married. Ever. I didn't play with dolls who got to walk down the aisle in pretty dresses I made for them out of my mother's old clothes or toilet paper or whatever."

He nodded, foolishness like hot pepper in his mouth. He coughed a couple of times, not sure what to say or do.

"Maybe I could...talk to your mom about it? Maybe she could help me set a realistic timeline. I mean, I'd need what? A dress, and flowers, and food, and maybe a band. I don't know how long it takes to do things or if they'll be booked out or what."

She pulled her hand away and wound her fingers together. "The whole thing is daunting."

"Yeah," Link agreed. "We really just need to show up in True Blue with Aunt Willa." He glanced over to her. "Everything else is just extras."

"But maybe I want the extras."

"And you can have them," he said. "If you ask my momma, she will cry in happiness, I can guarantee it." He nodded and smiled at her. "Guarantee."

"I really like your momma," Misty said quietly.

"She's the best," Link agreed.

"I'm going to text her," Misty said.

"No—maybe—" Link realized he'd practically shouted. His stomach swayed left and right and he told himself to calm down. "Maybe you should wait until we're actually engaged."

Misty's eyebrows went up. "Well, when will that happen?"

"I don't know," he said, his voice pitching up slightly. "I was told a proposal should be a fun surprise."

Misty started to giggle. "Who told you that?"

"If you must know," Link said, ready to stuff a sock in his mouth so he'd stop talking. "Your best friend." He really hit the D hard and threw a cocked-eyebrow look to Misty. "So stop laughing at Janie."

Misty zipped her lips, though her delight still filled the cab of the truck. "Do you have a ring?"

"Are you seriously going to ruin any and all surprises I may or may not have?"

She turned her head and gaped at him then. "Link."

"I need a drink," he said. "We're gonna stop here in Pampa, okay? You want anything?"

"Something to drink would actually be great," Misty said.

"Great," Link said, and he couldn't pull off the road fast enough. The wind blew in Pampa, and he faced into it, praying it would cool him off enough to finish the rest of this drive.

Yes, he had a ring. Yes, he'd brought it with him. No, he didn't have a plan for when or where or even how to ask Misty to be his wife.

* * *

Link went up to the second floor and back down to the parking lot with boxes, lamps, luggage, and more boxes. Misty wasn't bringing much furniture with her, thankfully. They'd been working for two straight days, and Link much preferred his ranch work to moving his girlfriend out of the apartment she'd lived in for the past seven years.

She hadn't moved fast the first day, going through everything, but today, they'd really gotten a lot boxed up. He estimated he had to make three or four more trips, and then they'd have everything in the back of his truck or the trailer he'd rented.

Misty came out of the apartment as he came up the steps. "I want that cabinet in my bedroom," she said. "It was my mother's."

"I'll get it," he said. He'd already emptied the drawers and taped them closed. It was just a matter of getting it out of the apartment and down the steps. He'd left a spot for it in the back of the truck, and it only stood to his chest, so it shouldn't give him too much trouble.

In fact, he didn't have a problem getting the cabinet down to the truck, and Misty brought down a box of her printer supplies while he covered everything in the bed of the truck with a tarp and tied it securely down.

"We just need to clean up," she said with a sigh. She tucked her hands into her back pockets and looked at the full bed and mostly full trailer. "We filled it up. I didn't think we would."

"Sometimes we have more than we think." He reached for her and added, "How are you feeling?"

"Fine," she said.

"Don't seem fine," he said.

"Don't I?"

"You won't look at me," he said. "Haven't looked at me for the past half-hour."

Misty still didn't immediately move her eyes to his. It took several seconds for her to get herself to look at him, and Link gazed at her. "There you are, love."

"I don't mean to get lost."

"You're doing a lot," he said. "Let's go get the place clean. You can take your pictures for the listing. Then we'll go to dinner."

"At the Four Seasons?"

"I checked that place," Link said. "No reservations available for tonight." He didn't tell her he'd booked another restaurant here in Dallas—one of the nicest places in the city—almost three weeks ago. "Don't worry, Misty. I've got dinner worked out."

"Okay," she said airily. "Now, come show me your muscles on my hard water stains."

He chuckled and followed her back up the steps one more time. She lightened considerably as they scrubbed countertops and wiped away fingerprints. Link did clean the bathroom while she started the vacuum in the back bedroom and worked her way toward the front door.

She'd never given him a definitive answer for when she'd like to get married, and Link reminded himself that she and

Momma would work out a date based on the timeline of how long it took to plan the wedding. "Summertime," Link murmured to himself. It was almost December now, and Link couldn't imagine the Glovers doing a wedding lickety split.

Of course, Oliver and Aurora had gotten married with only thirty days between the day Ollie proposed and the day they said I-do. So things could get greased if they had to.

Link didn't want a rushed engagement. He wanted to enjoy his time with Misty, and he wanted her to have every single detail of her wedding exactly how she wanted it.

As the vacuum went by the bathroom, Link muttered to himself, "You've got to ask her tonight." But he didn't want to put the ring in a glass of champagne or ask her in public. They were both staying in the same hotel that night, and he didn't want to propose there either.

So you're going to do it in the truck on the way home? he questioned himself. Irritated with himself, he finished up in the bathroom and took the bucket of supplies out to the living room.

Misty finished with the vacuum, and Link took the supplies outside. "I'll take the pictures," she said. "Be right down."

He hesitated. Did she want him to stay? Or would she prefer he leave so she could have one last moment in her apartment? Link took one look at her, and he knew: She wanted to be alone. So he took the vacuum and bucket and left her to herself for a few minutes.

When she didn't come down, Link's pulse beat at him to go check on her. He checked his pocket for the diamond he'd bought last week, and he hurried up the steps. He'd closed the door behind him, and instead of going right in, he knocked as if he'd just arrived to take Misty out for a fancy dinner at the nicest restaurant in Dallas.

He'd heard how Bear had proposed to Momma so many times, but Link didn't pull out the ring and get down on his knees right there on her doorstep. He waited, and Misty opened the door a moment later.

"I'm almost ready," she said. "I just realized I wanted that towel warmer in my bathroom." She hurried away from him and down the hall, and Link entered the apartment, his hand sliding into his pocket where the ring sat.

He pulled it out and looked at it. Uncle Preacher and Uncle Ward had gone with him to buy it, and they'd both assured him that it was beautiful, that it would do the job.

"Got it," Misty said. "Would you—?" She stopped only a pace from him, the bulky towel warmer coming toward him. "What is that?"

Link looked up and into her pretty eyes. Those eyes that had captivated him from the moment he'd seen them. "It's a symbol of my unending love for you." He held it up. "It's the long view, Misty, and I see me and you making a life together. And it might be messy, and I'll have to do overnight mowing every year until I'm, like, sixty."

He grinned at her, buoyed by the stunned shock streaming from her. So he'd surprised her, and everyone he'd spoken to about proposing had said no woman wants to know how things will happen. They wanted a good story to tell their friends, their kids, everyone.

"But whenever I think of that long view, and I reach really far into the future—and even into eternity—you're there. You're mine. I'm yours." He cleared his throat and finally remembered he should be down on at least one knee.

So he dropped to both and held up the diamond ring. Princess cut, with shining facets everywhere. "I'm completely in love with you. I don't know how to breathe through the immensity of my love for you. I feel like a new man every time I think of you loving me. It's just—it's mind-blowing."

You still haven't asked her, his mind screamed at him.

He cleared his throat and looked at his gorgeous girlfriend, still holding that towel warmer. "I love you, and I will love you for the long view, Misty. Will you marry me?"

She looked at him like he'd just asked her to cut off her own hand. She said nothing.

Link chuckled, because that was what he did when he was so far out of his comfort zone and had no idea how to get back into it. "Misty—"

"My face is wrong," she blurted out. "Look away."

"What?"

"Just look away."

"All right." He turned his head toward the pristine kitchen, wondering if he should get back to his feet. Shove that ring away. Hide his head. Cancel the reservation at Ember. Somehow make it home without losing all of his dignity.

"Okay, look again," she said. "I'm ready this time."

Link looked at her again. Gone was the towel warmer, her

anxiety, and that shocked look. She'd loosed her hair from its ponytail, and she grinned at him.

He smiled back at her. "I will always look again," he told her. "Will you marry me?"

"Yes!" Misty squealed. She clapped her hands and bounced on her toes. "Link, this ring is *gorgeous*." She held out her left hand, and Link slid the ring onto her finger. Then he reached for her, and she laughed as she leaned down to kiss him.

"I love you," he murmured.

"I love you so much." She kissed him and pulled back. "I just want you to know I'm not going to be good at this in the beginning. I'm really not. I'm so scared. But I'm in it for the long view too."

Link got to his feet and cradled her face in his hands. "I think we'll both have a lot to learn in the beginning."

"But we love each other."

He gathered her into his chest. "Yeah, I love you," he confirmed. "Because you're so special and so amazing and so brave."

"And I love you, because you're hard-working, and calm, and so, so special."

Link grinned, his eyes dropping closed, wanting and needing to simply be here with her, in this apartment in Dallas they'd never visit again, to feel the love she had for him and the love he had for her.

He could just see the two of them in a new house on the ranch, one with a big sunroom for painting, and bedrooms upstairs for the kids, and a big yard for the dogs who followed him home after work on the ranch.

"Can I text your momma now?" Misty asked.

"No," he said, stepping back and coming back to the present. "No, because we have our engagement dinner to get to, and you won't have time."

She blinked and grinned at him. "Are you going to tell me where we're going?"

"Ember," he said, ducking his head as if embarrassed.

But Misty made that delicious squealing sound again and launched herself into his arms all over again. "You didn't. Ember?" She searched his face, pure wonder on hers. "That's *such* a nice place."

"Yeah, I've got a jacket in the back of the truck," he said.

"You planned this." She gave him a look that said she appreciated the work he'd put into this proposal.

"Oh, don't go thinkin' you're special because I called and got us a reservation three weeks ago." He rolled his eyes. "Let's go. I don't want to miss it, and city traffic is not something I'm used to."

He bent and picked up the towel warmer, and they left the apartment together.

"I *am* special, though," Misty said once he'd put the towel warmer in the back and gotten behind the wheel of the truck.

He looked over to her. "Yeah, you are. You're the special-est."

"You're special too."

"Yeah." He took her hand and lifted it to his lips. "Okay,

now, text my momma and tell her I love you and you love me and we're going to get married."

Misty grinned and grinned, pulled her hand back, and said, "Okay."

I love second chance romances with my whole heart. And Link is one of my favorite cowboy heroes ever, and I love how Misty is just-right for him - and him for her! **I hope you loved them too!**

And keep reading for the first two chapters of the next book in the series, **THE COWBOY WHO LOVED TEXAS**, featuring enemies Dawson Rhinehart and Caroline Thompson!

Did you know there are chapters and chapters of extra content in small town Three Rivers? If you're interested in deleted scenes from this book, as well as bonus chapters before it and following it, **become a subscriber by scanning the QR code below with your phone.**

Sneak Peek! The Cowboy Who Loved Texas Chapter One:

Dawson Rhinehart pulled into the parking lot at the Three Rivers community center, coming to a stop right beside his parents. He got out and opened the back passenger door to collect the two pans of breakfast casserole his mama had made for this morning's New Year's Day breakfast fundraiser.

His father labored to get out of the truck only a pace away, and Dawson fought the desire to abandon the food and help his daddy. He succeeded, and he moved at the pace of a sloth behind his daddy as he took slow, stilted steps up to the sidewalk. He used the hood of the truck to help him get up that step, and then Daddy looped his arm through Mama's and used her strength to stabilize himself.

Inside, a flurry of activity told him where to take the food, and he handed it off to Ramona Whitely, who smiled and said, "Thank your mother, Dawson."

"Yes, ma'am," he said, wishing he could turn around and

walk right back out to his truck. He didn't care about this fundraising breakfast for the fire department, and he figured they'd already gotten the money for his ticket whether he ate or not.

He did want a bigger, nicer truck, as sometimes the wildfires out here in the Texas Panhandle could throw flames twenty feet in the air, if the summer season was long and dry and people didn't take proper precautions around their homes, farms, ranches, and vehicles.

Stuffing down his irritation at something that hadn't even happened yet, Dawson paused in the doorway and waited for a family to go by him. He had some errands to run after this breakfast, and because he couldn't put it off any longer, he joined the flow of people moving past the entrance to the kitchen and into the big gymnasium where he'd played basketball as a child.

His sports career had lasted until third grade, when he'd realized he didn't have the greatest hand-eye coordination—and his daddy wasn't going to drive him down to town for multiple practices each week, plus games on Saturdays.

He'd stuck to farm work after that, inventing games with his younger brother in the equipment shed, the barns, the stables, and simply the wide open land on the Rhinehart Ranch. Technically called Hidden Hollow Ranch, Inc for the taxes, Dawson loved working his family land that they all called the Rhinehart Ranch.

They had good neighbors and good soil, and Dawson would

rather be up there than down here. He wasn't exactly a people-person.

Still, he moved to the doorway of the gym and looked inside. People teemed around the long tables set up for the breakfast buffet. People moved along all the circular tables set up for eating. People laughed; people talked; people people people.

Dawson took a steeling breath and took the first step into the gymnasium. He couldn't see his mama or daddy, but he figured they'd saved him a spot. Perhaps if he just wandered around, they'd find him.

He nodded to family friends, then Judge Glover and his wife, then he veered over to Micah Walker. He was a decade older than Dawson, but they'd worked on building Mama's cabinetry together, and Micah had rebuilt the barn on the ranch after the summer flooding from a couple of summers ago.

"Howdy," he said to perhaps the one person he'd call a friend in Three Rivers. He had brothers, and Duke was married to a Glover, so Dawson had never hurt for company if he wanted it.

"Dawson." Micah half rose and shook his hand. "Are you looking for a place to sit?" Each table held eight, and Micah and Simone only had three children. No one else had sat with them, and Dawson nodded over to their oldest. Trap had finished high school last spring, but he'd been working with his father for years even before that.

"My folks are here," he said, glancing around. "Somewhere." He looked at Micah for a moment. "I was just wondering if you got that new cherry wood in. I want to try a cutting board with it."

"Not yet," Micah said. "Simone's been selling a lot of our checkerboard charcuterie boards at her shows lately."

"Yeah?" Dawson glanced over to Trap, who nodded.

"Cherry and oak," he said. "One lady bought one to use as a checker board."

"Light and dark," Dawson said, smiling at the younger man. He knocked on the table and straightened. "Good to see you guys."

He looked over his shoulder and found his mom with her hand in the air. "There's my mama. Enjoy breakfast."

"It's cold pancakes and burnt bacon," Micah said, to which Simone swatted him and said, "Shh."

Dawson chuckled as he walked away, because Micah had just vocalized his feelings about the breakfast. He moved over three tables and took his seat beside his daddy. "You're in the back," he said, working hard to keep the question mark off the last word. He managed too, in his mind.

"Yep," Daddy said. No further explanation. He never said more than necessary, and Dawson had definitely inherited that trait from his father.

No buffet ever had the back tables start first, and Dawson settled back into his seat and folded his arms, ready to deal with his grumbling stomach until he could get it some flaccid bacon and cold pancakes.

"You savin' any of these?"

Dawson shook his head at the Bellamores while Daddy said, "Nope, all yours." He immediately started engaging Brit Bellamore in conversation about their winter crops, and Dawson listened with vague interest.

"We're ready to begin," someone said into a microphone. "Please raise your hand if you have seats at your table, as we have more people coming in."

Dawson dutifully raised his hand, and a woman pointed toward him. She turned a little girl in that direction, and another woman came behind her. He put his hand down and nodded at the woman, whom he didn't recognize.

"These are open?" she asked.

"All yours," he said, and she pulled out the chair next to Gabi Bellamore. As she shifted, the woman behind the little girl came into view, and Dawson's flesh and muscles dang near flowed out of his skin.

Caroline Thompson.

Dawson felt everything inside him blazing, and as their eyes met, he wondered what she saw. Him, obviously, as she froze. The little girl, who was probably seven or eight years old, took the seat in the middle of the remaining three available while the other woman took her seat next to Gabi, and that left the only open seat next to Dawson.

Caroline's eyes narrowed then, and she practically stomped over to the chair and yanked it out. "Hello, Dawson," she clipped out.

"Caroline," he said easily. He hadn't seen her since their

impromptu breakfast together at the diner a few months ago. He hadn't filed any paperwork either, which was probably why Caroline now shot ninja stars at him from her eyes.

Their breakfast together had been fine, in his opinion. They hadn't talked much once the food had come, and he'd managed to maintain his dignity as they'd walked out together. He'd tipped his hat at her and gone to his truck while she went to hers. She'd sent him her half of the bill before he'd even gotten the air conditioning blowing in his truck, and she hadn't pestered him again about the missing paperwork.

They didn't have owls at the Rhinehart Ranch, plain and simple. And she couldn't make him file without proof of the endangered animals. She'd tried to say the ranch was prime habitat for the burrowing owls, and she needed him to file paperwork saying he wouldn't disrupt their habitat, but he'd ignored her.

In fact, he'd looked up the law, and he didn't have to file anything about a habitat, not even for an endangered animal—until the animal was there. Then, they couldn't remove the animals and destroy their habitat, but until the little owls chose the Rhinehart Ranch as their home, Caroline couldn't force Dawson to do anything.

"Thanks for coming to the firehouse fundraising breakfast," someone said. "We're going to go ahead and get started. Thank you for your support of our firemen and our efforts to improve our emergency services for the people of Three Rivers."

After a quick prayer, where silence descended on them, the

noise broke out as people stood and started talking. And talking, and talking, and talking.

Dawson should have something to say to Caroline, but for the life of him, he couldn't think of a single thing. He looked at the little girl next to her and found they had the same hair color.

"Your daughter?" he asked, not sure why he'd gone there. If Caroline Thompson had a daughter, she could have a husband, and that would mean Dawson's fizzing crush on the woman indicated he'd gone insane.

He glanced over to the other woman sandwiching the girl, and she looked like Caroline too.

"No," she said, but she didn't offer up any information about who the girl was.

"Niece?" Dawson tried again.

Caroline glared at him. "Yes, Mister Rhinehart. This is Judy. She's my niece."

He managed to smile at the girl as she looked at her aunt and then him. "Nice to meet you. I'm Dawson."

"Hi, Dawson," Judy said in a cute, high-pitched, little-girl voice. She looked over to her mama and back to him.

"I'm Dawson," he said again as he reached his hand across the table to Caroline's obvious sister. "You must be—"

"My sister," Caroline barked, cutting him off. "Bella. She's going to be living with me for a while."

Another smile manifested itself. "That's great," he said, shaking her hand. He pulled it back and noticed the two sisters exchange a glance. He ignored it and indicated his mama and daddy. "My parents. Wade and Abby."

"Great to meet you," Bella said. "How do you know Caroline?"

"Well, uh." Dawson shifted in his seat, wishing they'd somehow call their table up to get food. His eyes tracked over to the table where people had just gotten up, and they still had three to go until he could reasonably stand. "We had breakfast together once."

"No," Caroline said. "He's one of the ranches who won't file the endangered habitat paperwork."

Dawson looked over to his father, whose frown lines had deepened between his eyes. "*Ranches* can't file paperwork," he said quietly. "*People* file paperwork."

Caroline scoffed, but she didn't correct herself.

"Where are you guys from?" he asked Judy and Bella.

Bella didn't seem to have any of the tight-lipped qualities of Caroline, and she started telling him and everyone at the table about their move from Phoenix. She never mentioned a husband, and Dawson didn't have time to ask before their table became eligible to go get in line for breakfast.

He expected to be separated from Caroline then, because his parents didn't move fast at all these days, and he wouldn't just leave them in the dust. But Judy didn't move fast either, and with all the tables and chairs and people, they ended up joining the line in the same order where they'd been sitting at the table.

Which put Dawson right behind Caroline, with his frowny father hot on his heels. He wanted to say something to her, but all of the things that came into his head would embarrass him greatly.

Do you want to go to breakfast again? My treat.

Couldn't say that.

Your hair sure is pretty down like that, Caroline.

He hallucinated and pictured himself reaching up to tuck it behind her ear just before he kissed her. Certainly couldn't say or do that.

I'll file the paperwork, okay? Just don't be mad at me anymore.

But he'd been stubborn for too long about the paperwork, and he couldn't back down now. Caroline was a smart woman, and she'd want to know why he'd suddenly decided to file. He couldn't tell her it was because he found her gorgeous, even as unrelenting as she was.

She clearly didn't like him, though he'd never known someone to get so worked up over burrowing owls and paperwork before. She wasn't the first Wildlife Conservation Officer he'd worked with, for crying out loud.

"Oh, my goodness," she muttered ahead of him, and Dawson blinked to get himself out of the fantasy where he and Caroline held hands and shared intimate things about their lives —like the real reason her sister had come to stay with her in Three Rivers.

"This is a crime against potatoes," she muttered, some limp shreds falling off the spoon. They were white and obviously cold, not a stitch of browned, crispy goodness anywhere.

Without thinking, Dawson looked up and handed his paper plate of cold scrambled eggs to the woman standing there. "Can you take this?" he asked. She did, a squeak of surprise coming from her that wasn't really a protest.

He took Caroline's plate and handed it to her too. "Thank you." Then he took Caroline's hand, his skin burning where it touched hers, and said, "Come with me."

Sneak Peek! The Cowboy Who Loved Texas Chapter Two:

"Come with you?" Caroline Thompson stumbled after Dawson Rhinehart, because she had no other choice. The man had a grip on her hand she wouldn't be able to break even if she wanted to.

By some miracle in heaven, she didn't want to. His hand was big, warm, rough, and absolutely amazing surrounding hers. She just hadn't held hands with a man in a while, that was all.

She did not like Dawson Rhinehart. The man had been nothing but a stubborn mule for months now, and no one needed to know she'd often sat on her back porch, the sun sinking into the evening with her flipping her phone over and over and over, a text to him started but never finished and sent.

And now Bella was here, and she needed help with Judy. They both needed a lot of support as Bella navigated the divorce process and tried to keep herself and her daughter safe from her abusive ex-husband. Thankfully, Chuck hadn't followed them to Three Rivers, and Caroline hoped and prayed it could become a sanctuary for her sister and niece the way it had been for her.

"Where are we going?" she demanded as Dawson took her outside in the New Year's temperatures.

"I can't eat that garbage," he said. "We deserve a good breakfast." He cut her a look out of the corner of his eye, and how he looked so sexy and strong doing it, Caroline would never know.

"I'm not going to the diner with you," she said. "They have—"

"Home fries," he said. "I know." He clicked something on his key fob, and the closet truck to them beeped. He opened the passenger door for her, and Caroline simply looked at him.

He kept his head ducked down, his eyes barely able to meet hers past the brim of that deep, dark black cowboy hat. "Are you hungry?"

"Yes," she said without thinking.

"I'm not going to hurt you." He let go of her hand. "I can't stand breakfasts like this, and I'm starving, and we deserve to start the day with a good, hot meal."

Sparks popped through her blood, and she wondered if someone had poured baking soda into her veins, hoping for this kind of explosive, chemical reaction. "Where's the best place for breakfast in this town? Because it's my favorite meal, and I have yet to find somewhere that does what you speak of."

He grinned at her, and oh, that thing should be criminal.

Just like those cold, rubbery hashbrowns in the community center. "That's because you haven't eaten breakfast at my house."

Pure nervous energy ran through her, but Caroline thought it might actually be adrenaline. Excitement. She had the very distinct thought that this man could introduce some color and life into her existence, and she wanted that very, very badly.

"Okay," she said slowly. "I'll see where this goes, but I need to drive myself."

Dawson's face fell. "Can your sister get home without your car?"

Caroline blinked at him and said simply, "No, sir."

"I'll bring you back the moment you say," he said, and she didn't detect an ounce of dishonesty in him.

She still gave him a side-eyed look and squeezed past him to get in the truck. She honestly had no idea what she was doing. The Rhinehart Ranch sat forty-five minutes south of town. She couldn't just leave Bella and Judy at the community center.

Panicking, Caroline pulled her phone out of her pocket and started texting frantically. Dawson slid into the driver's seat and backed the truck out. He drove in silence, and Caroline had learned that he was familiar and comfortable and best friends with silence.

She wasn't sure how she felt about it, but she took the opportunity to text her sister where she'd gone and that her keys were sitting next to her plastic cup of water on that table.

I am going to get the whole story when you get back, Bella said. *Or I will fake a heart attack and interrupt whatever it is you have going on with Dawson.*

Caroline scoffed, which drew Dawson's attention. "You okay?" he drawled.

Okay, she tapped out quickly, and then she shoved her phone back into her pocket. "Yes," she said. "Just telling Bella what's going on."

"Mm. What did she say?"

"What are you going to tell your parents?"

"That something came up on the ranch." He grinned at her, that lopsided smile so adorable. "It's not exactly a lie."

"Do you regularly tell little white lies?"

"Technically, I haven't told either of my parents anything yet," he said. "So no." His smile remained as he turned to get on the road that led south. Caroline knew the area pretty well now that she'd been in town for nine or ten months, as she had to drive to a lot of the ranches and farms in Three Rivers for her job.

"Besides," he said. "I'm thirty-two years old, and if I want to take a pretty woman home for breakfast, I don't need to tell my mommy and daddy."

Ah, there was that familiar bite and fire. "Wait," she said as her brain caught up to her ears. "A pretty woman?"

Dawson's jaw jumped in that tell-tale way Caroline had seen in other men. He might not be a big talker, but he had plenty of non-verbal cues she could read just fine. Maybe she hadn't seen another man's jaw jump like that for her in a while, nor had she been called pretty by anyone but Bella or Judy in longer, but she wasn't new to dating and relationships.

"Yes, ma'am," he said. "I think you're pretty."

"Well...thank you," she said, not sure what else to say. Her momma had taught her that she could always be grateful, so "thank you" seemed appropriate.

"You ordered over-easy eggs at the diner a few months ago," he said. "Is that your favored way to take eggs?"

Caroline swiveled her attention toward him again. "Favored way to take eggs?"

"Yeah," he said without missing a beat. "Eggs are the most versatile food there is. You can—"

"Besides potatoes," she said.

He looked over to her. "Besides potatoes." He drove with one hand on the top of the wheel and the other draped lazily over his thigh. He seemed at-ease on this road, in this truck, with her. "So...how do you take your eggs?"

Caroline relaxed into the leather seat behind her. "I do like a really good over-easy egg. They're hard to do, and I'll admit I usually break mine on the flip."

"I've done that too," he said.

"If I'm going to be real honest, though, I'd go with a poached egg. Over a nicely toasted English muffin, with hollandaise sauce."

"So an impossible task," he said.

"So far in Three Rivers, yes," she said. "There was this cute little bistro in Sweet Water Falls that made the best Eggs Benedict I've ever had." She smiled, the morning sunshine of this

New Year streaming in through the windows. "Gonna be a nice day."

"Yep," he said. "Good day to be outside for sure."

He made the turn to go west from the highway, and they bumped along a nice dirt road and onto the Rhinehart Ranch. The homestead, a shed, and a barn sat straight ahead, with another much newer, nicer, and bigger house to her right.

Dawson didn't make that turn, and Caroline wondered who lived there. Obviously not him, and he went past another dirt road that went south again.

"Main house and barn here," he said. "Big vegetable garden back there my mama tortured us with." A smile cracked his face. "That place up front is my brother's. He's the foreman and runs the ranch. When Daddy dies, he'll own it outright."

"You won't share ownership with him?"

Dawson shook his head. "Daddy says it's just easier to have one owner. We have other clauses and whatnot in place to give us all a place here on the ranch."

"How many brothers do you have?"

"Two," he said. "One full sibling, one half. My daddy's first wife passed away, and he married my mama and had two more boys."

Caroline's heart expanded with emotion, because it seemed like Dawson had a good relationship with his family members, but she knew better than most that families were so complicated. Even when things were good, they were twisted and knotted and never simple.

"You?" he asked. "You've got Bella. Who else is in your family?"

"We have another older sister," she said. "Her name is Amelia. And I have a younger brother—my daddy's pride and joy." She heard the slight tang of bitterness in her tone as it landed on her tongue. "His name's Davy."

"A, B, C, D," Dawson said.

Surprise once again struck her right across the throat. He'd picked up on the alphabet in her siblings' names? Tall, handsome, and smart. A dangerous combination for her heart.

"Where do they live?"

"I grew up in Colorado," she said. "We're all over the Mountain West these days. Well, I mean, we were. Bella's here now. Davy's still in the Colorado Springs area. Abigail is in Boise."

"All good country," he said.

"Have you ever lived outside of Texas?"

He shook his head. "No, ma'am." He went around the shed and barn and continued down the road. "My brother, Brandon, and I live together. We've got a cabin out here. We have a man who works with us. Kevin Bentley. He had to give up his farm a bit ago, and he lived at Shiloh Ridge for a few months. His sister-in-law is a Glover. But we had a need, and he wants to work, so they moved up here. Him and his family."

Caroline had never heard him say so much, and it made her smile. "Is that everyone?"

"Yes, ma'am," he said. "We're not nearly the size of some other ranches. Five hundred and fifty acres. The four of us work it just fine."

She liked how he made a one-syllable word into two. "Just *fiy-yine*," she echoed, grinning at him.

"Are you gonna poke fun at how I talk?"

"Only when you make short words into long ones," she said, well aware of her flirting.

He pulled up to a cabin that bore blonde-wood logs, a sturdy roof, and bright blue shutters. He parked out front and killed the engine. "This is it. Don't be thinkin' it's gonna be nice. Two men live here."

"Give me a minute to prepare myself." She drew in a deep breath, as if she needed the oxygen as a shield against what she'd find behind that black door. Caroline held it for a silent count of four, then released it. "Okay, I'm ready."

"Dust and shadows," he muttered as he opened his door and got out of the truck. He slammed the door and glared at her through the windshield as he went round the hood. He dang near pulled her door off its hinges and looked at her again.

"Dust and shadows?" she repeated.

Dawson said nothing as he turned and headed for the cabin. She scurried after him, her stomach an empty well of nerves and hissing snakes. The cabin had a porch that ran the width of the house, with a swing built-in on one end and a rocking chair with a small round table on the other.

Shoes that obviously didn't belong to him or his brother sat on a mat a few feet from the door. Something fit for a teenager— or even younger. Not as young as Judy, but definitely not Dawson's age.

A football, a Frisbee, and several dog toys waited neatly in a bin, indicating more to Dawson than grumpiness and veiled invitations.

Caroline's interest piqued, and while Dawson had longer legs than her and a massive angry stride, he'd left the front door open for her. She entered and stopped to take in his space.

"Close that, would you?" he asked, his voice almost a growl. "I don't need to be heatin' the outside."

"Sure, right." Caroline moved out of the way and pushed the door closed behind her. She'd stepped into a living room, where he and his brother had a sofa and love seat set in brown leather. A coffee table sat in front of the couch, and it all faced the front window. No TV.

Caroline couldn't see one of those in the room at all. In fact, a radio sat on the back counter, and she watched almost in slow motion as Dawson reached over and switched it on. Something low warbled out of it, but it wasn't loud enough for her to make out words or a discernible melody.

A dining room table sat pushed against the wall in the kitchen, with the back door of the house behind that. Curtains hung on all the windows. Matching curtains in plain blue fabric.

The carpet at her feet looked clean, as did the kitchen when she reached the counter and leaned against it. Dawson had already started getting out breakfast foods, and he loudly put two pans on his stovetop and flipped on the burners.

The flames whooshed as they came to life, and Caroline took a seat at the bar to watch the show.

His fridge had colorful drawings and notes attached to it

with magnets. This man had children in his life, and for some reason, that made Caroline's heart soften toward him.

"I'm gonna do over-easy eggs," he said without looking at her. "I don't have English muffins, and I'm too hungry to go to the trouble of hollandaise sauce."

"Sounds fine," she said, not teasing him this time. She enjoyed watching him work in the kitchen, and he could apparently only focus on one task at a time, because he made no effort to speak.

She took in the hat rack with jackets and hats on it next to the back door, and she couldn't help wondering who'd given him the potted plant in the window above the kitchen sink.

A niece? Nephew? Sister-in-law? His momma?

Ten minutes later, he held two plates, one in each hand, and nodded over to the table. Caroline slipped from the stool and went to join him. She gave him a side-eyed look as she sat and he placed a beautiful plate of hot, perfectly cooked over-easy eggs—the yolks still whole—several strips of bacon, and a whole pile of crispy, browned, perfectly shredded hashbrowns.

"Do we get to talk over this breakfast?" she asked as he sat down.

"If you'd like," he said. He nudged the salt and pepper shakers closer to her and picked up his fork.

"No pancakes."

Dawson met her eyes, pure fire raging in his eyes. Blue-green fire was something she'd never seen before, but it felt like she could dive into the aquamarine color of it and swim around. Or get scorched.

She was up for either.

"Next time," he said, and he dropped those beautiful eyes to his plate. She hurried to pick up her fork too, her mouth watering for want of crispy potatoes with ketchup.

"Oh." Dawson got to his feet and went around her to the fridge. He returned with the ketchup she'd been about to ask for and set it in front of her. "Here you go."

"Thank you." She squirted it onto her potatoes and mixed them up a little, her smile growing. "This is so amazing, Dawson. Thank you so much." She took a bite, and instant rejoicing sang across her taste buds. They had the right amount of crunch to soft potato, salt, and pepper.

"Oh," she moaned, the ketchup adding the right amount of tang to the party already happening in her mouth. She swallowed and immediately scooped up another bite. "These are the best hashbrowns I've ever had."

Dawson smiled slightly, the left side tipping up higher than the right. "I'm glad you like them."

She liked every bite she put in her mouth, and she sat back when her plate had been emptied and pressed one palm to her belly. "Dawson, that was incredible. Thank you."

He'd already finished, and he picked up his plate and hers and took them over to the sink without accepting her gratitude. She twisted and watched him wash the dishes they'd just used. "Are you always this grumpy?"

"About," he said.

She got up and went to join him at the sink. She gently inserted her hands into the water and took the plate from him to rinse it. He looked over to her, and in that moment, everything softened between them. Caroline could certainly get her ire up too, and she'd been plenty irritated and frustrated with this particular cowboy.

But that melted away under the heat of his look, and Caroline forgot how to rinse a dish and set it to dry. All she knew was his eyes, that blue, the scent of his skin and the lingering scent of bacon in the air.

He leaned toward her, and Caroline tensed, ready to receive his kiss. Her eyes drifted closed, only to rudely fly open again when a shrill noise pierced the air between them.

Dawson likewise jumped away from her, and she winced at the sound of the plate clattering against the sink. She'd dropped it, and she hastened to pick it up while Dawson's phone rang again.

"What?" he barked into it, his back turned to her.

Caroline's nerves felt like flapping bat wings against her inside organs as she finished the dishes quickly and turned off the faucet. She grabbed a towel from the handle on the stove and faced Dawson.

He wasn't holding the phone to his ear any longer but staring at something on it in front of him. "This is not happening," he said.

"It's happening," a man said on the other end of the line, his voice echoing through the cabin as Dawson had put the call on speakerphone. "Where are you? I need you back at the ranch ASAP."

Dawson didn't answer, and Caroline was actually glad she wasn't the only one he stayed silent with.

"Daws," the man barked. Probably his brother. "Get up here. We need to deal with these burrowing owls."

Ice flowed through her, and she stepped right over to Dawson's side. She looked at his phone while her legs locked, and she couldn't remember if that was good or bad. Was she about to pass out?

His phone showed a picture, and Caroline had plenty of experience with the animal she saw. It wasn't a great picture, but she knew a burrowing owl when she saw one.

"Dust and shadows," she whispered, and Dawson finally looked at her. Only his eyebrows rose, slow and steady. In any other situation, Caroline might have given him a flirty smile.

"Dawson," his brother said. "I can see you're at your cabin. Get out to the West End Fence immediately." His brother sighed. "And call that wildlife officer. She's going to be the death of us, but we can't put her off any longer."

The call ended, and still Dawson held his phone in front of him.

Caroline plucked his device from him, which caused a growl to come from his throat. "I didn't think today was a good day to cause death, but it looks like it might be." She offered him his phone back, which he swiped from her. "Let's go."

Then she led the way out of his cabin with the longest strides she could.

* * *

Dust and shadows! There are burrowing owls on the Rhinehart Ranch! How are Dawson and Caroline going to navigate that AND a fledgling (see what I did there? Ha!) relationship when they can't see eye-to-eye on anything? Find out in THE COWBOY WHO LOVED TEXAS, which you can **preorder by scanning the QR code below with your phone!**

The Cowboy Who Came Home: A Second Generation in Three Rivers Ranch Romance™ (Book 1): He's been serving in the military for a decade. She's been quietly grieving a devastating loss. When Finn and Edith reunite in small-town Three Rivers where they grew up together, can their second chance romance provide hope, healing, and the happily-ever-after they both crave?

Scan this QR code with your phone to see this series in eBook, audiobook, large print paperback, or regular paperback:

The Mechanics of Mistletoe (Book 1): Bear Glover can be a grizzly or a teddy, and he's always thought he'd be just fine working his generational family ranch and going back to the ancient homestead alone. But his crush on Samantha Benton won't go away. She's a genius with a wrench on Bear's tractors...and his heart. Can he tame his wild side and get the girl, or will he be left broken-hearted this Christmas season?

The Horsepower of the Holiday (Book 2): Ranger Glover has worked at Shiloh Ridge Ranch his entire life. The cowboys do everything from horseback there, but when he goes to town to trade in some trucks, somehow Oakley Hatch persuades him to take some ATVs back to the ranch. (Bear is NOT happy.)

She's a former race car driver who's got Ranger all revved up... Can he remember who he is and get Oakley to slow down enough to fall in love, or will there simply be too much horsepower in the holiday this year for a real relationship?

The
CONSTRUCTION
of Cheer

USA Today Bestselling Author
LIZ ISAACSON

The Construction of Cheer (Book 3): Bishop Glover is the youngest brother, and he usually keeps his head down and gets the job done. When Montana Martin shows up at Shiloh Ridge Ranch looking for work, he finds himself inventing construction projects that need doing just to keep her coming around. (Again, Bear is NOT happy.) She wants to build her own construction firm, but she ends up carving a place for herself inside Bishop's heart. Can he convince her *he's* all she needs this Christmas season, or will her cheer rest solely on the success of her business?

The Secret of Santa (Book 4): He's a fun-loving cowboy with a heart of gold. She's the woman who keeps putting him on hold. Can Ace and Holly Ann make a relationship work this Christmas?

The Gift of Gingerbread (Book 5): She's the only daughter in the Glover family. He's got a secret that drove him out of town years ago. Can Arizona and Duke find common ground and their happily-ever-after this Christmas?

The Harmony of Holly (Book 6): He's as prickly as his name, but the new woman in town has caught his eye. Can Cactus shelve his temper and shed his cowboy hermit skin fast enough to make a relationship with Willa work?

The Chemistry of Christmas (Book 7): He's the black sheep of the family, and she's a chemist who understands formulas, not emotions. Can Preacher and Charlie take their quirks and turn them into a strong relationship this Christmas?

The Delivery of Decor (Book 8): When he falls, he falls hard and deep. She literally drives away from every relationship she's ever had. Can Ward somehow get Dot to stay this Christmas?

CHRISTMAS AT SHILOH RIDGE RANCH

The DELIVERY of Decor

THREE RIVERS

USA Today Bestselling Author

LIZ ISAACSON

The Blessing of Babies (Book 9): Don't miss out on a single moment of the Glover family saga in this bridge story linking Ward and Judge's love stories!

The Glovers love God, country, dogs, horses, and family. Not necessarily in that order. ;)

Many of them are married now, with babies on the way, and there are lessons to be learned, forgiveness to be had and given, and new names coming to the family tree in southern Three Rivers!

The Networking of the Nativity (Book 10): He's had a crush on her for years. She doesn't want to date until her daughter is out of the house. Will June take a change on Judge when the success of his Christmas light display depends on her networking abilities?

The Wrangling of the Wreath (Book 11): He's been so busy trying to find Miss Right. She's been right in front of him the whole time. This Christmas, can Mister and Libby take their relationship out of the best friend zone?

The Hope of Her Heart (Book 12): She's the only Glover without a significant other. He's been searching for someone who can love him *and* his daughter. Can Etta and August make a meaningful connection this Christmas?

CHRISTMAS AT SHILOH RIDGE RANCH

The HOPE of Her Heart

USA Today Bestselling Author
LIZ ISAACSON

Meet the cowboys who started it all at Three Rivers Ranch! Scan the QR code below with your phone to check out this complete series.

Scan this QR code with your phone to see and order this series in eBook, audiobook, large print paperback, or regular paperback:

1. Second Chance Ranch
2. Third Time's the Charm
3. Fourth and Long
4. Fifth Generation Cowboy
6. Sixth Street Love Affair
7. The Seventh Sergeant
8. Eight Second Ride
9. The Ninth Inning
10. Ten Days in Town
11. Eleven Year Reunion
12. The Twelfth Town

Seven Sons Ranch in Three Rivers Romance™ Series

Meet the cowboy billionaire brothers at Seven Sons Ranch! Scan the QR code below with your phone to check out this complete series.

1. Rhett's Make-Believe Marriage
2. Tripp's Trivial Tie
3. Liam's Invented I-Do
4. Jeremiah's Bogus Bride
5. Wyatt's Pretend Pledge
6. Skyler's Wanna-Be Wife
7. Micah's Mock Matrimony
8. Gideon's Precious Penny

About Liz

Liz Isaacson writes inspirational romance, usually set in Texas, or Wyoming, or anywhere else horses and cowboys exist. She lives in Utah, where she writes full-time, takes her two dogs to the park everyday, and eats a lot of veggies while writing. Find her on her website at www.feelgoodfictionbooks.com.